The Last Flapper

The Last Flapper

 by George Zuckerman

Little, Brown and Company-Boston-Toronto

FIRST EDITION

Published simultaneously in Canada
by Little, Brown & Company (Canada) Limited

PRINTED IN THE UNITED STATES OF AMERICA

for Blanche

Foreword

The last time I saw Harry Ingram alive, he told me that the living could not stand up against the dead, who no longer are buried deeply enough.

His own Montana grave shallow enough to serve him as a shooting box, he took aim and fired both barrels upon the ghosts of Davis and Rannah O'Donnell.

The publication, in 1966, of Harry Ingram's posthumous memoirs, *The Absent City,* and now, in 1969, of Rannah O'Donnell's *The Last Flapper* proves that it is, conversely, the dead who cannot stand up against the living.

I count myself among the culpable, for I had the wherewithal to prevent Harry Ingram's savage attack against the O'Donnells, and to keep Rannah O'Donnell's manuscript buried deeply enough in the Bank of Fifth Avenue, to whose vaults I had committed it in 1945.

The Davis O'Donnell legend, the myth of the American Adonis, the semi-divine martyr untimely slain and duly resurrected, is now full-fledged and beyond Harry Ingram's power to shatter it. Rather than legend, it is reputation that today sustains Davis O'Donnell and Harry Ingram, and affords them the readers lost to their neglected contemporaries.

My solicitude is for Rannah O'Donnell, to whom injustice has been done.

Henry L. Mencken wrote that without Rannah O'Donnell there would have been no Jazz Age. Harry Ingram damned her as "the mad bitch" who led her husband to ashes, his life unfulfilled, his great talent unrealized.

Rannah O'Donnell borrowed the form of her manuscript from the Civil War memoirs written by her paternal grandfather, Watson Gedney, Brigadier General, CSA. In describing her own four crucial battles, she overcomes prurience, a surfeit of Anglo-Saxonisms, and rashes of metaphors, which are as symptomatic of her schizophrenia as were her plagues of eczema.

The believers of Harry Ingram's charges may, from Rannah O'Donnell's testimony, gather further evidence of sin and guilt to uphold fate's verdict of dread adversity. The seekers after the obverse side of the truth may, with talmudic insight, observe that Rannah O'Donnell, for too long, dwelled upon the hidden name of the Lord.

That way, also, madness lies.

DELANO FREDERICKS

part one

The Battle of the Belle

1.

It is not the woman who holds a man by his prick, but the one
who holds him by his soul who is dangerous.

With this iron maxim I was branded for life. Borrowed from
the Russian author aptly named Maxim Gorki, it was delivered
to me in the white heat of agony on the darkest night of the year
1919 by Davis O'Donnell.

If General Sherman's best-remembered words — war is hell —
sum up the War Between the States, then Maxim Gorki's maxim
sums up the longer war between Davis O'Donnell and myself.

In the attic rooms where I am writing of my four battles the
wainscoted walls are covered with forty-seven oil portraits of
Davis, and his ninety-four eyes are upon me, the truest of blues,
the sharpest of agonies. The look in all of them is that of the
second lieutenant with whom I stood on the platform of the
Stephensville, Georgia, railroad depot on the night of January
17, 1919, and waited for the arrival of the northbound train that
was to take him, alone, from another Waterloo for an American
boy.

The khaki overseas cap, never worn overseas, sat carelessly on
strands of sand above the face of an Alexander belonging to
ancient coins, to Grecian marble. The khaki overcoat draped his

3

slender figure down to his brown cavalry boots. Too tall for a knight's armor, he stood four inches short of his dream of six-foot stature. The engines of his smiles and laughter ran well on whiskey. But when he was sad, as he was now, he was the saddest young man of all.

The wind from the Arctic north swept over the mushroom hat covering my auburn hair, over the dyed muskrat coat shielding my perspiring and shivering body. The banner of my bravado was a tasseled scarf that waved with the gossamer smile masking my heartbreak.

The railroad tracks ran above the banks of the Cherokee River and impaled me. The depot's red clay bricks wore soot and smoke as mourning bands for me. About us rose the laughter and chatter of this late hour in a party called war, a party from which we had fled in the midnight of reality. And now reason was summoning me to a battle with my beloved. Reason, damned reason, was bidding me to accept the crumbs of forever.

"God!" cried my heart. "Take me from my father's reason! Free me from his will! Freeze me in the cold of this moment! Stop the trains! Stop the clocks!"

I looked southward down the tracks, hoping to attract and to hurry the train that was yet beyond sight and sound. There was no sweet sorrow in this parting for me, only the foretaste of death, the death of a love fallen victim to time, distance, geography, and circumstance. And the trembling of my heart reached to the wash of my nerves.

To divert the drives of agony, I now turned to Davis and picked words as carelessly as a girl walking with her lover plucks leaves from hedges.

"Liz Cooper's right," I said.

"About what?" There was no timbre to his voice, no trace now of a smile on his handsome face.

"Liz says you remind her of her favorite movie actor. Wallace Reid."

"Swell."

"Wallace Reid has a better smile."

"What's a smile?"

4

"What I'm wearing. What you haven't worn in days."

He turned away from me to stare northward along the tracks, as if to take a reading on the course of sorrow. I tried again. "May I ask you something?" No reply, no turning of his head toward me. "Do you have a crush on Liz Cooper?"

Now Davis whirled his darkening frown toward me. "Why are you talking about her?"

"Most everyone falls in love with Liz before they fall in love with me. Didn't it happen to you that way?"

"I'm an idiot. I always pick the wrong girl."

I groped for and found crumbs of laughter. I said, "Oh, for sure. The truth now. How many girls did you make out with? Right here in Stephensville."

He was anything but the boastful male. "All of them. Except you."

I persisted, trying to disguise my jealousy as mere curiosity. "Really, how many? In round numbers."

I had hoped to spark a pun, but he only replied with an honest indifference. "I don't remember. Take a survey. See how many of the new crop of war babies look like Wallace Reid."

I said, "Oh, that's funny. Do you really think you put some girl in a family way?"

Davis studied me with disdain. "How can you laugh?"

"Why shouldn't I laugh? I have the best laugh in town."

He was bitter. "And you're having one on me now."

"You're so sad, Davis. I'm trying to cheer you up."

"Shouldn't I be sad?"

"Oh, of course you should. You lost the war."

The taunt hit home. "Tell it to the Kaiser."

I went on with the crosses of his Waterloo. "No wings. No overseas. No hero. No medals."

"And no girl," he added.

Ignoring this giant cross, I fled to the memory of a day the laughter had melted away to tears. "You shouldn't have been so smart-alecky with your noisy old aeroplane."

His resentment was cold now. "You and your big mouth."

"You and your big jokes. Bombing my lawn with that bag of chocolates."

"You didn't have to tell Major Daley who the sap was," he retorted.

"He took down the number of your aeroplane. I only told him what a great aviator you were and how you were sure to become an ace. I was only trying to help you. If only for you to die young."

Davis accepted this explanation now more readily than he had the first time I had offered it. "Anyway," he said absently, "you shouldn't have been entertaining the major on your front porch."

"What are porches for, if not for entertaining? Don't you entertain on your front porches in Milwaukee? At least in the summer? You do have summers in Milwaukee, don't you?"

"Come and see."

"Is that an invitation?"

Davis took my gloved hands and squeezed them. "Change your mind, please."

"There's snow in Milwaukee."

"It'll melt before your big, blue eyes."

I laughed. "Oh, you flattering Yankee!"

His voice was now soft with enticement. "We have heavy quilts. And warm beds."

"Oh, Lieutenant, how you do go on!"

He managed the smallest of smiles. "I wish I had a snowball right now. I'd wash your smile clean."

"Oh, you'll find plenty of girls in Milwaukee for that sport."

"Don't forget New Haven."

"Does it snow there, too?"

"Only when we play Harvard. They bring it down from Cambridge."

I laughed heartily. "Good! You haven't entirely lost your sense of humor. At least that's something you can take home with you."

Meaningfully he said, "You're what I want to take home."

I tried whimsy. "Why, thank you. But we're both failures.

6

You never got your varsity letter at Yale. I never got my scarlet letter in the war.''

''I tried.''

''You're a fool, a well-mannered fool. You should've done as Sherman's troops did. Or don't Yale men indulge in rape?''

He was unamused. ''Some Yale men fall in love.''

''With Indian princesses?'' This was a reference to a home-grown legend that I was descended from the Cherokees who long ago inhabited Georgia.

Davis frowned. ''Sometimes I think you really believe that malarkey.''

''Well,'' I jested, ''I have got your scalp.''

His cold hands touched my flushed face and I shivered. He whispered, ''I love your high cheekbones.''

I turned away to escape the cold hands and the burning eyes, then threw my attention across the river. ''Look over there. I can see the Cherokee campfires.''

Davis moved his face to eclipse the conjured Cherokee scene. ''We haven't much time left. I'd rather look at you.''

I wanted to hold and kiss him. Instead I said, ''The Chero-kees left Georgia on a trail of tears. Are you going to do likewise?''

''Come with me.''

''You know, don't you, that the Cherokees got their vengeance on the white man?''

''I love you.''

''For them,'' I went on with difficulty, ''Sherman is Tecum-seh, the Indian chief who avenged them. Isn't that an interesting thought?''

He said, ''Mine's more interesting. Come with me.''

''I can't. I own this town. And I can't take it with me.''

''You'll outgrow it.''

''Never. I'll always own it.''

''Milwaukee's an Indian name.''

I smiled and gathered leaves of faraway geography and cur-rent history. ''Davis, don't you wish you were now in France saying farewell to the Mademoiselle from Armentiers?''

7

He frowned. "I wish you were Liz Cooper. I'd be laughing with you now."

"Try," I implored. "Please, try."

"You're a fake. You play the Southern belle. But you're not."

Again the old refrain. "I'm a Cherokee princess."

"I know who you are."

"Tell me."

"You're the strange girl who feels the turning of the earth. The girl who rides the carrousel around the sun."

Remembering the terror of dark-of-the-night sensations, I said, without levity, "I'm not right in the head."

This old refrain, which he had heard before, angered him. "Shut up."

I didn't. "Are we making a pact of silence? Shall we stand here listening to the laughter? Waiting for the thunder of your train?"

"Think, Rannah. Think," he commanded.

"About what?"

Davis turned the hands of the clock forward, and my stomach turned with them. "The train has come and gone. I'm gone. Will you sleep tonight? Will you welcome the morning? Will you be waiting at your window for me to walk up Gedney Street to your house? Will you be able to walk alone in the woods beyond the street?"

My voice was tremulous. "I walked alone in the woods before I ever met you."

"It won't be the same any more," he prophesied. "It'll be a forest, dark with regret."

I fought him. "Good poetry. Bad truth. I'll go on. I have my town. My friends. My callers. My suitors. I may decide that June calls for a wedding."

"To Davis O'Donnell?"

"That's a Milwaukee name, isn't it?"

"It's an Irish name. And is that the problem?"

"What problem?"

8

"You don't want to marry an Irish Catholic. A renegade Catholic at that."

"That's silly, Davis. I have Catholic friends here in Stephensville. But they're here. And you won't be. The problem is Milwaukee."

"You don't want to live there."

"I live here!" I protested. "This is where I belong! Anywhere else I'd only exist. And endure."

Davis now took a new tack. "What if we forget Milwaukee?"

"I don't understand you."

"What if I don't take the train?"

"You have to. What will you do here?"

"Take a room. Find a job. Marry my girl."

I hesitated. "What kind of job?"

A bolt of anger. "What difference does that make?"

"Be practical. Marriage is a very practical thing. Especially here. What can you do?"

"I'm a Yale man."

I laughed. "Bulldog, bulldog, bow, wow, wow."

He glowered at me. "Don't you see a future for me here?"

"That's for you to see," I insisted. "Tell me what you see."

"I can teach school. Maybe get a newspaper job."

I took the cold of the night and chilled a mold of truth. "That's not a future. That's an exercise in futility. Which I don't wish to share. Not even with you."

"Do you love me?"

"I'll always love you. Always remember you."

Exasperated, Davis shouted, "What the hell *do* you want from me?"

"Lower your voice. You're disturbing the laughter."

His voice sank, but it was even more intense: "What do you want of me?"

I told him. "A smile. A last kiss. And a wave from a train window."

"Don't you want children who look like Wallace Reid?"

"How," I demanded, "would we afford to send them to Yale?"

9

"We'll have nothing but girls. And send them to Vassar."

I brought him back to earth, and to the pavement of reality. "I know what teachers and reporters earn. I can't live on peanut butter."

"You're not exactly an heiress."

"No, I'm not. My father has all the talents save that of gathering riches. But remember this: I'm a Gedney. And here in Georgia, it's a name worth more than riches."

Again the disdain. "And you're prepared to trade on it."

"Why not? My beauty, such as it is, will surely fade. But my name, never. The rich boys from here or Atlanta don't marry pretty girls from behind Woolworth counters. They marry heritage and grandeur. Why should I deny the legacy handed down to me by my paternal grandfather?"

Davis now put this question to me: "What do I have to do to win your hand?"

"Do you still want to, despite my crassness?"

His voice rose again. "What do you expect of me?"

I issued the order of the night. "Take a train. Sail a ship. Find a treasure. And bring it back to me."

"Trinkets for an Indian princess?"

I said, "No, coin of the realm. For the great house with a portico and pillars. For servants, sterling silver, and Pierce-Arrows for carriages."

"And how long will you wait for that phantasy?"

"I'm nineteen. I'm ripe for them now."

"Are you?"

"You doubt me?"

"Damned right I do. You're only a child, and I don't care if you're nineteen. You're still a child. Parroting the provincialism of your mother and father. You're all prattle and rattle. Yes, you'll marry. When your father and mother drop dead."

I was angry now. "Are you wishing them dead?"

He smiled sadly. "I wish you had brothers and sisters. You're entirely too precious."

Trying to sidestep the issue, I asked, "Are your sisters happily married?"

"They married. They're making their own lives. That's what counts. And remember this, next year you won't be nineteen."

"Nor will you be twenty-three," I countered.

Davis held his head high and directed toward the past. "I remember when I was seventeen and leaving home for college. My mother said to me, 'Darling, work hard. Yale can open all the right doors for you.' Poor mother, she never heard of Stephensville, Georgia, or of Brigadier General Watson Gedney." He now stared southward down the tracks. "I wish the damn train would hurry up."

At that moment I thought more of passing water than time. "Shall I kiss you now and leave?"

His demeanor Arctic, he merely shook my hand. "Good-bye, Rannah," he said, leaving me and all hope behind.

"No kiss?"

Without rancor, but with indifference, he now said, "We've had our share of kisses. Got enough money for a taxi?"

"I'm taking the streetcar."

His smile was lined with pride. "Have the motorman clang the bell for us. Just once."

"Yes, sir."

"I'll be back. Next time with Sherman. And the torch I'll carry will be only for burning."

I looked hard at him. "Do that, Lieutenant."

Davis looked away again, down the platform. Casually he said, "I see Charlie Nugent. Guess I'll go over and bum a Murad from him."

"Do that," I repeated, this time more as a dare.

"So long, Pocahontas."

The farewell was carelessly thrown over his shoulder. I watched him take three steps away from me. Then, with an instinct as ancient as man himself, I rushed toward him and clutched the wool of his overcoat. He turned to me without surprise or interest.

I said crisply, "Wait here."

He grinned. "Don't worry. I'm not about to throw myself under the train."

11

I winced at the thought. "I'll be right back."

"From where?"

"The ladies' room."

He said nothing, but he smiled the smile of the man who had discovered the Rosetta stone. I turned away and walked much too hurriedly to the waiting room. The abrupt change from the fresh, cold air to the stench and coal-stoved warmth of the waiting room sickened me. When I entered the ladies' room, I wasn't certain whether to vomit or urinate. I struggled with my clothes and my nerves and silently screamed at myself to hurry and hold the contents of my soured stomach. When I flushed the bowl, I heard the rush of water as the sound of a train. I hurried out of the toilet, out of the waiting room, and onto the platform where there was only chatter and laughter on the night wind. No train. No Davis.

I looked up and down the platform and saw nothing to lift the stone from my heart. I was like a child caught up in a foolish game of hide-and-seek, and my mind kept screaming, *Come out, come out, wherever you are.*

The steam whistle of the northbound train, muted by distance, answered me. Mocked me. I bit my fingers to keep from screaming, and my teeth tore through the wool of my gloves. I pulled at my scarf as if to strangle myself. And then I saw him — whom I loved — leaving the waiting room and marching toward me. Quickly I turned away from him to allow the wind to paint my pallor and dry my tears.

When I felt his close presence, I turned to him with a shoddy smile. "Where did you go? To the john?"

"To the ticket window."

Confused, I studied a ticket for Atlanta. I said, "You've got your ticket to Milwaukee."

"This is yours."

"Mine?"

He said, "You put on a good act. But your kidneys gave you away."

Still befuddled, I said, "Gave me away?"

12

"You love me as much as I love you. You know we have to be together."

Meeting his stare, I knew he spoke the truth. I studied the ticket again. "What'll we do in Atlanta?"

"First we'll find a preacher."

In control of myself again, I asked, "And then what?"

"We'll get a hotel room and put out a 'Do Not Disturb' sign."

And the parrot in me spoke again. "Then what?"

"On to Milwaukee."

The city with the Indian name held no magic for me. Again the parrot. "And then what?"

"Is that all you can say?"

I continued to taunt him, my voice now impassioned. "And then what?"

He said, "I have a big bedroom at home. With a big double bed." When he saw no reaction from me, he added rather bitterly, "Or would the Indian princess prefer a wickiup?"

Unmindfully, with a practicality I now damn, I posed this question: "And after the honeymoon?"

"I'll be a good husband and win bread."

"Where? How?"

"I'll go to work for my father."

"You hate the hardware business."

He hesitated. Making an end run around this truth, he said, "I'll think of something else."

I didn't desist. "What else?"

"Stop playing twenty questions."

"Please," I implored him, "can't you understand? I can't live in Milwaukee."

"A few hundred thousand manage to. It's a city. An American city. It's not Andersonville."

I pondered the allusion to stockades at Andersonville where thousands of captured Union troops had seen the bottom of hell. I said, "I'd rather take Andersonville. At least it's here in Georgia."

The coin of his face was tarnished now with black rage and I sensed an outpouring of invective, but it was forestalled by suc-

13

cessive blasts of the steam whistle heralding the onrush of the
northbound train.

Urgently now, Davis asked, "How about New York?"

"The Waldorf-Astoria?"

"As soon as we can afford it."

I said plainly, "When you can, send for me."

Again the prime question: "Rannah, do you love me?"

My reply, the one sentence I shall surely remember in hell, was
insipid and uncensored by reason. I said, "I do not *not* love
you."

"What the hell does that mean?"

I groped for reason. "Yes, I have kidneys. But I also have a
brain. I know that love's not enough."

"It's a beginning," he argued. "The only beginning for a life
for both of us. Don't you want that?"

"The piper must be paid," I said, not knowing why I said it.

He sighed. "And what the hell does *that* mean?"

"It's very simple. You can't afford me."

"Who are you quoting? Your father?"

"I'm speaking for myself."

"Are you really?"

It was the truth. "Yes, I am."

"You know what I wish?"

"What?"

"I wish I'd laid you," he said, using the verb for the first time
with me.

"You tried," I retorted coldly. "But I wish you had. Then
you might have lost interest in me. As you did with the other
girls you laid."

"Let's find out. In Atlanta. If it turns out that way, it's only
a short ride home."

"With a wedding ring? Or without my reputation?"

"You have your choice."

I didn't hesitate. "I'll stay here, thank you."

Davis persisted. "There's a hotel across the street."

I considered protesting that I wasn't a slut, but all I said was,
"What about your train?"

14

"There'll be other trains. There's no other girl, though."

"My father'd shoot you."

His grin was sad. "He might as well have that chance. The Germans never got it."

I managed laughter. "That's very funny. I'm glad — "

He interrupted me sharply. "Come to Atlanta."

Ignoring his demand, I casually said, "Will you write me?"

"From where?"

"Wherever you may be?"

"If I go alone, I go to hell." He seemed to speak with clairvoyance.

"Write me, please," I found myself pleading.

His reply tore at my entrails. "You'll never see me again. And you'll never hear from me."

"I'll write *you*." My voice was choked.

"Don't bother. Forget you ever knew me."

"How can I? I'm in love with you."

"Prove it! Get on the train with me."

"I thought I did prove it. Many times."

"How? When?"

I wanted to weep. "You know when."

"Those times we petted to climax?"

"Don't make it sound so clinical," I said painfully.

He touched memory. "Twice in the woods. Twice on your screened porch."

I turned away from Davis to watch the northbound train roaring and rushing toward the station, its beam of light a moon racing out of the cloud of night, its locomotive a gruff Gulliver thundering down upon us Lilliputians. My transfixion ended when Davis clutched my hand as if he never meant to free it.

"Come with me!"

"Come back for me."

"When?"

"When you've proven to the world what I know to be true: that you're someone special."

"If you know it, Rannah, then why do I have to prove — "

I interrupted him. "Prove it to yourself. You don't believe in

15

yourself. You look upon yourself as a failure. A failure at Yale. A failure at war. I don't want to share your Waterloos with you. I don't know where you're going. Milwaukee, New York, God knows where. But *go* there. Get there and build me an arch of triumph.''

I hated him when he answered, ''I can't do it without you.''

''You have to, Davis. If you can't, I don't want you.''

He regarded me with his own sudden hate. ''Who the hell are you, anyway?''

''Why did you buy the ticket for me?''

''I'll tell you what you are. You're a spoiled bitch.''

''Thank you.''

''You're Daddy's girl.''

Again by rote: ''Thank you.''

''Go marry some local oaf.''

I tried to taunt him. ''I may yet get married in Atlanta. I have several suitors there.''

''Good for you. Marry 'em all.''

I matched his childishness. ''A Yale man in Milwaukee ought to be a good catch for some rich bitch. Perhaps it's all for the best.''

''You said it.''

''You started it.''

''I'm sorry I ever met you.''

''Why did it have to be me?'' He said nothing. The train was roaring for him. ''I played hard to get.''

He said, ''I didn't realize how hard you were. How complicated. I thought you Dixie belles were soft and simple. I apologize. For being so obtuse.''

The train was at hand now. The ground beneath my feet was quaking, and I felt the train would jump the tracks and crush our lives and follies. I threw my arms about Davis and kissed him desperately on the mouth. He didn't respond. He was cold and dead to me.

I implored, ''Kiss me. Please.''

And the voice of the dead: ''We're out of the woods, you and I.''

16

"Don't be so damned clever!"

"Go back to your parties. Go to the woods with some other idiot."

"Are you going to kiss me or not?"

"Kiss you? I haven't even got a smile for you."

"I love you!"

"No, it's only that you do not *not* love me."

"I didn't mean it the way it sounded."

My voice was impassioned and frantic, but his was soft and quiet. "Good-bye, Rannah."

"Tell me you love me!"

"Right now I hate you. I look at you and remember what Gorki said about women."

"What was that?"

The brakes were on the wheels now and the train had stopped. Davis turned away from me. "I'd better get aboard now."

My fingers were claws on his sleeves. "Tell me!"

"Let me go."

"Tell me!" I screamed.

Davis turned on me. In that instant he appeared to me to reveal the demeanor of an old soldier leaving the field of his last battle. He said, more with resignation than with rancor, "Just this: Gorki said, 'It's not the woman who holds a man by his prick, but the one who holds him by his soul who is dangerous.'"

Overwhelmed, shocked by the toilet-wall word, I withdrew my hands. Davis turned away from me and I watched him calmly board the train. He took the steps like a condemned man climbing a scaffold. But the noose was around my neck, not his. I moved back to try to catch sight of him in the coach. I saw him enter and take a seat on the far side of the car. My heart screamed his name, but he, whose soul I held, didn't hear.

Panicked, I found myself boarding the train and entering the coach. I had the ticket to Atlanta in hand, but I didn't have a journey in mind. I rushed to confront Davis. Seeing my reflection in the car window, he turned and almost grasped a smile. But the smile was lost as he saw the fury clouding my face.

"Going to Atlanta?" he asked coldly.

17

"No, I'm not."

"Well, this train is. You'd better get off."

The coach was filling with passengers and I was blocking the aisle. I moved toward Davis and said, "No, I'm not about to go until I deliver a message. Not from Gorki. From Rannah Gedney." I brought up my right hand and slapped the stone of his face. "You go to hell!"

I didn't stir until I saw the rush of blood to the stone. Then I turned and fled, moving past voices and laughter and hands. Leaving the train I ran southward down the platform. I stopped when I heard the locomotive hissing steam and saw the wheels beginning to turn northward on the steel rails. Standing there, weeping freely, I watched the perceptible increase in speed, choked as the smoke rose above the lights of the depot, and sensed that the train was leaving me behind in hell. I watched the rear lights of the train until they were out of sight. The train was gone now, but its sound was still in my ears.

Deaf to the persisting bustle of activity at the depot, I stood there in a tomb of night eternally dark and silent. Then, out of the north, I heard a sound that seemed to rise from hallucination. I was truly hearing a train. The sound grew louder. Nearer. Nearer and nearer and nearer, louder and louder, bringing me waves of ecstasy.

And this is what I was thinking: Davis couldn't leave me. Miles of separation had brought him close to the point of no return. And he was returning. I saw him rushing from his seat, hurrying to the locomotive cab. Taking over the train from the engineer. Turning it around and returning to me. The northbound train was now racing southward. Back to me, bringing Davis back.

Almost at the precise moment when reason whispered to me that there was no turning of trains on tracks, I saw a beam of light piercing the distant dark and preceding the monstrous baying of the locomotive. The hallucination was revived again: this was the northbound train, my beloved's train.

I was crying and laughing as I watched the train emerge from the dark into the lighted oasis of the depot. As it slowed, I saw, with failing heart, that the locomotive and the trailing cars were different: this was a train from Atlanta heading south, bringing no one who answered to the name of Davis O'Donnell.

By the time the train came to a halt I had fled from the name of Davis O'Donnell to the name of Maxim Gorki, and then from Gorki to Leo Tolstoi and Anna Karenina.

And now the departed spirit of Anna Karenina entered into and possessed my body. I remembered and conjured the scene at the Russian station, the day I had first met Vronsky, when the workman had been accidentally crushed beneath the wheels of a train. To banish Anna Karenina's spirit, I turned to view the soldiers and civilians moving toward the train, and I saw them, with Anna's eyes, as lepers from whom I was desperate to escape.

I moved toward the train, which had now stopped, and the voice of Levin spoke to me. "In infinite time, in infinite matter, in infinite space, is formed a bubble-organism, and that bubble lasts a while and bursts, and that bubble is I."

Then, like Anna Karenina, I found myself silently crying, "Where am I, what am I doing? What for?"

I was close to the train now, close to the stilled wheels. I stood there waiting for the wheels to turn again, remembering Anna Karenina's memories of childhood, thinking how the fall beneath the wheels would be like the first plunge into icy lake water.

A warning bell sounded, but not for me. The locomotive belched. The wheels moved in reverse and then crashed forward with a strain of steam, a thrust of pistons. Now, now, I told myself, now is the moment to crush the body that held the soul that held Davis O'Donnell.

I dropped to my knees and was about to lurch forward when a hand reached out and grabbed me. It was not the hand of God, but the young, strong hand of a soldier whose horror was screened by freckles. Brusquely he pulled me to my feet and held me. He said nothing but the train whistle wailed for him.

Finally he found his voice, the voice of a Georgia country boy. "Hey, what's goin' on?"

I hated the sound of my own voice, which, but for him, would have been forever stilled. "Let me go."

19

He refused. "You outa your mind?"

I collected alibis. "I felt faint. I must have fainted."

He doubted me, but said nothing. The train was now beyond the station, beyond peril. Catching sight of the ticket for Atlanta which I still clutched in my hand, he took it and frowned over it.

He said, "This train went south."

"Thank you," I murmured.

He returned the ticket. Reaching inside his khaki overcoat, he withdrew a pack of cigarettes more crushed than I was. "Have a Pall Mall."

I had never smoked a cigarette in public before, but I took one from the pack. He mouthed one and then struck a match for us both. I took too heavy a drag and coughed.

"Easy," the soldier said with a country smile.

"I'm all right."

"You sure now?"

"Fine. Thanks for the smoke."

"I'm Ted Hawkins, stationed out at Hatton Field. What's your name?"

I found myself saying, "Anna Karenina."

"How do you spell that?"

I spelled it for him and broke the spell of Anna Karenina.

"You in the phone book?"

"Yes," I said softly. Then I embraced him and kissed him ardently, bestowing upon him the kiss intended for Davis. He blushed. "Good-bye, Ted."

Finding his voice, he said, "Can I take you home?"

I said, "I'm not going home, thank you."

"Goin' to Atlanta?"

"No."

"Goin' to be all right?"

"Yes, thank you."

"See you around maybe, huh?"

"Maybe."

"Thanks for the kiss."

"Thank you."

20

He wouldn't leave. "You maybe in trouble? You know what I mean, don't you?"

Casually I said, "I'm not pregnant."

The soldier blushed. "No offense."

"Good-bye." I gave him a smile without incandescence.

He grinned, nodded, and walked away from me. He stopped once to look back and wave at me. I returned the wave. When he was out of sight, I dropped the cigarette on the asphalt platform. With a toe I crushed the glowing life of the cigarette and, in that moment, I felt the train wheels rolling over and crushing me.

Sickness tore at my stomach and I ran to the dark beyond the depot and vomited. Faint, chilled, trembling, I then ran from my vomit. I slowed to a walk, and I don't remember how many times I paced up and down the platform before the cold drove me into the stench and warmth of the waiting room.

Blind to everything and everyone about me, I sat on a hard bench, lowered my heavy head, and closed my eyes.

A soprano voice, drawling alarm, roused me. "Miss Rannah?"

"Yes?" I looked up. An ancient black face, three gold teeth, two owlish eyes.

"I'm Louise Johnson. You remember me?"

I sat erect and studied her more closely, noting her white hair and the moth-eaten crown that was a floppy, velvet hat. Finally I said, "Yes, you used to work for Millie Bowden's mother."

Her smile was golden. "That's right, Miss Rannah. I seen you sittin' here and I says to myself, 'That sure looks like Miss Rannah.' Ain't set eyes on you for maybe three, four years."

"You left the Bowdens?"

She nodded and registered the sorrow of her race. "Three years. Mistah Bowden, he didn't take no more to my vittles."

"I'm sorry," I said.

"I misses the house. All you young chicks always gigglin', laughin', and dancin' to that Gramophone music."

"Yes," I said, in a voice that sounded as old as hers. "We had such fun."

First a nostalgic smile, and then a pursing of purple lips to express concern. "Miss Rannah, you shouldn't be in here."

21

I said, "It's warm. Warmer than under the train."

"This here's the colored waitin' room."

I looked about the room and saw, on another bench, a young Negro woman and her daughter eyeing me with awe and confusion. I said, "So it is."

"You best go on the other side."

"I'm comfortable here."

"It don't look right, Miss Rannah."

I said, remembering the Song of Solomon, "I feel black. Not black and comely, as the tents of Kedar, as the curtains of Solomon. Just plain, ordinary black."

I believe this was the first time in my life that someone looked hard at me and sensed madness. "Is you sick, Miss Rannah?"

To myself I thought: *By night on my bed I sought him whom my soul loveth: I sought him but found him not.* Aloud I said, "I'm sick of love."

She understood now. "A soldier boy?"

"He's gone. The train's so far away, but I can still hear it."

"Can I get you somethin'?"

I murmured aloud: *"Stay me with flagons. Comfort me with apples."*

Her fear of madness returned, and I could discern the sickly yellow of her eyeballs. She arose now and gently took my hand. "Come, Miss Rannah."

"Where are you taking me?"

"To the white folks' place. Come, child."

Rising, I freed my hand with equal gentleness. "I'm all right. Thank you. Very much. I can find my way." I turned from her, stopped, and faced her again. "What did you say your name was?"

"Louise Johnson."

"Thank you, Louise. You used to make good chocolate fudge. I remember."

She smiled and blinked tears. "Yes, child, and you gals sure loved it. Take care, Miss Rannah."

I nodded and left the colored waiting room and the chocolate color of my girlhood. I saw and felt the cold black of night and drifted into the white waiting room. I went straight to the ladies' lavatory, and when I left there I found myself hurrying toward the platform, as I had done before, in the hope that the clocks had been running counterclockwise, in the hope that the northbound train and Davis were there, awaiting my appearance. But the platform was vacant and the tracks empty.

Returning to the warmth, I sat down on a bench. In a moment I felt the softness of a train seat beneath me, the presence of Davis beside me. We held hands and felt the vibrations of the train and of our hearts. Then, abruptly, the vision faded. I was now on the platform and the hand of death was reaching out to me, enticing me to the chasm between the wheels. I fell to my knees and lurched forward and waited to be crushed.

I withdrew in time to run to the woods, and there Davis was waiting for me. Behind him the sun was streaking through the pines. He came to me, kissed me, and lowered me to the pine needles. I freed my hands, pulled at my skirt, and pushed my silk bloomers from the softness of my belly and the heat of my thighs. I felt him now, entering me.

Then I smelled chocolate and heard a Midwestern voice. Not the voice of my beloved. I opened my eyes and saw an unwrapped Hershey bar held in the hand of a boy in uniform. I met his eyes. They were brown and soft.

"Have a square," he said.

I shook my head, but I said nothing. My demeanor was flustered and my thighs retained the heat of the phantasy in the woods.

He persisted. "Sweets for the sweet?"

My voice, which I found before composure, faltered. "Have you a . . . have you a cigarette, please?"

"Sure thing." He produced a pack of Sweet Caporals as if it were a jewel box.

My hand was trembling when I took a cigarette. Deftly he followed with his matchbox and struck a match.

Blowing out the match and observing the wispy pattern of the exhaled smoke, he said, "Cold night, ain't it?"

"Yes."

23

"Them's good smokes."

I asked, "Where are you from?"

"Hatton Field."

I noted the sergeant's stripes on his overcoat. "Before that. Somewhere in the Midwest?"

"Chicago," he answered with the special pride given to denizens of big cities.

"You missed the train."

"Hell, no. Just came up from Columbus. Ain't been discharged yet."

"Have you ever been in Milwaukee?"

"Nah! They had to put a uniform on me to get my ass outa Chicago. I know a guy from Milwaukee."

"What's his name?"

"Joe Henrich."

"Know anybody else from Milwaukee?" I was attempting to conjure Davis, to block the image of the naked sergeant separated from me by only a wall of cigarette smoke.

"Got lotsa pals in Chicago."

"What does this Joe Henrich think of Milwaukee?"

"I never asked him. Lotsa breweries there, if you like beer. You like beer?"

"Hate it."

"Me, too. I like rye. Gimme some rye and a bottle of dope, that's for me. You like rye?"

I liked Coca-Cola better. That was the dope for me. But I said, "Bourbon."

The sergeant smiled. "That can be arranged. Interested?"

I feigned bewilderment. "I beg your pardon?"

"Like to have a drink with me?"

I found my smile. "Chocolate, cigarettes, and bourbon. Are you sure you're not a train butcher?"

He ignored my jest. "I ain't got a bottle on me, but I know where I can pick one up."

"Do you?"

"Yeah, from one of them bellhops across the street in the hotel."

24

"Really?"

He looked around the waiting room. "Stinks in here, don't it? Them lousy coal stoves sure smell up a place." He turned to me and in a tone befitting the announcement of the discovery of America added, "They got steam heat — radiators — in them hotel rooms across the street."

"How cozy," I said, the cigarette planted in my mouth like Theda Bara.

"My name's Pete."

"Pete what?"

He grinned. "What the hell! We ain't fillin' out a marriage certificate, are we?"

"That's a very interesting thought."

"I always sign the registers Pete Smith."

"How do you do, Mr. Smith?"

"How'm I doing, Miss What's Your Name?"

"Just call me Louise."

It pleased him. "You local gals sure got nice names."

"We try."

He moved closer to me. His mouth reeked of chocolate, tobacco, and whiskey. "How about us tryin' some bourbon for a starter?"

"Sounds marvelous. Hurry on back."

He frowned and whistled the opening notes of "Over There." Then he said, "You kiddin' me or somethin'?"

"No," I said absently. "I'd love some bourbon. And don't bother about the dopes."

"Hey, Louise. You takin' me for a chump?"

Innocently, I asked, "Why do you say that?"

"The bourbon ain't no good, not without the steam heat."

The cigarette dangled from my lips. "Sorry, I'm waiting for a guy from Milwaukee."

"A guy with a beer belly?"

"A Yale man."

"Brass?"

"Flesh and blood."

"Goin' to the hotel with him?"

"Where else?"

25

Sullenly he demanded, "Mind if I wait around? He just might not show."

"He'll be back," I said dully.

"Where'd he go?"

"Milwaukee."

The sergeant laughed the laugh of winners. "For beer?"

"No, for diamonds."

He had a question, but not about diamonds. "Know what they say about a bird in the hand?"

I played dumb. "What do they say?"

Impatient with this banter, he asked, "What do *you* say?"

More banter: "To what?"

"Ten bucks."

There it was. The backwash of the night of departure and despair. An ancient Negro woman, whose fudge I had tasted in yesteryears that danced to Gramophone music, had sensed I was mad. Now a sergeant with steam-heated loins was taking me for a whore.

Instead of raising a banner of dander, I welcomed the role and played the part. "You all right?"

"Clean as a whistle."

I smirked. "I hope you're not referring to your wallet."

He slapped a buttock. "I got a bundle. The dominoes gallop for me." He arose, and he was tall. "Let's go."

I stood up and was surprised to find that my knees didn't buckle. I said, "Why not? A bed's more comfortable than rails."

He jerked his head around. "What's that?"

"Oh, just some nonsense about a fate worse than death." My laughter sounded strange even to me.

The sergeant backed off. "You all right in the head?"

There it was again. He, too, sensed madness. I emitted more of the same strange laughter before I said, "No, but the rest of me is just fine. Just dandy."

When the sergeant and I passed from the erotic warmth of the waiting room to the winter of reality, I looked for a gust of wind to unmask me and reveal that the town whore was actually the belle who owned the town. But it didn't happen. Crossing the

26

street, I glanced up and down, searching for the straws of the familiar — the railroad yards and the slumbering freight cars, the warehouses from which the town issued cotton, peaches, and lumber to the market places.

Then I beheld the three-story, dirty yellow-bricked building that was the Cherokee Hotel, its legend faded by rain and sun and obscured by soot. Light from the windows was filtered by drawn green shades. In the distance I heard a shout and took it to be my father's voice calling me back from the quicksand of sin. But it was only one taxi driver shouting to another. I strained for the sound of Davis's train and heard only the nervous coughing of the sergeant beside me. My mind trailed the cough to the true source of his agitation.

"Ah," I exclaimed, as we reached the doorway, "the Waldorf-Astoria!"

The sergeant asked, "What's that?"

Remembering he was from Chicago, I said, "Pardon me, the Blackstone."

"That'll be the day." As we entered the small lobby, the sergeant turned to me. "Wait here."

The lobby was warm, its plaster walls painted a sickly green, the carpeting threadbare and stained, the mohair chairs and couches lumpy and misshapen. Only the spittoons and ashtrays had a sheen of currency. I sat down in a chair and saw an old brakeman peering at me over the top of his spread newspaper. I met his interested stare and made him wish he had a few dollars more and a few years less.

Turning to the desk, I observed the sergeant accosting the middle-aged, thin, bespectacled, balding clerk. The sergeant spoke softly to him. I was unable to hear what the sergeant was saying, but I saw the clerk raise his spectacles to appraise me. I met this stare, too, and watched the clerk abruptly grasp and remove his glasses, in the manner of an attending physician about to announce to a patient that a crisis was at hand.

I saw the desk clerk's lips moving, but I couldn't read them. But when the sergeant turned toward me, I could detect his chagrin and alarm. The desk clerk returned his glasses to his

27

wide eyes, and the sergeant returned to me, his flag down, his penis down.

"Let's go," he said glumly.

"No room at the inn?"

He took my hand and helped me to my feet. "Come on."

As the sergeant ushered me toward the entrance, the brakeman lowered his newspaper again. I waved to him. He didn't wave back. Outside, I glanced through the glass pane of the door and saw him crossing toward the desk to solve the mystery of the quickest arrival and departure of any pair of would-be sinners in the hotel's history.

"What's the matter?" I asked the sergeant. "Did the clerk tell you I was jailbait?"

He glared at me. "He knows who you are."

"Of course, I often frequent —"

"Aw, shut up."

"Where are you taking me now?"

"I'm puttin' you in a cab."

I persisted. "What did he say?"

The sergeant didn't answer me. We crossed the street to the depot and he opened a taxi door for me. "Get in."

"Now shall we try the Blackstone?"

He slammed the taxi door behind me and turned to the old, red-necked, cigar-smoking driver. "Six-thirty-three Gedney Street."

"Got you," said the driver. Taking the dollar bill the sergeant handed him, he added, "Much obliged, buddy."

I lowered my window and confronted the sergeant. "Is this good-bye?"

He said nothing to disturb his portrait of chagrin. The instant the taxi shot ahead, I saw the sergeant's lips form two words I had no trouble reading. I laughed and wished he had.

As the taxi climbed Main Street and sped toward Courthouse Square, I deduced what had happened in the lobby. The desk clerk, a total stranger to me, had recognized me as Judge Gedney's daughter.

I laughed. "Isn't that remarkable?"

28

The taxi driver heard me. "Miss?"

"What is the population of this town?" I inquired, as if I were a visitor from afar.

"Reckon about thirty thousand."

"Do you know who I am?"

"Can't say I do."

"Do you know who lives at 633 Gedney Street?"

"I'm new in town. I'm from down-country."

"Don't you even know the whores?"

"I know how to get to Gedney Street," he said coldly.

"Of course you should. That's the red-light district."

"You been drinkin', miss?"

"A little drinkin', a little fuckin'," I said airily. "What else is there?"

Not being a philosopher, he coughed and spat out of his window before he increased the speed of the taxi, as if he were anxious to discharge me from his care. When we came to Courthouse Square and I beheld the Johnny Reb statue, I began to recite aloud the lines of Henry Timrod chiseled into the marble base:

> *Stoop, Angels, hither from the skies!*
> *There is no holier spot of ground*
> *Than where defeated valor lies,*
> *By mourning beauty crowned.*

No applause from my audience, only a sharp turning onto Gedney Street. When the taxi pulled up and stopped at the curb before my house, I felt the charade coming to an end. The taxi driver reached back and opened a door for me.

"Good night, miss," he said with obvious relief.

Allowing myself one last whim, I asked, "Would you give me a puff of your cigar?"

His teeth bit through the cigar as he shifted into low gear, disengaged the clutch, made a U-turn, and raced back toward Courthouse Square. When the taxi was out of sight, I turned and faced my house, allowing it to recite to me the lyrics of my reality.

29

2.

The house in which I was born was built of red brick, stood two stories high, and was topped by a gabled attic and a slate roof. As I walked toward the open porch, I looked up and saw my mother standing at the window of her darkened second-story bedroom, and I was once again a nineteen-year-old belle, a virgin late coming home from the depot, as I had often been late returning from parties.

My father, who had apparently been standing in the vestibule waiting for me, opened the door. He was in shirt sleeves and wore his habitual string tie. At forty-seven he was a lean man built very much like Davis, but he had the eyes of a hanging judge and a Roman nose which I was fortunate not to have inherited. I looked like my mother, who now sadly looked as if time had tilled her beauty too often.

The Judge, who had never sat on a courtroom bench, but who practiced trial law, had a baritone voice designed for a rhetoric he invariably disdained. "Come into the study, please," he said in a tone which, had I been younger and a boy, would have directed me to the woodshed.

I followed him into the study walled with mighty books, the room in which he had directed my education, particularly in the

30

humanities, and only incidentally in such modern authors as Tolstoi and such compelling novels as *Anna Karenina.*

Breathing in the fragrance of pipe smoke, fresh coffee, and old leather, I sat down in the maroon chair close to the desk and faced my Socrates.

Settled into his captain's chair, he easily read my distraction. "You had a bad time."

"I'm all right."

"Remove your hat and coat."

I obeyed. And, in that instant, my mind tumbled and fell to plaguing memory, to the afternoon when my father had entered my mother's room and had come upon me standing before a mirror reflecting my budding breasts.

When I sat down again I was fifteen, naked, ashamed, and trembling.

"Coffee?"

I shook my head. "Bourbon, please."

He looked askance at me. "Why? Have you got the miseries?"

I laughed. "No, I'm only bleeding from the heart."

His demeanor pained, he said, "Discretion, Rannah. Always discretion."

"No bourbon?"

"For medicinal purposes only."

"I'm cold."

"Then take coffee."

"The hell with coffee."

He poured one cup. "The train left more than an hour ago. I heard it go by."

"Did you think I was on it?"

"No, I didn't. I had no such fears."

"I had a ticket in my hand."

His stare and tone were both harsh. "Purchased by Lieutenant O'Donnell?"

"Yes. For Atlanta. He wanted to marry me there."

I observed the tremor of his hand as he poured cream into his cup. "Determined, wasn't he."

"He's madly in love with me."

31

My father filled a pipe with tobacco from his pound tin of Prince Albert. After he had methodically sucked flame into the bowl, he blew out the match. "He's not alone, is he?"

I answered with conviction. "Davis stands alone. Far above all the rest." The blue, fragrant smoke drifted toward me. "Father, do you have any cigarettes in the desk drawer?"

"You know I don't keep them."

"I'll smoke one of your pipes."

He frowned. "I find pipes very unbecoming for women, even for mammies."

"I like your pipes. I confess I've smoked several of them. Please, may I?"

He weighed his decision. "Help yourself."

I arose, selected the longest pipe on the rack, filled it with tobacco, and lighted it.

When I had sat down again, he slid into interrogation. "Who put you in the taxi?"

I tried, without success, to blow smoke rings, but I did succeed in shocking him. "A soldier. From Chicago."

He strained for doubt. "Really?"

"We met at the depot. He picked me up. He thought I was a whore."

"Remarkable."

"Don't you believe me?"

"That you're a whore? No."

"He took me to the Cherokee Hotel."

Nothing is so sad as the deaths fathers die before their daughters' eyes. "And you went?"

The pipe made me brazen and the smoke was a screen for the truth. "He paid me ten dollars."

"Very generous of him."

"He's a gambler."

"And so, apparently, are you."

I asked, "You mean with my reputation?"

"No, with my credulity. Let me see the ten dollars."

I thought fast. "I was a sport. Like most whores. I gave the bill to the taxi driver."

32

Calmly he sipped his coffee. "Very generous of you."

"You don't believe me?"

"You forget, I'm a trial lawyer."

"I was in the Cherokee Hotel."

"How far in? The lobby?" I said nothing. "Charlie Musick's an old client of mine."

"Who's Charlie Musick?"

"The night clerk." My father described him perfectly. Noting my reaction, he said, "I see the description registers with you."

I laughed. "Yes. No wonder Charlie wouldn't give us a room."

"He knows who you are."

"It's a very small town, isn't it?"

"We're Gedneys," he replied, a simple statement of fact, not pride.

"Yes, and the Gedneys are very small people."

"Are we, Rannah?"

"Refute it if you can."

He said, "Some of us Gedneys are foolhardy and spirited. My father was, you are, but I am not."

"Davis says I'm Daddy's girl."

"We know how mistaken he is, don't we?"

"You know best," I snapped.

"Meaning what?"

"You know you're a coward. I didn't think I was. Not until tonight."

"Because you didn't take the northbound train?"

I now took a train of thought back to 1915, to the terrible time when my father had been sounded out on joining other lawyers in the appeal of the Leo Frank case. In Atlanta, Frank had been convicted for the slaying of fourteen-year-old Mary Phagan. The trial, in my father's judgment, was a mockery of justice. Yet my father refused to become involved and risk his political future. In the end, Leo Frank, his death sentence commuted by a very brave governor, was hanged by a lynch mob.

I said, "You once missed a train north, too. Remember?" As the pipe smoke rose about him, I saw him burning in hell.

33

"How can I forget?"

I didn't desist. "You were thinking at the time only of yourself. Of the Gedney name."

"Yes," he confessed. "All right. I'm a very small person."

"Don Quixote was shorter than you."

"Remember this: I'm still suspect and unforgiven in this town for having fought the Klan. I'm tolerated, being Watson Gedney's son."

I said, "One battle doesn't make a war."

"True. I've left the field to the demagogues and left behind a dream of the Senate."

"You made your bed," I said cruelly. "And Mother ran from it."

"Not for the reason you think."

"Oh, I've heard her carry on. Mother's disappointed in you. Besides, both of you got old and bored with each other."

He shook his head. "We're not all that old. Passion's not a preserve for youth alone."

"Then what happened?"

He told me. "About five years ago, at a dinner party given by the Hendersons, I voiced my belief that George Thomas, by giving his allegiance to the Union rather than to the Confederacy, acted with more valor and historic wisdom than Robert E. Lee. It was poorly received. I might better have said that Judas, and not Jesus, was the son of God. And that was the bitter end of the evening, the end of our long friendship with the Hendersons and with the Wardlaws. When your mother and I returned home, she became hysterical. It was frightening. I was afraid she'd lost her mind. You weren't home that night. You were sleeping over at Liz Cooper's." While my father paused to sip more coffee, I pondered the possible link between my mother's fragile mind and mine. My father now continued: "That very night your poor mother bolted the door between our bedrooms. It hasn't been opened since." A long, long pause. "I can't reason with your mother. The legend of the South is her religion, stronger than her faith in Jesus."

"Have you ever considered divorce?"

34

"Neither of us has. **Divorce is out of the question.** We both love you too much."

Anguished, I said, "I wish I had taken the train."

"You did well not to."

"Would the pillars of this house have fallen if I had left your lives?"

"That's not the point."

"Be responsive, Father. Isn't that what you demand of the witnesses you cross-examine?"

"We'd go on, without you, living out our days."

"God, what an awful thing you two make of life."

"Have we done so badly?" he asked. "You love life, don't you?"

"Do I?"

"You're beautiful, bright, learned, vivacious. And as you've constantly reminded the officers who came here, you own this town."

"I almost inherited a grave tonight," I said.

My father frowned. "How so?"

The pipe was sickening me now. I stood up, left the pipe in an ashtray, and went to the bookshelves to find and flip the pages of Tolstoi's novel. I said, "Anna Karenina did it. And there was no soldier to reach out his hand and stop her."

My father paled. "My God!"

"Are you thanking God, Father?" I knew that for him, as for me, God didn't exist.

"I'm thanking the soldier."

"You don't doubt me?"

"No, only your judgment. What happened to you?"

I returned the novel to the shelf. "I was mad. Not angry mad. I believe, in that moment, I was insane." He said nothing, but he did place his pipe beside mine in the ashtray. "Father, has there been any insanity in our family?"

"In all of us."

"That's an evasion."

"The remarkable thing about us mortals is that so few of us are locked away in asylums."

35

"Have you ever been mad? Insane mad?"

"No."

"Mother was that night, wasn't she? The night of the nonsense about George Thomas and Lee. You feared so, didn't you?"

"Morning follows night. Your mother lives, functions, and sleeps in a room without bars."

"She doesn't live. She exists. Endures."

"When you're older, Rannah, you'll realize that merely to exist, to endure, is to triumph over life."

"Isn't that a Pyrrhic victory?"

He didn't answer me. Instead he now became more candid with me. "I lied to you before. There was one time when I was insane mad, as you put it. August 17, 1915, in my office. A client I had successfully defended — a tenant farmer — came in and gave me, in lieu of cash, a shotgun and six boxes of shells. After he had left, the telephone rang. It was a reporter from the *News*, telling me Leo Frank had been lynched. I refused to comment and hung up. I sat there, with this sickness overwhelming me, and then I found myself breaking open the shotgun and injecting shells into both chambers. I don't know how long I contemplated shattering my shame and cowardice. Finally, I returned the shells to their box. The same afternoon I returned the weapon and the ammunition to the farmer."

I could say nothing. I could only regard him with understanding and compassion. Then he said, "You're not alone, Rannah. No matter what you feel, no matter what you do, you're never alone in your hell. There was Anna Karenina, there was you, there were and are legions who are confronted by Hamlet's dilemma."

Tears in my eyes, I implored him, "What do I do now?"

He rose, and for a moment I thought he was about to dismiss me. But he said, "I think the time has come for us to have a drink together." From his desk, he brought out a bottle of bourbon and two shot glasses. "Are you man enough to drink it neat?"

"Am I?"

"Any girl who owns a town must have a good deal of man in her. I know you do. You read, you absorb and you think like a man."

"So unlike Mother."

"Yes, but I'll say nothing against her. I fell in love with her at first sight. I knew who she was, what she was, and I wanted her. I never blamed her for her hysterics that night and all the emptiness that has followed. I was a fool to have said what I did. But what I said was true. However, it was a truth far beyond her capacity. You see, I forgot another truth: who she was, and what she was."

As we stood and faced each other across the desk, my father handed a jigger of whiskey to me. "Thank you," I said. "Shall we make a toast?"

"No toast. Let's just drink, man to man."

"I wish I'd been born a boy."

"Nonsense. You're what every woman should be. A man could — share, with a woman like you."

I never loved my father, before or since, as I did in that moment. We raised our glasses, eyed each other with a melancholy warmth, and sipped our bourbon. It was my first taste of liquor and it burned me. I smiled and exhaled heat.

"Drink it down," he urged. "It'll help you sleep."

"I don't want to sleep just yet. I must talk to you. I want to talk about Davis."

"Tomorrow. A little time, a little perspective never — "

I interrupted him with urgency. "Now, Father! Please!"

He sat down again. "All right."

Sitting on the edge of my chair, sipping the bourbon, I regarded my father a moment and said, "Make your case against him."

"Must I? You'll never see him again."

The judgment rocked me. "Why do you say that?"

"Summers end, wars end. Romance dies."

"The trains still run north and south."

"The biplanes aren't flying over us any more. The war was a

37

party for you, but the party's over, as you've sensed these past few weeks.''

"But Davis and I haven't changed. We still love each other."

My father selected another pipe from his rack, and I waited on my own rack for him to fill me with his wisdom. He said, "Tomorrow, or the day after, in Milwaukee, Lieutenant O'Donnell will put his uniform away. He'll pack it in mothballs. Along with his memories of Rannah Gedney and of Stephensville, Georgia."

"Can he forget me?"

Solemnly he said, "Yes, even you, like the rest of us, can be forgotten."

"I won't forget him," I vowed.

"I'm certain you will."

I emptied the shot glass and filled myself with resolve. "Please, Father, make your case against Davis. I want to argue it with you."

"Must we argue?"

"Must I accept your judgment?"

"Not at all. It pleases me that you have a mind of your own."

"Father, my mind's cracking! Please! Make your case!"

"You've known all along how I've felt about —"

"*Make your case!*"

Lighting his pipe, he leaned back and contemplated the blue smoke. "He's not a Southerner."

"That's a very unbecoming observation from a very unprofessional Southerner."

"Nonetheless, I am a Southerner."

"An accident of birth! You're a man of reason. A man of the world."

Unabashed, he continued his attack on Davis. "The man's a drinker."

"Isn't that terribly Southern?"

My father smiled to herald a jest. "He's sottish, not Southern."

"No jokes, Father. Please."

The smile was gone now, and the smoke seemed to paint sorrow

38

on his face. "I'm sorry, but I can't recall ever seeing him in this house, not once, when his eyes weren't glazed with drink."

"He was unhappy. About being eliminated from flight training. About his desk job."

"He could have wrecked his aeroplane and this house — let alone killed himself. The authorities at Hatton Field were not unjust with him."

"In war there are only the daring and the dead."

He countered, "In war there are only orders and obedience."

"What about your father?"

"Yes," he admitted, "he was an exception to the rule. But he proved himself in battle, not in high jinks."

Again I was unkind. "What great battles? They were raids, only raids. Was General Gedney at Shiloh, Vicksburg, Atlanta, Gettysburg?"

My father's mind fled to these bloody fields. "My father died believing he could have turned the tide in each of those crucial engagements."

"A belief you didn't share."

"I never argued the point with him. I only listened and wished I were he. I didn't collect facts about the stupidity and futility of the Confederate cause until he was long dead."

I asked, "Is Davis dead? So far as I'm concerned?"

"Rannah, he's wrong for you."

Stung, I said, "Arguments, Father! Not judgments!"

"The man's much too handsome, and being so, he's much too vain. Strange as it may seem, a too handsome man and a too beautiful woman rarely, if ever, make for a happy marriage."

"Why not?"

"Lieutenant O'Donnell —"

"The war's over. Call him Davis."

He nodded. "As you wish. Davis attracts many, many women, and you, my daughter, many, many men. There's bound to be trouble in paradise."

"Mustn't all good marriages begin with paradise?"

"A good marriage begins with reason."

"Did yours?"

39

He said, "Yes, it did. I reasoned that your mother would make a very proper wife for a politically minded lawyer."

"Back to Davis," I insisted.

"Yes. Have you applied reason to him?"

"I love him. Only him."

"Beyond that, what is there about him that makes you so certain he's the man for you?"

"He's educated," I began.

"True, he's a Yale man, but I must say, in all frankness, that I've failed to detect any intellect or erudition."

"You never saw the best of him."

"I never once heard him utter a single thought that commanded my interest or respect."

I said, "You probably did most of the talking."

"True. He was hardly loquacious with me."

"Didn't he have the ability to draw you out? To make you talk about wars?"

"War talk by men who've been to war is always interesting. Mark Twain said that. I found it so with my father and his compatriots. Neither Davis nor I had been to war."

I said, "I remember so much of what he said to me. Didn't he say *anything* to you worth noting and remembering?"

He shook his head. "No, I only recall a refrain of self-pity, which I very much deplore. Self-pity is pardonable, perhaps, in old men, but hardly in a boy of twenty-three. And remember this, Rannah, he is a boy. As for his drinking, he seems to be sipping either sorrow or laughter. This isn't the way of a man."

"It's the way of a poet."

"Perhaps. But hardly that of a man of reason. A man of reason would never have asked you to marry him, not at a point in his life when he is without means and without occupation."

"Father," I said regretfully, "I'm sorry you missed his magic."

"What magic? His personality?"

"Compared to Davis, Father, you and I are blind. I know. I've listened to him scores of times, and I've heard much I'll never forget to my dying day."

40

"For instance?"

"Damn the instances!" My voice rose. "I'm trying to tell you the effect he has had on me. And it wasn't because he was handsome. He has eyes to see the colors of life as painters do. He puts music to words and makes life a poem. He sees it all. He has the grace to stand apart from himself, to stand upon a hill, or outside a window, and look in on the drama of the moment."

"You've described a poet. Is he, in fact, a poet?"

"He wrote verse in prep school. And at Yale."

"In what vein?"

"Humorous. He has a marvelous sense of humor. Did you fail even to detect that?"

My father hesitated. "I can't recall that he ever made me laugh."

"He didn't try. He liked you, Father. You interested and intrigued him."

"I was most uncomfortable with him. I found myself saying more than I intended to say."

I said, "Wouldn't he be a son-in-law with whom you could sit and drink and talk from your heart?"

"I do that with you."

"Answer my question."

He said, "No, he wouldn't be. With Davis I don't believe I could ever have the feeling of father and son, of man to man, friend to friend. He doesn't share, at least he didn't with me. Let me put it this way: I sometimes had the feeling he had me in the witness box, cross-examining me, not for a jury but for a judgment from Saint Peter."

I laughed at him. "That's very funny."

My laughter perturbed him. "I didn't find it so. Let me try to put this in terms of war. The boy sits with you. By the light of the campfire you note he's wearing the same color uniform. But in reality he's a spy."

I laughed again. "For Saint Peter?"

Then came the admission: "No. For my conscience."

I drew the conclusion. "Davis drew out your guilt, Father. That's why you're afraid of him. That's why you hate him."

41

My father stood. "It's time you went to bed."

"I'm not a child!" I protested strongly. "Pour me another drink."

"You've had enough."

"Is court adjourned?"

"We'll talk again."

"One last question, please."

"What is it?"

"Would you buy me a one-way ticket to Milwaukee?"

"No, I would not. You couldn't live there."

"What am I? A tropical bloom?"

He merely said, "If it happens that you and Davis can't live without each other, then you must wait for him to return here, to make a life for both of you here. That's all I have to say for now. Good night."

"Good night? It's the worst night of my life!" My right hand seemed again to feel the pain of slapping Davis's face. "We don't have any of his books here, but did you ever read Gorki?"

"No. What's the point?"

"Do you think I'm a dangerous woman?"

"You're a headstrong girl, hardly a woman, let alone dangerous."

"Davis believes I am."

"I place no value on — "

I interrupted him. "Shall I tell you what Davis quoted to me from Gorki?"

"If you must."

I knew the maxim would shock and hurt him, and that was precisely what I intended.

My father was duly revolted. "Did you slap his face?"

"Belatedly."

Now came the judgment from on high. "Maxim Gorki, being Russian, confounds me. Lieutenant O'Donnell, being a Yankee, disgusts me, and I have no wish to hear his name again."

"Davis O'Donnell!" I cried out, and the cry tripped a barrier to respect. "I held his prick! I hold his soul!"

The daggers of truth found my father's heart. For a moment I

42

feared he would gasp and fall. Then, no longer able to bear the sight of me, he turned away and left the study in the halting manner of the walking wounded. The door slammed shut.

I stood there and wept into my hands and aimlessly washed my face with my tears. Then, with a resolve that seemed suicidal by nature, I went to the desk, removed the bottle of bourbon. Because my hands were trembling I spilled almost as much whiskey as I drank. I had three quick, scorching shots. And when I finally left the study, I had mindfully left the bottle and the pool of whiskey on the desk as evidence of my defiance and despair. Moreover, I left the lights burning in the room; there had been too much darkness this night.

As I climbed the steps to the second floor, I found my legs weakening, my breath short. Entering my room, I turned on the overhead light. Unable to face myself in the mirror, unable to accept the light and warmth of the familiar effects with the hardy roots of childhood and girlhood, I brusquely struck the switch and commanded darkness.

In the dark, I removed my dress, shoes, stockings, and then all of my damp underclothes. Naked and chilled, I stood there and felt the flood of whiskey lift the house from its foundation. I staggered from my room and walked naked through the corridor to the bathroom. Not bothering to bolt the door or turn on the light, I sat on the toilet seat and remained there to conjure specters, to behold the clawed feet of the iron bathtub as if they belonged to some forest beast poised to leap upon and ravish me.

I didn't leave the bathroom by the corridor door. Instead I opened another door leading to the guest room, and leading as well to the memory of a childhood night, almost ten years before, when, through the keyhole of this door, I had seen my Aunt Helen and Uncle Gerald locked in a carnal embrace upon the bed.

The memory very much with me, the bourbon now also rocking the guest room, I hastily pulled the bedspread away and left it in a careless heap upon the cold floor. Then I eased carefully between the soft of the mattress and the warmth of the blankets. The icy cold of the pillow melted before the heat of my face. I

43

shut my eyes and the bed suddenly seemed to be lifted by a giant Ferris wheel.

Escape, escape, I told myself. And my mind flew and intercepted a train rushing northward through the night. It brought me naked and burning with desire for Davis. In the conjured Pullman bedroom I lay on the bed and embraced my beloved. He hurt my mouth with kisses and crushed my breasts. I held him by his prick until I could hold him no longer. Then he became the forest beast with clawed feet and he ravished me with savage thrusts. The locomotive's whistle screamed my ecstasy.

Then I became aware of a weird moaning sound rising over the darkness of the guest bedroom. My first thought was that it was emanating from the beast of the bathtub, and then I realized with a shock that the beast was I.

Then another sound, that of the corridor door being flung open. Then a flash of light, a signal of doomsday. And there before me stood my mother, clad in her long cotton nightgown. I shut my eyes against the light and the apparition. When I opened them again, I saw that my mother was as real as the light.

She sat upon the bed and looked at me as if she discerned that I was the girl in the fairy tale who had turned into a forest beast. "Rannah, baby! Are you all right?"

Not certain what I might say, I merely nodded.

She shivered and sighed. "I heard an awful moaning. I ran first to your room. When you weren't there, I almost died. Then I thought to come in here. Rannah, baby, you must've been having a nightmare!"

I realized that my mother, in all her years of marriage, had not once cried out in ecstasy, that she had not understood the nature of the phantasy that rested as a fact on the freshly stained bedsheet.

Trying my voice at last, I weakly said, "Yes, Mother. A nightmare."

Tenderly she bent and kissed my fevered brow. Not so tenderly she suddenly withdrew. Her voice muted with astonishment and incredulity, she said, "You've been drinking!"

I lied as a child lies. "Father gave me a small drink. To help me sleep."

"The fool. I'll speak to him."

"Please don't. He only gave me one drink. I stole three others."

My mother was weeping now. "He's a fool. Every drunkard starts with the first drink. Do you feel sick?"

Another lie. The room was revolving and my stomach with it. But I wanted not to be nursed, but to be left alone. "I'm all right."

"Would you like some hot milk?"

"No, Mother. Good night."

She didn't stir. "Was the nightmare about him?"

"Him, Mother?" I feared she was referring to my father and hinting at a desire I had long buried.

"Lieutenant O'Donnell."

The name was a trumpet sound. "Yes, it was."

"Shall I tell you something?" Her voice was soft with secrets, dark with pathos.

"What?"

"I was praying you'd elope with him."

"Were you? Why?"

"Will it be our secret?"

"I swear it."

And she spoke to me as only unhappy women speak. "The thought of you running away with him was a delicious thought. Oh, to be young and run away. That's what I lie awake nights in my cold bed and think of doing myself. But I'm no longer young, there's nowhere to run and no one to run to."

The room was spinning again, and I raised myself and embraced my mother to still my soul and my surroundings. "I'm sorry, Mother."

She winced. "You're soaked. And no nightgown." She managed a titter. "Imagine! Sleeping like a hussy! You stay under the blankets. I'll fetch you your nightgown and some hot milk."

"No, Mother," I protested. "Just go back to bed. I'm going to sleep here."

45

"I can't argue with you, can I, Rannah, baby?"

"I'm nineteen," I said, as if I were ninety.

With sudden alarm, she said, "You won't tell the Judge what I said, will you?"

"Of course not."

She sighed again. And then, absently: "If tomorrow, or any day after, you wish to run away, I'll help you. Remember that."

"You won't miss me?" The child's voice again.

My mother's eyes held a sorrow I was to recognize years hence in my own mirrors. "Rannah, baby, you've been missing from me these many years. The Judge eclipses me, like the moon the sun. When my baby moans so frightfully, I run to her. As I used to run to her when she truly was a baby and cried in the night. Now my darling baby's all grown up and drinks hard liquor with her foolish daddy."

Softly I said, "Good night, Mother."

She rose and crossed her arms to warm her breasts. Looking toward the windows, she said, "He's happy tonight, isn't he? The Judge, I mean." Then she elevated words from the dungeon of her despair. "May his black smile never see the morning sun." I shrank before the curse and watched her turn, cross to the door, and extinguish the light. Then, turning to me and seeing me through the darkness as only a mother can see a child with a light of her own, she said, a little nervously, a little contritely, "You didn't hear me, did you, baby?"

A white lie to pierce the dark. "No, Mother."

Then, across the darkness, came her plaintive parting words. "Oh, dear Jesus, I hope my mother and father in heaven didn't either. They always so wanted me to be well-mannered, and always pleasant."

She opened the door, stepped into the corridor, and quietly shut the door behind her. My mind walked with her to her own bedroom and stayed with her until she had gotten into her lonely bed and had cried to Jesus to bring sleep and a dream of yesterday.

On this whiskey-dark sea of night, on the strange calm that had followed in the wake of the moaning winds, my mind fled

46

from my mother and rushed northward to lie across the tracks before the onrushing train bearing my beloved.

Hope whispered to me, reminding me that history can ever be mined for analogy. I went back to the time of my paternal grandfather, to the year 1864.

Somewhere in Georgia a regiment of a brigade commanded by General Watson Gedney had been dispatched to guard a mill that fed the starved Confederacy. One dawn a superior force of Sherman's troops attacked and captured the mill. The next day my grandfather ordered a counterattack. It succeeded all too easily, the Yankees retreating in short order.

What my grandfather hadn't realized was that the Yankees had been unable to operate the mill and convert the grain to flour. As soon as the Confederates had done with the milling, the Yankees, by design, reappeared with sufficient forces to retake the mill and the stores of flour which became bread for the terrible army marching from Atlanta to the sea.

So, I now reasoned, Lieutenant Davis O'Donnell hadn't been defeated by me in the engagement at the Stephensville depot. No, he was merely making a strategic withdrawal. In the North, he would regroup his forces, bide his time and wait for the mill of time, with its cold stones of loneliness, to grind away the grain of my adamant nature, and of the provincialism that walled me up in Georgia.

Yes, I thought, he would return to win me, the fair flour of the South. I laughed aloud at the pun, and muffled the laughter with my pillow before sleep, in its mercy, took me.

Somewhere on the night side of the spinning, racing earth, light-years away from laughter, I awoke to an awareness of hell. My head was a white-hot steel rail over which a thousand train wheels had passed. My mouth was a trap that had caught the foul ashes of defeat, and my eyes were lead pellets sinking in the quicksand dark.

A voice from childhood and terror arose in me, crying, "Mother, turn on the lights! I can't see tomorrow!"

47

3.

Love and war, wrote Cervantes, are the same thing; and stratagems and policy are as allowable in the one as in the other.

The blood of General Watson Gedney made me impatient with the lulls between battles. I found myself disturbed by the introduction of trench warfare with its sporadic artillery attacks, its exchanges of communiqués, and the sometime camaraderie of opposing soldiers exchanging smokes and rations, making a mockery of death-demanding, noble causes. Like my grandfather, I preferred the battle cry, the crackling of rifle fire, the charge of horses, the brandishing of swords, and the confrontation of chivalry.

Late the first morning after Davis had retreated to his own lines, after a breakfast of tea and toast to quiet a queasy stomach, I sat at the desk in my room and exhausted a box of stationery trying to fashion a letter that was more a missile than a missive.

I wrote, in my first and last letter to Davis in Milwaukee, that the sun, despite his absence, had appeared in the east as a golden apple, a gift of morning which I savored as always. I didn't tell him the sky was empty, or that I was hollow with loneliness for him. It was anything but a note of surrender.

48

A month-long week passed before Davis honored my communication, not with a letter but with an envelope containing nothing more than a clipping from a Milwaukee newspaper's society page. It told of the homecoming of Davis O'Donnell, the lieutenant, the Yale man, the handsome and eligible bachelor who was now making the rounds of the best local parties.

Thoreau was right. Time could not be killed without injuring eternity. And at first, in those early weeks, when I was wounded by our separation, I attended many, many parties honoring the return from France of warrior princes from Stephensville and from the neighboring kingdoms of Atlanta, Savannah, Macon, and Columbus. At one of these less than festive affairs, a Marine captain, on noting that I had difficulty owning a smile, let alone a town, inquired whether I had lost someone very dear on the Western front. I told him I was in love with the Kaiser, who was now interned in Milwaukee and spending his days chopping wood for fires that held no warmth for him.

Playing Davis's game, I forsook correspondence and only forwarded him my many invitations to parties, engagements, and weddings. I might as well have placed them in bottles and floated them down the Cherokee River. The postman rang the bell of the O'Donnell house, but it never sounded alarm for Davis.

Late in the spring of 1919, I suggested to my father that he allow me to become his secretary. He refused, believing my tenure in his law office would be short and ended by a marriage to one of the many serious and qualified suitors I had at the time. He did, however, agree that I was in need of a proper but temporary occupation. And so he spoke in my behalf to Brian Morehart, the editor of the Stephensville *News*, and I was hired as an assistant to the society editor. My wages were fifteen dollars a week.

I clipped the one-paragraph announcement of my adventure in journalism and forwarded it to Milwaukee, certain it would prompt a letter. It didn't. About a week later, in a large, manila envelope on which was a return address from Greenwich Village in New York City, I received an entire front page of a bogus

49

newspaper printed individually for tourists to Coney Island. At least the bannerlines were individual. This one read:

DAVIS O'DONNELL
ENTERS NEW YORK

Unable to bank my curiosity, I typed a note on copy paper reading: "What are you doing in New York?" For a reply I received a package: a shoe box stuffed with discarded Wall Street ticker tape. I showed it to my father, introducing it as evidence that Davis, a proper Yale man, was seeking his fortune in the lair of high finance. My father was neither impressed nor interested. I shot another note back to New York, reading: "Give my regards to J. P. Morgan, Junior."

And still no word from him, only envelopes containing a menu from the Plaza, ticket stubs from a Broadway theater, from the Polo Grounds, from the Yale-Harvard baseball game. One day I received a heavy package containing a newly published book. The title was *From Upton to Argonne*. It was a compilation of prose and poetry written by American doughboys, published by Albert Corbell and Son and edited by Delano Fredericks. The book, which disappointingly enough did not include a contribution from Davis, was inscribed not by Davis to me, but from Fredericks to Davis. It read: "For Davis, the boy who may make Milwaukee famous."

I recalled the many times Davis had told me about Freddie, whom he had described as the brightest boy of all at Yale, one certain to be a stellar name in American letters. In the offices of the Stephensville *News* one afternoon I happened upon a copy of *The Smart Set* containing an article by literary critic Delano Fredericks. It presaged a new golden era for American literature. The following day, from Davis, I received a copy of the same issue. No note, no comment. And I was left with perplexity about the meaning of the inscription in Freddie's book. I failed to understand how a literary man could feel that a boy from Milwaukee working in Wall Street could possibly bring fame to his hometown.

In the autumn of 1919 Davis and I exchanged ticket stubs

50

from football games, his from New Haven, Cambridge, and Princeton, mine from Atlanta and Athens. Christmas came, and with it a gift from Davis: a tin of tea, fashioned in the shape of a treasure box and containing not leaves for me to read, but doubloons that, in reality, were new and polished pennies.

He's trying to tell me something, I thought, but all of my conjectures were wide of the mark. Next morning I went to Farber's, the local department store, to select and send my Christmas gift to him. I chose three jars of peach preserves. The enclosed note read: "And a Merry Christmas to you. Trust you'll share the fruit with the bulls and bears."

1920 was only a few days old when I received a large package from Davis. I tore it open with excitement and an anticipation that hadn't dimmed in the long year of our separation. And I was dismayed to find a carton, formerly utilized to hold two dozen cans of Campbell's tomato soup, now loaded down with mementos from a New Year's Eve party: confetti, silly paper hats, and crushed cardboard horns. I looked in vain for a note.

Early in March, on a day blacker than ash buds, I sent Davis a clipping from the Stephensville *News* that I was certain would prompt a long-distance telephone call, a telegram, or at least a letter. The clipping, complete with a one-column cut of me, announced my engagement to Howard Franklin of Atlanta. The wedding was set for June 15th, and was to be held at the Piedmont Driving Club in Atlanta. The newspaper story detailed the social prominence of the Franklins and mentioned that Howard, a graduate of the University of Virginia, was now a vice-president of the Atlanta bank owned by his family. I enclosed no personal note, no explanation, no apology.

But the telephone didn't ring, the telegraph boys never came to my door, and the postman brought no letters postmarked New York. Days later, however, I received a huge package from Davis. Damn him, I thought, he's sending me a wedding present.

I damned him again and again as I unwrapped and opened the shipping carton to find a box within a box within still another box. The stupid, childish bastard, I thought, here we are playing with the matches of life, and he's reverting to boyish pranks.

51

I shivered when I opened the last and smallest of the boxes. It held a treasure beyond gold and jewels: a book.

The dust jacket, with a wash drawing of a soldier contemplating the vista of the Yale campus, heralded the title: *The Distant Spires*. The author: Davis O'Donnell. The publisher was Albert Corbell and Son. Opening the book, I saw that it had been dedicated "To My Mother and Father." On the flyleaf, written in blue ink, was this personal inscription: "For Rannah, who is Adele Garrett." It was signed, "Davis."

That and nothing more.

In tears I lay down upon my bed, embraced the book, and then, through more tears, through hours long past midnight, I read the novel. I must confess that I didn't recognize its worth at the time. But the magic that I had sensed in this strange boy from Milwaukee was now more than realized on the printed pages.

This first novel of a Wisconsin boy going to misadventure at Yale and coming of age and disillusionment in war was a far and different cry from *Stover at Yale*. The sad hero, Austin Fellows, was none other than Davis himself, cloaked by imagination. And the heroine, Adele Garrett, was the best and the worst of me.

As my eyes transported mind, heart, and memory through the paragraphs, pages, and chapters, and brought me to the closing, drifting words, I was prudent to wear blinders and block out my critical gaze. But once the book was shut and the lights out, I lay in my bed and assayed the coins of this treasure.

And these were my first and early conclusions: the novel had the bell sound of truth; the people were commanding; the dialogue was right; the memories perfect; the passions human and poignant.

But the book was flawed by its style. Davis erred in choosing to tell his tale in the manner of a bright boy at a party. The tone of the prose was that of the boy who has secretly spiked the punch, who has been imbibing too much, and who is talking too loudly, bent upon shocking the elders upstairs who can't help overhearing the revelations of the new generation: the drinking, the smoking, the kissing, the petting, the wild rides in motorcars, and the back seats of automobiles that had taken romance out of Victorian parlors and labeled it sex.

About a week later, on the morning of March 17, 1920, I was sitting in the kitchen, having a cup of coffee, when I heard the blare of an automobile horn. Not recognizing its pitch, I ignored it. But it sounded again and again. I rose, went to the front door and opened it.

Parked at the curb was a brightly polished, white touring car. Sitting proud and erect behind the steering wheel, the driver wore a tweed cap and a tweed suit. My mind told me it was Howard Franklin, for he had mentioned in his last letter that he was shopping for a new motorcar. My eyes, however, told me otherwise. It was Davis. He raised his right arm and waved to me as Robert Edwin Peary must have waved when he had reached the North Pole, the top of the world.

I couldn't speak. Too confused to cry, I waved back and waited for him to come to me. But he didn't. The king was on his throne. I wanted to rush to him, to kiss him, but Howard Franklin appeared when I rubbed my engagement ring. And I couldn't stir.

Finally, my voice uncertain, I shouted, "Coffee?"

"No," Davis responded. "It's an Apperson!"

We struck laughter together before he opened the door and started toward me. Rushing to each other, propelled by laughter and joy, we met, embraced, and kissed. After we had held each other long enough to accept the reality of the moment, I stepped back to admire his sporty civilian attire, for I had never seen him in anything but his army uniforms.

"I like your clothes," I said.

"Abercrombie Fitch."

I shook his hand. "How do you do? I'm Rannah Gedney."

"Care for a ride, Miss Gedney?"

"No, a walk, Mr. Fitch."

"Across the sidewalks and into the trees?"

"Only across the sidewalks, General Jackson."

We laughed again and began to walk in the direction of the woods whose trees still sheltered memories of yesterday. Davis

53

raised his eyes skyward, and in profile I saw him as a proud eagle commanding the heavens.

He said, "Great morning. Just as I planned it."

"And when did you plan it, General Jackson?"

Davis turned to me, his smile now bittersweet. "The name is Longstreet. I'm the general who hesitated and lost."

I laughed. "May I call you James?"

"Yes, Mrs. Franklin."

I couldn't smile now. "A bit premature, aren't you?"

"I pushed my Apperson up to seventy coming in from Atlanta this morning. That damn car dealer in Columbus Circle. He was all out of time machines." Again he was the sad young man. "I *am* too late, aren't I?"

"The morning's young."

He glanced about. "Nothing's changed. Except us."

"Why didn't you write?" I asked.

"I wrote a novel."

"But no letters."

"The book was an eighty-thousand-word letter. You know to whom."

"You tell me."

He said, "I wrote it to you, Rannah. Special delivery. From one special person to another."

"Thank you. The telephone and telegraph lines weren't down. Why didn't you let me know what you were doing?"

"I guess I was trying to surprise myself, even more than I wanted to surprise you. I had to prove I was someone special. Prove it first to myself."

"And you did just that, didn't you?"

"It wasn't easy. The nights have been long. Since I went away," he said, paraphrasing the war song.

I smiled again. "And I thought you were running with the bulls and the bears."

"It was tougher than breaking into the Yale backfield. But I did manage to pay the rent."

"I loved your book."

"Thanks."

54

"When did you decide to write it?"

"Hell, I'd been fiddling with it ever since my first semester at Yale."

"You told me that the second time we saw each other. I remember you saying you busted all your strings. But when did you really start it?"

"My first night in New York. Freddie talked me into it."

"But you suggested it to him, didn't you?"

Davis shook his head. "No, Freddie suggested it to me. We were drinking in his flat. Freddie, me, and Irene. Irene's his wife."

"I didn't know Freddie was married."

"She's a great girl. Could be your sister. They're very happy. I envy them."

"How did the book come up?" I asked, not wishing to contend with the matter of marriage.

"Well, I was doing most of the talking. Crying in my whiskey, I guess. Talking about Yale, the war, and then about you. Irene was fascinated, especially by you. Then Freddie put the cork in the bottle, told Irene to make some coffee, and cornered me. And told me what I had to do."

"Write a novel," I deduced.

"Yes. He put it this way: 'Davis,' he said, 'it's high time you took your Frank Merriwell malarkey about Yale and mixed it with the sassafras about that Georgia cracker in crinoline.' "

"How charming!" I regarded him with suspicion. "Or did you use that description first?"

"No, I didn't." He turned to me and took my hand. I shivered. "I only told Freddie how much I loved you. How much I missed you."

I freed my hand. "A man who can write a book can certainly write a letter."

"Freddie told me not to write you."

I frowned. "Why not?"

"He warned me not to waste time, words, or emotions. He told me to take my heart only to the manuscript. I worked hard. Nights and weekends."

55

"And the words flowed like wine."

He smiled wanly. "No, it wasn't like that at all. At first the words came like molasses. I ran to Freddie with the first chapter. After he'd read it, I ran from him. He hated it. I walked the city streets in the rain, caught a bad cold, and almost died. I wanted to die. One night, as a matter of fact, I decided in favor of the Brooklyn Bridge."

I ran from terror to humor. "For jumping, Mr. Brodie?"

"Exactly, Miss Bly. One awful night I sat down at my Corona portable to compose a suicide note. And then the damnedest thing happened. It turned out to be the new first chapter of the book."

"Then you ran back to Freddie. And he liked it."

"No. I didn't see Freddie for three months. I was afraid to. I knew his disfavor might direct me straight back to the bridge. I stayed with the book, with the Corona that was the only moon rising for me."

"Did you take the completed manuscript to Freddie?" He nodded, and I asked, "What did he say?"

The pain of the memory was etched on his face. "He flipped the pages. Said I was a lousy typist. Said I should be arrested for beating my typewriter ribbon to death. I left the manuscript with him, went home, and drank myself to sleep. I called him the next night. He said to come over. That and nothing more. And I knew I'd failed. When I got to his apartment, Freddie gave me two drinks and the bad news. He said I was close, but not close enough. He wanted me to start all over again. From page one. I told him to go fuck himself. And I left, without my manuscript."

"What happened when you went back for it?"

"I went back the next afternoon. Freddie wasn't in. Irene was. She'd read it. She told me she liked it. I kissed her, like a sister. Thanked her, and asked her for the manuscript."

A thought struck me. "Just a minute. Tell me this: why didn't you think of suicide after Freddie had told you the book was no good?"

After pondering my question for a moment, Davis said,

56

"Maybe Freddie wasn't impressed. But I was. Very much. More with myself than the book. I'd proved to myself that I could go the distance. The distance I had to go."

"Good for you. Did Irene return the manuscript?"

"No. She said she wanted to talk to Freddie about it. She told me to drop by about ten o'clock that night. I did. Freddie was cold to me. He'd had a big row with Irene. About me. About the book. Then Freddie sat me down and said, 'Look, you moron from Milwaukee, I'm your best friend, and I know what's best for you.' I asked him what he wanted me to do. And he told me. He wanted me to take my lunch hour the next day and walk from Wall Street down to Fourth Avenue and all those second-hand bookshops. He wanted me to browse there and study the trash I could buy for nickels and dimes."

Amazed, I asked, "He wanted you to give up writing?"

Davis shook his head. "No. He only wanted me to start again from the beginning. To rewrite with his objections, advice, and criticisms in mind."

"And, wisely, you did."

"No, I didn't. I asked him a favor."

"And what was that?"

"I begged him to remember he was my friend and forget he was God. I asked him to take the manuscript to his publisher, Albert Corbell and Son. To get me one rejection slip. After which I promised never to bother him again."

"Freddie did! And the publishers loved it!"

"No. Samuel Barrett, the chief editor, rejected it. Regretfully. I sent it out to two other publishers and got turned down. Then one day I got a note from Barrett asking me to drop into his office. He told me he couldn't put my manuscript out of his mind. Said he'd talked to Freddie. And Freddie urged him to write me, to see me, and persuade me to rework the book. When I said I'd do anything and everything he asked of me, he gave me a check for five hundred dollars. An advance against royalties."

I asked, "When was that?"

"Late last August."

57

The date angered me. "Why didn't you write and tell me? Didn't you think I'd be interested?"

"It was only five hundred dollars. Hardly enough to buy the Brooklyn Bridge."

"Enough to keep me from saying 'yes' to Howard Franklin." Davis regarded me with remorse. "I wanted to tell you. I wanted to pick up the telephone and call you. But I went out and deposited the check in a bank, bought six rolls of freshly minted pennies and put them into a treasure box. I had it all wrapped and ready for mailing when I had a change of heart. A premonition of failure. And I decided to wait until I'd rewritten the book, until it met with Barrett's approval. That's why I didn't send it until Christmastime. And when I did, I thought I was being clever. But I can see now, I was stupid."

I said sadly, "I wish you'd bought a telegram with those pennies."

"Tell me about Howard," he said, with equal sadness.

"Later. First I want to hear about Freddie. What was his reaction to Corbell's acceptance?"

"He invited me to dinner. Shook my hand, limply, and wished me luck. As if I really needed it."

"Did he help you with the book?"

"No, he didn't. He left me in the good hands of Sam Barrett. I worked only with him. I love the man. Like a father."

I persisted with my intrigue about Freddie. "But what did Freddie say when the novel was published? He read it, didn't he?"

"Sure. He reviewed it for the *New Republic*."

"And what did he say?"

"He wouldn't tell me. I'll know tomorrow. The magazine'll be on the newsstands tomorrow. At least in New York. Anyway, hear this: the reviews in the New York, Boston, Philadelphia, and Chicago papers were raves. Real raves. Barrett thinks the book may sell at least twenty thousand copies."

"Is that good?"

"The word is sensational. And just listen to this: I sold a short story last week to the *Saturday Evening Post*. For five hundred dollars. And they've given me a contract for six more, with the price going up two hundred and fifty bucks each time. I've got myself a New York literary agent. Ellis Mason. The best. Four days ago he called me at the brokerage office, and I quit my job on the spot. Why?'' He put an arm about me, more to support than embrace me. "Don't faint now. But Fox Films bought my book. Get this. For *twenty thousand dollars!*''

I was now glad he was holding me. "Congratulations. That's fantastic!''

He released me. "Thanks. I went right out and bought the Apperson. Took the high road south, and here I am.'' Now remorse overtook him again. "Tell me about Howard Franklin.''

My left hand trembled as I held it out to show him the engagement ring. It was less a gesture of pride than the reflex of a child showing a wound to a friend. "He gave me this.''

Davis glanced indifferently at the ring. "Is it real?''

"Of course it is. Ten carats.''

"I mean your love for him.''

"He's very sweet.''

"Where'd you meet him?''

"In Atlanta, last November. At the Georgia – Georgia Tech football game. I was with Dan McKissick. You remember Dan, don't you?''

"I found him easy to forget. Who was Howard with?''

"Liz Cooper. But he took an instant shine to me.''

He was sullen now. "You had no competition.''

"Liz is the most beautiful girl in — ''

Davis broke in. "She's a doll. If a man wants a wife to put on a shelf, she fills the bill.''

I mused about Atlanta. "We went to a dance that night at the Piedmont Driving Club.''

"Sure. Howard's a member,'' he said with envy.

"His family helped to found the club.''

"Must have millions.''

"You read the clipping. The Franklins own a bank.''

"And now they want to add a Gedney to their assets.''

"His family approves, if that's what you mean.''

59

"And your family also approves."

"Mother and Father are simply delighted."

He sighed. "What's Howard like?"

"Like the boy I always dreamed of marrying."

Davis frowned. "Even after you'd met me?"

My voice wavered. "You were an accident. An accident of war."

He was caustic. "And you've fully recovered."

"I love Atlanta."

"And Atlanta will love you. You'll own it in no time."

"Thank you."

"Where are you going on your honeymoon?"

"Europe. We're sailing on the *Mauretania*."

"Bon voyage."

Unable to take any more of this, I said, "Shall we turn around and go back?"

His voice was cold. "Can't be done. I've come a thousand miles. And each day comes up tomorrow. Not yesterday."

I thought, why can't Howard voice words like this? Then, caught in the tide of Davis's words, I said rather forlornly, "The night you left here, I couldn't see tomorrow."

But Davis dismissed my trauma. Without strain, he seemed casual. "How do you like working on a newspaper?"

"I gave up the job. Weeks ago."

"About the time of your engagement?"

"Exactly."

"Your decision? Or Howard's?"

"A girl needs time. To prepare her trousseau."

"Yes, I remember how much my sisters fussed about. And my poor, insecure mother. By the way, how is your mother?"

"She's fine, thank you."

"And the Judge?"

"Likewise."

"You never did tell me. Did you like working on the paper?"

I nodded. "Had you imagined I was getting drunk with the boys in the city room?"

"No, my imagination was otherwise occupied. With my book."

60

"How nice for you."

"And now you've left the job for the showers and parties. You'll be missed in these environs."

"I'm only going as far as Atlanta. Not to Milwaukee."

"So you are. I had a terrible homecoming. Hated Milwaukee. When I took off my uniform at home and changed into my college clothes, I felt like a kid back in prep school. No Yale. No Army."

"And no Rannah."

"Not in Milwaukee. It wasn't until I took the train for New York that I began to really miss you."

"And how'd you feel about me in New York?"

"You were always with me," he said. "Especially after I started the book. You are Adele Garrett."

"So you told me."

"Did you find the portrait unflattering?"

"I had to explain to Howard that it was only fiction."

He laughed. "You mean the part where Austin Fellows takes Adele to the seedy hotel across the street from the depot?"

I pouted. "It's tawdry. The least you could've done was have them married before they went to the room."

More laughter to grate on me. "I took out the wrong license. Literary instead of marriage."

"You described the hotel badly."

"Did I? How would you know? Are the town swells holding dances at the Cherokee now?"

"We're very democratic down here."

"Tell me, did the Judge read the book?"

"He has no interest in you. Or in your book."

"I thought I was very kind to him. In the book, I mean. Sam Barrett thought he was the best realized character of all."

"Really?"

"But you're the one the critics remembered. They were smitten by you."

"What did Flaubert say? Didn't he say *he* was Madame Bovary? Adele Garrett is as much you as she is me. Perhaps more so."

61

"Maybe."

"I never went to the Cherokee Hotel with you. I never slept with you."

He laughed again. "Was Howard really bothered?"

"Not enough to break off our engagement. He's no fool."

"Did you have to submit to a medical examination?"

I frowned. "Don't be crude."

"Sorry. Bad joke. And my apologies for causing you a bad time with Howard."

"I didn't say I had a bad time with him."

"He must be quite a fellow. I'd like to meet him sometime. Why don't you send me an invitation to the wedding?"

"Would you really come down to Atlanta?"

"How else would I ever get into the Piedmont Driving Club?"

"Seriously. Would you?"

"Sure. I'd like to be there when the minister asks if there is anyone present who knows any reason why Rannah and Howard should not be joined in holy wedlock."

I contrived a weak smile. "What would you do? Run down the aisle waving your book?"

After a moment he said, "Well, I could hide in the choir loft, fire a bullet into Howard's head, jump down to the pulpit, and shout —" He broke off. "What would I shout? *Sic semper tyrannis?* Doesn't fit. Any suggestions?"

"Yes. Shut up."

He said absently, "I hate churches. And church weddings."

I quickly changed the subject. "How long are you staying here?"

"Going back to Atlanta in the morning. When I get there, should I stop by the bank and say hello to Howard?"

"Don't bother."

"Why not? All Yale men are taught to jump over the net to congratulate their opponents."

"It's the winner who does the jumping."

"You're right. But, come to think of it, maybe I'm the winner."

I looked narrowly at him. "How so?"

62

"Why, it looks as if I've won my freedom. The episode's ended, the book's finished. Now I'm free to romp at the Plaza with all those Park Avenue debutantes."

"Then what are you doing here?"

"Research. For *Saturday Evening Post* stories."

I laughed. "Poor little self-centered me. I thought you'd motored all the way down here to steal me away from Howard."

He studied me sadly. "How could I do that? I know, I really know, from bitter experience, that you're anything but a compulsive, impulsive belle. You're Daddy's girl, remember? Always armed with reason. And I'm no match for the bags of reason in the vaults of that Atlanta bank."

I was bitter now. "Anything else?"

"Yes. The earth isn't flat. The next stop after Atlanta isn't the Abyss."

"Really?"

We had now returned to my house. Davis gazed at it and weighed it with his imagination. "This doesn't look like the house where Adele Garrett lives. No pillars, no great portico." He turned to me, and his smile jumped over a net. "Good-bye, Rannah. Best of luck."

I felt the chill of death. "Where are you going now?"

"I want to drive out to the airfield."

"There's no one there."

"I know. The abandoned and the deserted have a special appeal for me."

I turned to face the symbol of his success. "Nice car. What did you say it was?"

In the voice of a prep school boy, Davis recited:

Oh there are Appersons and Andersons, and Briggs and Buicks, too.
Cartercars and Cadillacs; of Garfords quite a few.
There are Hendersons and Hudsons; there are Hupps upon the floor.
And Jackson, Kings, and Keeting cars, and Loziers by the score.

I applauded. "Did you compose that at Yale?"

"No, it was written by a sportswriter named Damon Runyon.

Back in 1914." He turned to his car and proudly said, "I've wanted an Apperson ever since prep school."

I asked, rather uneasily, "Why don't you invite me for a ride?"

Davis looked at me with mock alarm. "What? In broad daylight? What'll the neighbors think? I only put scandal in books, never in Apperson touring cars."

"I'll chance it. Let me get a sweater."

"Better talk it over with your mother."

"Come in and say hello."

He said, "When we get back I'll say hello and good-bye. All at once."

"I'll be right out."

"Take your time. I'll polish the windshield and recite Emily Dickinson to myself."

I was actually afraid of going inside the house, afraid the closing of the door might shatter the mirage of his presence. I asked, "Any poem in particular?"

And Davis recited again, this time in a voice full of sorrow.

> *If I could see you in a year*
> *I'd wind the months in balls,*
> *And put them in separate drawers,*
> *Until their time befalls.*

I couldn't applaud, couldn't find a smile. And so I turned away from him, hurried into the house, and was careful not to slam the door behind me. I rushed upstairs to my room, snatched up a sweater, and went to the mirror to apply rouge to my pallor. In the mirror I suddenly saw the reflection of my mother, wearing a secret smile.

She said, "I saw him. My, he's more handsome than ever."

I strained for indifference. "Yes."

"And you're excited, my baby."

"I am not."

"Where are you going?"

"Just for a ride. Out to Hatton Field."

64

My mother's manner was graveside. "They're all gone, and it's been so quiet. You've been so quiet. I can't remember the last time you ran up the stairs."

"I'll be a bride in June, Mother. Leave me be."

"Such a wonderful car."

"It's an Apperson."

"And he drove it all the way down from New York?"

"Yes."

"I watched him from the window. After you went in, he looked like he was about to cry."

I wheeled on my mother. "Why are you always peeping through the curtains? Besides, you're imagining things."

With rare resolve, she said, "Invite him to dinner tonight."

"I will not."

"Don't run from him."

I could hear the railroad warning bells in her voice. "Mother, what are you saying?"

Again the secret smile. "Howard doesn't make you run up the stairs."

"Stop it, Mother."

"I'll speak to Hilda. We'll have a nice roast."

"I won't invite him."

"Then I will."

I was furious. "Don't you dare!"

I tried to move past her, but she caught and held my arm and commanded my attention. "I must. I dare so little these days. Listen to me, Rannah, baby. I say so little to you these days, and you have so little to say to me. But this time, please, listen to your shallow, stupid mother." She was weeping now. "Think about it, think about what's important and remember how you ran. Remember, please."

The instant she released my arm I hurried down the steps and out the front door, my pace then slowing until I seemed to be moving in time to a wedding march. Davis wore a smiling mask as he held the car door open for me. I sat down and settled back.

65

When Davis got behind the wheel and started the engine, I tested my voice. "Remember the way?"

"Like the milkman's horse." He shifted into low gear and the car shot forward. "You been out there lately?"

"Howard and I drove past it a few weekends ago."

"What does he drive?"

"A Buick."

"I'll race him any day."

"All the way to prep school?"

Davis laughed. "How tall is Howard?"

I hit him with the hard figures: "He's five-eleven, weighs one hundred and seventy pounds, and wears a size fifteen collar."

Recovering, Davis said, "Just remember what Jack Dempsey did to Jess Willard in Toledo last summer."

"Why should I? Are you thinking of fighting Howard?"

"Is he an athlete?"

"Captain of the tennis team at Virginia."

"Good for him. Probably got a court in his backyard."

"He plays at the club."

"Nice to belong to a club. I was thinking of moving into the Yale Club."

"You can afford it now."

"Yes, I can. But I'll probably lease an apartment on Riverside Drive. I like the view of the Hudson. Hey, how would you like a bedroom window overlooking Grant's Tomb?"

"It might be nice. If Grant didn't mind."

"I'm sure he wouldn't rebel against a beautiful rebel like you."

"Funny." I didn't laugh.

He said, "What I really had in mind was a suite at the Plaza. With windows overlooking Central Park."

I saw the park as if in a dream. "It's a nice park."

"You've never seen it."

"I've seen pictures of it in the *National Geographic*. And in the movies, too."

"How long'll you and Howard be in New York before you sail?"

66

"A few days."

"I'll let you know where I am. Maybe I can take you two to a speakeasy. You've heard about speakeasies, haven't you?"

"Yes, we got the news about prohibition and the Volstead Act. We're back in the Union again."

He smiled. "Stay at the Plaza. You and Howard'll like it there. It's got class, atmosphere, and the sweetest, saddest violins you've ever heard."

"I'll mention it to Howard," I lied.

"I want you both to meet the Frederickses. Well, you especially. You and Irene, you'd get along like twin sisters."

"What does she do?"

"She paints. Sells quite a lot. And she also writes about painting for the *Tribune*. Great cook, too. Knows all about wines."

I taunted him. "Too bad Freddie saw her first."

"Well, Freddie found his girl. And won her. I found mine. And lost her."

"I don't know anything about wines."

"And you don't paint."

"No."

"And you won't have to learn how to cook. Tell me, are you moving in with the Franklins?"

"It's a big house. Pillars and portico."

"That's the ticket. What should I send you for a wedding gift? A tennis racket?"

Containing myself, I said, "Thank you."

Davis now turned to me, and I saw that the flavor of his smile was bittersweet. "I'll send you one of Irene's paintings."

"Which one?"

"A real beaut. A watercolor of General Sherman's statue in the Plaza."

I wanted to laugh, but I didn't. "Funny."

"Well, instead of hanging it in the drawing room of the Franklin mansion, you can hang it from one of your trees suitable for lynchings."

I was about to say something about the Yankees having failed

67

to hang Jefferson Davis from a sour apple tree, but I discerned that Davis had fled to another and more recent war. His misty eyes were upon the airfield. A wind was sweeping across the terrain now given to weeds instead of wings.

"There's the field," Davis said with awe. "I'll never forget the first time I saw it. That summer of '18. All those hangars and barracks. All more beautiful than the castles on the Rhine. That's the way I saw it. As a knight sees a castle. A white knight to challenge the red knights of Germany." Suddenly he was mocking himself. "What a laugh! I never saw anything but red German noses in Milwaukee."

I said, "Baron Richthofen's dead. You're alive. And laughing."

Davis eased the motorcar off the asphalt road. There were tears in his eyes now. "Yes. The dead don't cry."

I said nothing. He stopped the car. We got out and began to stroll toward a hangar whose windows had been broken by vandals.

Davis said, "A broken window for every broken dream."

"Which one is yours?"

He ignored the jibe. "Did I ever mention Hall Bowen to you?"

"I don't recall."

"A classmate of mine at Yale. Rich bastard. Copper fortune. He was in the Lafayette Escadrille. Shot down three Kraut planes and one balloon. Bailed out once and broke his leg. Boy, how I envied him when he was talking about the war in the skies. I envied him that more than I did his Long Island palace. I was out there one Sunday last summer. Got too damn drunk and made a fool of myself. I wasn't invited again."

"You always drank too much," I said, wishing to turn the conversation back to the battle of the moment.

He glanced at me. "Does Howard drink?"

"Not so you can notice it."

"Most of the time I was writing the book, I was on the wagon."

"Good for you."

68

His eyes were strong upon me. "You're best for me."

I turned away from him. "Shall we go back?"

He said, "Not just yet. I want to see one of the hangars."

"Looking for ghosts?"

"I'm a pro now. I look for stories. With a professional eye."

As we crossed toward a hangar, I asked, "Will I be in any of them?"

He didn't reply, for he was now beyond the present. I observed him as he put his face to a window to peer into the dark of the hangar. At first I saw him as the small boy who was always looking into windows that faced the widening world about him. And then I saw him as a god, standing outside the world, outside of time, and measuring a strange and distant planet.

Finally he turned to me. "Know what I'm thinking?"

"I can't read your mind."

"Can't you?"

"What were you thinking?"

"I was making a wish. Fashioning a phantasy. I see a biplane inside. I open the doors, push the plane out. You and I climb into the seats, into the skies, and fly off to never-never land."

I let folly take the biplane from the skies. "And live in sin?"

Davis was not to be deflected. "You know what sin is for us. It's living our lives apart from each other."

"You're writing dialogue now."

He frowned. "And you'd better hear it. Good dialogue's a river of gold. A kind of gold you'll never find in the vaults of Howard's bank."

His voice, to me, was a roar louder than the Liberty engines. "Davis," I said warily, "I want to go home."

"That's where I'm taking you. I want to come back here alone." He turned away and began to walk toward the Apperson, his pace brisk, leaving me lagging behind.

"To cry alone?" I called to his back.

"No, to put pencil to paper. Maybe to put some sensible words in your mouth."

I implored, "What do you *want* me to say?"

69

"Tell me I'm home. Tell me you're home. When you're with me."

"It's too late." I got into the car.

Davis followed. When he had the engine idling, he faced me. "It's March, not June. The flowers for the bridal bouquet haven't been cut yet. They haven't even been planted."

"The engagement's been announced."

"Break it."

"Let's go. Please."

He drove the car much too slowly. "Aren't I someone special any more?"

"Where's the funeral?"

"I'm driving in a parade. Up Fifth Avenue. To the Plaza. Or isn't that grand enough for you?"

"It's not in Georgia."

His voice rose. "Damn it! Forty-eight states! Seven seas! Five continents! And you haven't got the courage to walk away from the family burial plot! Talk about funerals! Sure, I'm driving a hearse! And you're in the coffin!"

I lowered my head, shut my eyes, and imagined myself in a coffin. And the voice of my ghost spoke: "Make a right turn at the next crossroad."

"And where'll that take us?"

I opened my eyes to welcome the sight of Davis more than the sight of the sun. "There's a house I want you to see."

"What for?"

"It's up for sale."

He understood now, but didn't smile. "I'm not interested in settling down here."

"Not even with me?"

"I don't belong here."

"It's a beautiful house," I pleaded. "And it can be such a lovely home. And there's a carriage house. With a room where you can write in seclusion."

"That's a lousy address. Seclusion, Georgia."

"Take a look at it. What can you lose?"

"New York."

70

Davis was driving faster now. The crossroad loomed ahead. "This is the crossroad. Turn right."

He neither increased nor decreased the speed of the car. Deaf to my plea, blind to my desire, he kept his eyes on the road ahead. He didn't so much as turn his eyes.

I cried out, "Why didn't you turn?"

"I only saw dirty work at the crossroads."

"You'll never pass this way again!"

"I couldn't care less. I'm in love with New York."

"Marry New York!"

"You'll fall in love with it, too."

"Perhaps. But I'll wave a fond farewell to it, from the deck of the *Mauretania*."

The threat struck no fear in him. "That's not the boat for you. You're the kind of girl who books passage only on doomed boats. Like the *Titanic*."

"What is that supposed to mean?"

"I don't know. But it sounds good."

"Feeling very chipper all of a sudden, aren't you?"

"Why not? I'm now sure you love me more than Howard."

"You should've made the turn. This way leads to icebergs."

He said, "With our passion, we'll melt them all."

"You'll never have me," I vowed. "Except on paper."

"Well, maybe that's the best way."

"Go to hell!"

Davis was grim now. "I've been there. I left you at the depot two Januarys ago and went there. And then the keys of my typewriter opened doors beyond doors. And there I was. In heaven. And that's where I'll be returning."

I said nothing, and we rode in silence. I don't know what Davis was thinking, but my mind had fled from the Apperson and had gone back to make the right turn at the crossroad. I went through the empty rooms of the house and filled them with delusions.

Not another word passed between us until the Apperson had stopped before my house on Gedney Street. Davis shifted into neutral, left the engine running, and then casually stepped out

71

and opened the door for me. I stared at him and saw only the indifference of a boy taking leave of a first and disappointing date.

"Good-bye, Rannah."

My own voice was choked. "Is that all you have to say?"

"May you and Howard live happily ever after."

"Nothing else?"

He shrugged. "Just this. All of a sudden I feel taller than Howard."

With that he turned away from me, strode back to the driver's seat, and drove away without so much as glancing toward me. When the Apperson was out of sight, I wanted to fall down dead. Instead, I leadenly entered my house and climbed the hill of the stairs to lock myself in my bedroom.

In a moment I recognized the gentle rapping on my door. "Rannah?"

"Go away."

"Did you invite Davis to dinner?"

"No!" I screamed.

A long silence, and then: "Think, Rannah, baby. *Think hard.*"

And the afternoon came, and it was an afternoon when the clocks fell fast asleep. But I didn't. Lying there on my bed, I held the hands of the clock at morning. The Gramophone of memory played, over and over again, our voices. Questions and answers. Questions and questions. And no answers.

I was a girl at the crossroads, not knowing which way to go, knowing only that I would never pass this way again. At one moment, after consigning Davis to hell, I left the room to go downstairs to the telephone. I lifted the receiver and waited for the operator. By the time she spoke, I had changed my mind about placing a long-distance call to Atlanta. I had remembered that Howard was still at the bank, and I had no wish to disturb him there. Moreover, I had no idea what I was going to say to him. I only wanted to hear his voice, to drown out the voice of Davis.

As I slowly climbed the stairs, I became aware of the aroma of the roast cooking in the oven. I was in tears when I got back to

72

my room. Then, after a while, I dried my tears and the ink of my resolve.

I had made up my mind to invite Davis to dinner, to bring him into a confrontation with my father, to afford him the chance to defeat my father and win my hand.

After rehearsing my lines, I went back down to the telephone and called the General Hood Hotel. No Davis O'Donnell was registered there. I called the Wakefield Hotel. No Davis O'Donnell registered there.

My thoughts raced to overtake an Apperson speeding northward. Davis was gone. Gone North, gone forever.

Now I called Atlanta for reinforcement, for the sound of Howard Franklin's voice. The butler answered. Howard wasn't at home. He was attending a civic meeting in the city. I left a message for him to call me, no matter how late he returned home.

Replacing the receiver, I started up the stairs and then quickly retreated. I returned to the telephone and placed a call to Liz Cooper. I wanted to hear the sound of my own voice, my own laughter, as I told her about the surprise visitor of the morning. I meant to be cruel and gay, to be a girl with a girl, a belle with a belle, a fool with a fool.

Liz Cooper's voice was reassuring. "Hi, Rannah."

"Liz! Guess what?"

She guessed correctly. "Davis O'Donnell's in town."

"How did you know?"

She laughed. "Why, he's right here, out on my patio havin' himself a highball." I silently thanked God. Liz babbled on. "Rannah, he's positively darlin'! More handsome than ever! And so successful! I'm in love with him all over again!"

I was gay. "Marvelous! Did he say anything about Howard and me?"

"No, he just talked about New York, and I haven't stopped laughin' yet."

I wanted to throttle her laughter. "Liz, be a dear and ask him to the phone."

"Wouldn't you like to pop over?"

73

"I just want to talk to him. On the phone."

"All rightie."

The receiver was wet with perspiration before Davis came on. His voice was cheerful. "Hi."

My own wasn't. "I was surprised to hear you're still in town."

"I'll be gone by morning."

"Where are you staying?"

"I'll probably check in at the Hood."

"What are you doing for dinner?"

"I always liked the Cooper cuisine."

"I suggest the Gedney cuisine."

"Who's extending the invitation?"

"My mother."

"Is the Judge out of town?"

"He'll be here."

"Does he know I'm invited?"

"No, he doesn't."

He hesitated. "I'll stick with Liz."

"Are you afraid of my father?"

"No, I'm just afraid for you."

"Be here at six. We'll have cocktails."

"Manhattans?"

"If you wish."

"You know what I wish."

"Be here."

"That tells me nothing. I'm not interested in fighting the Civil War again tonight."

"All out of fight?"

"I'll be there."

I dried the telephone and my eyes and went to the kitchen to tell Mother and Hilda the tidings. Then I went into my father's study to survey our supply of liquor. I was appraising a half-empty quart of bourbon when my father, who had just returned from the office, entered and gave me a startled look.

"What's going on?"

74

I said, "We're having a guest for dinner. Would you call up and order a bottle of bourbon and a bottle of sweet vermouth?"

He smiled. "Howard in town?"

"Davis O'Donnell."

The name tore away his smile. "What's on your mind?"

"Manhattans. Three parts bourbon, one part vermouth, a dash of bitters, shake with ice, and serve with a maraschino cherry."

My father understood the recipe for hysteria. He said nothing, but his demeanor told me he was accepting the situation. And the challenge.

4.

Promptly at six o'clock Davis invaded our house, bearing a two-pound box of Whitman chocolates to delight my mother and a load of the Coopers' whiskey to disgust my father and dismay me. But the white flags of temporary truce were flying while we sipped Manhattans and discussed motorcars, highway travel, and the weather. What none of us dared admit was that the storm clouds were gathering, and that the sound of thunder was racing across dark March skies toward our dining room.

The roast that Hilda served was easier to cut than the tension in the room. It was Davis who fired the first shot with a careless yank of the lanyard.

Turning to me, he said, "Rannah, who owns that house you wanted to show me?"

I ignored the bemused glances of my parents. "Arnold Hoffman."

"Why is he selling it?"

I said, "The Hoffmans have moved to Savannah. Mr. Hoffman sold his furniture store in town. It's a beautiful house."

My father confronted Davis. "Mr. O'Donnell, are you thinking of settling down here?"

76

Davis smiled. "No, not at all. Stephensville's a great place to visit, but I wouldn't want to live here."

For the first time in years I heard my mother laugh at the dinner table. "Oh, that's simply charming! Isn't that what they say about New York?"

Appreciating neither the jest nor its reception, my father fixed Davis with a bleak eye. "Then why did Rannah want to show you the Hoffman place?"

I braced myself for the impact of Davis's reply. He said easily, "Rannah believes it's the right place for us."

My mother smiled. My father frowned before he overwhelmed me with his courtroom manner. "Is he making a whiskey joke?"

"No, Father."

"When did you break your engagement to Howard?"

"I haven't broken it."

"Whom do you intend to marry?"

"Howard."

My mother's smile died. Davis's whiskey grin persisted.

"Why have you wavered?" my father demanded.

"I was a fool."

"How so?"

"I thought I might persuade Davis to make our home here."

"Had you persuaded him, would you have married him?"

"Yes, Father."

My father said, "You're wearing Howard's ring."

I slipped the engagement ring off my finger and then quickly returned it. "It fits loosely. It can be removed."

"If Mr. O'Donnell removes his objections to living in Stephensville?"

"Yes. But he won't do that."

My father now faced Davis. "The asking price of the Hoffman house is twenty-two thousand dollars. Can you afford it?"

Davis said, "I can afford to live at the Plaza. And that's where I prefer to live."

"With or without Rannah?"

"Yes, sir. With or without her."

"Tell me, Mr. O'Donnell, why did you return here?"

77

"To take Rannah away."

"From Howard Franklin?"

"No, sir. From you."

My father's jaw sagged as if he had caught the thrust of a sword. My mother tried to mask her pleasure. I felt ill. For a moment, I thought I would have to run from the table.

My father glowered at Davis. "You're very impertinent."

"Am I, sir? Let's face it. You're the judge, you're the jury. Rannah won't make a move without your consent."

Methodically my father returned his knife and fork to his plate. I fully expected him to rise and leave us. But he remained and addressed himself to the argument: "I recognize your allusion to *Alice in Wonderland*. Are you also alluding to the Barretts? Do you liken yourself to Robert Browning? And me to Elizabeth Barrett's father?"

"I hadn't thought of it," said Davis. "But it fits, doesn't it?"

My father's eyes now summoned me to the witness box. "Rannah, did I urge Howard Franklin upon you?"

"No, Father."

"Wasn't it entirely your own decision?"

"Yes, it was."

Davis's voice rose to object. "She knew what you expected of her."

My father jerked his head toward Davis. "And what, might I ask, is wrong with that?"

"She loves me. Not Howard."

"Are you certain of that?"

"I'll rephrase that. Rannah loves me more than she does Howard Franklin. But she wants me on her terms. Because, in truth, they're your terms."

"And what do you presume *my* terms are?"

"Unworthy."

"You can be more responsive, Mr. O'Donnell."

"I want to marry Rannah. And take her to New York."

"Her life is here in Georgia. Why must she surrender family, friends, everything familiar, to go to a far country with you?"

78

"Is New York a far country?"

"Far and foreign."

"Sir, the armies are gone from the Potomac."

"Nevertheless, it's alien."

"And what's Atlanta?"

"Atlanta is Georgia, in and of Georgia. Well within Rannah's circle of friends and family."

Davis's expression was puzzled. "I can't make you out, Judge. You always struck me as the least provincial and chauvinistic man in this entire state."

"I am a Georgian."

"I've been in your study. I've seen your books. You're closer to Rome and Greece than you are to Atlanta. I know you're a man of intellect and letters. Don't give me the country boy act."

My father fumed. "Act, sir?"

"You know exactly what I mean. Rannah's your daughter. You've taken her up and down the steps of learning. She's no simpleton from Stephensville, she's a woman of the world."

"Not of *your* world, sir."

"I'm a writer," said Davis. "Justice Holmes — who was in the field with your father — said this: 'Life is painting a picture.' And what do writers do but paint pictures with words." Now he deposited his knife and fork on the plate. "Judge, consider Rannah's choices. What's Howard Franklin doing with his life? He's doing a sum. And remember this: your daughter isn't as straightforward as two plus two. Liz Cooper's the girl for a banker. Not Rannah."

My father demanded, "Why did you refuse to look at the Hoffman house?"

"If a painter wants to paint the sea, he doesn't run to the mountains."

"There are writers practicing their craft here in Georgia."

Davis said, "They're painting Georgia. I want to paint New York." He paused. "When I was a kid in Milwaukee, I always felt like Grant at Galena. Waiting for the call to command, to action. I missed the call at Yale. I missed the call in the war. Now I feel something about New York. I can feel the armies

79

converging. The battle of my generation. And it's not the trumpets that are blowing. It's the saxophones in the nightclubs. To hell with the medals and ideals and crusades. Now we shoot nothing but craps. Not for Christ's robes, but for the fast buck. The fast car. The fast crowd."

My father was reflective for a moment. "You've been most eloquent, but, I fear, self-defeating. I see you now as a drinking man who wants to drive his motorcar at a high and perilous speed. And to what destination? Not to home and hearth, but to a hotel, to a wild and endless party. Is this the path for a girl whom, as you put it, I have taken up and down the steps of learning?"

Davis was quick and sharp with his response. "What sort of world do you live in, away from your home? Don't you live in a court full of the sound and fury of murder, rape, arson, incest, robbery, assault, and what have you?" My father could say nothing. Davis continued. "I'm a writer. I work alone. In the quiet of my room. And that room, whether it be in a hotel, an apartment house, or a brownstone, must be in a home built by Rannah and me."

My father took another tack. With a calculated nonchalance he asked, "Tell me, how many drinks did you have before you came here tonight?"

"Four highballs. At the Coopers'."

"And you had two Manhattans here."

"Judge, you're doing sums."

My father shook his head. "I'm questioning your character. I contend you drink too much."

Davis retorted, "I'm not a banker. Sure, a banker has to starch his character with sobriety. He's got to stand upright under the weight of the money bags and the weight of the temptation to abscond." He paused to sip his water as if it were whiskey. "But I'm not Howard. I live with the angel of the backward look, and liquor's the rain and fog on the window of my mind. Byron said it: 'What's drinking? A mere pause from thinking.' I'm a writer, and I come sober to the sermon on the typewriter. The proof's not on the whiskey bottle label. The proof's in the cloth binding.''

"I read your book," my father said, much to my surprise.

Knowingly, Davis led with his chin. "I hope you enjoyed it."

"I did not. I saw through the thin disguises. I recognized your caricature of me in the character of Dr. Downey."

Davis smiled. "Who knows? Maybe I've touched you with immortality. Maybe the name of Dr. Downey will outlive, in time, the name of Judge Gedney."

"You've distorted the facts," my father complained.

"The book's plainly labeled fiction. True, the facts may be distorted. I prefer the word 'reshaped.' A biographer or a historian begins with fact and ends with fiction. A novelist begins with imagination and ends with truth."

My father's face was flushed. "I don't accept your thesis or your right to sully my character."

Davis leaped to his argument. "My right? I keep telling you: I'm a writer. I claim that right. As a bird claims the seed. As the fox the chicken." He paused. "And the guest his roast. You see, sir, you're the captive of my imagination. Dr. Downey is you, and yet not you. You should understand that. You're not a man of ledgers, you're a man of books. Besides, what do you do in a courtroom? In cross-examination are you gentle and kind when you thrust for the truth? Doesn't the hostile witness, when he stands down, leave the box feeling somewhat wounded and naked?"

"Why did you put me on trial?" my father demanded.

And Davis said, "Each and every story, each and every novel, is a trial. A confrontation between the imagination and the blank page. And each and every page presents a crisis. It either lives or it dies. I know you, Judge. I've heard the song of your thoughts. I've seen the body of your books. Your character lives. In the pages of my novel."

"Forget my character for the moment," said my father. "Tell me this. You said Rannah was the only girl for you. Is that a judgment rising from reason, or from passion?"

81

"I'll be pragmatic, Judge. I'll speak from experience. Without Rannah, I never could've written my book."

"You were without her. You were alone in New York."

For a long moment Davis said nothing. He merely sipped water again, seemingly not from the crystal glass but from the well of his mind. Finally he leaned back in his chair and stared at the chandelier. "Was the architect alone at Chartres? Or was the Virgin with him?" He faced my father. "You know the contention of Henry James."

"I take it you mean Henry Adams."

Davis gathered his best smile to take the correction with a good grace. "Right. I always confuse the two." He went on forcefully. "But I'm not confused about the source of my inspiration, my devotion, my work. According to Henry Adams, the Virgin was a greater force, a greater source of energy, than the twentieth-century dynamo. It was the Virgin who generated the power that went into the building of Chartres cathedral. And it was Rannah who generated the will and the force that moved me to write my book."

My father remained stoic to this testament. My mother was only bewildered. I, however, felt the full shiver of life, a sense of purpose, the grace of giving. At that very moment I knew that my life and my love were committed to Davis. But the struggle now was between Davis and my father. And the end was near at hand.

In the face of defeat, my father fought valiantly. He said, "You have at the moment the momentum of success. Won't that be sufficient to keep the wheels of your imagination turning?"

Davis was hard with him. "I fought my war, sir. I want my prize. I want Rannah. For my wife."

With an anguish that was a revelation to me, my father cried, "What shall I surrender? My peace of mind? The wisdom of my foreboding?"

"Foreboding what?"

"Armageddon!"

"I'm not taking Rannah to the plain of Esdraelon! I'm carrying her to Babylon!"

82

Quietly, now, my father said, "According to Isaiah, Babylon is fallen."

And Davis said, "I bear more recent witness. I've just come from there. Babylon is risen again." He paused. "Rannah belongs to me. Let her go."

Now my mother spoke, with familiar anguish: "Amen."

My father shot a glance toward her. His was the look of Caesar in the moment of Brutus's betrayal. Without a word he turned to Davis, rose, and said, "Excuse me, sir."

"Do we have your blessing?"

"Sir, I damn you."

Davis rose so abruptly that his chair toppled over. "Sir!"

My father, who had started toward his study, stopped abruptly and turned to him.

And Davis, seemingly on a stage of his own creation, quoted from Shakespeare, words whose prophecy escaped me at the time:

> *The weight of this sad time we must obey.*
> *Speak what we feel, not what we ought to say.*
> *The oldest hath borne most: we that are young*
> *Shall never see so much, nor live so long.*

Seeming to see only the specter of defeat, my father withdrew to the shielding walls of his study, to the Elba of his books. Davis, solemn in his triumph, set aright his fallen chair, and when he sat down again it was the throne of a newly crowned king.

My mother's eyes were tearful as she beheld the two of us. "Bless you. Bless you both." Rising, she went into the kitchen, abandoning the field to Davis and me.

We traded sad smiles. Davis said, "Hello."

"Who are you?"

"I'm drunk. Who are you?"

"According to one drunk, the Virgin."

He said, "I'm the Prince of Babylon."

Babylon fell again with the ringing of the telephone that

83

heralded the rising of Atlanta. Davis discerned my torment, but he said nothing. I left the room to take the call. It was Howard, of course. Over a hundred miles of wire, I spoke a thousand words and shed many tears. When I returned to the dining room, Davis was eating his pie. It was anything but humble pie.

Shortly after dinner Davis kissed my mother, kissed me, and made his conquistadorial way to the General Hood Hotel. My mother and I spent all the hours before midnight packing two valises to be taken in the Apperson and one trunk to be shipped to the Plaza.

That night sleep, like a restless hound, crept in and out of my bed. At dawn I quit the bed to bathe, dress, and feed tea and toast to the butterflies in my stomach.

Much earlier than was his habit, my father stole out of the house. I hadn't spoken to him again the previous night, and he was to deny me his parting words and a farewell kiss. From my window I saw him lugging the burden of his defeat as he marched off to his office.

At nine o'clock, the arranged hour, Davis swept up to the house in the Apperson. Ten minutes later, with my mother and Hilda weeping, we drove away, leaving the house, Gedney Street, and all the familiar streets of Stephensville behind us. The sky was overcast, the threat of rain persisted, and there was no sun to shine upon us.

We were miles north of Stephensville before we attempted conversation. I began it, bringing up questions that had tossed me from side to side, on a burning pillow, through the long night.

"Must we be married in Atlanta?"

Davis said, "We're expected in the chambers of Judge Harlan Thomason at two o'clock."

"When did you arrange that?"

"Day before yesterday. In Atlanta."

"And what else, my prince, did you arrange?"

"The Governor's Suite. At the Clifford Hotel."

"Also the day before yesterday?"

"Right."

84

"Sure of yourself, weren't you?"

"I'm like Sherman. When I make battle plans, I consider only the roads to triumph."

"Thank you, General. Did you steal my mother's silver before you left?"

"No. Only your father's thunder."

"So you did." After a moment I said, "The sweep of your arguments last night was more awesome to me than the sweep of Sherman's army."

Davis made light of it. "Gee, thanks."

"I kept looking at you, listening to you, and I said to myself, 'Who is this stranger?'"

"I was Delano Fredericks."

"I don't understand you."

Davis said, "Your father's a lawyer. But I had the edge on him. He wasn't prepared for a confrontation. I was. That's why I didn't let you know I was coming for you. Oh, yes, I was prepared. I'd played the scene over and over again in my mind. And when I came to it, I brought the power of Freddie's mind. I happen to believe Freddie has the best mind in the country, if not the world."

"The allusion to the Virgin and Chartres, wasn't that your idea?"

He shook his head. "No. Freddie said that. When he first urged me to sit down and write the novel. He said, 'Find out if the Georgia cracker can inspire you to build a book, as the Virgin inspired the building of Chartres.'" Davis laughed. "I'm so stupid I can't tell Henry James from Henry Adams."

I was angry now. "Was *anything* you said last night original with you?"

"Yes. My love for you."

"Nothing else?"

"My feeling about writing."

Assuaged somewhat by these answers, I changed the subject. "What did you do last night? Did you drink yourself to sleep at the hotel?"

"I worked. Till one in the morning."

85

"Worked on what?"

"A short story. About a man returning to a deserted airfield."

"Because you couldn't sleep?"

"I had to drink a pot of coffee to stay awake."

"After battle, sleep is best."

"I slept. After the battle."

"The battle at the typewriter?"

He nodded. "And I won it. Made a good start on the story."

"You say that as though you were telling a fraternity brother you'd made out with a girl."

Davis laughed. "I'll have to remember that."

"Can I forget it?"

He didn't understand me. "What?"

"Tell me a little more about it. How you feel. When you're working at the typewriter. Or is it working?"

"It's working. At living. I'm more alive at the typewriter than anywhere else. But let me go back. When I first started the novel, I felt I was alone in hell. The blank page turned my bowels to water. Then, after a week or so, after I had done a chapter, something happened. Hell became heaven. Down in Wall Street I was like a new groom who couldn't wait to get home at night and climb into bed with his bride. That's the way I felt about getting back to the typewriter. Back to the story." He turned to me and said, "Back to you."

"I believe everything you say, darling. Except the last phrase. You said that to placate me, didn't you?"

"I was writing about you."

"I don't come into the book until page 156. Remember?"

His grin was sheepish. "I remember."

"Were you writing about me last night?"

"Not even about myself. Every story doesn't have to be autobiographical. I'm a pro now. I'm using Hall Bowen as the hero and Liz Cooper as the girl."

I seethed. "Yet last night, after winning your girl in a duel with her father, you went to a hotel room, put it all out of your

86

mind, and began writing about Hall Bowen and Liz Cooper!"
My voice rose. "What am I supposed to think?"

"That you're marrying a writer, that's all."

"I'm trying to understand you. Trying to understand what
drives you to the typewriter. I know what drove you in New
York. But what drove you last night?"

"An Apperson."

"No bad jokes."

"The story drove me."

"And what's behind the drive?"

"I don't exactly know. Let me try to put it this way. I haven't
yet mastered my imagination. My imagination's mastered me.
What I imagine is real. More real than reality itself."

"You know what I think? You're cock-eyed about being like a
new groom who can't wait to climb into bed with his bride. Your
imagination's not a bride. It's a strange woman. No, that's not
right. It's a girl you're keeping. A clandestine love. A back-
street romance. It's the Other Woman."

Davis laughed. "That's great. I've got to remember that."

"To put it into a story?"

"Right."

"You think I'm ridiculous, don't you?"

"I love you."

"Shall I tell you something?"

"Make it funny."

"You won't laugh. That night at the depot I believed you
truly loved me. Right now I don't. Now I believe we're paying
the price of our long separation. You've found yourself another
woman. And I'm to be the wife from whom you'll run to this
other woman."

I was wrong. He did laugh again. "Are you going to name my
Corona portable as the corespondent?" I was silent. "Hey, I
think that's funny."

For a long while after that we said nothing. Through the
windshield now splattered with bugs I beheld the black ribbon of
the road and the distant green of a pinewood.

With sudden resolve, I said, "Stop the car. In the woods."

87

He said, "We'll be hitting Adamston in about ten minutes. You can use the rest room at the Inn."

"Stop the car!"

Davis looked at me with concern. "Are you ill?"

"Sick with jealousy. And don't you *dare* laugh."

He didn't. Soon he slowed down and eased the Apperson from the macadam road to the soft shoulder. I got out first and hurried off into the woods, feeling the wind in the trees, a wind cooler than that stirred by seraglio fans. I sat down at the base of a pine tree, on a bed of needles. I listened to the wind whispering a song of songs and waited for love to pass through the eye of one of the pine needles.

When Davis appeared and stood before me in perplexity, I said, "Do you have a bottle in the trunk?"

"I have a flask."

"Good. Get it."

Without a word he returned to the car. My hands went under my dress and tugged at my bloomers. Balling up the garment as Davis had balled up the months, I put it in my leather handbag.

Flask in hand, Davis returned. Still standing, he gave it to me. I drank fire. Then I said, "Take off your coat."

He smiled uneasily. "Anything else?"

"Yes. Unbutton your trousers."

"You can't be that drunk yet."

"I'm intoxicated." I breathed deeply. "The pines of Eden."

"No apple trees around."

Slowly I raised my dress. "Look at me. A Georgia peach. Ripe and fresh upon the orchard floor."

Davis sat down beside me. "Atlanta's so close."

"I'm Atlanta, and I'm burning."

The fusion of our mouths, then no more words, no more thoughts, only the groping, the clutching, the touching, and the climb toward ecstasy. Then the intrusion of guilt caused Davis to withdraw, to look at me and register his fear that this wasn't the right moment, the right Eden. I took my bloomers from my handbag and rubbed his face with the silken warmth. Quickly, urgently, he came over me and took me. And I waited to hear the moaning and the cries flying from my soul. But Davis's mouth was upon my mouth and stifled all sounds. Finally the wind and the woods returned, and there was no face before me to obscure the clouded skies beyond the treetops.

Tolstoi's Anna Karenina, by throwing herself under a train, had found the peace of the long eternity before birth. But I wasn't Anna Karenina now. I was Stendhal's Lamiel.

Told that love was a dangerous subject, and admonished not to wander into the forbidden woods, Lamiel nevertheless trespassed there with a peasant youth whom she enticed with a promise of monetary reward. The carnal act concluded, Lamiel asked the youth: "Is there nothing more?" He answered: "No." In surprise Lamiel asked herself: "What, is love no more than that? Why then do they condemn it?" When the youth went off with his ten francs, Lamiel burst out laughing, repeating to herself: "What! This famous love, is it only that?"

In the absence of ecstasy, I was Lamiel, until the voice of the peasant youth who was really a prince in disguise sang words that I knew I would take and hold to the last moment on my death bed.

"I love you."

I turned from the clouded sky to the sun of my beloved's face. "I love you," I said. The same lyrics from the same song, his sung like Caruso, mine like a child by rote.

We kissed again before Davis handed the bloomers to me. Rising, he turned away and strolled toward the car. I watched him stand by the side of the road, light a cigarette, and scan the scene with a professional eye.

I shouted, "Don't you dare!"

He wheeled toward me. "What?"

"Don't you dare. Get that writer's look out of your eyes. You've raised my dress, but never dare to raise the veil from the mystery of this Eden."

His smile was winsome. "Let's go. I have to marry you now."

"Funny man."

Davis pressed fuel to the engine, the speedometer rose, and the curves were taken in high. Around a bend of the road there suddenly loomed a slow-moving wagon piled high with ancient furniture. The old Negro on the high seat turned away from his tired horse when he heard the rising sound of the Apperson. I saw death in the Negro's eyes as Davis, unable to brake the car, swept past the wagon. The left wheels of the Apperson struck the soft shoulder, the car wavered, and I screamed before Davis once again had the wheels on macadam and under control.

"Slow down, please," I cried.

Davis laughed. "I'm Barney Oldfield." The speedometer climbed to danger again.

"Slow down!" I screamed.

Davis glanced toward me, saw fear and hate and relaxed his pressure on the accelerator. But he said nothing.

"Slower," I insisted.

"I'm only doing fifty."

"Slower!" My voice was pitched to panic.

Davis not only slowed down, he stopped the car and regarded me with dark concern. "Are you all right now?"

"We could have been killed."

"I'll be careful."

I said absently, as I folded my hands across my breasts to blanket the chill of death, "Know what I was thinking? I was thinking about that old bed. On the wagon. I was thinking: now we die, never to sleep together in a bed."

Davis kissed my trembling hand. "I'm sorry."

"Drive slowly. You can't kill yourself now and leave me with a bastard child."

Davis was patient with me, and he drove the Apperson now with an understanding of my panic, and with an awareness that death is forever waiting around the bend of a road. Once we entered Atlanta and were moving slowly down Peachtree Street, I experienced another kind of panic. I slid down on the seat and fenced my face with my coat collar and hands, a maneuver that was not lost upon Davis.

"What are you doing now?"

"I'm having hallucinations. I keep seeing Howard. I don't want to see him."

90

Davis said, "Wave if you see him. We need a witness."

I didn't laugh. When we stopped at a fine restaurant for lunch, I ordered a chicken sandwich but couldn't eat it. Later, when we ascended by elevator to the marriage license bureau, I felt sick. After the papers were signed, and after a drone of words which expunged fears of bastardy, Davis and I left the building, not by the elevator, but by the stairway.

At the Clifford Hotel I wanted to climb the eight flights of stairs, but Davis dissuaded me. Holding my breath, I survived to reach the plateau of our honeymoon without incident.

Its doors first opened during the Spanish-American War, the Clifford Hotel in 1920 was the Plaza of Atlanta, the correct address for visiting barons, and the local hostelry where the city's elite held its social and charitable functions.

The Governor's Suite struck me as the perfect setting for my honeymoon, for it belonged on the second floor of an antebellum mansion. The sitting room was rich with fresh cream-colored paint, shuttered windows flanking a great fireplace, French provincial furniture, lush red carpeting, and portraits of several former Georgia governors. The bedroom was majestic, with its great canopied bed, its huge mirrors, and flashes of matching blue satin on the bedspread, chairs, and settee.

Liberally tipped by Davis, the Negro bellhop departed and left us to contemplate the fruit, flowers, and iced champagne which Davis had arranged.

Within a half hour I was sitting in the bathtub. Moments later Davis entered. He was naked, and he carried the silver bucket containing the champagne and two glasses. He eased into the tub, sat facing me, and poured two glasses of champagne. We drank and behaved like two children playing house. Then, with the champagne bottle emptied, and with our passions flooded, Davis carried me into the bedroom.

We were both dripping wet and soapy as we lay upon the bed and made love. This time I freed my mouth and the moans of ecstasy escaped. It was the happiest moment of my life.

Afterwards, both of us lying there in the peace of Eden and smoking cigarettes, I uneasily asked Davis, "Did I scare you?"

91

"Scare me? How?"

"With my animal cries."

"Oh, that? I think I'll send for the ASPCA. You can sleep it off in the dog pound, you silly bitch."

"You've heard those sounds before?"

"Once."

"Who was she?"

"My first wife."

I slapped his flat abdomen. "Don't fool with me. Who was she?"

"An Italian girl. A waitress in New Haven."

"Where did it happen?"

"In the anatomy class. At Yale."

"Seriously."

"She had a room. Upstairs over a spaghetti joint."

"Did you pay her?"

"No, she paid me. You forget, I was a Yale man." I reached over and grabbed him. "Easy, you want me to yell?"

"Yell Maxim Gorki!"

"Maxim Gorki! Feodor Dostoievski! Leo Tolstoi! Anton Chekhov!"

I released him. We embraced. His head buried between my breasts, Davis fell asleep moments before I did, not realizing there was another bend in the road that day.

When I awoke, the sun was down and darkness had infiltrated the room. I reached for Davis and gathered emptiness. He was gone. I eased out of bed, went into the sitting room and found him there, battling the dark with a bottle of bourbon. I turned on a lamp and saw him take another pull from the bottle, which was almost empty. He looked dead and embalmed.

"Darling, what's wrong?"

His voice was thick. "I called New York."

"Who in New York?"

"My agent. Ellis Mason."

"Who died?"

"I did."

92

I knelt beside his chair. "Did they cancel the Hollywood sale?"

"No."

"Then what is it?"

"That no good son of a bitch!"

"And who would that be?"

"That fucking Freddie!"

Suddenly I remembered about the review. "The review in the *New Republic*. What did Freddie say?"

"Fuck him!"

"What did he say?"

Davis gurgled more bourbon from the bottle, and then spat words from the bottom of his hell. "Bogus! Fake! Ludicrous!"

"What else?"

"Mason read the entire review. But I couldn't make out what he was saying. All I kept hearing was bogus, fake, ludicrous. Over and over again. I don't know what the hell he said."

"And what did Mason say?"

"He thought it was a damn good review."

"Perhaps it was," I suggested.

"Bogus? Fake? Ludicrous?"

"Only three words."

"And I've got three more: fuck you, Freddie."

"You said the other reviews were raves. All right, then, to hell with Freddie."

With an awe that chilled my naked body, Davis said, "They won't let Freddie into hell. You know why? Freddie's God. That's what he is. God! All the rest of them — Barrett, Mason, the whole gang — they're nothing. They know nothing. Freddie's God. He knows all. I fooled the rest of them. Couldn't fool Freddie. Never could. Freddie knows. God knows. Bogus, fake, ludicrous. Can't fool old Freddie, no time, any time, never, ever."

His voice trailing off, Davis allowed the bottle to slip from his hand. His eyes closed, his head fell to his chest, and he passed out. In tears, I drew his robe about him and went to the telephone.

93

Ellis Mason's business card was resting on the telephone table, but I decided to try to locate a copy of the *New Republic* in Atlanta. Failing to do so, I placed a long-distance call to Mason in New York. When the call came through, I was ready with a pen and some hotel stationery. I introduced myself to Mason and then asked him to read the review to me, slowly enough for me to copy it down, word for word. I wept as I copied out the verdict of Davis's God. After I had replaced the telephone, I went to the bathroom, picked up the ice bucket, and removed the champagne bottle from the melted ice. Going directly to Davis, slumped and snoring in his whiskey sleep, I flung the icy water into his face.

He opened his eyes, wiped his face with a languid hand, and beheld me sullenly. "What the hell are you doing?"

"Can you hear my voice?"

"It's too loud."

"I want to read you something."

"What'd you write? A farewell note?"

, "Oh, shut up! I'm going to read you fucking Freddie's review. And you'd better listen."

"Why do you want to torture me?"

I shook him. "God loves you! You fool! He loves you! Freddie loves you! Listen!"

My voice quavering, I read the review, composed not by God but by a schoolmaster whose most talented pupil has fallen short of the mark of genius. The important word that Davis had not heard before was *despite*. Despite the bogus, the fake, and the ludicrous, Delano Fredericks had written, Davis O'Donnell had succeeded in his first novel. The book was alive and would endure as a testament of O'Donnell's generation.

Davis heard me, heard me well. He heard the praise and bore the reminders and the particulars of his shortcomings: immaturity, misuse of words, lack of true erudition. The review ended almost with a prayer, a prayer that Davis O'Donnell would grow, would command his craft, and would bring glory to American letters.

When I had finished reading I dropped the sheets of paper and embraced Davis. He wept, and I heard the weeping I felt I would one day hear from my children. I climbed onto the chair, sat across his lap, and held him as a mother holds a child until he remembered he was a man and I his wife.

I said, "Order some dinner, lover."

"I want to call Freddie."

"Sit there. I'll make the call. To room service. You'll call Freddie in the morning. This is our honeymoon."

He favored me with a look that sealed my love for him. "You look just like a girl I laid in the woods. Once."

"What do you want me to order? Steaks? Or some trees?"

Davis rediscovered his laughter, and we laughed and laughed and returned to Eden.

Hours beyond midnight I wandered from Eden to hell. I had a nightmare. I dreamed I awoke to find myself again alone in bed and to hear, emanating from the sitting room, the sound of Davis moaning. Not in ecstasy, but in the throes of death. In the nightmare I fled from the bedroom to the dark sitting room. There, in the dark, Davis was sitting in the same chair, his hands at his throat, his eyes distended, his mouth torn open and gasping for breath. I screamed, and in a voice muffled and obscured by terror he uttered a plea I had never heard before and heard again only in the belfry of my unsound mind.

Waking, I found Davis soft and silent in pillowed sleep, and myself drenched in sweat and trembling before the terror that was now mine alone.

I dared not wake Davis. I dared not sleep. I lay there in the dark, waiting for this longitude of earth to turn from night, waiting for the stillness to take away the voice of the nightmare that had cried out: "Save me! Save me from God!"

part two

The Battle of the Flapper

1.

On the golden morning of March 22, 1920, at Gettysburg, I succeeded where Pickett had failed. The soprano of my rebel yells preceding my advance, I braved the tongue-clucking fusillade laid down by General Davis O'Donnell, took Cemetery Ridge, and captured the Union battle flag that had been disguised as a blue cravat.

And, in the twilight of the same day, a day of magic if not history, I invaded New York.

From New Jersey we had crossed to Staten Island, and there, leaving our Apperson to ride the waves, we took our position at the bow of a ferry boat, stole past the Statue of Liberty and toward the Battery, toward edifices that were stalactites suspended from a cloud ceiling, and toward lights that began to flash in high and myriad windows, lights that were signals from our spies.

Once we left the bay to the waning sun, to the concourse of tugs, barges, ferry boats, ocean liners, and some schooners, our vessel reversed engines and impressed itself against the protesting black pilings. When the ramp was coupled to the bow, we returned to our Apperson and drove onto Manhattan. The streets, alive with the faces of five continents, gave proof through

99

the twilight that the skyscrapers were truly stalagmites rising from the bedrock of this treasured island. Overhead, on elevated tracks, an electric train retreated uptown; below, Klaxon horns heralded our triumph.

We led a parade up Broadway. At Union Square Davis stopped the Apperson and the traffic while, in swift ceremony, he rechristened it Confederate Square. Then we turned onto Fifth Avenue and moved northward. At Thirty-third Street I showed the magnanimity of Grant and dissuaded Davis from stopping and lowering the Union flag flying from a mast before the Waldorf-Astoria Hotel. At Forty-second Street we roared our triumph to the great lions fronting the library. Finally, in the Plaza, we took the sad salute from General Sherman and allowed him to keep his sword and horse.

Davis, for whom the skyscrapers seemed to be standing at attention, was at once the hero and villain of the day. Recalling the scandal that had beset the city many years before when Maxim Gorki had registered at a local hotel with his Russian mistress, Davis blandly signed the Plaza register as Maxim Gorki and Mistress.

The desk clerk, being unamused and unable to find a reservation in Gorki's name, forced Davis to try again. This time he wrote: Davis O'Donnell and Mistress. The clerk frowned at Davis and was placated only when I held up my left hand and allowed him to glimpse the wedding band on the third finger.

But an enterprising reporter from the tabloid *Daily News* noted the entry on the hotel register. That evening we were interviewed and photographed in our palatial tenth-floor suite, but not before Davis had removed and pocketed my gold ring and instructed me to play a poor country girl who had never heard of the Mann Act.

That was how the first days of our occupation of New York passed: with powder flashes from press cameras, the staccato of questions from reporters, the popping of champagne corks, the blaring of saxophones, the strumming of banjos, and the cash register recording mounting sales of *The Distant Spires*. And each night ended with the rituals of a ride in a hansom cab

100

through Central Park and a question from Davis: Where the hell's Freddie?

The very first telephone call we had placed in New York was to the Frederickses. But no one was at home. We checked friends and associates and heard nothing but conflicting and confusing rumors: the Frederickses were in Washington, with Freddie doing a series on the League of Nations; the Frederickses were in Hollywood, with Freddie penning an article on Charlie Chaplin; the Frederickses were in hiding, said one jester, hiding from the O'Donnells.

It was a metropolitan carrousel, with a brass ring for each day: always a new speakeasy, another foreign and exotic restaurant, another interview, another party. Through it all, the Corona portable sat silently on the desk in the sitting room of our Plaza suite. And the adding machines downstairs were clicking off reminders of mounting bills.

Several times that month the Apperson took us north to New Haven, where Davis belatedly reveled in the fame and hero worship denied to him in his undergraduate days. The new celebrity autographed scores of copies of his novel, sat down to write pieces for the various university publications, and lingered at tavern tables, spiking drinks with the booze from his long silver flask.

But where was Freddie? Where was God? His strange absence perturbed Davis. The stage was set, the curtain up, the play on, the spotlight on Davis — and no Freddie standing in the wings and waiting for his cue to enter. No Freddie to play Zeus to Davis's Adonis.

On April 21, I came at last face to face with Davis O'Donnell's God.

It was about four o'clock of a cool spring afternoon, siesta time at the Plaza for the night-prowling O'Donnells. Davis, insulated by five martinis, was sleeping soundly. I had had no drinks that day, excusing myself with the complaint of a stomach disorder. But it was more than that. I was very much awake with the sensation that I was pregnant, and I lay upon the bed pondering the prospect of motherhood and the problem of break-

101

ing the news to Davis. I wanted to tell him it was time to finish the honeymoon, end the party, pay the bills, and settle down in a home where the sounds of a typewriter and a child would rise with the sun.

The door to the sitting room was ajar. Hearing a knock on the corridor door, I left Davis asleep in the bed, put on a peignoir purchased at Bergdorf Goodman, slipped my feet into satin slippers from I. Miller's, and went to the door.

Opening it, I beheld an old man of twenty-six. His double-chinned face and portly body were molded from oatmeal. His brown suit was as rumpled as a pair of pajamas, his pushcart necktie indifferently knotted, his shoes unshined, and his black hair unruly. My initial impression was that the stranger was in the wrong hotel and had rapped upon the wrong door. But then, when I met his eyes — eyes that might have been stolen from a statue of Buddha — I realized that here, in the deceptive guise of a ghetto merchant, was God.

He spoke first, his voice deep, Bostonian, cold, and forbidding. "Mrs. O'Donnell?"

"Yes?"

"I'm Delano Fredericks."

I smiled, threw my arms about him, and kissed his oatmeal cheek. "Come in, Freddie."

When I had shut the door, I watched him survey the room and then fasten his gaze upon the Corona portable resting on the French provincial desk. He seemed to regard the typewriter as if it were a wild beast about to spring and attack him. Turning to me again, he asked, "Where's Davis?"

"Napping. I know how anxious he is to see you, but I hate to wake him. We've got another party tonight. Besides, I'd like to visit with you alone. For a while."

We sat down in matching wing chairs close to the Fifth Avenue windows, and I noted with surprise that Freddie's vested paunch sported no Phi Beta Kappa key and no gold football, and that his chubby fingers bore no Yale class ring. And then, as he stared appraisingly at me, I suddenly felt that it was I, rather than he, who was improperly dressed. Amid the ele-

102

gance of the suite I sensed that my flimsy peignoir was a highly improper attire for an audience with a man who had a papal presence.

I said, "Would you care for a drink? You have your choice. Gin, rye, bourbon, Scotch."

He shook his head. "Later. You and Davis running a speak-easy here?"

"Davis says, '*With* the O'Donnells comes the deluge.' "

"Enjoying yourself in New York?"

"Like a kid at the circus. I'm the little sister who was let in free because her big brother's the daring young man on the flying trapeze."

"How high is he flying?"

"He's conquered New York. And New Haven."

"What's next? Hartford?"

"Oh, that's the railroad!" I laughed. "That's very funny. You must tell Davis. I'm so glad you have a sense of humor."

"Didn't you expect me to have one?"

"You're much different from what I'd imagined."

"In what ways?"

"You don't look like a Yale man. You don't wear your class ring, your gold football, or your Phi Beta Kappa key."

"I have other affectations," he said. "I'm trying to be as grubby as Balzac. Playing the bohemian game with an address in the Village and a desk at a little, butcher-paper magazine."

"Where've you been? We've missed you."

"In seclusion."

"Davis was thinking of sending the Pinkertons after you."

"He didn't have to. He hounds me very well all by himself."

"How do you mean?"

Freddie smiled sadly. "Just an old campus joke."

"Davis loves you. He thinks you're God."

He winced as if I had uttered a blasphemy. "You said something about my not having the appearance of a Yale man. The fact is I come from a very long line of Harvard men."

"Yes, I know. Your father's a history professor there."

103

"Six generations of Fredrickses were churchmen before the line deviated from the pulpit to the classroom."

"Why did you choose Yale?"

"It was my father's decision."

"Which you regret?"

"Not at all. It was a wise decision. You see, my father took William James seriously when he said, 'Harvard is all thought, no college; Yale all college, but no thought.' My father believes that Herodotus and Spinoza sit with equal majesty in the libraries at New Haven and at Cambridge."

"Is that true?"

"That truth I discovered in my father's own library."

"So did I."

"Yes, but you were the belle of your town. I was hardly the big beau in Boston. I was a child prodigy, reading Latin and Greek before I went to prep school, always the bookworm, always the recluse."

"But not so at Yale."

"No. At Yale I made every attempt to join the human race, the race of boys. I learned how to smoke, how to drink, how to sing college songs, and how to laugh. I took my tapeworm fat to the football field and took my command of language to the college publications. Played poker, played with girls, and played at making friends."

"Friends like Davis?"

"Yes. Davis was a good part of my education. In Boston I had always given the upstart Irish a wide berth. They were always so alien to me. And then I met Davis." He paused, remembering. "One autumn night in my junior year I was working in the *Lit.* office, and there, at my desk, appeared this Irish boy, this freshman with an arm in a cast. He told me he'd broken his arm scrimmaging with the frosh football squad, and I told him to take the tale of his accident to the *Daily News*. He stammered something about having done some writing at prep school in Milwaukee, and about wanting to do something for the *Lit.* Coldly I told him to return the following week with whatever contribution he wished to submit. I never expected to see him

104

again, but he returned with a poem. It wasn't Byron, but it was good. It had a felicity of language, a rare sense of wonder and observation." Then, for a long moment, Freddie said nothing. He merely sat there. Finally he returned his gaze to me and said, "Yes. Davis was the perfect boy for Yale, handsome, personable, and gifted. The boy who, unlike me, had read dime novels, believed in Frank Merriwell and Dink Stover, and in the cause of beating Harvard. Had he been twenty pounds heavier and a few million dollars richer, he'd have been the big man on the campus."

I said, "He is now. Since the novel was published. We've been there several times."

Freddie was unimpressed. "That's the shame of it. I've put Yale behind me, but Davis never will. The college swallowed and forgot him, and now he'll always be going back, always be the Old Blue."

"Don't you ever go back?"

"Only in reverie."

"Unlike Davis," I said, "you also succeeded in the war. You got overseas."

"Not to the trenches, only as far as Paris and *Stars and Stripes*."

"Davis envies you that."

Freddie sighed. "He envies Eddie Rickenbacker and Hall Bowen much more. He's a fool."

"You say that with a passion."

With sudden sharpness, Freddie said, "The damned fool shouldn't be envying anyone, least of all me. The fact is, I envy him."

This revelation shook me. "What do you envy, Freddie? His success?"

"Damn his success. It could be his ruination." He turned to face the beast of the Corona. "What's he got in his typewriter?"

"A story for the *Post*."

He now directed his sharpness to me. "Exactly what I mean. It's a tragic mistake, a perversion of his gift."

"He's a storyteller," I argued.

105

"Do you read the *Post?*"

"I do now."

"Is that Davis's level?"

"He's proud of it."

"Don't you believe in Davis?"

"I married him."

"Do you have faith in him?"

"Why the inquisition?" I demanded.

"Either you believe in Davis, or you don't."

The harsh tone unsettled me, and I stooped to folly. I said, "I'm an agnostic."

"Who only genuflects to Mammon?"

"I bow only to reality."

His glare was accusing. "What happened to the reality you discovered in your father's library?"

The clarity of the question was lost in a fog of memory and despair, of guilt and regret. I said, "I don't understand."

"You embraced a body of literature. Now in bed you embrace a man who's obliged to leave more behind than dust and ashes. A man whose vision of life must be bound in books worthy enough to sit on your father's shelves."

"Davis? He's a boy."

"That's a temporary condition."

I smiled wanly. "Shall I confess something? When I first opened the door, you struck me as the oldest young man I had ever seen."

"I am and I'm thinking of growing a beard. But Irene's against it, believes it'll make me look like a bomb-throwing anarchist."

"You did throw a bomb at Davis." I recounted Davis's reaction to his review.

"You erred in phoning Mason."

"Why?" I asked. "It was my honeymoon."

"A transitory interlude, entirely divorced from the business of life. Or does that sound too puritanical to you?"

"Is life so stark to you?"

Freddie turned his head toward the window. "Down in the

106

Village we see the same stars from our windows as you do here at the Plaza."

"They seem brighter here."

Freddie jerked his head toward me and upset my smile. "Take down the tinsel before it's too late."

"Is this the message from Mount Sinai?"

"I deserved that. The fact is, believe it or not, the message comes from the Berkshire Hills."

"Never heard of them."

"You shall, I hope."

"About the tinsel," I said. "After I take it down, then what do I do?"

"You join my church and believe that Davis is God."

"There is only one God. And his name is Delano Fredericks."

"There are only pseudonyms for the name of God," Freddie declared, "and the pseudonym of the moment is Davis O'Donnell."

I shivered, and I reached for the warmth of absurdity. "Of course. And I'm the Virgin. With the power to inspire cathedral-like books."

Freddie gave me his best smile. "I see Davis told you about my allusion."

"That was the moment I decided to marry him."

"Good. That pleases me and makes me love you all the more."

I taunted him. "Remember me? I'm the Georgia cracker in crinoline."

He said, "The crinoline's gone."

"What should I be wearing now? Sackcloth and ashes?"

Again he delivered his best smile instead of the laughter he seemed unable to attain. "You're very lovely in your peignoir, and you make me wish I had a talent for seduction."

I laughed. "Oh, Freddie, I love you! Why don't you just say silly things like that? That's what I love to hear. What I want to hear. Why not leave the lamentations to Jeremiah?"

His best smile persisting, he said, "I'm a dirty old puritan with an Hebraic bent."

"Tell me about the girls in New Haven. Did you ever have an Italian girl?"

"I'll tell you only what my smile tells you, but let's continue with the prostitute in the bedroom."

"Davis!"

"Yes. His primrose path to Philadelphia troubles me. A story in the *Post* grieves me more than a story on the *Times'* obituary page."

I now saw Freddie as Michelangelo saw the prophets in stone. Somewhat in awe, I said, "No, you're not a Yale man."

Solemn now, Freddie said, "No, but Davis is. He turned defeat into victory. He knows what it is to miss making the varsity, what it is to bury the Merriwell dream, what it means to wear a uniform and not find the way to battle, what it means to love a girl and lose her, what it means not to be tapped for a secret society, what it means to be a Catholic in a den of Protestants, what it means to be an Irish outlander and be snubbed by rich snobs."

And I added, "And what it means to be a Yankee among Southerners."

"Yes."

"Freddie, shall I tell you something?"

"Please."

"All of a sudden you strike me as a man who knows more about defeat than anyone I've ever met."

He nodded again. "Yes. You see, I came to Yale too late, too late to be a man among men, too old to cry out in triumph, to scream in defeat. Yes, my kingdom was lost for want of a dime novel."

Before I could pursue this argument, I heard Davis's voice from the bedroom. "Rannah?"

"Yes!" I replied.

And Davis, with the imperiousness of a sultan, shouted, "Come in and say hello to Maxim Gorki."

The terrifying aspect of the moment wasn't my embarrassment, or the wildness of my laughter. It was that Freddie, who

108

had obviously translated the outcry, couldn't bring himself to laughter.

Cupping a hand to my mouth, I called back, "You come out and say hello to Freddie."

"Freddie!" cried Davis. "How the hell are you?"

"Fine." Freddie seemed unable to bring himself to shout.

In a moment Davis appeared, in terry cloth and brandishing the world's best smile. "Where's Irene?"

"Down in Park Row," said Freddie. "Working."

"How is she?"

"Fine, thank you."

"And how are you, you bastard?"

Freddie smiled the smile of a best friend. "As always."

Davis chuckled. "About Maxim Gorki."

"I know all about Gorki."

Davis and I laughed. Freddie couldn't, and again terror stalked the frivolity.

Davis said, "I didn't know you were here. As a matter of fact, I've been breaking my head all these weeks wondering where the hell you were."

Freddie's smile faded. "That's where I was. In hell."

Not comprehending the terror, Davis crossed to the telephone and ordered a bucket of ice from room service before returning to us and confronting Freddie. "In what corner of hell?"

"The darkest," said Freddie darkly.

"Doing what?"

"Going down to defeat."

Davis turned to me. "What's he trying to tell me?"

I burlesqued a Southern belle. "You Yankees talk so funny, a body can hardly understand a single word."

Davis leered. "I know what your body understands. But what does your first-rate mind tell you?"

"That you're crude, darling."

Davis laughed. "Where's Freddie been?"

I glanced at Freddie and noted his discomfiture. "He said something about the Berkshires."

109

With understanding, Davis turned to Freddie. "The family summer place?"

Freddie nodded. "Elementary, wasn't it?"

"Rannah, why didn't we think of that?"

"It's not summer," I said.

"Freddie, what were you doing there?"

Freddie looked baleful. "What have you been doing in New York?"

"Having ourselves one helluva honeymoon."

Without conviction, Freddie said, "That's what Irene and I were doing in the Berkshires, belatedly."

"Good for you!" Davis exclaimed. "Hey, you didn't get much sun."

Wryly, Freddie said, "You don't look very sunburned either, Mr. Gorki."

Davis said, "We missed you, Freddie. Really did."

"On your honeymoon?"

"Okay, wise guy. You're here. And I want to thank you for the review."

"You're welcome."

"You floored me with a couple of those adjectives."

"I tried. But I heard you recovered quite nicely."

Reacting to the expected knock on the corridor door, Davis turned to me. "Get that, honey, please. And tip him a fiver."

Dutifully I rose and went to the door. It was a familiar bellhop with an equally familiar bucket of ice and bottles of club soda and ginger ale. I signed the tab and tipped him one dollar.

"So long, Henry," Davis called to the bellhop, who waved and left. Turning to me, Davis frowned. "That wasn't a five-dollar smile."

I said, "Henry's bored with five-dollar tips. What are you drinking?"

Davis faced Freddie. "Scotch and soda?"

"Fine."

"Rannah, how much *did* you give Henry?"

"One Confederate dollar."

"You cheap rebels. No wonder you lost the war."

110

"Well, darling," I said, pouring Scotch into two glasses, "you must understand. We live so far from Wall Street."

Freddie was not attending. His eyes were once again on the typewriter. "Davis, what've you got in the machine?"

"A story for the *Post*."

Freddie's tone was frosty. "Why?"

"Henry lives in Brooklyn. With four kids."

"You're a fool."

I was slow making the drinks, for my mind was quick to sense a clash.

"Yes, but a rich one," Davis said.

"Why aren't you working on your second novel?"

"Freddie, did you come here to lecture me?"

"Precisely."

"I'm on my honeymoon."

"With Rannah? Or with the *Post*?"

"I can't write a line. Not even for the *Post*."

"That's a good beginning."

"For what, Freddie?"

"The second novel. Put a fresh sheet of paper in your Corona and do what you must do."

"I've got six commitments with the *Post!*"

"Break them."

Discernibly upset, Davis appealed to me. "Honey, hurry up with those drinks. This man's too sober." To Freddie he added, "And too somber. Hey, you have a row with Irene?"

"No. And don't change the subject."

Agony in his voice, Davis demanded, "What's with you?"

"When are you checking out of here?"

Davis strained to keep his temper in check. "What the hell's gotten into you? We're having a ball! I love the Plaza! It's the top of the world! I'm bigger right now than General Pershing!"

As I served their highballs to Freddie and Davis, I observed casually, "Davis is bigger than Maxim Gorki."

It fell flat. Davis peered at me suspiciously. "Have you been crying on Freddie's shoulder?"

"Don't be ridiculous," I said.

111

Davis faced Freddie. "She's a spoilsport. Always reminding me I'm tippling too much. And tipping too much."

"I've explained that," I said. "I'm from the impoverished South."

Davis sipped his drink and looked at me as if he would rather be drinking my blood. "Rannah," he began — it was never "honey" when he was angry — "are you against my writing for the *Post?*"

"You haven't even written your mother."

Davis sighed in confusion. "Why is Freddie lecturing me?"

"Ask him. He's the bright man over there. Behind the highball glass."

Freddie said, "Rannah didn't complain to me."

"Then what's the beef?"

"You made a promise."

More confusion from Davis. "To whom?"

"To your readers and your critics."

"And what was that?"

"You understand me perfectly."

"The hell I do!" Davis was in a rage now. "The book's selling big! Hollywood's buying! The magazines are buying! What's all this crap about promises?"

"Do you feel fulfilled?"

"I'd like a Pulitzer prize."

"You won't get one, not for *The Distant Spires.*"

"Thank God you won't be on the committee."

Calmly Freddie said, "Davis, I'd like to see you win all the prizes. I think you can do it."

"Thanks, God."

"I don't appreciate that."

"Is that blasphemy?"

"Your smirk is blasphemy and you're a damned fool."

Davis now tried to throw a cloak of humor atop the muddied moment. "In the words of Owen Wister, Mister, smile when you say that."

"I don't feel like smiling."

"Aw, come on," Davis pleaded. "Let's get drunk."

112

"Where would that get us?"

"To Brooklyn. We're going over to the Crescent Athletic Club tonight. Remember Alvin Rodgers?"

"Not kindly."

"Alvin's got himself engaged to a Brooklyn heiress. Standard Oil money. Be a helluva party. Big crowd from Yale."

"No, thank you, I've been to Yale."

"Don't you want to see the old bunch?"

"Not particularly."

Davis looked stung. "Does that include me?"

"Yes, unless you kiss the *Post* good-bye."

Davis turned to me. "Honey, why aren't you drinking?"

"I'm listening," I explained.

Returning his attention to Freddie, Davis asked, "What the hell does the *Post* have to do with our friendship?"

"As friend to friend, you're a stupid bastard."

"Are those your parting words?"

"Only my overture."

"What the hell are we fighting over?"

"Radium."

Davis glanced toward me and noted a perplexity matching his own. "Honey, you know this guy?"

"To know him is to love him."

Now Davis asked Freddie, "What's all this about radium?"

"Radium's a radioactive element obtained from uranium pitchblende and discovered by Madame Curie."

Raising his right hand, as if he were taking an oath, Davis said, "I swear it. I didn't steal it."

"You have it," Freddie said with a trace of bitterness.

Davis grinned mirthlessly. "You want to search the suite?" He turned to me. "You know what the hell this idiot's driving at?"

"Something tells me you'd do well to listen."

Turning again to Freddie, Davis said, "I'm listening, *God*."

"You discovered radium, only you were too stupid to recognize it. You mistook it for a Roman candle."

113

I understood Freddie, but Davis, the backward boy, did not. "Radium! Roman candles!"

Freddie said, "Radium is genius — an element very much present in your novel."

At first Davis seemed awed by the revelation, but then he seemed to hear the Sirens of absurdity and he laughed with abandon. "Hey, that's funny! Are you saying I'm a genius, God? Hey, Freddie, this is Davis O'Donnell you're talking to! Remember me? The stupid oaf from Milwaukee!"

"Davis, you're a long way from home and from New Haven."

"Sure! And I'm the lucky son of a bitch who's cashing in on his luck! What the hell's wrong with that?"

"Everything," said Freddie. "It's a question of luck when a bellhop runs into a five-dollar tipper, but luck had nothing to do with you. With you it's a question of a great matter, a grave matter, and a very grave gift."

Davis studied Freddie and came to his own grave conclusion. "You look dead, Freddie. When did you die?"

"Last night."

Both Davis and I felt the finality of this confirmation. I shivered in the tomb at the Plaza. Davis's laughter sounded like graveyard whistling. "Tell me, Freddie," he finally asked, "how did the death certificate read?"

Freddie's gaze seemed to have been fixed by the hand of an embalmer. "Massive pitchblende."

Davis turned to me and went into a low Dutch comic routine. "Gott in Himmel, Madame Curie! How you like *dot?*"

My voice was feeble. "Call me Marie."

More laughter. "Once more, dear wife, into the bottle. Damn the icebergs. Full speed ahead."

Davis held out his glass, but I refused to take it.

Cross now, Davis said, "The hell with both of you." He went to the bottle and poured straight Scotch. Then he rounded on Freddie. "Okay, pal, translate that death certificate for me."

Freddie said, in the manner of a coroner at an inquest, "The morning you left for Georgia, Irene and I left for the Berkshires: Irene to do some painting, I to write a book."

114

Davis's eyes widened. "What kind of book?"

"A novel."

"A novel!"

"Yes."

"What's it about?"

"Charles Whittlesey."

The name didn't register with me, but it did with Davis. "The major who commanded the Lost Battalion! The guy who later killed himself!"

"The same."

"Christ! That's a great story. Ought to make a great novel."

"That's what I thought," Freddie said.

"Didn't it?"

"No, I failed."

"How much did you get done?"

"Fifty thousand words."

"I want to see it."

"You can't. I put a match to it last night."

"Christ! Talk about stupid bastards!"

"It was no good."

"I don't believe it, God."

Freddie sipped again. "The language was faultless, the construction artful, the spelling and grammar correct. It contained nothing that was fake, bogus, or ludicrous. Nonetheless, it was all pitchblende, no trace of radium."

Davis asked, "Did Irene read it?"

"Yes. She loved it. Said it was masterful."

"Then why the hell did you burn it?"

"I'm the critic in the family."

"You can't judge your own work." Then, with sudden inspiration: "You have a carbon copy."

"No carbon, save in the ashes. The book never came alive, save in flames."

"Maybe I could've helped you."

"Thank you," Freddie said stiffly. "I've tried to learn from you, to borrow from you. I'd been doing that ever since we first

115

met at Yale, but it can't be done. You have the gift and I don't."

"Bullshit! Compared to you, I'm an amateur."

Freddie stood and looked at Davis with disdain. "No, compared to me, you're God." While Davis remained stunned, Freddie came to me and kissed me. "Good-bye, Rannah."

I said, "When will we see you again? I do want to meet Irene."

"Davis has our number. Call us."

When Freddie turned to him, Davis said, "Come to the party with us. I think you need to get drunk."

"I've got some reviews to write."

"The hell with that! Come on, we've got to celebrate."

With anguish Freddie said, "Celebrate what? The terrible truth that I now envy you more than you ever did me?"

Blood rushed to Davis's contorted face. "Christ! I must be asleep and dreaming. I never thought I'd live to hear you say that."

Freddie held out his hand. It seemed more a gesture of surrender than a farewell.

Davis withheld his own hand. "Call Irene. Tell her to come over. We'll have dinner up here. The hell with the party in Brooklyn. We'll sit and talk about the novel. Your novel."

Freddie shook his head. "You can't talk novels. You can't drink them either. And forgive me if it appears I came here to cry on your shoulder. That wasn't my intention. I only wanted to let you know about the radium and the Roman candle. Good-bye, Davis."

Davis trailed Freddie to the door. "What time do you want us over tomorrow night?"

"We're busy tomorrow night."

"Name the day."

Freddie closed his eyes wearily. "I don't want to see you."

Davis would not relent. "I'll call you tomorrow."

"Don't. I don't want to talk to you."

Tears in his eyes now, Davis cried, "Are you *that* fucking envious of me?"

116

"I'm beyond envy," Freddie said softly. "I don't wish to hear you tell me about the Yale crowd, about Hollywood, the *Post*, or any of that nonsense. When the honeymoon's over, and you've started on your second novel, you can pick up the phone and ask the operator for my number."

Having delivered his ultimatum, Freddie exited. When Davis turned to me, he saw tears to match his own.

"Pinch me," he said.

"That's unnecessary. You've just had your behind kicked. Good and proper."

Davis regarded me more in anger than in sorrow. "You taking Freddie's side?"

"What other side is there?"

"Mine!"

"My, how explosive! Must be the Roman candle going off in your hand."

"You looking for a spat?"

"You just had one." I watched him cross to the Scotch bottle. "And you're about to have one too many. The sun isn't down yet."

"Another lecturer heard from." He poured the whiskey like water, then moved to the typewriter and slammed his free hand down upon the keys. "Christ! What the hell does he want from me? Why the hell doesn't he leave me alone?"

"A little louder, darling. They can't hear you in Philadelphia."

And now the perturbed, petulant boy went to the open window, leaned out and down, and shouted, "Fuck you, Freddie!"

"That's loud enough."

Retreating from the window, Davis threw himself into the wing chair previously occupied by Freddie. He took several gulps of whiskey before he said, "What an afternoon! When I woke up, all I wanted was you."

"And what do you want now?" I asked.

"Why's he rushing me? What difference does it make if I knock out a few stories for the *Post*?"

"Did you notice how old Freddie looks?"

117

"He looked dead."

"He looked old."

"His suit needs pressing."

"Was it a good idea?" I asked.

"What?"

"Was it a good idea Freddie had about the novel?"

"Great."

"Don't you want to talk?" He said nothing. I tried again. "At Yale, did Freddie ever talk about writing novels?"

"Yes. He was going to be the American Dostoievski."

"A pity."

"A great idea. This Major Whittlesey, a great character. Won the Congressional Medal of Honor. Big hero. But not to himself. Blamed himself for giving out the wrong position of the Lost Battalion. Our own artillery hit them with a barrage. Lots of casualties. Whittlesey never forgave himself. Took a boat trip and jumped overboard." He drank more whiskey. "He was a New Englander. Like Freddie."

I said, "Perhaps Freddie'll give you the idea."

"Why?"

"Sounds like something you'd like to do. As a second novel."

There was hate in his eyes now. "Does it?"

"I can tell by the way you talk."

He erupted from the chair. "Shit! You're stupid! How the hell can I write that story! I never even got to France!"

"Freddie," I said calmly, "never got to the trenches."

"He was there! Over there!"

"You, darling, have the radium."

"Beat it! Before I throw the typewriter at you!"

Then and there I decided to desist, realizing it was futile and graceless of me to add my bark to the pursuing hounds of his conscience. Instead I tried to divert him with the balm of the marital bed. "What do you hear from Gorki?"

Davis looked at me as if I were mad. He said nothing, and somewhere in that strained and sullen moment our honeymoon came to an end.

118

2.

Hours later, hours that had passed into a darkness which had been ours earlier, we left the suite, Davis in his tuxedo and I in my evening gown, neither of us with a smile. Not a word passed between us until Davis had turned the Apperson onto the Manhattan Bridge.

His eyes upon the traffic, Davis finally said, "Say something funny."

"I'm pregnant."

He didn't laugh. "I'm Maxim Gorki."

"I know. That's why I'm pregnant."

Davis glanced at me and saw the glint of truth. "Impossible."

"Somewhere south of Adamston, Georgia."

"Yes. South of contraceptives."

I said nothing. I was blind to the vistas of the beautiful Brooklyn Bridge to my right and the Manhattan skyline behind me. I saw only Davis and observed the birth of a smile upon his brooding countenance.

He said, "What'll we call the little bastard? Maxim Gorki O'Donnell?" He laughed. "May the saints forgive me. That's a terrible name. Forget it."

"How about this? Adele Garrett O'Donnell."

119

Davis shook his head. "Couldn't get in Yale with a name like that."

"Sorry. Hadn't thought of that."

"Happy about it?"

"Yes, I am," I said. "I want to have four children."

"Sure. We'll have our own backfield."

"Two boys, two girls."

"I'll speak to Gorki about it."

"Please do."

Davis took his right hand from the wheel and squeezed my left thigh. "Honey, I'm sorry about before."

I played dumb. "Before what?"

"Freddie castrated me."

"I understand. I only wanted to show you he really hadn't."

"I'm all right now."

"Both hands on the wheel, please."

He relaxed and I relaxed with him. "We'll have to get a chauffeur. Anyway, that's what I like about hansom cab rides around the park."

"I think the horses know." We laughed together. "Darling, do they deliver babies at the Plaza?"

"I think so. By the trade entrance."

"I wouldn't want it any other way."

But then Davis must have seen tomorrow beyond the traffic, for he said, "Shall I make a U-turn?"

"On the bridge?"

"On the Brooklyn side."

"And then what?"

"Greenwich Village."

"Freddie?"

"I want to borrow something."

"Like what?"

"That summer place in the Berkshires."

"So far from Fifth Avenue?"

"It'll be quiet there."

"You want quiet?"

"A must. Always before the storm. Babies cry a lot."

My voice was now choked. "And before the storm?"

"By day we'll listen to the Corona. By night to the crickets."

"Do you write?"

"Used to, before I got married. Well, you know how it is. A wide circle of friends. People popping in and out."

"Like Maxim Gorki."

Davis hooted. "Honey, I love you. Don't ever lose your sense of humor."

"No, only my figure."

"Do you mind?"

"No, darling. Not if you don't."

Davis said nothing. The full measure of his attention, as we left the bridge behind, was given to the wide, cobblestoned street and new patterns of traffic. After some blocks, I said, "I thought you were making a U-turn."

"Tomorrow the Village."

I felt my heart sink into a dark tunnel, like the subway train that had crossed the bridge with us. "Changing your mind about the Berkshires?"

"I can't ask Freddie for the house."

"Why not?"

"I've got those *Post* stories to do."

"Let's say farewell to the Plaza and to the *Post*. I'll have a baby, you have a second novel."

"I haven't got one in mind. Not an idea," he said forlornly.

"You'll find one," I assured him. "Once you forget the *Post*."

"Babies are expensive."

I said, "I want to give you a baby. Not an excuse."

"Hey! You been to a doctor yet?"

"No."

"Then how can you be sure? Maybe you're just late."

I felt fright. "Is that what you're hoping?"

"I don't know. It's all too much for me. It's been quite a day. First I'm proclaimed God, then God the Father."

"Perhaps there's no such thing as a pregnant Cherokee princess," I said.

"Let's find out. I'll stop at the next cigar store."

"The cigar store Indian never talks."

After a pause Davis said, "Freddie talks. Too damn much. Christ! How am I going to sleep tonight?"

I had no answer for him, so I said nothing. For the remainder of the ride to the Crescent Athletic Club we spoke only of street directions.

Davis's spirits revived when he parked the Apperson among the luxury cars outside the country club on Shore Road. We sat quietly a moment, taking in the scene: the rambling wooden clubhouse on the bluff above The Narrows, the great hedged-in polo field, the boathouse and landing at the water's edge. I turned to Davis and saw that he was in the heaven of his vision.

Arm in arm we approached the Japanese lanterns strung along the porch of the clubhouse and then followed the music inside. Appropriately enough, the band was playing *Japanese Sandman*. We moved into the ballroom and joined the dancers beneath the glittering chandeliers. We had one dance, and then went to the punch bowl. To Davis's delight, the punch was spiked with rum. And to my chagrin, after some chitchat with some of Davis's college friends, I found that Davis had disappeared.

Now I felt lost, alone, tossing restlessly upon a sea of strange faces. I drained another glass of punch, for the first time in my life a wallflower.

My glass emptied, my heart heavy with a longing for home and the parties of my girlhood, I quit the ballroom and retreated to the porch to stand alone beneath the Japanese lanterns. With one ear I listened to the band, with the other I heard the sounds of boats in The Narrows. Far to the west I saw the lights of Manhattan, distant and ethereal.

Then into my line of vision came a man who was a stranger, yet whose face was familiar to me. After a moment I realized I had seen him before in the pages of *Vogue*. He was Claude Terrence. Six feet, four inches tall, he looked like Francis X. Bushman's brother. In fact he was a ten-goal polo player, a Princeton man, the scion of a New York banking family, married to an aristocratic girl from Tennessee.

Unmindful of my presence, Terrence lit a Cuban panatela and surveyed his kingdom.

I tried my voice. "Beautiful evening, isn't it?"

He started slightly. "Yes, I was admiring the view." He moved closer and noted I was strange to him. "Do cigars bother you?"

"Only when *I* try to smoke them."

He smiled, but all he said was, "Charming." Then, obviously not as smitten with me as I was with him, he went back to his contemplation of the boathouse below the road.

After a while I asked, "Expecting someone?"

He blew a perfect smoke ring before he said, "I hear this O'Donnell chap's here."

I played dumb, played the game. "Who is that?"

"Davis O'Donnell. The writer."

"Oh, him."

"Have you read his book?"

"No, have you?"

"Yes, I have. Quite entertaining."

I asked, "You a Yale man?"

"Princeton."

He turned away again, inspected the array of lanterns as if they had been hung expressly for him, and edged away.

I called after him. "I didn't catch your name."

He stopped and wheeled about gracefully. "Oh, I'm sorry. I'm Claude Terrence."

Matching his casualness, I said, "I'm Mrs. Davis O'Donnell."

He returned to my side. His demeanor, at last, was now lantern bright with interest. "Well. I'm pleased to meet you."

"My name's Rannah."

"Yes, I know. I've been hearing about you."

"Hearing what?"

"You're from Georgia, aren't you?"

"A long way from."

"Would you care to dance?"

"I'd love to."

Having slain me, Claude Terrence killed his cigar, then led me

123

into the ballroom, onto the powdered dance floor, and into the steps of a fox-trot. And, like a fox, I ran from the orchestra's hunting horns, southward across state lines and all the long way back to my lair in Stephensville, where my dancing days had begun.

While dancing a waltz with Claude Terrence, I kept searching the scene for Davis, wishing he would appear out of the dark, tap Claude Terrence's shoulder, and waltz me about until my head spun with love for him. Then, with a resolve born of dismay, I began to catch the eyes of other young men. I enticed them with smiles and winks I had never dared or needed to dare in Stephensville.

Before long Claude Terrence was gone from my arms, and in his stead came a steady stream of young men snared by my wily airs and graces.

In the intervals when the musicians shook the spit from their horns, the pianist planted a fresh cigarette in his mouth, and the violinist took the handkerchief from his chin and mopped his sweaty brow, I found myself again in this strange splendor, wondering where Davis was and why I had wandered so far from home.

I drank too much spiked punch, took many drags from cigarettes held by the boys in the orchestra, and danced some more to the tunes I was now calling.

I danced as if I were naked and performing at a smoker, and my audience increased with each burst of my laughter, each bar of music, each chorus of whispers. And then, finally, to cap the evening, I pulled a stunt I would never thereafter be allowed to forget.

After I had danced my last dance, I reached under my gown and drew down my black Parisian panties. With a host of eyes upon me, I balled up the silk and tossed it up onto a chandelier. One awed group remained beneath the chandelier to ogle what I referred to as the black flag of the Confederacy. Another, bolder group followed me from the ballroom, hoping no doubt for further and madder follies.

At the entrance door I stopped, struck a pose, and dispersed

124

them all by announcing I was rejoining my husband. Imitating Ethel Barrymore, I croaked, "That's all there is. There isn't any more."

Alone again, in a darkness that led east, west, north, and south, I searched for Davis. Long, anguished minutes later I found him alone on the dark expanse of the polo field, at a remove from where he had vomited.

"Davis?"

"Yes?"

"Are you all right?"

"Let's go home."

I deferred all questions until we were once again in our Apperson and gliding through Brooklyn streets.

I began with an idle comment. "Nice party."

"Sure." His voice was listless.

I laughed. "I had loads of fun."

"Good."

"Got the blues?"

"Uh-huh."

"Freddie?"

"Guess so."

I said nothing. I wanted to talk about the party, not about God and radium. But I decided to leave Davis to his sickness and silence.

Then, after a while, he asked, "Feel like talking?"

"Always. With you."

"Can we talk about secret things?"

"Darling, do we have secrets from each other?"

"I mean like sex."

My intuition chilled me. "I guess we all do."

"Do what?"

"Keep secrets from each other. About sex."

"Meet anyone interesting tonight?"

"Someone who attracted me sexually?"

"Yes."

"Claude Terrence."

Davis flicked a glance at me. "I didn't know he was there."

125

"We danced. He dances very well."

"Then you enjoyed yourself."

"Hugely, darling."

He hesitated. "Didn't miss me?"

"No, I was having a lark."

"I'm glad."

"So am I. I thought, for a while, I'd be lost tonight."

His guilt was evident. "Aren't you going to ask me where I disappeared to?"

"I didn't know you'd disappeared, darling."

"I went down to the landing."

"The landing of what?"

"The boathouse."

"Oh!"

"I wasn't alone."

"It was a big party, darling. You weren't supposed to be alone."

"I was with Joanne Fabian."

The name didn't register. "Who's she?"

"A girl I first saw from afar at Yale. One of the rich Eastern crowd. Vassar girl. Always with Hall Bowen's gang. Society swell."

Jealousy registered. "Beautiful?"

"More than that. Inaccessible. The girl at the other table. In other company. At the party seen through the window. From the cold outside."

"That was Yale. Is she married now?"

"Yes. To Pete Fabian. One of the Hall Bowen crowd."

I wanted to caution Davis that he was repeating himself, but all I said was, "Good for her."

"I laid her."

The declaration had a simplicity all its own, and a sharpness that easily penetrated the skin, the flesh, and the bones shielding my heart. "Good for you."

His eyes on the traffic, Davis said, with contrition, "I didn't mean to."

I bit a finger. "These things happen."

126

"It was so easy."

"Like breaking the glass on a fire-alarm box?"

"No, it was more like breaking the window between us. With my success."

"Thunder does that, too."

"We went aboard this yacht. Down to one of the cabins."

"I can imagine the rest."

"Can you?"

I gave a poor imitation of laughter. "It's easy, darling. You're a celebrity. All girls desire celebrities."

"You understand?"

"Of course, I'm Mrs. Understanding."

My sarcasm eluding him, he said, "Know what her exact words were?"

"I won't spoil it for you. You tell me."

"Joanne said: 'Now I'll be a part of everything of yours I read.'"

"Touching."

"You're bitter. I shouldn't have told you."

"I'm glad you did. Now I'll understand *everything* of yours I read."

A moment of painful silence. "Can you forgive me?"

My voice was sharp now. "What sort of game are we playing?"

"Game?"

"Yes!" I screamed. "Are we setting up new rules? You tell me your conquests, I'll tell you mine?"

Davis looked as if he might be sick again. "It won't happen again."

"Want to bet?"

"You'll always think the worst now, won't you?"

"We both shall."

"Anyway, try, if you can, to forgive me."

"Oh, shut up."

Davis did shut up, but not for long. "What do you want to do about it?"

"Do about what?"

"Thinking of leaving me?"

127

"You bastard! I'm pregnant!"

"What if you weren't?"

"I want a drink. Right now."

"I don't know any speakeasies in Brooklyn."

"Well then, let's get the hell out of Brooklyn."

I was cowering in my seat. Davis said, "We're taking our usual ride around the park, aren't we?"

"Not tonight."

"Please, honey."

"Not ever again."

"We've got to talk this out. I feel guilty as hell."

"Save it for the confession booth."

"Yes. Maybe it's time I went again."

I sat now with my spine stiffened, my anger arched. "You'll go again! To bitches like Joanne Fabian!" Then, with both hands, I tore at my gown and raised it to my navel. "Hey, Gorki, take a look!"

Davis jerked his head toward me. "Where's your pants?"

"I had ants in them." I lowered my gown and allowed Davis to cultivate some jealousy of his own.

"Claude Terrence?"

My laughter was genuine now. "Oh, you great American authors! So perceptive!"

He believed me, and I let him wallow in the muck of that belief. "What's happening to us?"

"Success, you dumb bastard! Now shut up and find a speakeasy! Right here in Brooklyn!"

Davis stopped the Apperson when he saw a uniformed patrolman standing idly on a street corner. The policeman accepted a five-dollar bill, and Davis followed his directions to a speakeasy in Brooklyn Heights. Meanwhile I opened the glove compartment, withdrew Davis's flask, and drank off the remaining gin.

Parking the Apperson at the curb before an innocent-appearing brownstone house, Davis and I got out. Like two duelists marching to the field of honor, we crossed to the basement door. Davis belabored the door with his knuckles, not gently, but

128

rather with the authority of the law. In a moment the peephole was opened.

Davis spoke the passwords. "Greetings from Patrolman O'Rourke."

The door was opened by a brute of a man whose menace I didn't readily detect, for, having been to other speakeasies, I was familiar with the inevitable typecasting of bouncers. Without a word the brute led us to a table to one side of a dead, marble-faced fireplace, and we sat down upon a leather-upholstered bench fixed to the paneled wall.

Dim, dull light emanated from small pink-frosted bulbs that bloomed from wall fixtures and played upon banks of tobacco smoke. At the bar, at the far corner of the room, sat a blowzy woman flanked by two men who took turns whispering obsceni-ties in her ears and detonating bursts of giggles. At the table next to ours was a stern, middle-aged couple lending Gothic presence to what prohibition had wrought in place of the corner saloon: mixed company, mixed drinks, and mixed whispers.

The waiter who came to our table was a young Sicilian born for vendettas. "What'll it be?"

Davis asked, "What's your name?"

"Angelo."

"Got a watch, Angelo?"

"No."

Davis slipped off his wristwatch and handed it to the bewil-dered boy. "Here. It's yours. Now listen carefully. Every five minutes, on the dot, I want you to bring us two glasses of rye and soda. Understand?"

"Got you."

"All right, Angelo, we're going over the top."

Angelo retreated to the bar. I was prepared to begin my own war with Davis when a swarthy stranger moved toward our table. Squinting at Davis, he smiled and said, "Sorry, Bud, I thought you was Larry Jennings."

Assuming the role of tough guy, Davis retorted, "Who says I ain't? And who the hell are you?"

"Honest mistake, Bud. It's kinda dark in here."

129

I asked the man, "What's a Larry Jennings?"

"One of the best lightweights in the business. Went six with Benny."

Another question from me. "Benny who?"

"Benny Leonard," the man said. He turned away and went back to his table.

Davis enlightened me. "Benny Leonard's a prizefighter."

I shrugged. "You're a prize Gorki."

Davis said nothing, for Angelo had appeared with our drinks. When he set my glass down, Davis instantly picked it up and sampled it. "What brand is this, Angelo?"

"I don't know. Can't read."

Davis persisted. "Did it come out of a bottle? Or a kerosene can?"

"Where you people from?"

"Chicago," said Davis. "And the lake's full of guys like you."

Angelo stabbed Davis with the stiletto of his dark eyes, and we watched him cross to the bouncer. A whispered conference, and the bouncer cast a cold, wary glance toward us. He watched Davis empty his glass and then fling it against the fireplace, where it smashed dramatically.

With giant strides the bouncer came toward our table, placed two ham hands upon it, and breathed fire at Davis. "Look, mister, we run a quiet place."

Davis said, "I didn't catch your name."

"Hoxie. Now behave, huh?"

Davis saluted him. "Yes, sir."

The brute left us. In exactly five minutes, when Angelo returned with the second round of drinks, Davis inquired, "Who's Hoxie?"

"Ace? He used to be in the ring. Ain't you never seen Ace Hoxie fight?"

"He ain't Dempsey," Davis replied.

Angelo merely shook his head and went on about his business. Davis lifted his glass and emptied it. He was about to hurl it into

130

the fireplace when I caught his arm and restrained him. "Hold it, Yale."

Davis sneered at me. "I'll have you drummed out of the regiment."

"Don't do it for me. Just for God, country, and Yale."

Davis nodded. "That's different."

I sipped my drink and kept a watchful eye upon the empty glass now resting upon the table. Imperiously Davis snapped his fingers at Angelo again. Davis said to him crisply, "A change of orders, Angelo. Every two minutes. *Capish?*"

Angelo regarded Davis with disdain. "*Capish.*"

As Angelo moved to the bar, Davis turned to me again. "That's Italian. Means, do you understand."

"Understand what? Adultery?"

Davis said nothing, merely cradled his head in his hands and sulked. When Angelo delivered the third round, Davis raised his glass, tapped it against mine, and said, "To Claude Terrence."

"To Joanne Fabian."

"I *capish.*"

And again I had to restrain him from hurling his empty glass into the fireplace. "Break marital vows. It's more fun."

"We're not married."

I said, "We're not *not* married."

"You and your double negatives."

"I do not *not* hate you."

Davis laughed loud enough to draw the attention of everyone in the speakeasy. "You know what J. P. Morgan said?"

"I long to know."

"You can't really afford a yacht if you have to consider the wages of sin."

I didn't respond. I was occupied with a restraint that kept me from smashing his laughter with my highball glass. However, the next time Davis obeyed his compulsion to smash his glass, I, by a design tempered in alcohol, neither said nor did anything to deter him. The sound of the shattering glass was a bell Ace Hoxie instinctively answered. He came out of his dark corner straight toward Davis, but he disappointed me by sitting down beside

131

Davis and speaking softly. "All right, Bud. Pay up and beat it."

"One last round?" Davis asked with a smile.

"You've had it."

Now I addressed the brute. "Careful, Ace, lover boy here once went six rounds with Dempsey."

Hoxie regarded me as if I had told him the Brooklyn Bridge was falling down. "That so?"

"You doubt me, Ace?"

Ignoring me, Hoxie faced Davis. "Gimme the cash. I'll bring you change."

I nudged Davis. "Darling, give him your Sunday punch. He doubts you."

"Today's Friday," said Davis.

"Yes," I agreed, "but Ace wants to sleep till Monday morning."

Davis turned to Hoxie. "You in shape, Champ?"

"Just reach for your money."

"Give it to him, darling," I said. "Right in the solar plexus." I turned to Hoxie. "Brace yourself, Champ."

Davis, the fool, made a fist and drove it with all his might into Hoxie's abdomen. Hoxie gasped, and then, with professional dexterity, countered with a blow to Davis's abdomen.

Agony tore Davis's mouth open. He gasped, fell forward, and, carrying the table down with him, lay inert in his spew. Now I, sick with a remorse that ran to frenzy, got to my feet and struck Hoxie in the face with my glass. He reacted with a push of a ham hand under my chin that sent me sprawling backward to pain and then nothingness.

Lost hours later I awoke with a never-before, never-again sensation that my head was held in a giant and invisible hand remorselessly turning in a winding motion before it tossed me against a black and endless sky.

My head rocketed through space before my eyes opened upon the awesome sight of Jesus descending from heaven and flying toward me on a collision course. Closer and closer came the flying cross from Calvary and the crucified Son of God. I screamed and saw, in another dark, the hooded figure of Death moving between Jesus and me. A skeleton hand reached out to touch my face and terror closed the lids of my eyes.

Then, hearing a gentle voice that seemed to rise from my childhood, I tried my eyes again and this time saw a young Negro nun in a white habit. I was in a dark hospital room. And the Jesus whom I had seen falling from the sky was now nailed to a cross nailed to a gray wall.

It was late morning before I awoke again and, in a strange blur, saw the crucified Davis O'Donnell sitting in a chair beside my bed.

I tried my voice. "Hello."

"Hello, honey."

"Where am I?"

"In Brooklyn. Saint Anne's Hospital."

"What happened?"

"You had a concussion."

"How?"

"I didn't see it. They tell me your head struck the fireplace."

"What fireplace?"

"The speakeasy. Don't you remember?"

"No." I felt a crown of thorns pressing into my scalp. "My head hurts."

"You'll be all right, honey."

"I'm dying."

"No."

Then, as memory returned, I said, "I want to die."

"Don't. I love you."

"Darling, I want to confess. It was my fault."

"Mine."

"I wanted the brute to hit you. Forgive me."

"Forgive me."

"I lied to you. About Claude Terrence."

"I know."

"How do you know?"

A small grin. "I know where you left your pants."

133

"Where?"

"On the front page of this morning's *Daily News*."

"I don't understand."

"There was a photographer at the club. He sold the picture to the *News*."

"What picture?"

"Your pants. Hanging from the chandelier."

"Oh, no!"

Davis said, "We're all over the papers this morning."

"The speakeasy fight, too?"

"That too."

"Oh, God, I want to die!"

Davis grasped my hands and waited for me to open my eyes again. "I'll make it up to you. I swear it."

"Swear what?"

"Never again."

"Drinking?"

"Other women."

I freed a hand and brushed his pale lips. "The brute. I thought he'd killed you. I struck him."

"So I heard. It was foolish."

"I'm a fool. I don't deserve to live."

Davis kissed my hands, and then a white nun interceded and gave me more sedation. When I had taken it, I saw Davis rising from his chair.

"Darling!" I cried. "Don't leave me."

"I'll be around. Rest now. Get well. I love you."

"I love you."

He bent over and kissed my mouth. My leaden arms were too heavy and too late to embrace him. I saw him step back, wave an uneasy hand, and leave the room. I turned my head now to find the nun.

"Sister?"

"Yes?"

"Am I dying?"

"Hush now and sleep. Close your eyes."

134

"A favor, please," I implored, fighting sleep, a sleep I feared was the sister of Death.

"What is it?"

"The crucifix. On the wall. Take it away. Please."

"Sleep." The voice was distant and fading.

My eyelids fell, shutting me away from Christ on the Cross, from the Brooklyn hospital room. I heard an orchestra playing *Japanese Sandman,* and then I was dancing in a great ballroom with Davis. We were the only dancers on the floor, and he whirled me about and the chandeliers were comets rushing through vast meadows of skies.

And then I heard Davis saying something about Adele Garrett O'Donnell not being a name to take to Yale. I laughed, but my laughter stopped when I saw that I was now dancing with my father, and that he was holding me as if I were dead. The last thought that struck before sleep took me was that the best of me had been murdered in a Brooklyn speakeasy.

3.

The compost of days built an arch for the years, an arch so fragile that it quaked above the fault of memory and was swept away by a flood of legend.

After a week in which Death had turned away from me, I was discharged from the hospital. And Davis drove the Apperson not to the Plaza but to a haven some forty-five minutes from Broadway, to a century-old stone house sitting on a knoll overlooking the Hudson River. The house, filled with ghosts of Dutch patroons, had been leased by Davis for one year and had been staffed with a Scandinavian couple.

The misadventure in Brooklyn, the full bill for which I hadn't as yet received, did result in mounting sales for *The Distant Spires* and inspiration for Davis's second novel, *Violins at the Plaza*.

In that year of strained isolation, Davis and I stooped to duplicity. Six mornings a week, while Davis was free to pursue his second novel, I trembled in another room, at another desk, and tried to write Davis O'Donnell short stories for the *Saturday Evening Post*. In the evenings Davis would slash his pencil across my pages and fire epithets and revisions at me. After his final editing of each story, he always sat down and rewrote the

136

opening and closing paragraphs with a stamp I could never duplicate.

Once a month the Frederickses came out to spend a weekend in the country. Freddie never failed to lament the time Davis was supposedly wasting with the magazine stories, but we never let on that it was Davis who served God and I who appeased angry creditors.

On several weekends, well spaced, we went back to the Plaza to recapture moments and moods to be distilled into the novel and into the stories. We went to the theater, to expensive restaurants, danced to the violins at the Plaza, but stayed away from speak-easies and out of the newspapers.

It was a time of truth for both of us, a year of haven to which we would often, in later and darker years, return in reverie. But we were too young to appreciate its value at the time, too wounded to be completely at ease with each other.

Nightly, ritually, we had two martinis before dinner. Before and after that the liquor cabinet remained locked. That was our agreement, the rule of an asylum in which we acted as each other's keepers.

Early in our stay in the country I menstruated again and wrongly supposed I had never been pregnant. About six months into the year, on a night fresh with snow, Davis and I decided to buy the stone house and make it a home for our children. Spring came with its verdancy, but with no sign of pregnancy for me.

On successive weekends we drove into New York to visit a Park Avenue obstetrician. There we were to learn that I had indeed been pregnant, that I had suffered a miscarriage in Brooklyn, and that I would never again be able to conceive a child. According to the physician, I had apparently inherited a condition from my mother, which he described as one-child sterility.

We returned to the house in the country that night, and when I had asked for a third martini the walls of our asylum came tumbling down. We ran out of gin, never made it to the dinner table, and in the sunless morning that followed we came to a

137

decision to close up the house and close out all of the dreams that had gone with it.

Back to the Plaza we went. We remained there for two years and made the city our estate.

In the spring of 1922, *Violins at the Plaza* was published. Its measure of success fell short of that attained by Davis's first novel, perhaps because it was more fun to read about the O'Donnells in the tabloids.

The second novel not being a sequel to the first, the critics were kind. All but Freddie. He noted the improvement in Davis's craftsmanship, admired the reach of the theme, but deemed the work a failure. The novel, according to Freddie, did reach pathos, but fell short of tragedy, its implicit intention.

The hero was based on Claude Terrence, the heroine on Joanne Fabian. In the end, however, the hero evolved into Davis and the heroine into me. The adventures were truly ours, based on our first months in New York.

The couple in the novel, Earl and Elizabeth Lawler, both from the Chicago social register, come to postwar New York to spend an inheritance of one million dollars. They remain to waste their money, their passions, and their lives.

What was missing from this work was Davis's view of the boy looking through the window. It was not a heartbreaking story of an American Dream, but rather a cold tale of an American Nightmare.

Meanwhile, in what was passing for reality, Davis and I remained a team, dancers in the vaudeville of the times. We had our love to warm and to warn us, and we were ever careful to know where the stages ended and where the pits began.

Leaving the New York scene, we took our act abroad to the capitals of Europe and had clean, capital fun. Returning to America, we bought a Pierce-Arrow and motored across the country to Hollywood to mingle with the celluloid faces. And then we went on to Santa Barbara and Pebble Beach to continue our romance with the very rich.

On our return trip eastward across the continent we stopped off at Stephensville, where we were hailed and welcomed by all

138

save my father, who cared not at all for the notorious flapper and her famous consort.

From my hometown we went north to Atlanta for a return engagement in the Governor's Suite at the Clifford Hotel.

It was there that Harry Ingram invaded our lives. As a reporter for the Atlanta *Constitution,* he came to our suite and went away with a page one interview. When we left for New York we carried with us the manuscript of Harry Ingram's first novel. Looking back now, I can't recall any sense of foreboding. I never expected to see Harry Ingram again.

When, days later, we returned to Manhattan, we checked in at the Plaza. Within an hour Guy Thurlow appeared, this time not in the role of William Randolph Hearst's star reporter but as a friend bearing booze.

A string bean of a man, Guy was six feet, six inches tall, bald, and saw himself in his own mirror as the ugliest man in captivity. To Davis and me, and to his wife and three young daughters, he was a beautiful boy of forty.

Within a week we had rented and settled into a cottage on Long Island's North Shore to become Guy's neighbors and drinking companions.

It was the best of our moves, and the worst of our moves.

The crucial date was June 28, 1924, a Sunday night, a night that was Gettysburg for Davis and me.

Dressed to attend a party, Davis and I, because it was fashionable to be late, decided to drop in and have a drink with Guy Thurlow. Edna, a good Methodist and a better mother, was a teetotaler.

We roughhoused with the three little girls until Edna led them upstairs to their beds. Then we entered Guy's sanctum, a room paneled in knotty pine and containing paintings by Remington and Russell, ancient rifles and Indian relics, and one of the finest libraries of Americana extant.

Guy was seated at his desk, a cigarette drooping from his mouth, as he pounded his Underwood with his two long forefingers. Seeing us, he arose with his finest smile, playfully jabbed Davis's jaw, and then, in the manner of Valentino, swept me into

139

his arms and kissed me fervently. As Guy and I went through our routine of silently mouthing dialogue and affecting the exaggerated gestures of the silent screen, Davis went to the bar and set up three drinks.

As we crossed to the bar, Guy asked Davis, "Where's the party tonight?"

"The Swopes."

"Hate that hotel," said Guy. "Sound of croquet balls keeps me awake all night."

"Come on along," Davis urged.

I said, "You must meet Sally Sinclair."

Guy sipped his drink. "I got three little girls right here. Prettier, better dancers. And they think I'm handsome. Sally Sinclair won't. She likes a handsome face." He jerked a thumb at Davis. "Like yours. Your James Montgomery Flagg face."

Davis said, "I'll bet you say that to all the boys."

"Love this booze," I said.

"The best available. Courtesy of Joel Stone."

"Who's Joel Stone?" Davis asked.

"A wandering Jew, newly domiciled down the road a piece in the old Parton mansion."

"International banker?"

Guy laughed. "Purveyor of bootleg spirits to the North Shore majesties."

"Bootlegger!" I exclaimed.

Guy said, "He wears bench-made shoes from London."

"At today's prices, why not?" Davis said.

"I get my booze now at cost."

Davis asked, "Will he do the same for Guy Thurlow's best friends?"

"It's a thought. Drop in some night. A party's always going on there. Doesn't make the gossip columns like Swope's shindigs. The Swopes have superior silver, but you can't beat the hardware at Stone's."

He lost me. "Hardware?"

Guy turned to me. "Underworld characters."

140

"Real gangsters?" I asked.

Guy said, "Are there any other kind? These boys are definitely in touch with reality. The finest types. From Chicago, Detroit, Brooklyn, and other such cultural centers."

"You been there?" Davis inquired.

"Never to the parties. I drop over for lunch on occasion. I mix with the underworld only in Broadway restaurants."

Strangely enough, Davis lost interest in Joel Stone at this point. There was another name more pressing on his mind. "Listen, Guy, I've got a manuscript I want you to read."

"Yours, pal?"

"I didn't write this one. But I wish I had."

Guy smiled. "I can fill Yankee Stadium tomorrow with writers who make that statement about your books."

"Thanks. But this one was written by someone down in Atlanta. A newspaperman. And a big fan of yours."

"What's his name?"

"Harry Ingram."

"Never heard of him."

"You will," Davis declared with a certainty I didn't share. "He's written a helluva novel about the war."

"Which war?"

"Wilson's war."

"Oh, that one," said Guy. "I remember I did see some shooting while I was over there. Pity they shot the wrong guys. Everybody with a war novel in his head seems to have escaped."

Davis said, "Ingram's from Montana."

"A statement Custer could never make."

"You've got to read this one."

"The hell I do. I'll save my bloodshot old eyes for your next book."

Davis poured more whiskey into his glass. "The way it looks from here, you'll have a long wait."

This being a poor prelude for a party, I changed the subject. "Guy, get dressed. Take us to the gangsters."

"Rannah, you don't need me. You've got a beau."

"I love you," I said with some truth.

141

"I love you too. Send Boy Wonder to the Swopes. Then we can be alone."

"What about Edna?" I asked, playing along with him.

"We'll run away." He turned his smile to Davis. "You know, pal, I'd sure take her away from you if I could. But I think it'd be easier to carve the Siamese twins apart."

Davis laughed. "Come on, Guy. Let's away to the party. You deserve a bigger audience."

"Joel Stone never laughs."

Davis said, "I mean at the Swopes."

I pursued the matter of Joel Stone. "Why doesn't Stone ever laugh?"

"You can't get laughs from a stone," he quipped.

"Why not?" I persisted. "No sense of humor?"

"Wrong." Guy drank and considered. "He has a talmudic sense of humor, whatever the hell that is. Anyway, he says he has it. I never argue with people who claim they have gout or a talmudic sense of humor. Stone tells a good story. Makes me laugh quite often."

I remained puzzled. "Why can't you make him laugh?"

Guy lit a cigarette. "He's too busy to listen. When you're talking, or trying to slip in a wisecrack, the wheels are turning over in his brain like a cylinder in a revolver. Just waiting for you to finish talking so that he can tell you what's uppermost in *his* mind."

"And yet you like him?"

"He keeps me in stitches. And in bottles."

Davis said, "Sounds like a phony to me."

"I don't patronize phonies. You know me better than that."

"Then what's the big attraction?" Davis demanded.

Guy took more whiskey. "There's a little bit of Madame Defarge in me. I like to knit my brow and wet my whistle while the tumbrels bring on the next act."

"Has the revolution come?" Davis asked.

"It's on the march, and not through Georgia this time. This time the rabble's on the North Shore and in the White House. I wonder if Coolidge has found a use for the poker chips."

I asked, "What has Stone got to do with all of this?"

"The booze barons," said Guy, "are pinch-hitting for the robber barons. They're busting down the fences from Puritansville to Methodistville."

Davis shook his head. "That's you all over, Guy. Ask a serious question and — "

"I am serious. I'll take the booze barons over the robber barons any day. Take Joel Stone. He hasn't legions of moles working down in mines. No kids wasting away at sweaty looms. No robots on assembly lines."

I said, "Guy, you sound like a Red."

"Just like Freddie," Davis said.

Guy frowned. "Is he a Red?"

"Pretty radical. For a Yale man."

"Me, I'm just a far western Wobbly. The Chief thinks I'm a nihilist."

I asked, "What are you?"

"Rannah, if I were the President of the United States, I'd open the next baseball season by throwing out the first bomb."

Davis frowned. "You sound as if you mean it."

Guy said, "I do."

For the first time Davis and I were seeing the darker side of his character. Davis was quick to lecture him. "Why are you so damned bitter? You've got a lovely wife, three fine kids, a big house, money in the bank, and a great curve on your typewriter."

Guy said, "You caught me too early into the bottle for me to answer that."

"I'll wait," said Davis.

"Pal, go to your party."

"The hell with the party. You interest me more."

Guy grinned. "Take in the Stone party."

"The hell with Stone, too. I want to hear you talk."

"Drunks should never ever stand on soap boxes. How about me telling you a talmudic joke?"

Davis refused to accept the evasion. "No, damn it! Let us in on the big joke. The big joke on Guy Thurlow."

Guy turned to me and wrapped the truth in a funny face. "I love your wife."

"I love you," I said.

"You must teach me how to Charleston."

Davis broke up the love scene. "Try making a pass at the truth."

"For the Hearst papers?"

"For the O'Donnells."

Spilling rather than pouring more whiskey into his glass, Guy said, "You know why I can't sleep? I spend my nights weeping for Shoeless Joe Jackson and for Warren G. Harding."

Davis demanded, "Is that a talmudic joke?"

Unperturbed, Guy continued. "First the bastards fix the World Series. Next they fix the White House. And now they've fixed my wagon, torn down the bunting and draped it with the black of their hearts."

"You're making a hundred grand a year," Davis reminded him.

Guy gazed unhappily into his glass. "I'm too tall to stand on my money. Besides, even idiot authors like Davis O'Donnell make it big these days."

"Why'd you call me an idiot?"

"All the Irish are idiots. You. Wee Willie Hearst."

"He's not Irish."

Guy laughed. "I'm afraid Tammany Hall beat you to that conclusion, pal."

"Why am I an idiot?"

"You flunked American history."

"I got straight C's in my history courses."

"So what does that prove? That you're a gentleman? You're blind, pal, blind to American history. And all the vitamin C you picked up in New Haven won't help you."

"What will?"

Guy raised the whiskey bottle. "There's a genie in here somewhere. Find it."

"Have you found it?"

"Find it for yourself, pal. Go over to the Stone party."

144

Exasperated now, Davis asked, "Why are you so damned fascinated with gangsters?"

"You've got Frank Merriwell. I've got Jesse James. My frontier heritage."

"I've grown up," said Davis. "I've got a yen for Sally Sinclair." He turned to me. "Let's go."

Recalling the beauty and vivacity of the Broadway musical comedy star, I said, "To the Stone party?"

"Afraid of Sally Sinclair?"

"Darling, chastity belts aren't fashionable any more."

Guy said quietly, "Pal?" Davis glanced at him. "This Joel Stone, he's a war hero."

Davis registered instant interest. "That so?"

Guy nodded. "I figured that'd get a rise out of you. He was with the Lost Battalion."

The spark of interest was gone. "I know that joke of yours. About filling the Polo Grounds with all the phonies who claim to have been in the Lost Battalion."

Guy said, "Stone was there. I checked him out."

"For real?"

"For real."

Davis turned to me. "Could be interesting. For Freddie."

"Why Freddie?" I asked.

"Don't you remember that novel he tried to write? The one about Whittlesey and the Lost Battalion?"

I said, "Well, I'm for it. Let's go to the Stone party. And then we'll have a good excuse to call up Freddie. God knows we need an excuse these days."

"What do you do?" Davis asked Guy. "Knock on the door and say Guy Thurlow sent us?"

"Just say you're Spike O'Donnell."

"Who's Spike O'Donnell? Not that outfielder who — "

Guy interrupted him. "You and your lousy Yale education. Spike O'Donnell's a Chicago booze baron."

A boy's pleasure in his eyes, Davis said, "Great! This could be fun. Sure you don't want to come along?"

"No," said Guy, with a meaning that, at the time, evaded us.

"I'm going to have too much fun just sitting here, drinking all by myself and laughing myself sick."

I asked, "Laughing about what, Guy?"

"Davis could pass for one of Spike's brothers. All he needs is a shoulder holster."

Armed only with his intrigue, Davis rushed me out of the Thurlow house and into the Pierce-Arrow, which sped us to the lair of Joel Stone.

Some ten minutes later we passed through a commanding gate and moved past sentinel trees toward a great Tudor mansion with bay windows, many gabled roofs, and fantastic chimney treatments. This, truly, was a sixteenth-century castle befitting the nineteenth-century magnificence of a Morgan partner more than the twentieth-century munificence of an American bootlegger.

After parking our car alongside limousines, we crossed to the entrance. When the imposing door had swung open in answer to our ring, a tall, graying English butler saw Davis biting a cigarette in the manner of a wounded man biting a cartridge. I also sported a cigarette.

"Good evening," said the butler.

Davis talked out of a corner of his taut mouth. "Joel in?"

"Yes, sir, Mr. Stone is at home. Whom shall I say is calling?"

"Spike O'Donnell."

The butler reacted as if he were the butler in the mystery play who had committed the murder, and who was now confronted by the master detective.

"Would you wait here, please?" He hurried away.

As we waited in the foyer we studied the oak wainscoted walls and the molded plaster ceilings. Instead of a string quartet or a lone harpsichord, we heard the syncopated rhythms of a jazz band, and we knew we were still in the twentieth century when we beheld dark gangster faces smiling at young, highly attractive blondes and redheads in stylish gowns.

Davis whispered to me, "They look like actors who've wandered onto the wrong movie set."

146

The butler was now whispering to one of the actors. The bad actor turned to us, and we saw his hard, flat eyes.

This barrel-chested man, in his early thirties, with a jowly, fullmouthed, olive-skinned face, came toward us. He wore a double-breasted, pinstriped blue suit, a striped shirt, and a garish Broadway necktie complete with huge pearl stickpin. Confusing the Sicilian with the Semitic, I took him to be Joel Stone.

As he drew near, he assumed the smile of a poker player disclosing four aces.

"Hi, folks. I'm Frankie Yale," he said, extending his hand to Davis.

Davis, the fool, shook his hand and said solemnly, "I'm Eli Yale. Class of '18."

His own smile unwavering, Frankie Yale asked, "What's that handle again?"

"Spike O'Donnell."

Frankie Yale guffawed, flashing the gold in his teeth. "Got a great sense of humor there. I know you two characters. Davis and Rannah, ain't it?"

I asked, "How'd you guess?"

"I seen your pictures in the papers. And I got a special interest. Nineteen-twenty. A speak in Brooklyn, down on Henry Street."

Davis asked, "Vas you dere, Sharlie?"

"No, but I got a piece of the action. You cost me plenty. But who invited you tonight?"

"Guy Thurlow," said Davis, subdued now. "He wanted us to meet Joel Stone."

"How is Guy?"

"Halfway into the bottle by now, I guess."

"Great newspaperman. Real moxie. And you're from the same college, ain't you?"

"Yes, we're both Yale men."

Frankie Yale grinned. "My real name's Uale. That's Sicilian. But I don't take sides. Had a spot in Coney Island called the Harvard Inn."

147

"And what've you done for Princeton?"

Frankie Yale roared. "Come on over and have a drink." We followed him to the bar. He asked Davis, "How is it with you writers? Who puts in all the periods and commas in all that stuff you write?"

Davis, no fool now, didn't stoop to condescension as he discussed his craft. The conversation had turned to the financial mysteries of the writing profession when Frankie Yale was summoned by one of his young lieutenants to attend to a pressing matter.

Davis and I remained at the bar drinking fine Canadian whiskey and observing the scene. Then, with flaring interest, I saw a man who stood out like one white sheep in a herd of black. Seemingly oblivious of all the other guests, he moved gracefully across the dance floor toward us.

He was athletically lean, blue-eyed, with wavy blond hair and a full British mustache. His fair skin was tanned by sun and wind. He wore a crested blue blazer, a tailored white shirt, and an English school tie. When he addressed us I noted that his diction was studied and precise.

"Good evening. I'm Joel Stone. Welcome to my house."

Davis said, "You know us, don't you?"

"Guy Thurlow and I have often talked of the O'Donnells. And of your books."

With a wrong, skeptical note, Davis asked, "Have you read them?"

"Yes. And I enjoyed them thoroughly."

Fearing a further and embarrassing probe by Davis, I said brightly, "Guy suggested we drop over tonight."

"I'm delighted," Stone said.

Davis said, "You seem more relieved than delighted."

"I beg your pardon?"

"Relieved that we're not really the Spike O'Donnells from Chicago."

Stone was graciousness itself. "I prefer the Davis O'Donnells. May I show you to the library, please?"

"We'd rather see your wine cellar," said Davis.

148

"You shall."

Stone ushered us into a spacious library, the size and grandeur of which caused Davis to say, "This a branch of the New York Public Library?"

"In a sense," said Stone, with some nostalgia. "I'm a public library boy."

I watched Stone remove from a shelf two books with familiar bindings and titles. He carried them to his desk, took a pen from a marble and gold holder and extended it to Davis. "Mr. O'Donnell — ?"

"Call me Davis."

"And I'm Rannah."

Stone looked pleased. "Thank you. And I'm Joel. Davis, would you kindly inscribe a few words in your books?"

Davis took the pen, examined the books, and exclaimed, "Hey! First editions! I take it back. This isn't a public library." Seated at the desk, Davis noted the date and then scribbled this whimsy: "To Joel, my old Chicago pal, Spike."

Looking over Davis's shoulder, Stone smiled good-naturedly and asked, "Would you mind adding your own John Hancock?"

Davis, the clown, wrote: "John Hancock."

I said, "Quit it, darling. Joel's serious. Now behave."

Davis now added his own signature. "Okay, Joel?"

"Fine. Now the other one, please."

In *Violins at the Plaza,* Davis wrote: "To Joel, who owns his own Plaza, Davis O'Donnell."

After Stone had thanked him, Davis inquired, "Which book did you like better?"

"*The Distant Spires.*"

"Why?"

Stone gave it some thought. "I liked the feeling of the outside boy at Yale and his attitude toward the rich snobs. It moved me. It educated me."

"How?"

"Well, this is my own present attitude about the rich — and a very correct one, I believe. The rich have no reality. When you move among them, it's as if you are moving within their dream.

149

And, while you're in their midst, you find it difficult to remember that you yourself are also dreaming."

Davis beamed. "I like you."

I said, "Hold on, darling. Perhaps Joel didn't like *Violins*."

But Joel did, and this is what he said to Davis: "You tell a marvelous story. You've a gift for transporting the reader, and for inducing him to return again and again to your pages to find jewels previously overlooked. As for your wealthy hero and heroine, you made me feel empathy for them. But the failing — and it's mine, not yours — lies in what I believe to be the unreality of their existence. The specter of their tomorrows is boredom. Never the reality of life and death, never the universal concern with food and shelter, sickness and health, or love. Lastly, unlike the boy at Yale, they never pose the prime question: What does a man do with his life?"

Davis and I regarded him with amazement. Davis said, "Look, Joel, any time you want to chuck this bootlegging racket, you can qualify as a literary critic."

Stone's smile made him look very old and tired. "You flatter me. And yet you return me, painfully, to the prime question." Then, to me, he said, "Would you too sign these books?"

"So happy you asked me," I said. I took the pen and the chair and inscribed my signature in both novels.

After returning the books to their places on the shelf, Stone gave us a tour of the house. Then we went out to see the garden.

The evergreen garden, more befitting to a Roman palace than an English country house, sloped gently toward the placid waters of Long Island Sound and the lights on the mainland beyond. At the hub of the garden was a replica of the Temple of Love in the Borghese Gardens in Rome. About it were spoke-like paths that led to statuary, knots, mazes, labyrinths, and dovecotes.

Stone guided us along the broad path leading from the main house to the boathouse and landing. Davis and I were startled when, from a none too secluded spot, we heard a man gasp as if in agony. Looking in that direction, we discerned a man sitting in a wrought-iron chair, clutching the blonde head of a girl kneeling at his feet.

With a measured detachment, Stone went on with his guided-tour description of the garden. Then, with only the slightest of pauses, he gave us details of the sleek sailboat moored at the dock, and of the two powerful motor launches in the slips below the boathouse.

Stone said, "Would you like to see my hideaway?"

I said, "Yes, we would."

Stone led us up the steps to the boathouse, unlocked a door, and we entered a room outfitted in the manner of a master cabin on a great yacht, with nautical fixtures and portholes for windows.

After we had sat down in leather chairs redder than the mahogany walls, Stone said, "There's no telephone in here, no means of communication with the house. And I've left orders never to be disturbed when I'm here, except in cases of the most extreme emergency. I like to come here in the mornings, after some sailing. I read in here. But mostly, I daydream."

I asked, "Daydream about what?"

"A girl."

Now Davis, his mind on something else, brought the moment down to earth and to the earthy. "Joel, what about that couple in the garden?"

Joel made a small gesture that bespoke embarrassment. "I apologize. A case of careless navigation."

Davis asked, "Did we come on the wrong night?"

Joel shook his head. "Not if Guy Thurlow meant for you to glimpse some of my associates: the bootleggers, the executioners, the gamblers, the bookies, the racetrack touts. Those Harlem musicians play five nights a week here. No parties on Monday or Tuesday nights. Four nights a week I entertain high society, with a liberal sprinkling of talented and beautiful faces from Broadway and Hollywood. Sunday evenings are reserved for my associates, many of whom are from distant places."

"Like Chicago and Detroit?" Davis inquired.

"Yes, those cities are well represented tonight."

151

I asked, "Are we keeping you from your guests?"

"Not at all, Rannah. I welcome this visit. One of my day-dreams."

His smile and his voice built a wall between us. Davis shattered this wall with a curt question. "Joel, can I be frank?"

"Please."

"Who's Mr. Big here tonight? You?"

"No. That would be the gentleman from Brooklyn, Mr. Frank Yale."

Davis pursued the theme. "Who's the big man in Chicago? Spike O'Donnell?"

Stone grinned. "Spike O'Donnell, in the current war between the Sicilians and the Irish, is the name of the archenemy."

Davis snorted. "No wonder Guy's laughing to himself. Hey, what if one of your crowd took me for the real Spike O'Donnell?"

"Catastrophe."

"Would I've been shot?"

"Not at this address."

This delighted Davis. And while I directed my attention to Joel Stone, Davis remained riveted to the underworld. "Who is Mr. Big in Chicago?"

"John Torrio."

"Yes, I've heard of him."

"Shall I tell you something surprising? Mr. Torrio doesn't like Davis O'Donnell."

Davis looked his astonishment. "I've never met the man!"

Stone explained. "He found one of his adopted daughters reading *The Distant Spires,* took it from her, and burned it. He thinks you're a bad influence on the youth of today. Deplores your laxity of morals."

Davis and I exploded with laughter. I said to Stone, "Isn't this Torrio a man with blood on his hands?"

Stone said, "Indeed."

"That's marvelous," said Davis. "Tell me, Joel, how'd you get mixed up with Torrio?"

"Through his lieutenant. Al Capone."

152

"Capone! I was reading about him. Recently. Something that stuck with me. Yes, I remember now. Something about him serving with the 77th Division. With the Lost Battalion. I guess that explains it."

"It doesn't," said Joel, nervously clutching a thigh with a hand I wished, at that instant, were mine. "It's only legend."

Davis was confused. "Guy says you were with Whittlesey."

"Yes, but Capone wasn't. He registered for the draft, but he was never called up."

"Then Capone's using *your* war background!"

"I might say we both are. Among the many contributions I make to our enterprises, I've also contributed my war record to Mr. Capone."

"Beats a prison record," said Davis. "Tell me, Joel, where are you from?"

Stone impaled me with his languid blue eyes. "I'm afraid I might be boring Rannah with — "

I quickly interrupted him. "Nobody bores the O'Donnells. We hold the record for dashing to the nearest exit." I made my point stronger by kicking off my pumps, and then by turning to Davis and saying, "Fire away, Spike."

This was to be a nickname often substituted for the shopworn Maxim Gorki, but the first utterance of it served only to return to mind the dark picture of perverse dalliance in the garden.

Then I heard Stone answer Davis. "I was born on the lower East Side of Manhattan. The ghetto."

"Are you Jewish?"

"Yes," he replied with no trace of pride or shame.

"You look British," I said.

He took it as a compliment. "The name on my birth certificate reads Joseph Steinberg."

"Immigrant parents?" Davis asked.

"Russian-Polish."

I said, "Polish! Does that explain the blond hair and blue eyes?"

Davis, the history expert, answered for him. "Sure! Raping Jewesses is an old international sport. There were a few of them in Milwaukee I wished I could get in the sack." Davis sighed and returned to more mundane and immediate matters. "How large is your family?"

"I have three married sisters, and a younger brother who's studying at Cornell."

"How much formal schooling did you have?" Davis asked.

"Two years of high school."

"And then what?"

"Correspondence courses. I was the boy who clipped coupons from magazine advertisements, such as Sherwin Cody's English courses."

"Did you quit school to go to work?"

"Yes. My father became ill, and I took a job in a butter-and-egg house on Greenwich Street. Three years later, with my father well again, I decided to try Wall Street."

Davis said, "I worked there. What house were you with?"

"Benjamin Fresco and Company. Mr. Fresco was a great philanthropist, but not so far as I was concerned. I started as a runner and remained a runner until I left."

"When was that?"

"April 6, 1917, the day war was declared. I enlisted in the Army."

"Why?" asked Davis. "Were you that patriotic?"

Joel was reflective. "I suppose I was, but the deeper truth is that I sensed opportunity."

"In the war?"

"There was none for me in Wall Street. There I worked hard, studied hard, haunted the public libraries. But you can understand my failing: I was competing with bright lads from the best universities."

"I understand," said Davis. "But how did you use the war to your advantage?"

"Happenstance. Before our battalion was beleaguered, as the Germans correctly put it, I was only a lowly enlisted man, serving as runner for Major Whittlesey. Afterwards, the Major won the Congressional Medal of Honor and I was awarded a

154

Distinguished Service Cross and a battlefield commission, thanks to the Major. May he rest in peace.''

More with envy than with admiration, Davis said, ''How great for you. How lucky to be able to prove your valor.''

Stone, more with humility than with pride, said, ''There was a personal — yes, a selfish design to my valor. I believe I feared failure more than I did death, and I consciously took the road to heroism, believing it to be my best route, my only shortcut to success.''

''I know what you mean. What happened after the war?''

''Following the Armistice, I used my new status and my shiny medals to gain enrollment in the American Army University at Beaune, in France. Beaune, to me, was what New Haven was for you.''

Davis asked, ''How so?''

''Because of my association with Whittlesey, I was afforded the opportunity to mix with American aristocracy. At Beaune I met and befriended men from the best families, the best schools. And there, also, I met a girl, a sister of one of my fellow students.''

''The love of your life?'' I interjected.

Stone gave me a sad, surprised look, as if seeing the ghost of that girl in me. ''Yes, Rannah, perhaps you've met her. Her name is Patricia Standley, or was until she became Mrs. Harper Wentworth.''

''I've heard of the Harper Wentworths,'' I said. ''But I don't believe we've met.'' I turned to Davis. ''Have we, darling?''

Davis shook his head.

''They're very much on the move,'' said Stone, ''from one resort to another. They do have a home in Oyster Bay.''

''Have they been here?'' Davis asked.

''Not yet.''

Davis, still on the scent: ''After the Army University, then what?''

''I spent some time in England, improving my mind at the British Museum and my manner in Bond Street. Bought all the correct clothes, grew this mustache, and adopted this accent.''

''When did you get back to the States?''

155

"In 1920, the year Patricia Standley was wed."

I asked, "Did you take it hard?"

Stone glanced at me and nodded grimly. "Very."

Davis asked, "What did you do then?"

"Made the rounds in Wall Street, with disappointment. Reluctantly I accepted a position in a bucket shop, never realizing what strange doors were opening for me. Through my immediate bosses I met Al Capone, and my talents, such as they are, were put to use."

"What are your talents?" I asked.

"Actually very meager. Style, front, name. My superiors, confidently enough, have entrusted me with a North Shore mansion, a Wall Street brokerage house, and a racing stable. But I'm merely a bootlegger."

Davis said, "You seem to say that with some shame."

"My family is ashamed of me. Their pride goes to my younger brother."

"Guy Thurlow's all for you," Davis told him.

"So am I," I said.

Stone smiled. "You're both very kind. But, please, no medals."

"Only a prize named Patricia Standley," I said.

"A foolish dream, isn't it?"

"Not with a garden like yours," said the bitch in me.

Stone was pained. "The best people once walked those paths. And now —"

Davis said, "Quit knocking yourself."

"The splendor is lost, and I with it," said Stone. "One day, perhaps, you'll read that I came to a violent end. Please remember it was in the wrong war, and for a very ignoble cause."

I was quick with argument. "Is Patricia Standley an ignoble cause?"

Davis said, "I don't think so."

Stone appealed to Davis. "You're Davis O'Donnell, not Horatio Alger. I should think you'd understand."

"I'm trying to," said Davis. "Do you or don't you believe in the Horatio Alger dream?"

Stone lowered his head. "Decidedly I do. But consider this:

156

Alger's heroes, however impoverished at the start, had nobility of character. I fled from honor when I walked into the bucket shop."

Davis was derisive. "The hell with that. You peddle great whiskey."

"To the rich, yes. To the poor, no. Our lesser brands, it grieves me to admit, blind and kill."

Recoiling at the thought, I asked, "Why don't you quit? Aren't you rich enough yet?"

"I can assure you, Rannah, it would've been simpler to quit my beleaguered battalion in the Argonne and walk through German machine-gun fire."

Davis said, "Speaking of booze — good booze — have you a bottle in here?"

"I'm sorry," said Stone. "I don't drink. And, believe it or not, this is the first time I've entertained in here. Shall we return to the house?"

"No," said Davis, "I don't want to break this up. I've got more questions. If you don't mind being grilled."

"Not at all. I enjoy talking to both of you."

I stood. "Will your bartender give me a bottle?"

"Of course. But — "

"No trouble," I said quickly. "I'll find my way through the garden."

Davis said, "That's my girl scout."

"I may lose my merit badge along the way."

The quip amused Davis, but Stone was expressionless. The truth was that I wasn't fleeing from the sexually disturbing presence of Joel Stone, but rather that, in fancy, I was taking him with me into the dark and lustful garden.

My passage to the house was uneventful, save for the sound of giggling emanating from an unseen corner. Entering the house I attracted interested glances from several of the men, but I was more attracted now by the buffet. I was helping myself to a plate of boiled shrimps and remoulade sauce when I noticed a woman near me holding an empty plate.

Diminutive, in her late forties, she stood not five feet tall in

157

her high-heeled slippers. Her face, not too beauteous, was that of an aging doll. She wore a diamond tiara in her raven hair, diamond rings on her small fingers, and diamond bracelets on her thin wrists. My initial impression of regality vanished when I saw her beholding me with a tea-leaf smile which told me she knew my fortune.

In possession of the serving fork, I asked her if she would care for some shrimps.

She spoke Russian, but I readily translated her smile. *"Pajalesta."* When I had filled her plate, she said. *"Spaseeba."*

I smiled. "Sounds like Russian."

"My English she sound Russian also."

"I'm Rannah O'Donnell."

She nodded. "I know you are. I am Tania."

I recognized the name at once, for it rang with notoriety. She was the madam who ran Manhattan's finest bordello.

"The Tania?" For reasons of her own, she never used her family name.

Unlike Joel Stone, she had no sense of shame. "The others, they all fakes. You sit down with me?"

"Yes, I'd like to."

We crossed to some chairs, sat down, and pitched our voices to surmount the blare of the band.

I asked, "How did you know who I was?"

"Ah, you! You like picture star. Picture in papers. I know you. I hear your name. You be surprised."

"In what way?"

"Men, they say: 'Get me girl like Clara Bow. Get me girl like Rannah O'Donnell.' "

I almost choked on a shrimp. "Seriously?"

"Tania never say no. Tania got all kinds girls. Just look around."

I looked, but my mind's eye saw only the fellatio in the garden. I said, "Are these some of your girls?"

"All my girls. You not."

"Tania, if I *were* one of your girls, what price would I command?"

158

"You talk too hard English. Say again."

"How much would you charge for me?"

She said, "I get you t'ousand dollars."

"For how long?"

"One night."

"What do these girls get?"

"Not t'ousand. But plenty. I get big check from Mr. Stone. Do big business with him. All big people. Even from Washington. Very big people."

I turned to study some of the girls. "Which one is Joel Stone's favorite?"

"He never touch my girls."

The revelation shook me. "Is he a pansy?"

Tania shook her head. "No pansy. I know pansies. He not pansy. He all business. Big man. Big danger. He want, he put me out business. Tomorrow if he want. Big — how you say it? — connections?"

"Yes, connections." I sighed and found the taste had returned to the shrimps.

Tania said, "You come wrong night, yes?"

"Oh, no. I'm glad we came tonight."

"Where is husband?"

"With Joel."

"Husband, he have good face. Good smile. You watch him."

Tania's delivery was champagne to me and I giggled. "He's a big boy."

Again the tea-leaf smile. "I got big girls. Make big pleasure. This not like parties you go. Believe me."

Accepting the admonition, I said, "You must pardon me now. I'm supposed to deliver a bottle of booze to my husband. He's in the boathouse with Joel."

She nodded approval. "Take bottle. Stay there. Make own party. These wops." She made a deprecating gesture with her free hand. "Stay away. Keep husband away. No trouble for Tania. Just big checks."

I rose. "It's been pleasant talking to you."

159

"*Spaseeba*. That mean thank you. You beautiful girl. Be good wife."

"I shall," I said without much conviction. And when I turned away from her, I found I felt very unsettled.

The bartender graciously gave me a bottle of Canadian whiskey, and scores of eyes followed me out of the house. As I moved along the garden path toward the boathouse, I conjured danger lurking for me among the evergreens. I dashed up the steps to the boathouse, opened the door, and hurtled into the room.

Davis was gone. Joel Stone, smoking a pipe, stood facing me, exhaling fumes of rage as much as tobacco smoke.

"Where's Davis?" I asked uneasily.

With no eyes for me, he said, "He left a minute ago."

"Why'd he leave?"

Joel stared out a porthole window. "I'm afraid Davis is upset with me."

"Why?"

Stone turned to me. "He asked me some questions I refused to answer."

"Questions about what?"

"My operations."

I tried to make light of it. "Only a woman talks about her operations."

"I understand him. A writer must probe."

"Was he nasty?"

"Well, his parting word was an epithet."

"I can imagine." And my imagination moistened the hand that held the whiskey bottle. I handed it to him. "Pour me a drink, please."

Reading my face, Stone said, "Shouldn't we return to the house?"

"No," I said flatly.

I sat down in a leather chair and noted Stone's discomfiture as he opened the bottle and fixed me a drink. In the queasy silence my eyes drank him in and saw the bunk as a garden of desire.

160

When he served me, I bestowed upon him a covetous smile. "Why don't you have one?"

"I'll have some White Rock."

"Jump off the wagon."

Deftly he retreated to nostalgia. "As a boy, on religious occasions, my father would pour some wine or brandy for me. Now he refuses to drink with me. Which, in part, explains why I'm now a teetotaler."

I didn't want, then and there, to think about fathers, his or mine. I said, "I met Tania."

Stone sighed. "I was hoping you wouldn't."

"Why not? She's fascinating."

He said, "Now you know what kind of party this is."

"Cheer up. I'm not Patricia Standley."

"You're very much like her."

"No, I'm not. I'm white trash. From the South."

"I don't believe that."

"What do you believe, Joel?"

"What I read in Davis O'Donnell's books."

I said, "It's not at all true. Davis exaggerates."

"You must come another night. We get the best people here."

"Are you sending me home?"

"Davis might be concerned."

Remembering Tania, I said, "He's a big boy."

"I've incurred his wrath. I have no wish to incur his jealousy."

"May I ask you a nasty question?"

Stone looked pained. "Must you?"

"Why don't you consort with Tania's girls?"

"Frankly, they revolt me."

"Do you practice continence?"

"No comment."

I persisted. "Do you sleep with rich bitches who remind you of Patricia Standley?"

He hesitated a moment but did not seem offended. "I never supposed you'd be more probing than your husband."

"Forget my husband. What did you suppose? About me."

161

"I supposed I'd like you."

"Do you now?"

"Very much."

"Tania says she can get a thousand dollars for me."

Stone sighed again. "Forgive me."

I laughed. "Don't take it so hard. I was flattered. I'm flattered right this minute."

"I'll have a talk with Tania."

"Don't be so stuffy."

"Shall we go?"

"Another tour about the garden?"

"Some morning, perhaps."

"What about now?"

"Hardly the time."

"For dalliance?"

He said, "I go sailing every morning at eight. How would you and Davis like to join me tomorrow?"

"It's a date. But what about now?"

"I have guests."

I kicked the crutch of his lame excuse. "I know who your guests are."

"Yes," he said. "And I sometimes wonder if Patricia Standley knows."

"Oh, the hell with her!"

"I wish I could say that." He set his glass down and moved to the door. Opening it, he turned to me. "Shall we go?"

I took a last sip of my drink and rose. As I crossed toward him, I released a smile intended to fly in the face of the truth of the moment. "Friends?"

"Yes, I'd like us to be friends. I'm sorely in need of real friends. Will you try to make Davis understand?"

I didn't stir. "Understand what?"

"My reluctance to blueprint my shady business."

"Joel, you'll never be Davis's friend. Not unless you take him into your confidence."

"Must he know everything?"

162

Absently I said, "When he sits down at the typewriter — which is rarely these days — he plays God to the blank page."

He nodded. "Very well put. But has a god need for all secrets? Doesn't a god divine the truth?"

"Perhaps."

He asked, "If I had an affair with you, wouldn't Davis divine it?"

"Good question."

"And what is the answer?"

"I don't know. You see, I've never had an affair. Not with anyone."

He regarded me more with disappointment than bewilderment. "Then you were toying with me."

My laughter spun a lie for me. "I'm only a flirt and a tease. The honest girls here tonight work at being whores. I play at being a flapper. Forgive me."

Stone forgave me. And, as we left the boathouse and followed the straight path toward the house, I felt forsaken, too. I kept wishing he would take my hand and lead me toward a maze in which I might lose my inhibitions.

But only Davis was lost, nowhere to be seen in the house. My first conjecture was one I dared not reveal to Stone, but he sensed and shared my fears. Leaving me at the bar, he went off alone to seek out my errant husband. Drink in hand, I watched Stone approach Tania. After an exchange of words, I saw, even at the distance, a degree of rage possess Stone before he turned away from the distraught madam and departed in the direction of the garden.

At the height of my own distraction, I was approached by a young man who had the smile if not the allure of Valentino.

"I'm Archie," he said. "What's your name?"

I told him.

He moved closer, his eyes electric with lust. "Where you been all night? Out in them gardens?"

"You must be Italian."

"Born right in Chicago."

"With a name like Archie?"

163

"It's a nickname, stupid. My name's Arciero. Wanna have me spell it for you?"

Sensing the worst about Davis brought out the very worst in me. "Can you?"

He glowered at me. "Don't get smart with me. Lucky you're a good-looker."

I pressed my luck. "I wish I could say the same."

A little white around the mouth, he said, "You like workin' for Tania?"

I raised my glass and drank. Then, lazily, "Got a better idea?"

He fell back upon a crooked smile. "You got spunk. Let's quit fightin'. Let's fuck."

I didn't blink. "Sorry, Archie. I'm all booked up."

"Who with?"

I thought fast. "Is your name Yale?"

He paled perceptibly. "Do me a favor?"

"Do yourself a favor. Get lost."

"Forget what I said. Okay?"

"Okay."

After the bartender had served me another and badly needed drink, I quit the bar, found Tania, and cornered her.

"Did Joel ask you about my husband?"

Tania played dumb. "Ask me? Ask me what?"

"I'll ask you. Did my husband go off with one of your girls?"

"No."

"You're lying, aren't you?"

She huffed. "I should lie! I see him. With one bottle. With *two* girls. They go out."

Flushed, I asked, "To the garden?"

Tania grabbed my free hand. "Do not go there. You sit. You wait. I wait. You get husband. You go home. I get check. I take girls. And I go home."

I sat down. "Who are the two girls?"

"You like my rings?"

I repeated the question.

"So I tell you names. So what? You arrest them?"

164

"Why two of them?"

"You nice girl. Don't ask."

"Lesbians?"

Ingenuous Tania asked, "What means that?"

"Why do you play so dumb?" I demanded.

"Excuse me. You play dumb, I play dumb."

Bitterly, gracelessly, I said, "Yes, *madam.*"

With grace Tania held out her hands again. "You like my rings."

I fled from her and had started toward the garden when I heard Stone's voice. "Rannah!"

I stopped, dared not turn about to reveal my ugliness, and waited for Stone to deliver himself and his sordid tidings. Instead he posed a question. "Can you drive?"

I studied his face and lost the question. After hearing and now understanding its reiteration, I said, "Yes."

Stone said, "Davis is in the car."

"Is he plastered?"

"He's passed out."

Stone saw me to the Pierce-Arrow and gave me a last despairing stare that told me he never expected to see either of us again. As I drove past the gate, I stopped the car to see if the road was clear, and then I turned to Davis, asleep and snoring beside me on the front seat, and registered the thought that I never wanted to see him again.

I wept now as I guided the car through the Sunday night traffic, driving slowly, observing countless automobiles passing me, trying to keep their bright, oncoming headlights from blinding me. The pattern led to peril, for with a pair of headlights rushing toward me, I had to struggle with a perverse and morbid impulse to twist the wheel left and bring a smashing end to our lives.

Reaching our cottage, I parked close to the front door. I turned a key to quiet the trembling of the motor, but there was no key to quiet my own trembling. In a strained voice I called Davis's name several times, but he heard nothing. When I

165

reached over and slapped his ugly face, he reacted and mumbled a protest before he lapsed into sleep again.

Leaving the car, I entered the house, rapped on a bedroom door, and roused our German couple, Otto and Bertha. A few minutes later I led the way upstairs to the guest bedroom. Otto, sullen and panting, dumped his burden upon the bed and left before I could dismiss him.

My ensuing irrational actions caused me to make several trips between the guest room and the master bedroom, each time carrying bundles of Davis's belongings and throwing them in a heap on the floor. When I had done with this I felt the first pangs of contrition, and I decided to undress him and properly put him to bed.

Davis was of no help as I struggled with his coat, his shoes and socks, and then his trousers, all of which I added to the heap on the floor. Then I saw something that at first I believed to be a hallucination. But it wasn't. With all contrition drained from me, I viciously slapped his limp face before I fled from the room.

I went to the master bedroom, undressed, got into the big bed, snapped the bed lamp off and, despite the warmth of the night, shivered in the bedlam of the dark. After a long, long while I turned the bed lamp back on, set the alarm clock for seven, went to the medicine cabinet, constrained myself, and swallowed but two of the dozens of red pills in a deathly green bottle.

Sleep overtook me at last, and the next sound I heard was the ringing of the alarm. The sound that followed was a mournful tolling of bells which rose from a mind lost in hell and blind to the beam of the morning sun.

Recollecting my design for the day, I got up, showered, and left the bathroom naked. Reentering the bedroom, I saw Davis standing there, shaky and disheveled, still wearing his shirt, his undone black tie, and his undershirt.

"Get out of here, you son of a bitch!"

"What did I do?"

"Go to the bathroom!"

He laughed. "Is that what I did?"

166

"Take a good look at yourself. In the bathroom."

"Why?"

"Because I say to."

Shaking his head, he trudged into the bathroom. Meanwhile, from a bureau drawer, I selected a brand-new pair of panties and a brand new brassiere. I was dressed in my white sailor suit and was slipping on my tennis shoes when Davis emerged.

Damning his sheepish grin, I said, "Did you take a good look?"

With a humor I disdained, he said, "I found it."

"Can you explain it?"

"Guess I must be a boy."

I railed at him. "You son of a bitch! Why is Gorki wearing two shades of lipstick?"

Davis said nothing. I sat down at the dressing table and, as I applied my own brand of lipstick to my mouth, I felt revulsion. I was brushing my hair when Davis found his voice.

"Where are you off to?"

"Sailing."

"Joel Stone?"

"Not Henry Hudson."

"Wait for me."

"You're not invited," I lied.

"I seem to remember I was."

Pointedly I asked, "What else do you remember?"

He relented. "Be a good sailor."

I rose and regarded him with scorn. "I won't do anything you wouldn't do." As I tried to move past him, he grabbed my arm. I jerked it free. "Don't touch me! Don't ever touch me again!"

Leaving the room, I slammed the door behind me. I went down to the kitchen, drank a cold bottle of Coca-Cola, took three bites of a piece of Danish coffee cake, and rushed out of the house.

I was seated behind the wheel of the Pierce-Arrow when I saw Davis at the front door with a Svengali stare meant to penetrate deep into my conscience. The clutch insufficiently disengaged, I made a hellish grating sound as I shifted into second and

167

escaped from him. I did not look back nor did I consider turning back.

On the road to Stone's mansion I realized it was desire for revenge rather than desire itself that was driving me. About a hundred yards before Stone's gate I felt I lacked the courage to pass through it. But I managed the turn.

When he swung the door open, the butler was less than arch with me. He beheld me with a condescending droop of his eye as if he were an Anglican vicar and I the village trollop. I followed him to the library and found Joel Stone seated behind his desk, attired in a robe, pajamas, and slippers. Sackcloth and ashes would have been more suitable.

"Good morning," I said.

"Good morning, Rannah."

"What's wrong?"

"Forgive me, but I can't sail this morning."

I frowned. "Did Davis phone you?"

"No, he didn't. I did receive a long-distance call from Detroit."

"And?"

"There's been trouble. One of our trucks was hijacked near the Canadian border."

"Is that such a calamity?"

"There was a killing."

"One of your men?"

He nodded gravely. "A boyhood friend. His name was Marty Ross. They stabbed him to death with ice picks."

He swiveled his chair so that I might not see his guilt and torment. In my mind's eye, however, I saw hands plunging ice picks into a body, saw blood and heard animal screams. And I smelled death. But in that moment, rather than chilling and sickening me, it was the most potent of aphrodisiacs.

I crossed trembling hands, drew my blouse over my head, and allowed it to fall silently to the floor, where it cushioned the fall of my brassiere. Then I moved around the desk, spun the chair about, and, before Stone could give voice to his astonishment, buried his face between my breasts.

168

An hour later, as I sat again behind the wheel, Stone kissed me for the last time that day. Then he stepped back into his grief and watched me drive away.

I thought I was calm and knew I was not when, on passing through the gate, I steered the car in the wrong direction. Before long I changed course and started homeward, driving now at a funereal pace to keep the motor from growling like a cornered beast and to defer my confrontation with a wounded husband.

The instant I braked the car in the driveway of our cottage, the front door opened and there stood Davis, wearing a polo shirt and slacks. Avoiding his gaze for a moment, I left the Pierce-Arrow and stood on jellied feet. When I dared to face him, I saw that he had divined the truth. As I boldly and yet warily crossed toward him, Davis contorted his face, spat at me, and then threw the door against me. The door slamming against the frame, shook the house and loosened it from its foundations.

As I went into the house, I heard the door to his study slam shut. Then I heard the softer and more terrifying sound of a key turning in its lock.

Within the hour, after the German couple had deserted the sinking house, I ran a bath. The moment I locked the bathroom door, something I had never before done in my years of marriage to Davis, I realized that the enemy was within the house, and that the siege had begun.

At noon I ventured downstairs. The house seemed to hold the lull that precedes storms. The door to the study, from which no sound issued, remained closed and locked. All this oppressed me unbearably and caused me to flee to the Thurlows.

Edna and the children had gone to the beach, but Guy, who readily sensed my turmoil, invited me into his warm sanctum. He sat behind his cluttered desk wearing a sweat shirt, corduroy trousers, and moccasins. As I sat in a club chair, he watched me with a paternal concern.

"What's the score?" I didn't answer, for I hadn't selected the key in which to sing of my dilemma. Guy essayed a pleasantry. "I can tell you're behind."

I told Guy everything, and he listened without once interrupt-

169

ing me, but with no screen of a confessional booth between us, it was an ordeal for him.

After I had ended my account, Guy managed a disarming smile as he reached for his whiskey bottle. "It's time for my all-day succor."

I tried to smile, for I was beholden to him for not having responded with fatherly wrath.

"Can I pour you one?"

I shook my head and loosened beads of tears, especially when I saw how Guy's hands were trembling.

Downing his double shot, Guy stared at the empty glass rather than face me. In the saddest of voices, he said, "I'm sorry about last night. About sending you over to Stone's place. I thought I was just setting up some laughs."

I asked, "What do I do now?"

"What are you thinking of doing?"

"Leaving."

"Georgia?"

"Yes."

Guy tore off a corner of a sheet of copy paper and chewed it. "Where's Davis?"

"Locked in his den. With his booze."

"Rannah, don't leave him."

"I'm afraid. Afraid of being alone in that house with him. Isn't that a terrible thing to say?"

"Do you hate him now?"

"No. I hate myself."

"He won't hurt you. I've never covered a murder trial in which the deceased was the victim of a slamming door."

"He's drinking."

"That — in the latrines of science — is known as O'Donnell's Law: if you don't have paper in your typewriter, you can't wipe your guilty ass."

"Is it my fault he's not writing?"

"No, only your problem."

"What can I do about it? I gave up nagging him a long time ago."

170

Guy poured himself another drink. "I'll tell you what you should do. Remember the times. This — with apt obscenity — is called the Jazz Age. And remember the place. Coolidge's Republican Cathouse. Where all clocks are set on double standard time."

"Yours, too, Guy?"

He said, "I'm no exception. I don't spend all my energy pimping for Willie Hearst. If the whores were delegates to this summer's national conventions, I'd be nominated for president by both parties." He gulped whiskey. "And remember this, Rannah. Upstanding American boys like Davis don't carve whores' names on the trunks of trees. They forget 'em in the morning."

Bewildered, I asked, "What's your point?"

"You in love with Joel Stone?"

"I loved making love to him."

Brushing his free hand over his bald head and face, he said, "He is handsome."

"Pour me a drink, Guy, and I'll take off my dress."

He borrowed my father's eyes and stared me down. "The bar's closed."

"Don't you want me?"

"Once I have you, I lose you. And Davis." I could say nothing to refute him. "You caught the smell of death this morning in Stone's library. I catch it every morning. Then, when I see my little girls, the smell leaves me, and I take on courage for the day."

"Yes, you have your children."

Guy said, "Why bust up the team? Just change the act."

My voice was listless. "What's the use?"

"Hell! Philosophers strike out on that question, but I'll take a swing at it. Take a morning like this. You drag your beautiful ass to another man's bed. And if you love it, as you say you do, then what the hell! Pretend you got the best spot in paradise. Now get back home and fix your boy some lunch."

I got up. "Thank you, Guy."

"I thank you, Rannah. It's nice to know you'd go to bed with

171

me. I might start singing in the shower again. Or even take to smiling at mirrors.''

I said, ''You're beautiful.''

His smile was fleeting and soon lost. ''Rannah, if there's trouble, phone me. If you can't phone, run here.''

I tensed. ''You expect trouble, don't you?''

''I know this,'' said Guy. ''When you were telling me about you and Joel Stone, I wanted to hit you with a mashie niblick.''

''And what might Davis do? Come after me with a kitchen knife?''

''If he loves you the way I love you.''

I kissed him tenderly. ''Make a pass at me. Sometime soon.''

Sadly he said, ''I'll be thinking about it.''

He came with me to the car, kissed my hand, and watched me drive away. When I entered the cottage, my hand was perspiring and trembling. The key slid into the lock. I turned it slowly and quietly and opened the door that led to the door of the cage of the wounded tiger.

The house was quiet. I went to the kitchen, made a ham sandwich and poured a glass of milk, then carried the tray to the door of the study. I knocked lightly. No reply. I knocked again to no avail.

''Davis?'' No answer. ''I have your lunch.'' Still no answer. ''I'll leave it by the door.''

I set the tray down, retreated to the staircase, and waited long moments for the study door to be opened. When it was not, I went upstairs to the guest bedroom and busied myself for a time taking Davis's belongings and returning them to their proper places in the master bedroom.

An hour or so later, in stockinged feet, I went downstairs and saw that the tray outside the study door had not been touched. I went to the kitchen and lunched on a bottle of Coca-Cola.

Returning to the bedroom, I locked the door, took two sleeping pills, and escaped. It was after six in the evening before I awoke.

The tray at the study door remained untouched, save by summer flies and ants. I returned it to the kitchen, the milk to

172

the sink, the sandwich to the garbage pail. Then I tried again. I broiled two sirloin steaks.

Arriving at the study door with the dinner tray, I knocked. No answer. I called Davis's name in vain, and then announced the contents of the tray. Still no response, no sound.

I tried to eat my dinner alone in the kitchen, but there was no savor to the steak, whose blood rareness I now found sickening.

Darkness fell upon the silence of the house. Before I retired for the night, I checked the tray again. It remained untouched. I left it there.

In the bedroom, I locked the door again and opened the windows wide, for the night was hot and humid. I looked out, hoping at least to see light spilling from the study windows below. Darkness.

At about three o'clock in the morning a clap of thunder returned me from a dream of Stephensville to the waking nightmare of the Long Island cottage. Lightning brought flashes of brilliance and left the dark tingling with terror. The ensuing sound of rain prompted me to leave the shelter of the bed and shut the windows. Naked, I left the bedroom and scurried about closing other windows. Downstairs I saw, again to my dismay, that the tray hadn't been disturbed.

More thunder from the skies, and then thunder in my voice: "Davis!" I pounded on the study door. No reply. "Shut the windows!" With my ear to the door, I waited to hear the sliding sounds of windows being shut. Hearing nothing, I was struck with sudden horror. Through the solid door I saw him lying cold and dead on the couch, empty whiskey bottles attending his wake.

Anguished, I tried to break down the door, or at least his reserve of silence. Finally I desisted, returned to the bedroom, and listened most of the night to the rain and my heart.

Tuesday, the longest day of my life, came into the cottage tracking rain, remained to drip rain from dark to light to dark again, and all the awful while I sensed that the roof was holding up better than my mind. Twice I answered a ringing telephone and heard only rain. Once I answered the doorbell and saw

173

nothing but rain. Otherwise I remained abed, leaving it to prepare breakfast, lunch, and dinner trays for Davis, only to feed the garbage pail.

It was past midnight when, suddenly waking, I felt as if I had been sealed up in a tomb. The rain was over and the bedroom was humid and stuffy. When I opened the windows and allowed the fresh wind to wash my face, I suddenly heard the sound of static emanating, through open windows, from the study below.

Davis was alive, awake, and playing with the three dials of the Atwater Kent radio in the study. Soon the static gave way to dance music, and then to the dulcet voice of a Los Angeles announcer identifying Abe Lyman and his orchestra playing in the Coconut Grove of the Ambassador Hotel.

I sat down at the window and danced with Davis in that ballroom across the dark continent.

On Wednesday the sun shone again. I was removing an untouched breakfast tray when the telephone rang. It was Edna Thurlow, and she induced me to join her and her three daughters for a day at the beach. Alone under an umbrella, Edna sat and watched four little girls build an elaborate sand castle.

Thursday morning, five minutes before two o'clock, I half woke from a drug-induced sleep to hear what I imagined to be the patter of rain upon the roof. Moments later I realized the storm was centered in the study below. Davis was at his typewriter.

This night my heart danced to the music of the Corona, and my mind announced to me the call letters of a station on another planet, in another galaxy, in another time, when smiles were in season.

Twice more before dawn I woke and rushed the dials of my mind to catch and hold the tapping sounds telegraphing the soul of a story.

At nine o'clock I left a breakfast tray outside the door of the study, as usual. When I returned from marketing I found that the tray, for the first time in the siege, had been accepted. I fixed lunch and dinner trays that day and three trays on Friday. But

174

I never saw Davis, spoke not a word to him, allowed him to work, nap, eat, drink, and work again.

I needed no pills that Friday night, and felt no need to bolt the bedroom door. Shortly before three in the morning I was torn from a placid dream and cast into a waking nightmare.

The bedroom door swung open and, in the chasm of dark, I saw a black face descending upon me. I screamed, and the black face bellowed with the laughter of Davis O'Donnell.

I turned on the bed lamp and saw the swollen, blood-red eyes and the bearded face of the lord of the manor. He took his laughter to the bathroom and left me with the stink of sweat upon sweat and whiskey upon whiskey. I listened to him sing in the shower, heard him whistle as he shaved, and then saw him emerge to command his bower.

This god, up from an invaded and conquered hell, down from his arch of triumph, brought the pink marble of his body down upon a bed of roses. As an offering to my god, I gave him a cup of tears and the talons of my passion.

Then, in a dark disturbed only by the glow of two cigarettes, in a time for talk, I tried my voice.

"I love you," I said, and the cigarette smoke danced.

"I love you," said Davis in a voice so distant that I turned and saw that his eyes were in another world.

Both cigarettes burned and marked time before I took a second chance. "What are you writing?"

"Notes."

"Short story?"

"Novel."

"Wonderful."

"Heard from the German spies?" he asked, in reference to the departed servants.

"No. Shall I hire another couple?"

"Can you manage without help?"

"I can manage."

"Just for the summer."

I said, "Anything you say."

"Bring in a cleaning woman. Once a week."

175

"All right."

"We won't be entertaining much. And don't accept any invitations. We won't be going out."

"I'm delighted you're back at work. Especially on a novel."

"Yes. Feels good."

The peace of this utterance should have led me to sleep, but curiosity, tainted with doubt, killed the kindness of the night. I asked, "Care to talk about it?"

His own question arose slowly from somnolence. "What do you want to know?"

"What's it about?"

"You and me."

"Who am I this time?"

"Constance Albright." I heard the name and my mind ran to mirrors to view the mountains and the valleys of my new incarnation. And then Davis spat upon the mirror. "Yes, Constance Albright. A cunt from Dixie."

I tried to be casual. "And who are you?"

"James Barrow. A bootlegger."

This pulled a string of guilt, and the naked body of Joel Stone materialized before me. I had to speak to break the spell. "And what happens between Constance Albright and James Barrow?"

"Tragedy."

I now felt the dead weight of Joel Stone's cold, dead body lying full length upon me. "For both of them?"

There was now an edge to his voice. "You want the plot?"

"Have you got one?"

"Afraid I'm overplotting again?"

"No. I didn't mean it that way. I'm sorry. Please, just tell me simply. What it's all about."

Absently, awesomely, he said, "The American Dream."

"Tell me more."

"I'm putting myself in Joel Stone's shoes. And I'm telling the story through Guy Thurlow's eyes. Understand?"

I didn't understand, for all I could discern in that dark and awful moment was a jumble of reality. "How does it end?" I asked, as if my own fate were involved.

"The bootlegger gets killed."

I wrote the ending I wished. "By gangsters?"

"Fuck you."

"I asked a simple question!" I protested.

"You're goddam simpleminded. Good night."

No need for the call letters from hell. I was back there again. Among other fatalities, we killed our cigarettes. I left the bed and flushed the ashes and the butts down the toilet. Returning to the bed, I vowed silence and listened as Davis courted sleep in vain. Finally he sat up, swung his feet over the side of the bed, and lit another cigarette.

My voice was soft and imploring. "Davis?"

His was indifferent. "What?"

"Can we go back?"

The question, meant to be vital, seemed instead to be borne on a catafalque that held the corpse of my fidelity, and to be drawn by the power of prayer to the crossroads of resurrection.

"Sure," said Davis, not stirring. I stirred and prematurely loosed tears. Davis rose now, turned, and faced me in the dark. As he inhaled, I saw a smile in the momentary glow of the cigarette that caused the catafalque to plunge over a precipice. He said, "I'm going back Sunday night. You can go Monday morning."

4.

This, in my purple testament of bleeding war, is *The First Book of Harry*.

It spans an era — not years of Our Lord, but a time of Satan — from the autumn of 1924 to a cruel, April afternoon in 1930, in the devildom of Spain, not far from the Roman ruins at Tarragona, where, in a grove of hazelnut trees, I buried all my clocks and calendars.

In October of 1924 Davis completed the first draft of his third novel, *North Shore*. Reading the pages for the first time, I had the eerie feeling that the hands of Harry Ingram, not those of Davis O'Donnell, had played the night music on the Corona. Gone were the faults and furbelows of Davis's earlier style. No longer was Davis the dashing, plumed Jeb Stuart. Now, like Harry Ingram, like General Grant, he knew his strength and expended it with frontal attacks that led to ultimate victory, a victory which I was slow to comprehend.

As I read the manuscript, which ran to seventy thousand words, I found myself thinking of Harry Ingram, of Joel Stone, of Guy Thurlow, and of myself, forgetting the genius of Davis O'Donnell. When later in the day I had to confront Davis with my reaction, I lied to him with superlatives.

On the waxen wings of my praise, Davis flew to the Thurlow house to deliver the manuscript to Guy. At about four o'clock the following morning the telephone rang. Ten minutes later, in robes and slippers, Davis and I were in Guy's den. He poured drinks and words golden with prophecy. He said he wished he had written *North Shore,* the first and last time Guy Thurlow ever stooped to envy. Davis got drunk quickly, acknowledged his unpayable debt to Guy, and, true to his word, dedicated the novel to him.

Early in November, without his wife, Harry Ingram came north from Atlanta. He was accepted by Davis O'Donnell's agent, publisher, and wife. Like a good Eskimo I took him to my bed, the first liaison occurring on a Sunday night which found Davis once more in Joel Stone's garden.

Harry read *North Shore,* and this is what he said, this in a time before success fired his volcano, before the fruits of his wisdom were brandied in the cesspool of his lexicon: "I'll tell you how good this is. I'm going back to Atlanta to start my book all over again. From page one."

Neither Davis nor I believed him, for his book seemed altogether ready for publication.

In the spring of 1925 *North Shore* was published. Delano Fredericks, now reviewing books for the New York *World,* said this in his opening paragraph: "The promise of Davis O'Donnell has been fulfilled. With the publication of his third novel, *North Shore,* he has made the first advance in the American novel since Henry James. He has caught in the snare of his genius the tragedy of our time. He has evoked the spirit of the era with a book perfect in its feeling and its symbolism."

But this was the paradox of the strange hour. While Davis had earned the highest praise from Delano Fredericks, Guy Thurlow, and Harry Ingram — the trinity that had directed him to the spire of genius — he was quick to tumble down to earth and allow himself to be kicked and spat upon by the corps of critics and pundits, by the keepers of the myths who frowned upon this tale that dared to suggest the waste of the American success story.

179

Also, in the midst of a prosperity without parallel, those educated and affluent Americans who bought and read novels were in no mood to accept a story in which the hero was a bootlegger who wanted wealth only to buy back the happiness he had lost, and who dies at the hands not of the underworld but of the *haute monde.*

By Christmas of the same year, *North Shore* had sold a disappointing twenty thousand copies before it was forgotten and left for dead. Davis and I endured the first act of the Broadway play of the same name. The second and third acts found us drunk in a nearby speakeasy. We saw the motion picture of the same name in Paris. We were drunk before we entered the movie house, and we left sometime after the third reel, a short moment after Davis had vomited into his straw boater.

By then, in the long summer of 1926, we felt the heat and force of Harry Ingram, the sales of his belatedly published first novel, *A Pattern Called War,* having passed the one hundred thousand mark, and the critics having proclaimed homage and fealty to the new prince of American letters. King Davis was dead, long live King Harry.

The winters became colder and longer, with the bills piling up as high as the snows. The cold wave had started in Philadelphia, in the offices of the *Saturday Evening Post,* the editors suffering the publication of *North Shore* with the same shock as the 1920 bombing in Wall Street, and then taking to the barricades of their rejection slips.

In 1927, on Long Island, Joel Stone shut down his mansion and disappeared from the scene mere days after Frankie Yale had been machine-gunned to death in Brooklyn. In the same year *The Knockout,* a collection of short stories by Harry Ingram, was published. It not only endeared him further to the critics and the public, but it went on to sell more copies than had *North Shore.*

In 1928 the motion picture of *A Pattern Called War* was hailed as the greatest achievement since *The Birth of a Nation.* We saw the film in Charleston, where Davis was working on an antebellum novel. When we left the theater we found our way home again, but Davis never found his way to chapter four.

In the unblessed year of 1929, the fault at Armageddon slipped twice. In April, Harry Ingram's second novel, *The Lost Generation,* shook the literary world. Late in October the high towers of financial Babel crashed in Wall Street.

In November Davis and I went to Milwaukee to bury his father, a man who had never owned one share of prosperity, and who could not survive one month of depression. In December we left the sidewalks of New York to those human lemmings who followed one another from high windows just around the corner from prosperity.

We set sail for the Old World and established a colony for American expatriates in the South of France. There Davis wrote very little. Instead we drank too much, committed adultery too often, took to the insulting and losing of friends, and, more terribly, to the wasting of time and the spilling of the salt of our spirits.

In this atmosphere of exile and decline, our tempers were short and the days were long before word came from Spain that King Harry would deign to receive us at his court at Tarragona during the first week in April.

We had to see Harry. From time to time Harry would send, via couriers, cases of muscatel wine to help cure me of my champagne sickness. But now Davis, crippled by failure, had need to drink success from the secret grail possessed only by Harry.

It was simple to conjure grails in the ancient city of Tarragona, which stands on limestone rock overlooking the Mediterranean Sea and the Roman yesterday which rests in the stones of its tumble-down walls.

We drove our Renault through the Iberian city, the windows of its whitewashed houses screened by cedar jalousies, its streets alive with women in red skirts and black shawls carrying pottery jars on head or hip. We found the road to Lérida, bordered by tilled fields, orchards, and groves of hazelnut trees. Two miles out of Tarragona we came upon the triumph of some forgotten

181

twelfth-century architect who had built a villa for a Spanish knight returning from the Crusades.

As we drove through the gate toward the singular house with its turrets, narrow windows, pebbled floors, and great beams that bespoke a shipwrecked history, we came upon another triumph of Harry Ingram's: an outdoor prizefight ring, its canvas catching sun instead of wind.

On that early April afternoon in 1930, Harry Ingram was thirty-one years old, four inches taller and forty pounds heavier than his vanquished rival from Milwaukee. But in the ring Harry stood three inches shorter and thirty pounds lighter than his sparring partner from New Orleans, the onetime heavyweight champion of the world, Dandy Flood.

Besides us, the cast of characters at ringside included the following: Charlotte, the flaxen-haired, flat-chested dancer from Dublin who was Harry's second wife; Beatrice Smith Flood, the wealthy Chicago matron who was the third white wife of the Negro fighter; Alex and Sandra Martin, he an untalented homosexual poet, she a talented Lesbian sculptress; two bullfighters from Pamplona; an American foreign correspondent and his bride; and a sportswriter from Barcelona.

Harry, wearing white boxing trunks that were a gift from Jack Dempsey, carried the frame and mien of a champion, his hair blacker than his opponent's skin, his bronzed arms and legs muscular, his abdomen as flat and hard as a shield.

Bald and forty, Dandy Flood looked overage, overweight, and overmatched. The sportswriter from Barcelona, serving as timekeeper, rang a bell that resounded with nothing but boredom for me. Flood gave proof through the four three-minute rounds that he still retained much of his former grace and prowess. But it was all very polite and bloodless, much like a modernistic ballet as they danced about the ring, Harry stalking the black man, his arms mapping out intentions for mayhem. But nothing happened, save in the fourth and final round when, it appeared to me, Flood, by design, took a glancing blow on the head and fell to one knee. There were a few gasps from the spectators, but I glanced at Mrs. Flood and unraveled the secret of her smile.

182

King Harry took his huzzas, helped Flood out of the ring, and listened and laughed as the black man raved about the punch of an author who could hit as hard as Dempsey. I was happy to leave the sun, to find the stone coolness of the house and the solace of chilled muscatel.

Talk of boxing and bullfighting spilled with wines into a long evening, through a late Spanish meal. Davis, unlike me, was intrigued. He drank well that night, and he listened well to the tales of the bullring's great Belmonte and the prizefight ring's great Flood.

It was past one in the morning before King Harry blew out the party candles and all his guests fled to their appointed bed-chambers.

Davis and I undressed and came naked to the antique bed. In the dark we lay not as lovers, but as a married couple worn by time and spent by defeat and regret.

"Good night," said Davis.

"Glad you came to Tarragona?"

"I enjoyed myself today. I don't know about tomorrow."

"More boxing. More bombast. You'll never get to talk to Harry."

"Good night."

I said nothing and turned my back to him. A few moments later we heard a rap on the door. Davis turned on the bed lamp. He called, "Come in."

The door opened and King Harry entered. Still attired in his polo shirt and white duck pants, he carried an uncertain smile, a bottle of brandy, a bottle of muscatel, and three glasses. "Can we talk?"

Davis, suddenly radiant, said, "Sure, Harry."

Harry came around to my side of the bed and proffered the muscatel bottle and a glass. As I sat up to accept them, I unthinkingly bared my breasts. Damning rectitude, I did nothing but say, "*Gracias.*"

Concerned rather than embarrassed, Harry asked, "Sure it's all right with you?"

"I love muscatel," I said.

Davis frowned at me, but he lost little time in returning his attention to Harry, who found a chair and sat down at Davis's side, where they more easily could share brandy and talk.

Uncomfortable in the straight chair that lacked the dimensions of a throne, Harry stood up, turned the chair around and straddled it. The back of the chair now served as a railing for the hairy arms that held the brandy bottle and an inhaler. After pouring brandy for Davis and for himself, Harry glanced at me.

"Rannah, your hair's getting darker."

"The hair on my chest?"

Harry laughed. "Reminds me of Atlanta. Our first meeting. Davis taking me in the bathroom to introduce me to you. And you sitting in the tub and sipping champagne."

I said, "Champagne's a dirty word."

Davis said nothing. Harry said, "You're getting to look like a Cherokee princess."

"I'm thirty years old."

"My first yen, back in Montana, was for Indian girls."

I said, "Shall we chase Davis? Or is this to be a *ménage a trois?*"

Davis played deaf and dumb. Harry chortled. "Just old friends. Just talk."

"Ah, these tourist folders!" I exclaimed. "I was certain you were going to exercise your *droit de seigneur.*"

Harry guffawed. Davis, at last, said, "Harry exercised his right on Dandy Flood's jaw."

More laughter from Harry, followed by brandy, then a shift of mood as he gazed at Davis with concern. "What are you working on, *amigo?*"

"A nervous breakdown," said Davis.

"What's in the machine?"

"A novel."

"Good."

"Machine keeps stalling."

"Keep punching."

"Harry, how do you punch a glacier?"

"You don't. A glacier moves on its own."

184

I listened and said nothing, forgoing cleverness and sarcasm and trying to remember that a dialogue between success and failure can be like the blending of vintage wine with vinegar.

His confidence crushed more thoroughly than the grapes that had gone into my bottle, Davis now said to Harry, "I'm about to chuck it. Three ideas for novels, and I'm about to take a third strike with my bat on my shoulder."

"What's this one about?" asked Harry.

"The Snyder-Gray case."

"Good. Solid. What's your angle?"

Davis said, "I put the story in Milwaukee. German Catholic background. Shame of divorce. The sin worse than murder, worse than adultery."

"Middle-class background?"

"Yes. The Albert Snyder character is a head bookkeeper. Prussian in personality. A burgher who misses his beer and the corner saloon. He won't break the law by going into a speakeasy or patronizing a bootlegger. He's a dull son of a bitch who comes to life every Saturday night for five minutes when he bangs his wife. With the lights out. And without any preliminaries."

Harry asked, "What about the insurance angle?"

"I threw it out."

"Why?"

"Was that my mistake?"

"I don't know," said Harry, exercising patience now. "Tell me why you threw it out."

Davis said, "The character I have in mind isn't after money. She's not even after love."

"What's left?"

"Life."

"Go on," Harry prompted him.

"My woman is dead in Milwaukee. Her husband won't even take her to a movie. What she wants is life. The Jazz Age life. Dancing, petting, bathtub gin. Matinees in hotel rooms. Dirty jokes. Back seats of motorcars. Cigarettes. Cosmetics. And, most important of all, she wants the release of laughter."

"Good," said Harry. "What about Judd Gray?"

185

"He's a drummer out of New York. The guy who brings the Jazz Age to Milwaukee and Ruth Snyder."

"Who plans the murder?"

"She does."

"She murders her husband to become a flapper?"

"Yes. What do you think?"

Harry addressed himself to his brandy. "Right up your alley. You know Milwaukee. You discovered the flapper. What the hell's wrong?"

"Rannah gets in the way," Davis said.

"In the way of what?"

"The Ruth Snyder character. My character keeps coming out too bright."

"Thank you, *amigo,*" I said sourly to Davis.

Davis said, "I don't know. What the hell am I blaming Rannah for? I just think something went out of me after *North Shore.*"

"What something?"

"Confidence."

"*Merde,*" said Harry.

Davis, the bookkeeper from Milwaukee whom I wanted to murder, said, "My first book sold seventy thousand. My second forty. My third twenty. Get the picture?"

"Sure," said Harry. "You're getting better with each book."

"It's not funny."

"*Amigo,* I didn't mean it to be. You want to know something? I read *North Shore* again last week. It's brandy in the barrel. Gets better every year."

Davis, in torment, asked, "Why didn't it sell big?"

"What's this crap about selling? Are *you* a drummer from New York?"

"Your two novels sold big, Harry. As they deserved to."

Harry nodded. "All right, get it said. My collection of short stories sold better than *North Shore.*"

"Yes," Davis admitted. "That was a wallop."

"And I get bigger money from Hollywood."

I said, "And better pictures."

186

Harry glanced at me, perusing my naked breasts with the eyes of a sultan whose thoughts were a long way from his harem. Then he focused upon Davis. "It's all in the handling, *amigo*. You've always been too quick with the buck. Too quick to grab it, too quick to spend it. I play hard to get with Hollywood. I make sure I get the top money, the top director, the top cast, and the big promotion."

Davis, the beggar thrown from his horse, held out his inhaler and Harry poured more brandy into it.

"I figured *North Shore* to make a mint," said Davis. "To win all the prizes. Damn it, Harry, that was my Sunday punch."

Quietly Harry asked, "Who'd you want to knock out?"

Davis dropped the other shoe of truth. "You, Harry."

"You knocked me down. The bell saved me. And I went back to my corner for a year and rewrote my whole fucking book."

Davis nodded. "Over a hundred thousand copies sold. That knocked *me* out."

Harry grinned. "Yelling foul?"

"*The Knockout. The Lost Generation.* Harry, you hit me when I was down."

"*Merde!*"

"You're the champ. And I just want to say this —"

"No fucking speeches. Just talk. Just pitch without a windup."

Davis now chanted his litany of envy. "Three books, three knockouts. A champ is a champ is a champ."

"What are we talking about? Making money?"

"Isn't that the game?"

Harry frowned. "You son of a bitch! You look like Davis O'Donnell. But you talk like a stupid prick. Know what I get asked a couple of times a year? Did Davis O'Donnell really write *North Shore?*"

"And what do you say to that?" Davis asked.

"I have a joke. I say, 'Hell, no. Bacon wrote it.'"

"What do you say when you get bored with the joke?"

"I say there are two Davis O'Donnells."

Davis asked, "And which one's the impostor?"

"Neither," said Harry.

"What's the joke?"

"You hear me laughing?"

Davis was pitiful now. "Harry, what's the answer? What the hell do I do now?"

Harry, slowly and deliberatively, said, "I like the Snyder-Gray idea. Could be an American *Bovary*."

"Or another *North Shore*?"

Harry answered bitterness with envy. "I wish I'd written it."

"Why?" asked the idiot boy.

"Look, we're writers. Agreed?"

"You're a writer, Harry. I'm a hack."

"Let's stay with the first can of beans. When we beat the typewriter, who the hell are we trying — really trying — to beat?"

"Each other."

Harry studied Davis as if he had discovered a third Davis O'Donnell whom he despised. "Funny man."

I said to Harry, "You should see him in blackface. He's the Two Black Crows."

Neither heard me. Harry said to Davis, "*Amigo*, try that question again."

"Harry, I'm sick of questions. I came across the border for answers."

Harry emptied his inhaler, spilled in more brandy, then spilled the truth to Davis. "This is the answer. The one and only answer to explain bastards like you and me. We're trying to beat Death."

I understood Harry, but Davis was beyond understanding, and he could only play jester to the king. "Are you Death, Harry?"

"Go fuck yourself."

Davis rammed his left elbow against the oaken headboard as if he were trying to sound an alarm. He looked hard at Harry. "I don't want to hear about immortality. Just tell me how I get to sell a hundred thousand copies of my next book."

"Take the first step," said Harry. "Finish it."

188

Davis voiced his agony. "I can't get past chapter two!"

"What's the block?"

"I don't know what street I'm on. I was slapped in jail two weeks ago. Drunk and disorderly. Christ, that's the story of my life. Drunk and disorderly."

Harry turned to me for confirmation. I said, "He was in the can. In Cannes. One night."

Harry looked hard at Davis. "How much money have you got?"

Davis turned to me. "How much?"

"Billions. In German marks," I said.

Davis addressed my breasts. "How much?"

"Two billion," I said to Davis. To Harry, I made more sense. "We mailed off a short story last week. If Mason sells it for three thousand dollars, we'll be about a thousand dollars ahead of bankruptcy."

Harry said, "A story for the *Post?*"

"If they'll have it," I said. "Which they won't."

"Why the hell not?" Davis demanded of me.

"Darling, they don't love you any more."

Harry parroted Davis's question. "Why the hell not, Rannah?"

I told him. "Two words. *North Shore.* Those two words were translated in Philadelphia to mean: screw you. Anyway, they've got a stable of writers who write Davis O'Donnell horseshit better than Davis O'Donnell himself."

Davis, the keeper of the lists, said, "I sell to *Collier's, Cosmopolitan, Redbook, Liberty.*"

Harry looked sick. "Please. Not while I'm drinking."

"I can't afford to write for *Harper's, Scribner's,* and the *Atlantic Monthly,*" Davis retorted.

I said, "Of course he can't. The *Atlantic Monthly* can't keep me in Kotex."

Harry laughed. "That's funny." He said to Davis, "Don't you laugh any more?"

"I took the cure," said Davis. "That night in jail."

189

Harry said, "Let's talk about champs. There are three of us here. You, me, and Dandy."

I asked, "What did Dandy write?"

"History," said Harry gravely. "In Carson City, Nevada, on Labor Day of 1913, Dandy Flood left the ring —"

I broke in. "No speeches, Harry. You promised."

Desisting, Harry raised his inhaler to me. *"Salud."* Turning from me, he began to stalk Davis. "Now about champs."

"I know all about champs."

"Like what, *amigo?*"

"Dandy Flood threw the title in Australia. I threw in the towel in New York. What did you throw, Harry?"

"What did I throw? A lot of bullshit about myself. But it's all part of the bread and circuses. All part of the emptiness that has to be filled before a champ gets back and accepts the challenge of the blank page."

"You made a speech," I chided Harry.

Harry ignored me. "A champ gets off the floor and comes back."

"How did Dandy Flood come back?" Davis countered.

"By marrying three white women. One after the other."

"And what did that prove?"

"Defiance," said Harry. "Defiance of the black man for the white bastards."

I said, "Harry, how dark you've become!"

Harry said, "Sherman made one mistake. He forgot to burn Stephensville."

"Atlanta's survived Sherman. And Harry Ingram."

"I wrote in Atlanta. More than I ever did in Paris. I love Atlanta."

"Bully," I said. "I'll consider that your Confederate Memorial Day speech."

Davis had a question for Harry. "About Dandy. He did throw the title, didn't he?"

"They scared him. With statistics."

"What statistics?"

"More than a hundred blacks were killed in riots around the

190

country after that fight in Carson City. That so-called defeat for white supremacy."

I put this to Harry: "Did Dandy fake it this afternoon? Or did you really knock him down?"

Without hesitation, Harry said, "He faked it."

Davis cringed. "You asked him to?"

"No. He just did it for me. Because I'm his friend. Because that sportswriter was here. They'll be talking about it in New York in a few days."

"Harry," I said, "why are you his friend?"

"He's a champ. A man without a country. That gets to me."

"Does Dandy ever get to you for real?" I asked.

Harry said, "He loves me."

"And you love to show off."

Harry met my stare, lowered his gaze to the breasts I was showing off, and said, "I'm human. But I don't show off when I write."

Davis asked, "What are you working on?"

"If I were working, *amigo*, you wouldn't be here. This is holiday time."

"Do you work well here?"

"Damn well. Only reason I'm here. If I could write in Montana, I'd be in Montana."

"Think I ought to try it?"

Harry shook his head. "This isn't your continent. Go back home."

"Milwaukee?"

"Any place in the States. You're an American writer. I'm not. I'm like Dandy. A man without a country. Both of my novels and the best of my short stories take place in a no-man's-land called Europe. You're an American writer, *amigo*. The best American writer. The champ."

Harry believed what he had said. I believed him, too. But Davis didn't. "Harry," he said sadly, "tell me something. Why didn't *North Shore* sell a hundred thousand?"

Harry lowered his head to sniff brandy. "I've got some

191

thoughts about that. It should've sold a million. And won all the prizes."

"Why didn't it?"

Harry said, "Because it was written by Davis O'Donnell."

"Instead of Harry Ingram?"

"No. This is my point. Before *North Shore,* Davis O'Donnell was a trade name. Like Jell-O. The Yale guy who discovered the flapper. The drunk, the joker, the sophomore, the guy in the *Saturday Evening Post,* the guy with his picture in the papers. The guy in the raccoon coat with the flask on his hip. You were liked. You were the life of the party. Everyone laughed with you." Harry paused to imbibe. "Then *North Shore* is published. Not *about* New York. *Against* New York. And who the hell does Davis O'Donnell think he is? Why, the mad son of a bitch thinks he's Jeremiah! Yeah, Jeremiah! Shouting from the rooftops: 'Woe unto us, for we are spoiled.' Yeah, Jeremiah writing in a book that all evil should come upon Babylon. Babylon on the Hudson. Jesus Christ, you handed us a wallop. Me included. I couldn't believe that Davis O'Donnell, the happy drunk, had turned out to be the wet blanket at the prosperity party. The big feast of the twenties. Bigger than Belshazzar's. When you got up at the banquet table, everyone — including me — expected to hear either a funny or a dirty story. Or maybe we half expected to see you fall on your face. Or piss in your pants. But what did you do? You walked away from the table, went over to the wall, and wrote *mene, mene, tekel, upharsin.* The American Dream's been shat upon." Harry took more brandy. "You with me, *amigo?*"

"With you," said Davis, holding out his inhaler for a refill.

Harry's voice boomed again. "Jeremiah! A prophet without honor in his own country. A pariah. And take Daniel, the boy who came to read the handwriting on the wall. To interpret it. Sure, they gave him a chain of gold and proclaimed him the third ruler of the kingdom. Then, when realization hit the powers that be, they threw him to the lions." Harry pointed a finger at Davis. "You're Jeremiah! You're Daniel! You have the dreams, the visions. You charge. You accuse. Sure, *you* have the dreams, the visions." Harry dropped his hand and rubbed his abdomen with it. "Yeah, I have only the nightmares: the dead being taken from the battlegrounds and stacked onto trucks like cordwood."

Davis broke through the nightmare crust. "Harry, what the hell are you trying to say?"

Harry pressed his chin against the rail of his chair. "We'll never know. You and I'll be dead. We'll never know."

"Know what?" Davis insisted.

Harry said, "I keep chastising myself. I keep seeing the golden door. It opens for Davis O'Donnell. Not for Harry Ingram. *Amigo*, that's a thought I find harder to take than the stink of death."

Davis was derisive. "Harry, you're drunk!"

"Didn't you hear me? Didn't you understand?"

"I understood," said Davis. "You were talking about immortality. About Shakespeare and all that crap. The perfect subject for drunks. All I know is that I'm dead and buried, and you own the world."

His eyes strong upon Davis, his arms outstretched, a Samson straining at the temple pillars, Harry cried out, "You stupid son of a bitch! When did you stop believing that Delano Fredericks was God?"

"After *North Shore* died."

"Time out for a prayer." Harry lowered his head. "Please, God, may all my books die the death of *North Shore*. Please, God."

I had something to say, and I said it. "Freddie doesn't answer letters, let alone prayers."

Harry glanced at me. "That's clever."

"Why didn't you laugh?"

I felt my breasts wither before Harry's wrath. "I never laugh at tragedies. And to me the great American tragedy is the two of you."

Davis interposed. "Let's get back to books."

Harry jerked his head toward Davis. "That's my message, you dumb bastard! Let's get back to books!"

193

"Tell me how!" implored Davis.

"You and Rannah stop beating each other. Break up the fucking marriage."

I tried a tired joke. "If you have Harry for a friend, you don't need an enemy."

Harry whirled on me. "You've had ten years together. Call it off. What the hell have you got to show for it? What the hell's keeping you together?"

"A funny thing called love," I said.

"That was sure a fucking, funny scene down at that depot in Georgia. You had your love, your ticket, and you still couldn't get your ass on the train."

"I married Davis."

"You married success. Now divorce failure."

I glanced at my husband and saw him savoring his brandy as if he were drinking the wisdom of Solomon. I turned to Harry, withheld rage, and tried to score with my own wisdom. "What failure, Harry? The failure that'll take Davis through the golden door?"

Harry was jolted, but not for long. "Rannah, it's 1930. This prick here hasn't written a book since 1924. Six fucking years. Christ! How many years can a writer piss away?"

I waited for Davis to answer that. He said nothing. I said to Harry, "Are you blaming me?"

"Who the fuck's talking about blame? I'm not blaming you *or* Davis. I'm just saying things that have to be said. Since 1924 you've had no marriage. You had an arrangement. Think of it! What the hell are you actually breaking up? Are you still lovers?"

Silence from Davis. I said, "We're free lovers. As you damn well know."

"Everybody knows," Harry said regretfully, as if in apology to Davis.

Now I decided to attack. "What prompted this, Harry? Are you so marvelously happy with your new wife?"

"I love Charlotte. More important, she loves me. She thinks I'm God."

194

"She must be stupid."

"She's young. That's the secret. Being young and seeing God in your bed."

"And what happens when Charlotte ages and wises up to you?"

Harry said coldly, "When she gets to be like you, Rannah, I'll divorce her."

"And marry another young girl?"

Now the king talked of kings. "A writer, no matter what age, is like the dying King David. A young virgin must be sought to warm and cherish him."

I looked at Davis again and wondered if he were listening at all. He appeared like a prisoner in the dock, attuned only to the verdict.

To Harry I said, "Why marry at all? Writers should have nothing but mistresses."

"Bullshit! Mistresses are worse than wives," Harry declared. "They're more demanding. They eat up your time and attention. No, a young wife's better."

"I heard your first wife left you," I said.

Harry flinched. "True."

"Why?"

"She thought I was crazy."

"And how did she tumble to this truth?"

Harry smiled wanly. "By seeing me sentencing myself to another year of hell. Another year of rewriting my first novel."

I laughed and tried to infect Davis with my laughter. But he was dead, floating face down in the brandy inhaler.

Harry wasn't dead. "What the hell's so funny?"

I said, "I get it now, Harry. The O'Donnells and *North Shore* broke up your first marriage. Now you want retribution. You want to break up ours."

Harry looked at me as if I were mad. Then he turned toward Davis and roused him. "*Amigo?*"

"Yes."

"You never met Francine —"

"Francine who?"

195

"My first wife. Pretty girl. I loved her, too. That November of '24, when I got back to Atlanta, she wanted to hear nothing but good news. I told her all that was good. And I told her I was going to take another year with the book. She couldn't understand that at all. If the publisher, the agent, and everybody else who'd read the book — including Davis O'Donnell and Delano Fredericks — liked it fine, then why in hell was I sitting down to rewrite it from page one? And this is what I said to her: 'I have to.' And she said: 'If you do, I'll walk out on you.' I sat down to a pint of booze, thought about it, and then I told Francine: 'I want you to go. I don't write to exist. I live to write.'"

"Beautiful," I said, mocking him.

Harry grimaced, swallowed brandy, and then said, "Look, let's nobody get sore at nobody. I love you both. And I'd like to keep you both for friends. But Christ, remember the facts, remember the dates. Chuck the damn wedding ring into the Mediterranean. Better yet, pawn it for a couple of bottles of booze or wine. Have a farewell fling and then leave each other alone. For good."

I said, "Fuck you, Harry."

"Rannah, you're only thirty years old."

"Oh, shut up!"

He didn't. "You're still damned attractive. You can find another man. The kind of man you need. And always have needed. A rich man."

I said, "A rich man? Are there any left?"

Harry said, "The real rich weren't hurt in the crash. They seldom are. The real rich, I've been told by one of the Rothschilds, live on the interest earned by the interest on their capital."

I said, "Don't bother to instruct me, Harry. I can't distinguish a bull from a bear."

Harry went on. "Remember that stunt you and Davis pulled on the Vincent Zacharys?"

I nodded. "Such fun."

"Weeks of fun. You two idiots chasing a yacht with honeymooners aboard from port to port."

"Oh, yes," I said. "Every night the Zacharys saw us, we'd tell them we were heading back to New York. But we went all the way. All the way to Palm Beach." I reached a hand to Davis. "Remember, darling?"

Davis only nodded. Harry said. "Next time around, Rannah, marry the guy who can afford the yacht. Not the writer who can't afford not to get up in the morning. And not to face the blank page."

Instead of thanking Harry for the sermon, I decided to laugh in church. "Such fun! We drove the poor Zacharys out of their minds! Each time they saw us, we had a new disguise. A new bag of tricks."

Harry said, "The Zacharys don't remember it as fun." Having had the last word on the subject, he concentrated on Davis. "*Amigo,* do you need a year for the book?"

Davis was lost. "Book? What book?"

Harry was patient. "The Snyder-Gray case."

"I can't get past — "

"How about trying again? Alone."

"Where?"

"How about Milwaukee?"

Davis shook his head. "I'm a boy in Milwaukee."

"You name it."

"New York. The Plaza."

"You can't afford it."

Taking the cue, I said, "He can't afford a divorce."

Harry was patient with me, too. "I'll foot the bills for the divorce."

"Bless you, Harry."

Harry veered away from my sarcasm and faced Davis, who was now very much with us again. "I'll stake you to a year in San Francisco, New Orleans, or You Name It."

"How much of a stake?"

"I'll have Mason send you five hundred a month."

"What about the small print?"

"I don't get you."

"The conditions of the contract. No strings, Harry?"

Harry poured brandy. "I've got conditions. You work only on the book. No short stories." Harry came back to me again. "And no Rannah."

I had something to say, but I waited for Davis. Davis continued to stare at Harry and out the window overlooking his tomorrows. "And no mistresses?"

"Stick with whores."

Davis laughed, and for a moment I thought his laughter would save me. "Joel Stone doesn't live there any more. Oh, come into the garden, Maud." After another burst of laughter Davis finally said, "What do you think, honey?"

"Think about what?"

"Splitting up."

"Do as Harry says. Always do as Harry says. Stick with the whores." I looked at Harry. "By the way, the virgin didn't do a damn thing for King David. I think the old bastard died of shame."

Harry said, "Davis is only thirty-four."

"Well, let's find out about that, Harry," I said. "Be a good little boy, run back to your bedroom and fetch your new wife. Fetch her and bring her to the bed of King Davis O'Donnell. Then we'll take it from there. How about it, Harry?"

Harry seemed chagrined, but he made no answer. To Davis he said, after a pause, "Think it over."

I tried again. "Harry, if you're afraid to ask your wife, then stay here with me. Let Davis go to Charlotte."

Harry stood up now, pushed the chair aside, looked down at me, and said, "Good night, Rannah. I love you."

I said, "Prove it. Make love to me now. Like you used to."

Harry tried to feint. "I'm in training. Got to go four rounds with the champ tomorrow."

"Only one round with me, Harry. You never take more than three minutes."

Harry turned to Davis. "How'd you live ten years with her?"

Davis said, "I've had lots of wives. Rannah's had lots of husbands. The mornings after find us with strange faces to confront mirrors. And each other."

198

"Darling," I said, "don't be surprised if tomorrow morning you find yourself greeting Lord Nelson in the bathroom mirror."

"Lord Nelson?" Davis was puzzled. "What does she mean by that?"

"Ask Rannah," said Harry.

I said, "Tell him, Harry. I won't mind if you cite scripture again."

Harry said to Davis, "When Nelson was killed, they preserved his body by stuffing it into a cask of brandy."

"Am I dead?" Davis asked.

"You've been murdered. By the bitch in your bed." Now to me: "Here I go quoting scripture again. This time from a bible called *North Shore*."

"Hallelujah," I said flatly.

Harry spoke only to Davis. "Take your hero, the bootlegger. His death is your death. His love brought him death. His love of that fucking rich bitch who's Rannah all over. And this is the genius of the scene: you didn't have the bootlegger fucking the rich bitch when her husband comes to the yacht with murder in mind. No, she's fucking another rich guy, and your bootlegger is covering for her when he takes the bullets in his guts. That's the greatest fucking scene ever written in any American book. But this is my point, *amigo:* You've got to leave this bitch. She's your death!"

"Hallelujah," I said again.

Harry was done. He stood there for a moment, the brandy bottle held over the inhaler, his eyes darting between Davis and me as if he were trying to sift reality from phantasm. "Hell," he muttered to himself as he turned and hurried from the room.

I said, "Turn out the light, darling."

In the ensuing darkness I waited for Davis to say something, to say anything.

Finally I said, "You can go straight to sleep without saying your prayers."

"What?"

"You were a good little boy tonight. You ate up all your bible lesson."

199

"Good night."

"I'm not going to shut up. I'm going to talk you to death."

"We're both drunk."

"Darling, I'm drunk with joy, with ecstasy. I've been to a revival meeting, I've heard Harry the preacher, and the sermon of the fox without a fresh piece of tail." I laughed alone. "You realize what he said to you?"

"Good night."

"Harry was saying: I'll take the cake. I'll take the gold. You, Davis Idiot O'Donnell, you keep looking for the golden door, and wait around for the pie in the sky, by and by."

"Good night."

"The son of a bitch, he's jealous of you. He's jealous of *us.*"

That roused Davis. "Jealous of what? Our failure?"

"What failure? Our marriage?"

"Yes, our marriage. My career. What've we got? Where are we going?"

"Where the hell do you want to go?"

"To chapter three!"

I felt cold and sick. "You're thinking divorce, aren't you, darling?"

"Harry makes sense."

"Sense? He's a fool. He knows about dying and the dead. He doesn't know about life and living. Or about women. Why, the stupid bastard divides all women into virgins and bitches. You and I — we know it's more complicated than that. And he doesn't understand love. To Harry, love's nothing but a wet dream."

Davis said, "He lives to write."

"Of course. And in between chapters he knocks down Dandy Flood."

"He writes."

"*Mene, mene,* tickle my ass."

"Harry wants me to write."

"Before you get to chapter three, darling, you can get in practice by writing some I.O.U.'s for the money he's going to lend you."

"You don't care if I write or not."

I said, "If caring made a difference, I might care. I can't get through to you, you can't get through to me. We send each other messages in the bottles we float down our kidneys. Like tonight. Like now."

A moment of silence. "Let's try separation."

Now it was my turn to say, "Good night."

"Go home for a while," said Davis.

"Go home? Have you looked at me lately? I'm no belle any more. Not even a flapper. Have you listened to me lately? I'm a bitch. A foulmouthed bitch. What can I bring home? Children? Money? A happy smile?"

"Good night," Davis said from the cellar of his unhappiness.

I wouldn't let go. "Good night? Yes, it was! For you! Where are you now, my darling? In San Francisco? In that secret room with the secret window, watching the rain of secret words?" I felt hysteria rising in me. "Lo, the winter's gone from the wintry blank page! Davis O'Donnell springs into action! Davis O'Donnell fights another summer! Another fall! San Francisco, open your golden gate! Open your golden door! Here comes Davis O'Donnell!" I reached across the bed and thumped my husband's back. "Do you hear me?"

"I've heard enough."

I sat up now and drank muscatel from the bottle. Then, falling back upon the burning pillow, I spoke softly. "Sleep, darling, if you can, on this strange bed. On this, our deathbed."

But Davis didn't hear me, sleep having insulated him from me. After minutes measured by the dripping of perspiration and fouled by the odor of fear, I left the bed and curled up like a child in the rocking chair. I was afraid of the deathbed, and fearful of the snare of sleep that was the twin of death.

But I did sleep, and I did wake to find dawn routing darkness and death. Leaving the womb of the rocking chair, I stood up and watched Davis's chest rise and fall before I went to the narrow window to look at a sky from which the stars were gone.

Then, as I lowered my gaze to the Spanish terrain and tried to breathe in the salty freshness of the Mediterranean, I saw that I

201

was being observed. The man outside the villa wore a brown beret, a tweed jacket, tweed knickers, brown stockings, and brown-and-white shoes. He held a walking stick in his black right hand, and he smiled at me with his black face. I smiled back at Dandy Flood and watched him turn away and cross toward the road. My eyes now went to the boxing ring, and I painted death on its canvas.

Careful not to wake Davis, I dressed myself in a peasant blouse and bright skirt, forsook shoes and stockings, and left the room and house in pursuit of Dandy Flood. He was walking slowly, and I caught up with him a few hundred yards away.

"Good morning," I called to him.

He stopped, turned about, and gave me his heavyweight smile. A man educated by success and by contact with the Broadways of the world, he had the air of a master rather than the grandson of a slave.

"Good mornin', Mrs. O'Donnell."

"Mind if I walk with you?"

"My pleasure."

We walked together, his cane tapping the stones whose coldness I felt with my bare feet. I asked, "Is walking a pleasure?"

"Real pleasure. Walkin's good. Runnin's bad. Used to run five miles every mornin' when I was in trainin'. Long time ago. But that wasn't bad runnin'. Not with nobody chasin' you. And I been chased."

"Where are you from?"

"I was born in New Orleans."

"We're both from the South."

Dandy shook his head dolefully. "Not my South, you ain't. Railroad cops. Prison guards. Billies busted over your head. Eatin' dirt and wishin' you had a stein of rye and a bushel of fries. Or dreamin' about a settin' of eggs and a skillet of pork chops."

"How'd you become a professional fighter?"

"Made my first five bucks fightin' at a county fair. In Oklahoma. See, they'd pay five bucks to anyone who'd go four rounds with this white giant. Inside a tent. Cost you four bits to get in

202

and watch. Nobody ever made four before me. They'd see that you didn't, one dirty way or another. I was smart. I went out and nailed him in the first round. Man, he went down. And I went up. Before you knew it, I had me a white manager, and we was ridin' inside a train goin' north. Fightin' here, fightin' there. Eatin' big, thick porterhouse steaks. Then Carson City. And everybody yellin', 'Kill the nigger.' "

"When did you get your first white wife?" I asked.

"After I was champion. Had to beat it outa the country. Looked like jail for me again. They didn't like for me to have a white wife. I had me white whores, and nobody said nothin'. But a white wife? Kill the nigger."

"When did you meet Harry?"

Dandy Flood's smile returned. "About a year ago. We was introduced in Paris. He — Harry — he says to me, you come on down to Spain sometime. He says he's got this painting this painter George Bellows did in Carson City. Then he tells me he's got this here boxin' ring and he works out every day. Come on down, he says, we'll spar. And, sure, bring the wife." Dandy tossed his walking stick into the air and twirled it like a happy boy. "Harry's my friend. Best white friend I ever had. That man talks to you, pours you a drink, and listens when you talk. And you feel like you're the champ again. That's the big thing. Bigger than marryin' a white woman. Bein' champ."

I said, with calculated indifference. "You're just like me."

"How's that?"

"We were both fooled."

"Fooled by what?"

"By Harry. He's not my friend. He's not your friend."

Dandy Flood reacted as if I had plucked the rising sun from the Spanish sky and left him with a universe as black as his skin. "I don't get you."

"Don't misunderstand me," I said. "I like Harry."

"So do I."

"But the truth's the truth."

"Me bein' black?"

"Black? You're whiter than Harry."

203

"Say that again."

"You're whiter than Harry."

"You're mixin' me up."

"You're Harry's friend. But Harry's not your friend."

I had him on the ropes of confusion. He asked, "If Harry's my friend and — "

I interrupted him. "Harry has no friends."

"Ain't you his friend?"

I repeated my contention, word for word.

He said, "All them people at the house. You mean to tell me — "

"We're not people. I'm not flesh and blood. You're not flesh and blood. Not to Harry."

"What are we?"

"Characters." Dandy shook his head to tell me he didn't understand. I went on. "Think back to the times you were in the ring. Was your opponent your friend? Any of your opponents?"

"No, they wasn't."

"Harry's a writer. You know that, don't you?"

"I seen his books."

"You know that I'm married to a writer, don't you?"

"I know that."

I said, "Let me tell you about writers. They're not like fighters. A fighter like Dandy Flood, when he's not in the ring, he's a nice guy, a good guy, a white guy, a swell guy looking to be a friend to a friend. But a writer — a guy like Harry, or like my husband — he's always in the ring. And he's got no friends. He's like the giant at the county fair. He doesn't want you to go four rounds with him."

Again the complaint: "You got me all mixed up."

"Would you hurt a friend?"

"Never."

"Harry wouldn't either. That's why he doesn't have any friends. We're just characters. Just setups for him. And he's got us in his ring. Slugging us hard. Hurting us."

Dandy shook his head again. "Harry never tried to hurt me."

"Harry hurts all of his characters. All of us suckers. He rips

204

our bellies open and smears our bowels all over his books."
Dandy looked at me as if I were a fishmonger in the Tarragona
market place shouting at him in Spanish. "All writers do that.
Including my husband. You know what writers are?"

"What?" he asked, his chin exposed.

"They're mother-fuckers."

Dandy clucked. "Please, don't talk like that."

"I'm your friend, Dandy. Are you my friend?"

"Sure."

"Friends can talk and listen. Harry's not your friend. He's
using you. He'll break your bones, grind you up, and make ink
of your blood for his typewriter ribbon. Can you read?"

"I read some."

"Harry's easy to read. He uses small words. Small sentences.
And you know what he'll say about you? In a story? In a book?
He'll call you a black bastard and write about how the white
world wanted to kill the dirty nigger."

"Not Harry," Dandy protested.

"You're not his friend. Remember that when you get in the
ring with him later."

"You think I'd hurt Harry?"

"A nigger wouldn't. A man would."

"Why would a man?"

I told him. "A man wouldn't want a story going around the
world that he, a man who'd been a champion of the world, had
been knocked down by a drunken writer. All around the world
they're laughing at you. Laughing at the nigger with the yellow
streak who ran into one of Harry Ingram's punches. That's your
friend. A man who brings a sportswriter from Barcelona to tell
the world who's the *real* champion of the world. Harry, the he-
man! The muscle-man! The great white hope of the Western
world! He knocked down that black-and-yellow nigger, that
black son of a bitch who up and married three white women!
Bring him back to Louisiana and we'll cut off his black balls and
string him up!"

Dandy Flood stopped walking. He blinked at the morning sky

and gasped for fresh, clean air. Turning around, he said, "Let's go back to the house. You makin' me sick."

I said, "I'm your friend."

He walked faster. "You talk crazy."

"Break his jaw."

Wishfully he said, "Harry's my friend."

"No, he ain't. You understand the word *ain't*, don't you? Harry ain't your friend. Ain't never going to be your friend. He's the great white prick!"

"You're talkin' dirty again," he said sadly.

He hadn't heard anything yet. I asked, "Dandy, where was your first wife from?"

"North Dakota."

"Your second wife?"

"She was Italian. From Milan."

"And your present wife?"

"Chicago."

"Shall I tell you something?"

"What?"

"You've never slept with a white woman. Italian and Yankee women — even Yankee whores — they're not white."

Dandy said, "They was white."

"You're a black boy from Louisiana. I'm a white girl from Georgia. Remember back to the South and think about the time you got hot and bothered looking at the white girls. I'm one of those white girls. You fuck me and you've fucked a white girl."

Dandy struck the stone road with his walking stick. "Please, don't *talk* like that."

"Don't you want me?"

"I got me a white wife."

I turned to glance at the hazelnut trees. I said, "See those trees? How'd you like to meet me there this afternoon? How'd you like to fuck me under one of those trees?"

Dandy Flood, flooded with anguish, slammed his walking stick against the stone road and snapped it in two.

I persisted. "You get in the ring with Harry this morning. You hit him good. Knock him down. You knock him down and

206

hurt him and I'll be waiting for you. Under one of those trees. At four o'clock. Think about it."

He retrieved the broken end of the walking stick. "Forget it."

"I won't. And you can't. See you in the ring," I said, leaving Dandy and heading for the grove.

"Where you goin' now?" Dandy demanded.

"I'm going to sit under a hazelnut tree. And dream about this afternoon."

"You got me all bothered."

I laughed. "Knock Harry down. Then you can knock me down. Four o'clock."

He shook his head. "Can't."

I withered him with scorn. "Can't what? Knock Harry down? Or fuck me? It's easier than you think." I laughed again, and my laughter sounded harsh to me. "Come on, be a champ! Knock out the white giant at the county fair! And win yourself a doll from the South with the whitest ass you ever saw."

Dandy Flood stood there on the road, rubbing the two pieces of the walking stick together and letting the pitch of my laughter and the sight of my body enflame him.

When he took one tentative step toward me, I said quickly, "Four o'clock."

Turning away, he removed his coat, folded it over his left arm, thus concealing his agitation, and started toward the villa.

I lay alone for a while under a hazelnut tree and smelled blood. I saw Harry lying dead in the ring, dead in his coffin, dead in a grave filled not with earth but with stones from Roman ruins, carried and cast by me.

I fled from the grove when I recalled the words I had used with Dandy Flood. I took a bath to wash away the dirt from my feet. At eleven o'clock that morning, however, when I saw Harry enter the ring, the sight of him overwhelmed and routed my shame.

Davis was in Harry's corner, lacing the boxing gloves for him. The sportswriter from Barcelona assisted Dandy Flood in the other corner.

I was sitting alone at ringside when I sensed the presence of Alex Martin, who used perfume as an after-shave lotion and held a cigarette between his thumb and forefinger as if it were a phallus.

As Alex Martin sat down next to me, he said, "Good morning, Rannah."

"Hello, Alex."

"Delightful morning, isn't it?"

"Yes," I said, moving away from him. "Where's your wife?"

"Might I ask you a slight favor?"

"Of course."

"Please don't refer to Sandra as my wife. If you don't wish to call her Sandra, you might refer to her as Mrs. Martin. Thank you. And, to answer your question belatedly, Sandra's to be found on the opposite side of the ring."

To sustain the inanity I asked, "And why is Sandra sitting on the opposite side of the ring?"

"She wants to see Harry against the sun. And don't ask me why." He paused, leaned his head toward me, and whispered, "By the by, Sandra's interested in you."

In the reality of a morning in which I wanted to see Harry Ingram murdered in the ring, in which case I was to submit to intercourse with a Negro, I could only smile at this genteel whisper of perversion.

I said, "Who do you like? Dandy or Harry?" Alex Martin frowned. I added, "In the ring."

"In and out, I'm just wild about Harry."

"Doesn't Dandy interest you?" I asked.

"Have you been to the museum in Tarragona?"

"Not yet."

"You must go. There's a rather exciting piece of sculpture there, after Praxiteles, of Bacchus playing with a panther." Alex Martin turned toward Harry. "I see Harry as Bacchus, ever young, ever fair." He nodded toward Dandy. "And there is the brute, the beast, the black panther."

I now turned my head to watch Davis kneading the muscles on

208

Harry's shoulders with sophomoric enthusiasm. I asked Alex Martin, "How do you see Davis?"

"I'm jealous of the attraction he has for Harry. And vice versa."

"Are you suggesting they're fairies?"

"As Browning wrote, every wish is like a prayer," Alex Martin said with regret.

Then the bell sounded and the fairies fled before the onrush of brutes. In the first round I saw again the ballet of boredom. In the second round I saw the farce of Dandy Flood taking punches from Harry.

Between rounds, while Davis ministered to Harry, I turned to Alex Martin and said, "Harry packs a wallop."

He said, "Nonsense. The three-legged beast's an excellent actor."

"Three-legged beast? Is that fact or phantasy?"

He glanced toward Mrs. Flood and whispered: "What do you think attracts those white pigs who marry him?"

My mind raced back to the road at morning and the sight of Dandy Flood retreating from me with his coat held before him.

The bell sounded again and brought me back to the present, and to the presence of the boxers, with Harry taking the offensive again and Dandy retreating before him.

Between rounds three and four, Alex Martin delivered the hardest punch of the morning. He said to me, "I believe Sandra and you have a mutual friend."

"Who would that be?"

"Stephani Baroni."

"Sandra must be mistaken. But, of course, so many people claim friendship with the Davis O'Donnells."

Alex Martin fell silent, and I left the sun and the ring to return to the night of a party in Paris, a night in which I vaguely remembered stealing away and going to bed with Louis Baroni, and vividly remembered waking up in a bed with Louis Baroni and Stephani Baroni.

The bell announcing the fourth and final round stemmed my revulsion and alerted me to the action in the ring. Again Harry was the aggressor, the great white hunter stalking the black panther. Then, rather abruptly and deftly, the charade came to an end. Dandy Flood took a flurry of punches and Harry kept bearing in, only to move into the path of a black gloved hand that caught him below the heart.

Harry doubled up and sank to the canvas. At the same instant I rose to my feet and cried, *"Kill him! Kill him!"*

From the floor of the ring, Harry glared toward me. Before he could express his rage, he bowed his head and vomited up his breakfast. Davis rushed into the ring, threw a towel over the vomit, and helped Dandy raise Harry and assist him to the stool in his corner.

Still standing, I observed the scene in Harry's corner and listened to Dandy Flood trying to explain the accidental knock-out. Davis helped Dandy again, stating that Harry had imbibed too much the night before. Harry broke off the apologies and explanations, good-naturedly grazed Dandy Flood's jaw with his taped right hand, and left the ring to retire to the privacy of his bedroom and the support of his brandy.

Dandy Flood protested too much to everyone but me. Davis was later given an audience by Harry and allowed to apologize for my barbaric outcry for his blood. But neither Davis nor Dandy could forgive me. I comforted myself with the rock-hard reality of the moment when Harry had fallen to the floor of the ring, with the fleeting instant in which I had pronounced him dead.

When luncheon was served, Charlotte apologized for her husband's absence. I ate and drank the explanation of Harry's nonappearance. As for the luncheon itself, I remember it for cold beef, cold salads, chilled drinks, and icy stares.

In our bedroom, later, Davis announced to me that we were cutting short our visit and leaving in the morning.

And I said, "That's the nicest thing you've said to me all day."

Then he sat down and probed me with reproachful eyes. "Are you all right?"

"I'm fine."

210

"You don't look well."

"What do you suggest, Doctor? An ocean voyage?"

"You hurt Harry."

"That's dandy," I said.

Then and there, for the first time, Davis voiced a suspicion bordering upon diagnosis. "Rannah, I think you're mad."

I protested too loudly. "I'm mad at Harry! And you too! Get the hell out of here, you fairy!"

Davis said nothing. And I saw not anger but sorrow in eyes that told me his love for me had died. When he was gone from the room, I was left alone with a mirror I was able to turn toward the wall and a clock whose hands I couldn't turn back.

At fifteen minutes before four, when Davis was with Harry in the latter's den, I left the villa with a sketch pad to draw an alibi, and with a bottle of muscatel to dull my fear. Barefoot, I walked on the stony road toward the grove of hazelnut trees.

It was four o'clock. A church bell in Tarragona sounded the hour as I sat with my back against the trunk of a tree and searched the grove for Dandy Flood. Seeing nothing but the symmetry of the grove, I opened the bottle of wine and drank from it.

With each swallow the wine seemed to sour more and more to vinegar. The sky turned from a rich blue to a sickly green. The sun lost its yellow in a rage of red. The leaves darkened to black. The grove sprouted into a jungle, and in the heat I heard the death cries of animals, smelled spilled blood, and then flung myself face down upon the earth, pressing my nose into the palms of my hands to keep from smelling the stench of my animal sweat.

I heard a voice. "Rannah?"

"Who is it?"

"It's Daddy."

"Daddy, can you hear me?"

"I can hear what you're thinking."

"Daddy, take me home."

"Yes, Rannah, I'll take you home and bury you by the river."

"Daddy! I'm alive! I'm in Africa! Lost in Africa!"

211

The sound of my voice fell upon deaf trees, and my hands clawed into the soil, at first to dig myself a grave by the river in Georgia where all the Gedneys lay buried, and then to take myself to the South Shore of Long Island and the building of a sand castle on the white strand where the waves washed me with the salts of life.

Then it happened, with the crash of a wave that flung me back to the African jungle.

From an orange sky a black panther sprang upon me. My scream never passed the black paw slamming against my mouth. Another paw swept under my skirt and clawed away my silken leaf. Swiftly, deftly, my knees were sundered as the black panther, who had also clawed the sun from the afternoon sky, impaled me against the midnight earth, stiffened sinew, summoned blood, and delivered me to a hell in which I cried for God, and then to a heaven in which I laughed with the Devil.

The thrust that broke the back of ecstasy freed other screams. My assaulted mind, rocking with my body, heard the black panther say: "It's me. Daddy. Only me. Daddy. It's Daddy."

A last scream shattered awareness and flung me into infinite space, where I became a dead moon orbiting a dead planet.

My return to awareness was as slow as the sprouting of a seed. Sound and pain led me to the thought that I had returned to life disguised as a clapper in a cathedral bell. When I opened my eyes and my mind, I saw that my hands and my feet were bound, that I was in a narrow bed, in a narrow room with quilted walls and one narrow, barred window, through which freely passed the pealing of the bells of Barcelona.

part three

The Battle of the Madwoman

1.

William James said: "The Lord may forgive our sins, but our nervous system never does." And the Lord, according to Matthew, said: "I was sick, and ye visited me: I was in prison, and ye came unto me."

It is my father's recollection, not fond and not mine, that the date of his first and last visit to the prison for the deranged occurred on December 18, 1930. By then clocks, calendars, newspapers, magazines, and radios were added to my list of forbidden artifacts, such as matches, razor blades, knives, scissors, pills, glass, and pieces of string.

My corner of hell, camouflaged by cakes, candies, and Cadillacs, rested upon five acres of Pennsylvania countryside seventy miles northeast of Philadelphia as the bats fly to the belfry.

The name of this secluded rendezvous for the affluent mad was Hollow Grove. Outsiders saw the hollow as a deer park. I, as an insider, saw it as a natural pit in which I was entrapped, and from which there was no escape over the high fence designed to keep us from disturbing the peace of the outsiders whose depression was merely economic.

A gate almost as imposing as that at Joel Stone's quondam estate on Long Island opened onto a macadam road that wound

215

down a steep grade to the sylvan hollow and the French château and its fourteen satellite cottages.

The château would have been a dream house for the Marquis de Sade; there were rooms where the walls were padded, the windows barred, the straitjackets handy, the baths tepid, the sheets icy, and the shocks from insulin or electricity readily available. Visitors, however, were impressed by the great library, the stately dining room, and a kitchen manned by an Austrian couple who roasted geese, ducks, and chickens, simmered sauces and gravies, and whipped up cakes and pastries.

Save for hypomanic periods, the inmates, euphemistically called guests, resided in the splendor of two-room cottages with their individual keepers, laughingly referred to as companions, who slept on Murphy beds in the sitting rooms.

My keeper, whose name was Sophie Neff, I saw as a creation of Vincent van Gogh, who painted peasants to look like potatoes and potatoes to look like peasants. In her fifties, Mrs. Neff was a mass of starch and muscle engineered to withstand the day-and-night stress of contact with godforsaken creatures given to hysteria, violence, depression, silence, withdrawal, aphasia, and other vagaries of the human mind.

And, lest I forget, while she was anything but a companion to me, Mrs. Neff was a human being with a history of her own.

She had lived with dirt, disgrace, and death. Her eldest son, a doughboy gassed in the Meuse-Argonne sector, had died in a French hospital. Her two youngest children had died during the Spanish influenza epidemic of 1918. For Christmas that same year her husband, a coal miner, had spent ten cents for a bullet, borrowed a pistol from a friend, and fired the shot that made her a widow. And she now lived with the knowledge that her eldest daughter was a prostitute in Jersey City.

Yet Mrs. Neff was happy at Hollow Grove, and she thanked God for delivering her to a place where she had found another daughter who returned her love and kindness with familiar abuse, and where, in a time when bread was to be found at the end of long lines, she was able to eat cake.

216

Hollow Grove had first opened wide its gates in 1927. It had been established by a husband-and-wife team of psychiatrists.

Dr. Dominick Patrone had escaped from an Italian ghetto in Philadelphia by reason of his talent for making touchdowns. Dr. Marybelle Ware Patrone had blossomed in the Tidewater country of Virginia in the knowledge that she was a daughter and granddaughter of Old Dominion physicians. He, who was born with shoulder pads and looked like one of Frankie Yale's underworld lieutenants, brought the language of the street corner and the locker room to psychotherapy. She, the petite, attractive belle, had lost her Virginia accent and charm somewhere in the labyrinths of psychiatry.

Before my incarceration it had been the firm and fast rule that Dr. Dominick ministered to the madmen and Dr. Marybelle to the female of this species. The revolution came with the Battle of Lexicon, in which I used Anglo-Saxon invective to rout Dr. Marybelle and her array of Greek and Latin incantations. Peace came with Dr. Dominick.

And this December morning he came to my cottage, hardly the very model of a modern, major psychiatrist. He wore a sweat suit, sneakers, and a towel for a muffler, his uniform for his morning workout, a mile run around the grounds.

I was having coffee and fresh croissants in bed when Mrs. Neff ushered him into the bedroom.

"Good morning, Spike," he said.

"Good morning, Frankie," I answered. I had no delusion that I was Spike O'Donnell or that he was Frankie Yale, but the salutations were spades of dirt thrown on the graves where we had buried the ancient enmity between physician and patient.

He sat down, broke off a piece of croissant and dunked it into the coffee. His mouth full and working, he said, "You patients sure know how to live."

I smiled. "You're a nut."

"Takes one to know one."

I tugged at his sweat shirt. "Look at yourself. Is this what Freud has wrought?"

217

"Siggie's got his ways, I've got mine. I'm thirty-eight years old and I like to run in the morning."

I said, "If you were married to me, you wouldn't have the strength to chase a streetcar in the morning."

He blew on the embers of my desire. "You keep talking like that and you'll wind up in a hotel room in Philadelphia."

"Threatening me, Frankie?"

"No threats this morning, Spike." Signaling an end to the game, he took my pulse. "How do you feel?"

"Itchy," I said. "This damned eczema."

"You're using too much lotion."

"You bring back my sanity. I'll take care of my vanity."

He smiled. "You're saner than I am." His smile faded. "Seriously, to be clever, to make couplets, you have to have all of your marbles."

"Then why am I here, Doctor?"

"Because I love you and don't want to lose you."

"Seriously," I reminded him.

"Because you can't beat the food," he said, filching the last of my croissant. "How'd you sleep last night?"

"With my eyes shut."

"Good. Any nightmares?"

"Yes. I was in a Philadelphia hotel room with —"

"Shut up. I've got some news for you."

I reached high for a wish. "I'm leaving!"

"You've got a visitor coming this morning."

I frowned. "Visitor's a dirty word."

"This nut claims to be your father."

"You did write him!" He nodded and I pressed his hand. "Thank you, Doctor. I love you."

"Take a nice bath. Doll yourself up and get out of bed. Put on your best duds and visit with your old man in the sitting room."

"Visit?"

"Entertain him."

"I entertain notions of freedom," I said as I began to scratch my arms. "This damned eczema!"

218

"Rannah, stop with the big words. You're getting like Marybelle. You've got a rash. A plain, lousy, itchy rash, that's all."

"Is there a chance?"

Dr. Dominick played the dumb doctor. "A chance for what?"

"My leaving here with my father. Today."

"Where would you go?"

"Home."

His following question was anything but simple. "And where is that?"

I thought hard and said, "Stephensville, Georgia."

But he took me back to the underworld. "Spike, it's not true about Southern cooking. All that grease'll kill you."

"Frankie, it's the way I wanna go."

He nodded approval of my reading and then, in an instant, he revealed a brother's love for his sister. "Rannah, you know I love you. Nothing'd make me happier than if I could touch your face and take away your rash. Or if I could send you away today with your father."

Dismally I said, "But you can't."

"It's up to you. You persuade your father that you're well enough to come home, and you can go. Today. But you'll have to take your rash with you. If you want, you can drop it off in Virginia."

We laughed together, and then I asked, "Doctor, will I truly ever get well?"

He said, "It's a good sign when you want to go home. When you think you're not ill and that we're just keeping you here to get your money."

"Answer my question, please."

He was frank and honest now. "There's no cure today. Not for cancer and not for that word you hate so much."

"Schizophrenia."

"As my wife says, there is no *restituto ad integrum*."

Deaf to Latin tags, I asked, "Can I make a life for myself again?"

"What sort of life?"

"A quiet life. No more drinking. No more parties. No sex. I'd get a job. Perhaps on the newspaper again," I said, feeling I had cleanly fielded the question.

"What about your husband?"

There was frost on the window of recollection. "I'd let him divorce me. And make his own life without me."

"Would you want to marry again?"

"No."

"You still love your husband, don't you?"

"Yes. If I didn't love him so much, I couldn't hate him as I do."

Dr. Dominick leaned back in his chair, scratched his navel, and contemplated me. "Don't tell that to your father. You have no hate, you can't afford hate."

"Will you be here when my father comes?"

"You talk to him alone. Then the three of us can have lunch in the château."

"I don't like the château."

He frowned at me. "You *hate* the château?"

"We'll have lunch," I said, "in the château."

"Good."

"Doctor, what else must I do to convince my father I'm well enough to go home?"

He hesitated, and then spoke with caution. "Be yourself. Be honest with him. Don't try to fool him. Don't patronize him. Don't demean yourself. Confess your guilt and your awareness of it. Your illness is your fault. Remember that. Yours and yours alone."

"I'll remember. Do I tell him I'm well?"

"No, you don't. But you can tell him it's better for you to be at home than here. It's far better to have contact with reality. He'll understand. I'll make sure he understands that."

"Anything else?"

He thought a moment. "It's been six years since you last saw your father. Be prepared for a change in him."

"I don't understand. What sort of change?"

"He'll be older. Lonelier. Sadder. He won't be as you've seen him in your dreams and nightmares."

220

"I understand."

He assessed me. "Feel excited?"

"My heart's pounding. I feel I'm going to be born again."

The smile waned. "Spike, you're thirty years old. A big girl. You've got to promise me something."

"Anything, Frankie," I said.

"You may not make it today and —"

I was quick to scream. "What are you saying?"

Dr. Dominick was sharp with me. "Quiet down! I'm saying this: from what I know of your father, it won't be easy to convince him to take you home."

"Aren't you putting me on the defensive?" I complained.

"Rannah, listen to me. You'll have to learn to live with a defensive attitude if you leave here. Just imagine the looks Lazarus got from people when he returned from the dead. You'll be returning from the second greatest fear of man. Madness. And you'll have to defend yourself against inhumanity, insensitivity, the fear of contagion, the lack of trust. You'll be the woman from Bedlam, the mad Rannah. It won't be easy. It never is for the afflicted."

I said, "But he's my father."

"Your father died when you and Davis O'Donnell drove off in your Apperson ten years ago. You told me that."

"If he's dead to me," I argued, "then who's coming to see me today?"

"Judge Gedney, a very clever lawyer coming to contest a claim."

"A claim?"

"A claim that you're his daughter and he's obliged to take you back into his home."

"Is he obliged, Doctor?"

"No, Rannah, he is not."

My voice rose. "Then why should he do it? Why should he want to take me home? For my mother's sake?"

"No, not for your mother's sake," he said plainly.

"Why then?" I screamed.

"Don't yell!" He pointed an admonishing finger at me.

221

"Don't snap at me! Or at your father!" He lowered his hand and his voice. "Your father may want to take you home if you remind him how much he once loved you. If you remind him how bright, witty, and vivacious you can be. What good company you can be to him again. To sit in his study with him and sip bourbon and talk about life and books."

I was confused. "You make it sound as if I were applying for a job. As if my father were looking for a companion."

"A very good analogy," he said. "But let's say friend. Our keepers, may the saints forgive Marybelle, are companions. But then it's Marybelle's money."

"Speaking of money, Doctor, who's paying my bills?"

He hesitated. "I want you to answer that."

"As I would to my father?"

"Yes."

"I don't know."

"And how would you answer me?"

I was certain, then and there, that Harry Ingram was barricading me at Hollow Grove with his bars of gold. But I said again, "I don't know."

"Your monthly bill," Dr. Dominick informed me, "is sent to New York. And we promptly receive a check signed by a man named Ellis Mason."

And I smartly said, "Yes, he's my husband's agent." I thought of Mason, then and there, as Harry Ingram's agent. Then I asked, "And how large are the bills?"

"Very large. A thousand dollars a month."

I was thinking about the high measure of Harry Ingram's hatred for me, but I said, "My father could never afford that, could he?"

"No, he couldn't."

Then I posed this question: "If my father took me home, and if I couldn't control myself, he could commit me to the state hospital, couldn't he?"

"He could. Does that frighten you?"

"A prison is a prison."

"You said a mouthful, Spike. Now let's see you bust out of

222

here." Dr. Dominick squeezed my hand and got up to leave. At the door he stopped, faced me again, his expression somber. "Rannah, remember to speak slowly. No rushing of words and no obscenities. Please."

An hour later I was at the sitting room window watching the December wind sweep the landscape for winter's arrival. Time was a kite caught in a tree, and almost another hour passed before I saw my father walking toward the cottage, marching to the cadence of defeat.

I fled from the window to the bathroom mirror and saw only a poor likeness of the girl who had once owned her hometown and the love of her father. The belle was gone, the flapper gone, and the madwoman hid behind the fan of a smile.

When the door swung open, it failed to swing away the years. I saw my father as my grandfather, and he saw me as an impostor. We embraced cautiously, being careful not to chip the china of our emotions. I introduced Mrs. Neff, showed him the bedroom, and chattered about comforts of home before Mrs. Neff retired to the bedroom and left us alone in the sitting room.

My father settled into his chair, filled his pipe and lit it, and the aroma of his tobacco took me home.

My question skipped homeward. "Did Mother send me anything? Is there something from her?"

He blew smoke signals I couldn't read before he said, "No, Rannah."

I dared the truth. "Is she ill?"

"She was."

I went to the wishing well. "She's better."

My father removed the pipe from his mouth. "Your mother's dead."

I wanted to run from my father, to rush back to bed, to pull the sheets over my head and wait for morning and the song of my mother waking me. Then I buried my dead mother and felt the earth quaking with a realization that my father had come to Hollow Grove only to inform me of my mother's death. I stared sadly at my father, nailed his presence, and decided to pursue my quest for freedom.

223

I now struggled to feign concern about my mother. "When did she die?"

"A week ago. A coronary."

"At fifty-one? I don't recall Mother ever having a heart condition."

"We buried her Tuesday."

Allowing the evasion, I followed the trail of his words. "What sort of day was it?"

He returned the pipe to his mouth. "Sunny and warm."

"Who was there?"

My father indifferently listed the names of the mayor, a congressman, relatives, friends, and then, quite casually, recounted the services at the Episcopal Church and at the cemetery.

I said, "I'm sorry I wasn't there."

"Everyone understood your absence."

"Including you?"

"Yes."

"Did you miss me?"

"Yes."

I wanted to smile, but I was careful not to. Instead, rather solemnly, I said, "Thank you, Father. I'm ready."

He regarded me quizzically. "Ready?"

"For your questions. I know you must assure yourself that I'm well enough to be taken home."

His eyes were strong on me. "Are *you* assured you're ready to come home?"

"Father, is that your first or your last question?"

"The first."

I asked, "Am I wrong to want my freedom?"

"Freedom from what?"

"This prison."

"Do you feel you've been unjustly imprisoned?"

"Not unjustly," I lied. "The decision to place me here was a wise one. Dr. Dominick's been very good for me. But, for me to remain here any longer would be very unwise."

"Why?" he asked gently.

I spoke the truth now. "I have a faith in home. I utter the

224

names Stephensville and Gedney Street, and I hear hope. A hope for a miracle of healing. Father, perhaps home is where my Lourdes lies."

"Do you believe in miracles?"

Again I suppressed laughter. "No, I'm my father's daughter. The dead don't rise again. The crippled never throw away their crutches." Sensing I was defeating my own cause, I pleaded, "Father, let me try again." He said nothing, and as I groped for reason I noted the rhythm with which he puffed on his pipe. Finally I said, "As a child, first learning to walk, I used the walls of our home to support me. Is it too much to ask of the walls again?"

"You can't return as a child."

"I know that. But reason with me, Father. Which makes more sense? That Mrs. Neff should be my companion? Or that I should be your companion?"

"Rannah, what sort of pact are you trying to make with me?"

"I'm not asking you to be my keeper. If you see yourself only as my keeper, then I don't want to come home again. Not ever again."

"What do you want of me?"

I said, "I want to be there when you light your pipe. When the light comes into your eyes. I want you to talk to me, to listen to me. You're alone now, Father, and Hilda's no companion for you. And I'm alone too. And Mrs. Neff's no companion for me."

As I waited for my father to speak again, I realized I had traded on my mother's death.

My father said, "I have my law practice. I'm alone only when I wish to be alone."

"I'll work. I'd like to work for the *News* again. We could breakfast together, walk downtown together, you to your office, I to the newspaper. Then we could have dinner together."

"Yes," my father said with grave deliberation, "that would be very nice." I smiled too soon. He now added, "Rannah, tell me about your illness."

Then and there I decided not to tell him more than he had

225

asked for. I didn't want him sifting through my verbosity for clues to my insanity. "Didn't Dr. Dominick —?"

"Dr. who?"

I explained about the two doctors Patrone before I tried again. "Didn't Dr. Dominick tell you about me?"

"I want you to tell me about yourself."

I wanted to tell my father to go fuck himself. Instead I said, "Shall I be frank with you, Father?"

"Please."

"This," I confessed, "is very trying for me. I understand your concern, and the wisdom of it. But you do have me at a disadvantage. You do have me on the witness stand. I'd prefer not to ramble and pluck wild arguments. I'd prefer it if you'd be frank and direct with me. If you'd ask me questions."

My father smiled and I loved him again. "Good reasoning. Good awareness. I'm pleased." He paused to structure his attack. "How would you label your illness?"

I uttered the hated word without hate. "Schizophrenia."

"Meaning what? For the layman."

"A split personality. A break with reality."

"Anything else? As it pertains to you."

"I withdrew within myself."

"When did you first sense this illness?"

"In Spain. Do you know about Spain?"

My father said, "Mr. O'Donnell wrote me about your being in a hospital in Barcelona."

"What else did he say?"

"That you had suffered a nervous breakdown, and that you were being given the best of care."

I was suspicious. "Nothing else?"

"Only generalities. No specifics."

"And what you want now are the specifics."

My father nodded. "Who do you blame for your illness?"

"No one. No one but myself," I replied casually.

"You don't blame your heritage?"

"I don't blame anyone but myself. Blood tells me nothing."

My father tapped the stem of his pipe against his teeth.

"Aren't you trying a little too hard to absolve your mother and me?"

I embraced the question, for the answer had come to me at the window shortly before his arrival. I said, "Are you Adam? And was my mother Eve? Did creation begin with you? Life's too brief to search back millions and millions of years with one candle of awareness. No. I blame myself."

No smile, no applause, only another question. "For sins you've committed?"

"Sin is very unoriginal. I don't believe in it, Father."

"There is no right or wrong?"

"Yes, right and wrong, good and bad. I was wrong. I was bad."

"To do what?"

I said, "To question your judgment."

"My judgment about what?"

"Davis O'Donnell. Marrying him was wrong for me. Bad for me."

My father didn't believe me. "When did you first divine this — error of judgment?"

"The first morning I left home. On the road to Atlanta."

"What happened?"

"I slept with Davis. In the woods."

I heard a snap. My father had cracked the stem of his pipe with the reaction of his teeth. "He forced you?"

Equivocating, I said, "I was confused."

"Had you slept with him before?"

"No."

"What confused you?"

"Davis. He wasn't anything like the boy I'd fallen in love with."

"How so?"

"You remember the last dinner at the house? Don't you remember how different he was? How much wiser? It was borrowed wisdom."

My father was intrigued. "Borrowed from whom?"

"A man named Delano Fredericks."

227

The name registered. "I've been reading about Mr. Fredericks."

I winced. "Is he dead?"

"No. But he's announced the death of capitalism."

I was incredulous. "Freddie?"

My father put Freddie out of his mind and asked, "After the incident in the woods, before Atlanta, why did you marry O'Donnell?"

"I was afraid he'd made me pregnant."

"An unfounded fear."

"No, I was pregnant."

"You never mentioned it in any of your letters to your mother."

"Did you read those letters?"

"I did."

I wanted to kiss him. Instead I told him about the pregnancy, the row in the Brooklyn speakeasy, and the miscarriage.

He asked, "What was the extent of your physical injuries?"

"I suffered a concussion."

"Is it possible your brain was damaged then?"

I avoided the pitfall of an easy answer. "Oh, I'd love to say yes and wrap it up in that simplicity. But I don't think that's true at all. Yes, I had a concussion when my head struck stone. But no, that wasn't the reason for or even the beginning of my madness. The fall that hurt me was the fall from grace."

"The grace of God?"

"No," I said, "the grace of conscience. The Gedney conscience."

"Who made you fall?"

"I blame no one but myself."

"What made you fall?"

I had known that question was forthcoming and I had baked an answer for it. "Booze. Bootleg booze. I drank too much. Everybody was drinking too much. I drank *much* too much. For me. Too many lost nights. Too many days without mornings. Too many aspirins and too many hairs of too many dogs. Too many wet towels. Everything was too much. The telephone rang too much. The music was too loud. The motorcars were too fast. Too many parties. People inviting you and trading empty glasses for filled ones. I was too long at the fair."

"You were too long with O'Donnell. Did you ever consider divorce?"

"In 1924. That was when I almost left Davis."

"For what reason? Infidelity?"

"Yes, Father."

"Why did you change your mind about divorce?"

I said, "I made infidelity a two-way street."

My father winced. "At O'Donnell's suggestion?"

"No, to spite him."

"Were you still in love with him?"

"It wasn't a question of love, Father. I was on. I didn't know how to get off."

"On what?"

"The stage of the times. The Jazz Age. I was one of the dazzling O'Donnells. Lee got only as far north as Gettysburg. I invaded and conquered New York."

For once in his life my father wasn't interested in Lee or Gettysburg. He asked, "When did your health really begin to suffer?"

"In France."

"What year?"

"Nineteen twenty-eight. A vintage year for Harry Ingram."

"What was the nature of the ailment?"

Without thinking I said, "Envy."

"Envy?"

"That was Davis's sickness," I explained. "I had the champagne sickness. Then I gave up champagne for muscatel. Harry used to send cases and casks from Tarragona. Tarragona! That used to be such a beautiful name."

"Used to be?"

Warily I said, "That's where it happened. My breakdown."

"You remember it clearly?"

I remembered Dr. Dominick's admonition to speak slowly. "How can I remember clearly what was never clear?"

229

My father pursued me. "How do you remember it?"

"Must I remember it?"

"Please. I know it's difficult for you."

"Then why must I — ?" I stopped, took a deep breath, and said, "Yes, I understand why I must. The witness must be responsive." My body began to itch again, but I only scratched my mind. "I drank too much. I drank mandragora to sleep out this great gap of time. From the gap to the hollow. Hollow Grove! How quaint the names of hells on earth! This is the crater at Petersburg! The sunken road at Waterloo!"

There was no approbation in my father's eyes for a daughter who remembered her Shakespeare and her history. "Rannah, on that day in Tarragona, when did you first suspect that your mind was disturbed?"

I dared not mention that I had heard his voice in the grove. I said, "Something went awry with my senses. Sight and sound and smell. And touch. The sky was green."

"Were you drunk?"

"I was drinking. Muscatel. Under a hazelnut tree."

"And then what?"

"I must've fallen asleep."

"And then?"

"I was attacked."

"By whom?"

"A panther."

"Do you still believe it was a panther?"

"No. I don't believe the sky was green, either."

"What do you believe now?"

"That I was very sick."

"Who attacked you?"

"Madness."

My father tried again. "Who attacked you?"

"Harry Ingram."

"Is that what you believe now?"

"It was Harry. He drove me mad."

"And raped you in the grove?"

"The panther raped me."

230

"There are no panthers in Spain."

"When the skies are green, there are."

My father frowned. "Rannah, I want to be fair. I want to take you home. But you must remember this: I'm cross-examining you. When I ask you a question, I know the answer. And I want you to tell me the truth. To reassure me that you're well enough to distinguish between phantasy and reality. Is that understood?"

"Yes, Father."

"Who attacked you?"

"Will the truth set me free?"

"Yes."

I told my father the truth, and I was amazed by his stoicism, by the absence of his revulsion, and by the depth of his understanding.

Then he asked, "What do you remember after the attack?"

"The sound of bells. From the churches in Barcelona. I was in a hospital. In a padded room. Strapped to a bed."

"Who brought you there?"

"I have no recollection."

"Do you know who found you in the grove?"

"No."

"How long were you in the Barcelona hospital?"

"I don't know."

"Where were you taken from there?"

"Davis took me to Switzerland. To a sanitarium in Zurich."

"How long were you there?"

"Must've been weeks. Then we took a train to Le Havre. And then a boat. The *Majestic*. To New York."

"Do you remember anything about the trip?"

"Yes. I tried to kill myself." I held out my wrists so that he might see the thin white scars.

"Why did you try to kill yourself?"

"I wanted to die. And I couldn't understand why Davis prevented me from dying. Why he wanted me to live."

"Do you understand now?"

"I don't try to."

231

"Rannah, do you remember how you got here?"

"We were met at the dock by Ellis Mason, Davis's literary agent. We got into Mason's car. Davis gave me a pill. I fell asleep in the Holland Tunnel. When I awoke, I was undressed and in bed." I pointed. "In that bedroom."

"Do you remember the date?"

I shook my head. "The last date I remember is April 1, 1930. The day Davis and I set out for Tarragona."

"What is today's date?"

"Today has the look of December. Beyond that what does time matter to me, Father? I know day from night, summer from autumn, winter from spring."

"How've you been treated here?"

"Royally. I have only one complaint."

"And what is that?"

"Hollow Grove is no different from Andersonville. It's a prison. And there's only one way of escape."

"One way?"

"Yes. Through the kindness of your heart."

My father smiled and I felt the warmth of spring. "Very well put."

"Take me home, Father. Please."

Although he failed to respond to my plea, I felt assuaged by a change in his manner. The next question was casual enough to make me believe the inquisition was over. "What's the average stay of a patient here?"

"I don't know."

"Do you know any of the other patients?"

I said, "I see them from time to time. When I quiet my mind by looking out the windows, I see them walking. With their keepers. To the château. I watch them sit under the trees. Watch them throw leaves to the wind, and see the leaves rush over the wall. To freedom."

"Do you go to the château?"

"I'm taken there. For treatments."

"Why haven't you used the library?"

"I don't wish to consort with the other patients."

232

"Why not?"

"Father, why do you think they have cottages here? The design is to separate the patients. I don't believe the company of the mad is conducive to recovery."

"Is it a contagion you fear?"

"Not a contagion. It's nothing you can see under the microscope. It's just strangers huddling together in the cold."

"Who are the other patients?"

I smiled. "You can't accuse me of being a snob. They're all richer than I am. They're filthy rich."

"What are some of their names?"

"I know only one woman by name. Augustine Rivard. The others? The men here include a retired admiral, a rabbi, a steel magnate, a surgeon, an heir to a railroad fortune, and —" I laughed, "a lawyer."

My father smiled. "And the women?"

"One college girl. An English actress. And five wives of wealthy men. Two of them widows. Including Augustine Rivard."

"How do you know Augustine Rivard by name?"

"I was walking one afternoon with Mrs. Neff. And Mrs. Rivard saw us and invited us to visit her cottage. I scowled at her and walked away."

"Why?"

"I don't like July 4, 1929. That's the day Augustine Rivard prefers and preserves behind windows shuttered to keep out the snows that never fall in July and to keep time from bringing her to the winter day when her husband came home from his brokerage office to fire the shot that shattered his head and her mind."

My father watched me draw breath before he casually asked, "Where's your husband?"

"In San Francisco."

"What does it cost to keep you here?"

"A thousand dollars a month."

"And your husband has no problem paying the bills?"

"Oh, he's not paying them. Harry is."

"Harry?"

233

"Harry Ingram."

"Tell me, why is Ingram responsible for your bills?"

"He's doing it to help Davis."

"What is your husband doing in San Francisco?"

"He's working on a novel. About the Snyder-Gray case."

"Do you have his address?"

"No."

"Does he write to you?"

"When he's writing a book he never writes letters."

"And Ingram sends the checks here?"

"No, Ellis Mason pays the bills. He's also Harry's agent."

"How do you know that Ellis Mason pays your bills?"

"Dr. Dominick told me."

The retort shattered my father's head. I saw him dying and heard his dying voice. "Didn't Dr. Patrone also tell you —"

I tore into his question. "Father, what's wrong?"

"Answer my question," he ordered me, and his voice broke the windows, pulled the door from its hinges, and allowed winter to rush in and witness our deaths. "Didn't Dr. Patrone tell you he corresponds regularly with O'Donnell?"

I brought heat to the cold. "Why do you insist on calling him O'Donnell? He was your son-in-law! Can't you call him Davis?"

"Didn't Dr. Patrone tell you that Davis was in Hollywood?"

"Why in hell would he tell me that? Davis is in San Francisco!"

"Rannah, don't excite yourself."

"You're exciting me!"

His voice now had the softness of rot. "Davis isn't in San Francisco. He's in Hollywood, employed by a motion picture studio. He — not Harry Ingram — is paying your bills. Dr. Patrone told you all of this. Don't you remember?"

I didn't remember and I was quick to demand, "Why would Davis want to pay my bills? Is it part of the divorce settlement?"

Sadly my father said, "Your husband hasn't divorced you."

I was confused. "Why? Because he's Catholic?"

"He's made no mention of desiring a divorce. And, moreover,

he can't divorce you now. In the state of California, incurable insanity is grounds for divorce only after the wife has been committed for a period of three years to a recognized mental institution, private or public.''

I shouted, ''Are you saying I'm incurably insane?''

''Please, lower your voice.''

''My God! You come here, raise my hopes, dash them, and then tell me to lower my voice! Are you or aren't you taking me home?''

''One day soon perhaps —''

''Today! Make it today!''

My father wept a lone tear for me. ''Forgive me, Rannah, but you're not well. You can't be and fail to distinguish between reality and phantasy.''

''Are you real, Father?''

My father rose, crossed to the bedroom door, knocked, and opened it. He said, ''Mrs. Neff, would you summon Dr. Patrone?''

Mrs. Neff appeared, looked obliquely at me, and touched a bell that sounded in the château.

I confronted my father again. ''What do you want with Dr. Dominick?''

''I merely want him to join us. Perhaps we can set another date. Perhaps next spring.''

The words wound about me. ''Date? Spring? What are you talking about?''

''Rannah, you need more time to recuperate.''

''Dr. Dominick wants you to take me home! Today!''

''If he tells me that, I'll do so.''

I folded my itching arms and scratched them. ''You're too sure he won't!''

''Rannah, we'll let him decide.''

''Damn you! You know you're not about to take me home. You never wanted to. You tricked me with your questions. I know your courtroom tactics. Relax the witness, divert him, lull him, and then in all innocence pose the question that will destroy him. Where's Davis O'Donnell? Is that a question a loving

235

father asks his troubled daughter? Isn't it rather a courtroom question?''

"I love you. I'd give my life to bring back yours," my father said.

But it was too late in the morning, too late in time, for I was trailing the tobacco smoke to phantasy. "You want to bury me. You spoke to me in Tarragona. You told me you were going to bury me by the river. Why are you burying me alive in Pennsylvania?"

I saw the inquisitor's alert look. "I spoke to you in Spain?"

"Yes!" I screamed. "Before and after you raped me!" The mask of the inquisitor fell away, and I saw my father put his head upon the block and wait for the blow that would sever his head and take him from the sound of my voice. "You murdered Mother! You wanted her out of the way! You wanted me! You've wanted me ever since the day you saw me naked in Mother's room! Standing before the mirror! In my white bloomers! And my budding pink breasts! You wanted me and you took me in Tarragona! I heard you! You spoke to me! 'It's me. Daddy. Only me. Daddy. It's Daddy.' I heard you!"

He heard me and must have wished he had never been born. He shut his eyes to dam his tears.

But I didn't desist. "How did you murder Mother?"

"With silence. *Mea culpa.*"

"Don't speak Latin! I hate the Latin of priests and physicians and lawyers! And incestuous fathers! You're afraid to take me home! You're afraid I'll tell the police you murdered Mother! You're afraid!"

My forearms were bloody now as my nails tore at my flesh. Opening his eyes, my father frowned at the sight. He spoke to me now as a father to an errant child. "Rannah, stop it."

I fell to my knees, assumed the height of a child, and let hysteria have its way with me. "Take-me-home-Father-I-won't-tell-the-police-I'll-be-good-I'll-sleep-in-your-bed-and-we'll-make-love-in-all-the-ways-of-love-that-I've-learned-you'll-love-me-Father-and-I'll-love-you-and-we'll-keep-the-shutters-closed-and-the-doors-shut-and-we'll-drink-bourbon-and-muscatel-and-read-books-

236

together-and-we'll-be-so-happy —" The door to the cottage burst open and I saw Dr. Marybelle enter, her face set and her thin lips white as snow. I screamed, "Father, save me!"

He said nothing, did nothing. He hardly stirred as Mrs. Neff pinned me and muscled me into the bedroom and into bed. After she had stabbed me, Dr. Marybelle said, "Rest now. Close your eyes."

I heard her voice as a reprimand from a schoolroom drifting past me. "I hate you," I said. "I'm never going to bring you an apple again."

Three days later, after swimming that branch of the Nile that flowed through the château, I was borne back to the palace of my cottage. I was lying in bed and wondering about the phantoms of reality and the flesh and blood of phantasy when Dr. Dominick came in. Instead of a smile, he brought me contrition.

"Rannah, forgive me. I didn't know your mother was dead, and I didn't realize the nature of your father's visit."

I said, "I have no father."

"I had a cup of coffee with him."

"Doctor, I don't want to hear about my dead father."

He regarded me sadly. "I coached you and coached you. Was the truth so difficult?"

"When will I stop thinking Davis is in San Francisco?"

"When you stop believing that Harry Ingram is paying to keep you here."

"Paranoia?"

"If you can spell it, you can think it." I said nothing, and he continued. "About those voices. I thought we had it straight. Who spoke to you in the grove at Tarragona?"

"Dandy Flood," I said correctly.

"And what did he say?"

" 'It's me. Dandy. Only me. Dandy. It's Dandy.' "

Dr. Dominick sighed. "You tried. That's the important thing, to try and try again."

"Doctor, will my father come back for me?"

"Do you remember what you said to him?"

I remembered and I said, "I have no father."

237

"That's true, Rannah. He'll never come here again, and I doubt if he'd ever consent now to take you home."

"If you should write to him, tell him I understand. Tell him I'm sorry."

I was back in Stephensville ringing the doorbell when I heard not the sound of a bell but the softness of a simple question. "Where is Davis O'Donnell?"

"In San Francisco."

The question, honed with pain, was repeated. "Where is Davis O'Donnell?"

I looked at Dr. Dominick and gasped. "Hollywood!"

Now he sang the song of inquisition. "And where is Mrs. O'Donnell?"

"Hollow Grove."

"And where does Mrs. O'Donnell want to be?"

"He doesn't want me. He doesn't love me any more."

"Your father?"

"My husband."

"Listen to me, Mrs. O'Donnell." He stared at me with Mesmer's eyes. "Your husband loves you and wants you in Hollywood. Is that understood?"

"I understand. But when?"

"When you're well enough again."

"The other day you thought I was well enough to go home with my father."

"It was a try."

"A lie?"

"I said *try*. T-R-Y."

"Doctor, I don't understand you."

"I was for Stephensville, but I'm not yet for Hollywood."

"Why not?"

"It's too soon for both of you. Your husband is having his own problems. The adjustment to a new career is very difficult for him. His sense of pride is failing and he feels a loss of status. Moreover, he has tremendous guilt feelings about your illness."

I asked the key question. "Does he really want me?"

238

"He misses you. And, let's be frank about it, he misses the thousand dollars a month it's costing him to keep you here."

"How long will it be before I can go to Davis?"

"I don't know."

"Make a guess, please."

"Rannah, I can't. It depends not only on your progress, but on your husband's."

"What are you saying? You're making it sound as if Davis is sick. As if he's in a sanitarium in Hollywood."

"He lives in an apartment in Hollywood. He works in an office in a movie studio. He's working hard, and it's hard to work when you're sick."

"Sick? What's wrong with him?"

"I want you to tell me."

I told him. "His wife's mad. His career's shot."

"And he drinks too much," Dr. Dominick added. "But I don't want to worry you unnecessarily. He's functioning, he's trying his damnedest, and he loves you. Does that make you feel better?"

"Some."

"Well enough to have another visitor tomorrow?"

I leapt for the moon. "Davis?"

"What's your second choice?"

I fell to earth and felt battered and bruised. "I don't want to see anyone. Not the way I look."

"Not even Guy Thurlow?"

The name held music and magic. "Guy! Is Guy coming here? Why is he coming here?"

"He's leaving for California in a few days to cover the Rose Bowl game and visit a friend named Davis O'Donnell."

I clapped my hands. "What time will he be here?"

"About noon. I'm just as anxious to see him as you are. He once gave me a nice write-up in a big game against Cornell in —" He checked his exuberance. "Rannah, I'm sorry about your mother. We'll talk about —"

"Doctor, did I kill her?"

"You were right here."

239

"Wasn't that exactly what killed her? My being right here?"

"Your mother was bedridden for months."

"Since last April?"

He shook his head. "You should've practiced law instead of the Charleston."

"No jokes, Doctor."

"Your father blames himself and not you. So what do you make of that, Portia?"

I didn't answer. Dr. Dominick departed. Once I was alone again, I said, "I make nightmares."

Sleep redeemed my presentiment and took me directly to Stephensville, to the bed where my mother lay with death.

"Rannah, baby, stay with me."

I escaped her outstretched hand, stole a dime from her purse, and ran away. I gave the dime to Guy Thurlow, who was the man at the box office window of the Bijou Theater in Stephensville. Inside the theater I found that I was alone and afraid. I could hear the music, but I could see no one at the piano. I could see the screen, and I saw Davis making love to Anna May Wong in a San Francisco Chinatown opium den. Then the screen went black and darkness enveloped the theater for a moment in which I broke from my seat and attempted to flee. I was pounding against barred doors when I saw the arc light of the projector pierce the dark. The beam struck not the screen but the floor of the seatless theater. And now I saw my mother sitting beside an open coffin. She was calling me.

"Rannah, baby, come here."

I ran to her. "Mother, what are you doing here?"

"I died. Look at me. I'm dead."

"Mother, you're talking to me."

"Oh, my baby, look inside the coffin."

I looked and saw my mother lying there dead. Then I turned to my mother sitting in the chair. "You are dead, Mother. What did you die of?"

"Shame, my baby."

"Shame?"

"Jesus heard you, I heard you. Jesus saw you, I saw you, Oh, my baby, my poor baby, who ran from the hazelnut grove to hide behind walls with crazy folks.''

"Mother, I'm here."

"Don't stand there, Rannah, baby. Come with me to Jesus to wash away your sins. Get in the coffin. Lie down with me."

I turned away from my mother sitting in the chair and stared at the body in the coffin. Then, as I stood petrified, the arms of my mother in the coffin rose slowly to embrace me, to draw me into the coffin.

I screamed and opened a door at Hollow Grove. Mrs. Neff rushed into the bedroom. She tried to comfort me. At length she moved away.

The child in me protested. "It's too dark. Don't leave me."

Mrs. Neff sat down in a chair. "I sit here. I wait for you to sleep. Close your eyes. Sleep."

"Sing to me," I said to my mother.

And Mrs. Neff answered, "I can't sing. I never sang, even as a girl. Never any singing in my house. My father was very strict."

"You like singing?"

"I like to listen."

I said, "My mother used to sing to me. She had a lovely voice."

And then, in the awesome dark, in the coffin of the cottage bedroom, I opened my mouth and let my mother's voice rise and leaven the nightmare into a dream.

Early in the morning the December winds delivered a rain that flirted with hail and snow. After breakfast I took up my vigil at the sitting room window, spending the hours chasing the clouds and trying to clear the roads from New York for Guy Thurlow, the confederate certain to deliver me from evil. He arrived shortly before noon in a Peerless sedan which I saw as the getaway car. I was as warm as the sun as I watched him extract his tall frame from the automobile. Holding a package under one arm, he walked on the water of the rain with a majesty that knew no barriers.

I was at the door to greet him and, when he removed his battered hat, I saw the crown of snow on his bald head marking the winter of his life. As always in the flush of reunion, we kissed as lovers. Then, as we sat down with reality, I listened to Guy give me tidings of his wife and his three growing daughters. Ruby was fourteen, Anita twelve, Lucy eight, and I was much younger and left alone on a Long Island beach with a sand castle crumbling in the rain.

Then I said, "Guy, if you passed me on Fifth Avenue today, would you recognize me?"

242

He smiled. "You think you've changed. You should see Fifth Avenue."

"What's New York like today?"

"As gray as my pallor. I'll be glad to get to California for a while."

"When are you leaving?"

"Sunday night."

"Alone?"

"Yeah. It's a little early for the other boys going out to cover the game. I have to go up to San Simeon to see the Chief."

"You stop first in Los Angeles, don't you?"

"Right. I wrote Davis to meet me for dinner Thursday night at the Biltmore Hotel."

"I want to be there," I whispered.

"I want you to be there. Next year in Los Angeles."

The door to the bedroom was shut, but I whispered again to keep Mrs. Neff from overhearing. "Take me with you."

Guy averted his face from my stare and glanced about the room. "Nice place you've got here. You'd have to be crazy to want to leave."

"No, Guy?"

His face was drawn. "No, Rannah. Next year. Even the Count of Monte Cristo wouldn't try it this year. It's been a lousy year."

I looked out the window and saw Guy and Davis dining at the Biltmore in Los Angeles. "Guy, you won't tell Davis, will you?"

"Tell him what?"

"How horrible I look."

Guy waited until I turned to him again. "How can I? You'll always be beautiful to me."

"It's my skin. This terrible eczema."

"Tell Guy the Medicine Man if you itch."

"I itch."

"Good sign. Means you're itching to get well."

I smiled with Guy and remembered how I hadn't smiled with my father. I said, "Where you're sitting now, my father sat the other day."

243

"I heard he was here."

I didn't know what he had heard, and I told him all about the inquisition that had left me upon the rack. Guy listened and looked at me with love and compassion.

Finally he said, "I'm sorry about your mother."

My mind flooded with my father, I asked, "What about my mother?"

"I'm sorry she's dead."

I smiled to assuage him. "It's all right. She's all right this morning. She only died in my nightmare. Only a nightmare." Guy's face now looked like rainswept marble and his eyes were blind and searching for light. "Guy, you look so very, very sad."

"That's what the Chief says. And that's why I'm going to San Simeon."

"I don't understand."

"Rannah, I'm losing touch with reality. I have to get away from New York. Have to touch and feel the reality of San Simeon. I have to find out that prosperity hasn't left us, that it sits on a hill overlooking the Pacific." He laughed. "The Chief wants me to be funnier than ever."

"Doesn't he understand how sad you really are?"

"If he did, he'd never renew my contract. The Chief's an optimist. He believes the jester can save the king."

I remembered a time when Delano Fredericks referred to Guy as "the jester." And I asked, "Guy, do you ever see Freddie?"

"Not in over a year. And I miss him. Freddie has no time for Hearst hirelings. He's too busy beating the drums for Marx. And I don't mean the Brothers."

I plucked another memory. "I remember you once saying you'd throw out the first bomb if you were President of the United States."

And Guy said, "I remember that. I remember everything I said to you, and everything you said to me." He clapped his hands to chase reverie and summon humor. "Yeah, but Herbie's in the White House. And he can't throw a chicken over the plate."

244

"Guy, you're not making sense."

"What the hell, it's raining."

I now asked, "Ever see Harry Ingram?"

"Don't expect to. Not till they extend the subway to Spain."

"Is he still in Tarragona?"

"Tarragona? I thought he was in the money."

"You know he's the reason, don't you?"

"The reason?"

"Harry's the reason I'm here."

Guy shifted uneasily. "Well, that's a lousy reason."

We weren't connecting. "What is?"

"Harry. He's a lousy reason."

"Don't you like Harry?"

"I'm just mild about Harry."

"Guy, why don't you like him?"

"Any reason of yours is a reason of mine."

"Guy, you keep talking like this and they'll put you away."

"Who's They? Harry Ingram and who else?"

"Dandy Flood."

"He's dead," said Guy indifferently.

"Dandy Flood? Are you sure?"

"Somebody must've been sure. They buried him last October."

"You're joking."

"I am, but I shouldn't be. I covered the funeral."

"How did he die?"

"Hard. It took three white punks with pistols. Happened in a speakeasy in Harlem. A place run by Willie Brant, one of Dandy's old sparring partners. The punks were sticking up the joint. Willie opened the cash register. Dandy opened his mouth and took on three guns. It was the mismatch of the century. Dandy went down and the hospital surgeon counted ten slugs."

I asked, "Did you like Dandy Flood?"

"A great heavyweight. To the last," he said seriously.

"He knocked out Harry Ingram."

"Like I said, a writer should stick to his last."

"Did you like Dandy as a person?"

"Outside the ring?"

245

"Yes."

"Nobody likes a tiger outside his cage. If you mean did I like Dandy Flood the way I liked Bert Williams, the answer is no."

Contrite, I asked, "Did you hear about Dandy and me?"

The question jolted him. "I heard, and I wept."

"Who told you?"

"Davis, and he wept."

"And who told Davis?"

"Harry."

"And who told Harry?"

"Dandy Flood, who also wept."

"Did Harry weep?"

"Yeah. For Dandy and Davis, but not for you."

I returned to Tarragona. "Did Davis tell you about the night before? About Harry coming to our bedroom?"

Guy nodded gravely. "I heard. I heard everything."

"From Davis?"

"Yeah. Before he left for the Coast."

"San Francisco?"

"Hollywood," he corrected.

"Why Hollywood?"

"Because Hollywood wanted him. The way Dandy Flood wanted you."

I winced. "Guy, that's cruel."

"It's the truth."

I looked out the window and saw Davis swimming in a Hollywood pool. "You're not happy about Davis being out there, are you?"

"Why should I be? He isn't."

"Why did he go? Just to support me and keep me here?"

"He had to go somewhere."

"What happened to San Francisco? Harry was going to lend him the money to finish the novel."

Guy said, "Harry also wanted to lend him the money to pay your country club dues."

"Why didn't Davis take his damned money?"

"For one thing, Davis had given up on the Snyder-Gray novel. He had another one in mind."

246

"And what was that?"

"A novel about you, and your breakdown."

"And Harry discouraged him," I concluded.

"No, he encouraged him. Harry's sore as a son of a bitch that Davis sold out to Hollywood."

"Someone must've discouraged Davis," I surmised.

Guy nodded slowly. "Freddie."

"Freddie! Why would —"

"Freddie told Davis to forget the novels. Both novels. Freddie said the twenties were dead, to hell with the era. He advised Davis to get religion."

"Religion?"

"Marx."

"Did Davis tell Freddie — did he ask him about going there? To Hollywood, I mean."

"He did. And Freddie said Hollywood was just the place for him. He did everything but put Davis on the train."

"Why?"

"He knew Davis'd be of no use on the barricades."

"Guy, was Freddie right about Hollywood?"

Guy was pained. "What difference does it make whether Freddie or Harry was right or wrong? What bothers me is that Davis had to cry for help."

"Did Davis ask you what to do?"

"He did. But I'm a lush. I give booze, not advice. Then Davis said to me: 'You know, I've got to do this for Rannah.' Sure, I love the guy. But I gave him a dirty look and said to him: 'What about God, country, and Yale?'"

"Did he laugh?"

"No. And then I said: 'You sure you're not doing this for spite? You sure you're not just spiting Rannah?'"

"And what did Davis say to that?"

"He yelled. Loud enough to wake God, country, and Yale. What was he supposed to do? I told him to go home. I was just chasing him, and he took it for a piece of advice. 'What home?' he asked. And I tried to make it funny. I said: 'All you need is four rooms. One for the booze, one for the typewriter, one for the plumbing, and one for the dame from Georgia.'"

247

I stirred from my chair, fell to my knees, took Guy's hands and kissed them. "And then what did Davis say?"

"He said: 'One of these days.'"

"How long must I wait?"

"Rannah, I don't know. When I see him next week, I'll tell him how anxious you are to leave."

I turned to the window again and saw Davis dancing with a girl in the Coconut Grove of the Ambassador Hotel. "Maybe he's happy without me."

"Listen to me, Rannah," Guy said. "He's not at all happy. He's boozing it up worse than ever."

"Guy, whatever became of Joel Stone?"

"I don't know. He's either in hiding somewhere or locked in a barrel of cement on the floor of the East River."

I looked at Guy and laughed loud and long. "It was all a joke, wasn't it?"

"What was a joke?"

"Your sending us over to Joel Stone's. That Sunday night."

He nodded. "It's all in a joke book now. The Great American Joke. The Great American Novel, which it is. I'm talking about *North Shore*."

I said, "I don't read any more."

Guy glanced at the easel near the windows. "I see you paint."

"I don't paint."

"How do you spend your time?"

"I don't spend it. I *do* time. I'm a prisoner. I think of escape. True escape. Not the escape of daydreams, nightdreams, nightmares, hallucinations. Dr. Dominick wants me to paint. But I don't want to paint. I don't want to weave baskets or paint pretty pictures. It's part of the trap. The trapdoor that drops you back to childhood."

Guy nodded sagely. "We all play games, and some of us get to the Rose Bowl. Who do you like? Alabama or Washington State?"

"How fares Yale?"

"They had a great season. Frank Merriwell came back enrolled as Albie Booth. A thin and obvious disguise."

248

I looked out the window and saw Davis and me sitting in the rain at Yale Bowl. "Davis must be happy about that."

Guy nodded. "Sure. You see, this Albie Booth is about Davis's size. Another Davis against the Goliaths."

"Or Davis against Rannah."

"He loves you."

I said forcefully, "Tell him this for me: if he loves me, let him send me a one-way ticket to Hollywood. That's what I want for Christmas."

This demand was followed by the entrance of Dr. Dominick, and for the next hour, over lunch, I listened to Guy and him talk football. Loving them and the sound of their voices, I was able to comprehend the legends of the shoulder-padded heroes. Also, because it was the kind of talk that Davis always enjoyed, I imagined, in the moments when I had my eyes on my veal cutlet, that Davis was with us and we were all sitting together in the tavern warmth of a Manhattan restaurant. Truly it was a good hour, and when Dr. Dominick opened the door to return to the château, I was grieved to feel again the chill and fright of Hollow Grove.

I turned my alarm on Guy. "Please tell Davis this: if he doesn't love me, but only has pity for me, he's to stop sending the money that's imprisoning me." I found myself laughing. "I want to be evicted from the premises. For nonpayment of rent. Thrown out on the sidewalk." Again I laughed. "Guy, I'm laughing. But I'm serious. Please, don't make a note of my laughter."

"No laughter," said Guy soberly.

"You understand, don't you, Guy? The longer I stay here, the worse I'll get."

"I understand. I'll try to make Davis understand." He stood to prepare me for his leavetaking.

I embraced him. "Oh, Guy, I love you."

He spoke in another voice, perpetuating the illusion of our love. "I love you, Rannah."

"I love you as much as I love Davis. You understand that, don't you?"

249

"I understand. It's like I told Edna once."

"Edna?"

"My wife."

I laughed nervously. "I'm sorry. My mind —. My mind. Period. What did you tell Edna?"

"I said, 'Rannah loves me as much as she loves Davis, because Davis and I are one and the same person.' And Edna said to me: 'And who would that be?' And I said: 'We're both the Phantom of the Opera. Davis is the masked phantom and I'm the phantom unmasked.'"

Although it was one of the saddest things I had ever heard, I absolved us both with laughter. I said, "I'm sorry, Guy, but there's a long waiting list for these cottages. You certainly qualify, though."

Guy laughed along with me. "You make me want to cry. You say such nice things."

I embraced him again. I whispered in his ear, "You'll save me, won't you?"

And he said, "If Davis doesn't listen to me and take you away from here, I'll throw him to the M-G-M lion."

I was all right until Guy crowned his unmasked face with the battered hat and then drew his overcoat over his lean frame. He opened the cottage door. I looked through the rain and saw the Peerless, a carriage that had grown from the pumpkin of my dream of escape.

I rushed past Guy, startling him. As I ran, the rain felt gentle on my eyelids. I opened the rear door of the Peerless, shut it behind me, and lay down on the floor of the car. Guy finally appeared. He slid behind the wheel.

Sadly he said, "Rannah, where do you want to go?"

Still lying on the floor, I said, "Philadelphia. Take me to Philadelphia. I'll take the train from there to Stephensville."

"Your father doesn't want you at home."

"I know. But I'll hide in the attic. Mother will hide me."

I heard the rain, but no one heard me. And then I heard the thunder of doors and gates clapping shut.

250

3.

The corpse from California, who each and every month of my stay at Hollow Grove had sent me candied fruit that gave no sweetness, delivered himself for his wake on the dusk of an otherwise lost June day in 1933.

With Mrs. Neff shadowing me, I had taken a long, lazy stroll about the green and blooming grounds. Returning to the cottage, I saw a maroon Studebaker with New York license plates parked outside. Instead of entering the cottage, I went to the window and peered into the sitting room. I saw the corpse standing and beholding, with eyes crying for the cover of pennies, the two books in my library — the Holy Bible and a novel by Davis O'Donnell entitled *In Battalions*.

When I entered, the corpse embraced me with a tenderness appropriate for distant cousins. I introduced him to my keeper, who quickly retired to the bedroom to leave me alone with my late husband.

I said, "Don't you recognize Rannah Gedney?"

"Three years."

We sat down. "It's my head, too."

"I don't understand," he said warily.

"Dr. Dominick told me about a madwoman who couldn't

251

recognize herself in a mirror. She came to believe she'd been guillotined, and that the wrong head had been sewn back. She went around saying: 'Mine was so beautiful.' "

Despite *rigor mortis,* he managed the ghost of a smile. "I recognize your gallows humor."

I had no answering smile. "I avoid mirrors."

He said, "I look in the mirror and see my father."

"How old were you when you died?"

They say the nails of the dead grow. I can attest that their smiles also grow. "I'm thirty-seven. And I detect a faint heartbeat. At times."

"You'd better rap hard on the coffin lid. You look dead to me."

I saw the teeth of his smile now and I imagined the skeleton face. He said, "The dead don't acquire second chins. Or pots."

"You are dead. Even your smile is dead. What killed you?"

He shook his head. "You're performing the autopsy. You tell me."

"You were stabbed to death."

"By whom?"

"By guilt," I declared.

"Guilt about what?"

"Conspiring with Harry. To smite me with madness. To imprison me. To free yourself from me."

"Rannah, I'm not free of you."

"The dead are free. Shall I tell you what also killed you?"

"Please."

"Success and failure. Harry's success, your failure."

"True."

"Harry has a new book out, doesn't he?"

Davis said, "I thought you didn't read the papers."

"I don't. I just read the news printed on your dead face. What's Harry's book about?"

"A bullfighter."

"What's the title?"

"*Duel at Pamplona.*"

"And you thought the book was great."

Davis nodded. "The reviews were raves. And it's selling big. Very big."

"And Hollywood wants it, of course. How much has Harry turned down so far?"

"A quarter of a million. From Paramount."

I took a dagger to the corpse. "And how many readers have paid two dollars and fifty cents for your latest novel?"

He said, "You're holding the inquest. You tell me."

I contradicted him: "It's an Irish wake we're holding. And you can bring in your whiskey bottle, your flask, or whatever the source of your fragrance is."

"I don't need a drink."

"Your book is dead. And it probably didn't sell ten thousand copies."

"Just under nine," he said from just under the lid of his coffin.

"Who gave you the title? Harry?"

"Shakespeare. From *Hamlet*. 'When sorrows come, they come not as single spies, but in battalions.' "

"Good Shakespeare. Bad O'Donnell. Lousy title. Who found it for you in *Bartlett's?* Harry?"

"I found it myself."

I laughed. "You may've opened *Bartlett's,* but it was Harry who placed your finger upon that particular quotation. *In Battalions!* Sounds just like Harry Ingram. The ring of war, battle, and soldiers. You must've shivered with discovery and delight. Eureka! A title for your novel. Your *war* novel!"

"What war?" Davis demanded.

"Freud sees life as a battlefield. Dr. Dominick told me that. And, oh yes, he liked the book very much. So did Dr. Marybelle."

The praise meant nothing to him. "So they wrote me."

Continuing the inquest, I said, "And Guy loved the book, didn't he?"

Davis nodded.

"And Harry said the book'll never die, didn't he?"

"Something like that."

"But the reviews were no good, were they?"

"They stank."

"And Freddie never bothered to review it at all, did he?"

Davis regarded me with amazement. "How'd you know that?"

"I remembered something Guy told me. He said you'd told Freddie the idea of the novel. And Freddie advised you to forget it and go to Hollywood."

"That's close enough to the truth."

"But you didn't forget it," I said. "You worked on it for two years. Nights and weekends when you weren't working at the studio."

"Thanks. You're very kind."

"Isn't that the truth?"

"No. I wrote the novel in my office. At the studio. On company time."

"With the studio's permission?"

"No. They were paying me a thousand a week to adapt other writers' novels."

"You were fired, weren't you?"

"The contract was terminated. Three months ago."

"They found out you were writing the book on their time."

Davis shook his head. "Worse than that. They found out that dead men tell no tales."

"That's clever," I said.

"Just another way of saying I never wrote anything that got on the screen."

"Perhaps you never were in Hollywood. I was sure you were in San Francisco."

"I heard about that."

"I couldn't imagine you in Hollywood."

"Why not?"

I said, "I knew how Harry felt about Hollywood. I couldn't imagine Harry allowing you to go there."

"Harry was against it. He fought me hard."

"Why did he lose?"

"Can't you understand why?"

254

"You couldn't bring yourself to borrow the money from Harry. To pay my bills here at Hollow Grove."

Davis sighed. "Harry never offered to lend me —"

"I remember, in Tarragona, Harry saying he'd give you five hundred a month to — "

"He never offered to pay your bills," Davis said sharply. "And he thinks I've been a fool to keep you here."

I had no difficulty remaining calm. "What alternative course did Harry suggest?"

Davis looked away. "What's the difference?"

"Did he suggest pushing me overboard on the *Majestic?*"

"No. Harry told me to take you home."

"What home?"

"Stephensville. To your family."

"And then what? Have them commit me to the state hospital? Is that what Harry wanted?"

"No. But it was what I was afraid of."

"Did you voice this fear to Harry?"

"Yes."

"And what did he say?"

"He told me to save myself."

"And to hell with me," I concluded.

"Harry was right about Hollywood."

Swerving abruptly, I asked, "How much money do you owe the Patrones?"

"Your bills are all paid up."

"You make that sound as if I were checking out of here tonight. Am I?"

"Are you ready to leave?"

I hesitated. "Is the choice mine?"

"All yours."

"And if I left here with you, where would you take me?"

"First to New York."

"The Plaza?"

"If you wish. We'd see the Thurlows, the Masons. And then we'd take a boat to California."

255

Quickly I jumped ship. "I don't like boats any more. I didn't like the *Majestic*. I don't like the ocean. The waves beckon me."

With the indifference of the dead, Davis said, "We'll take the train."

"To San Francisco?"

"To Woodland Hills."

"Woodland Hills. Where is that?"

And Davis answered with the exuberance of a cemetery-plot salesman. "In the San Fernando Valley. Less than an hour from Hollywood."

"Who's buried there?"

Ignoring my jibe, he said, "There's a ranch house there. Two bedrooms and a den. An acre of land. A beautiful hillside setting."

"And what will *you* do there?"

"Write."

"Write what?"

"Original stories. For the movies. I sold one last month for five thousand dollars. I figure to —"

I interrupted him. "Whose house is it?"

"I've leased it for a year, and I've got an option to buy it. For six thousand dollars."

I smelled death. "What kind of story did you sell for five thousand dollars?"

"Warner Brothers bought it. It's called *Highway to Hell*. What it really is is my old Snyder-Gray idea turned into a gangster picture. Madame Bovary meets the twentieth-century Jesse James."

I rallied a touch of pity. "Don't you write any more?"

He said, "I've got lots of ideas for original stories. I can open the morning newspaper and come up with at least one good idea."

I repeated the question for the West Coast. "Don't you write any more?"

And the sage answered, "Times've changed. Do you realize how many millions of people see a movie? All around the world?"

256

"Why'd you give up?"

"You know what the royalties on nine thousand copies are?"

"Why'd you give up?" I repeated.

Allergic to the dust of his tomb, he coughed. "Freddie gave up on me."

"You wrote *In Battalions. After* Freddie gave up on you. Why'd you surrender your life?"

"Surrender my life? I'm alive."

I had no compulsion to shout. Instead I spoke gently. "You're dead. If you don't have a novel in the typewriter, you're dead. You know it. Why'd you give up?"

"You tell me."

"No, I'll tell you if you're lying to yourself."

And the tattered and tarnished soldier said, "I've been to Appomattox."

I was cruel. "Don't hide behind metaphors."

"I've surrendered my pen to Harry."

"That's the same metaphor."

He said, "I don't write any more. I can't write any more. Harry's made my writing unnecessary. Is that plain enough?"

"I recognize stupidity."

"That's the way it is."

"And I recognize cowardice, but I don't understand it. Because you're not a coward. You're just stupid. You rival Harry the way Yale rivals Harvard."

"I hear you," Davis muttered.

"And I've heard you, O'Donnell, when you were alive and made more sense. I know where your war is, where your battle is. It's not you against Harry. It's you against the blank page. And I don't mean movie scenarios or magazine stories. You know exactly what I mean."

Pained, he asked, "Do you know what year this is?"

"I couldn't care less."

"It's 1933. There's a depression on. Freddie's on a soapbox, and there's a Harvard man I voted for in the White House."

I said, "It's very difficult for the mad to have a dialogue with the dead. I think we need an interpreter."

257

Davis waved an impatient hand. "I'll agree you're not mad if you'll agree I'm not dead."

"And then what shall we do? Take a year's lease on a sand castle?"

Davis stood up and stalked about the room. Continuing the charade of persuading me he wasn't dead, he brought the anguish of the wounded to his voice. "What do you want of me? I've been trying to explain to you that it no longer profits me to write novels. There's a life to be led in California, gold to be mined in those studios. And —"

"Thank you, Horace Greeley."

"You want to talk about *art*?"

"I'd love to, Mr. O'Donnell."

"Now I'm going to express a fresh opinion to you. But one that I've honestly come to believe. The motion picture is the finest art form yet invented by man. Far superior to novels, to plays, to opera."

I said, "I believe you. I sense your conviction. But you remind me of a horse in a pasture watching a motorcar pass by. Does the horse think he's obsolete? Does the horse rush down to the blacksmith and trade in his horseshoes for four balloon tires?" Again a charade, this time Davis bursting his coffin with laughter whose authenticity shocked me into raising my voice. "You're a novelist! Run! Run to the nearest typewriter! Run over the Freddies and the Harrys! Run! Die running!"

Davis sat down again. "I wish I owed Corbell a book. But all I owe them is money. And they don't want another book from me. At least they haven't asked for one. And Mason? He's a realist. He knows what year this is. He's for the Hollywood gold."

With scorn I said, "Hollywood gold! How about the Hollywood girls?" Davis neither replied nor indicated that he had heard me. I tried again. "How's your sex life?"

Davis faced me and I saw tears in his eyes. "My sex life?" He paused like a boy called upon to recite before the class. "I shook hands once with Greta Garbo. No erection. Danced with Jean Harlow at a party. No erection."

"You are indeed dead," I said.

258

"I had my orgies," he said absently. "I'd ring for my secretary. Marge. She's twenty-two. I'd dictate a few paragraphs of a treatment. Study her breasts. Her legs. Then I'd find myself telling her the latest dirty story going around. She'd only smile. So I'd dismiss her and take my erection to the couch. Shut my eyes, fade out Hollywood, fade in exterior Georgia highway. Day. Camera holds on a 1920 Apperson. Pans to the woods, and dollies in for a close-up of a boy and a girl making love. Yes, I have my orgies. I masturbate."

"And what do you do for penance?"

Davis didn't hear me. "When I was writing the book. Writing those love scenes in —"

"What book are you talking about?"

"*In Battalions.*"

"Oh."

"Do you remember the love scene in the Paris taxi?"

Bewildered, I asked, "What year was that?"

"I'm talking about the book. The scene in the book."

"I haven't read the book."

This revelation caused Davis to blink, to glance at the table where his book stood next to the Bible, and then to turn to me again. "You've had the book since early March."

I was unabashed. "Yes, and Dr. Dominick wants me to read it."

"Then why haven't you?"

I said, "I'm in the middle of a ghost story."

"A ghost story?"

I got up, took the Bible, and handed it to Davis. "Here."

He studied me rather than the Bible. "No desire at all to read my book? Or should I say *your* book?"

I grabbed the Bible from his limp hands. "*This* is my book."

"I had such hopes," Davis said forlornly.

"About what?"

"*In Battalions.* I hoped for a miracle. A sale of a hundred thousand copies. A Pulitzer prize. A big deal with Hollywood. I hoped for a miracle. I worked for a miracle."

I turned the dagger. "You were only masturbating."

259

Now I saw the miracle of a smile on the face of the dead. "I was trying to tell you before that when I was writing that Paris taxi scene in my book — that scene between you and me — I had an orgasm at the typewriter."

"Perhaps that was the miracle you were really working for."

"Very funny. I'll have to remember that. I may tell it over drinks. To drunks. No, that wasn't the miracle I was working for."

"What was?" I was curious now.

Davis took and held the copy of his novel as a father might hold a sick child. "You see this book every day, don't you?"

"Of course."

"Yet you never tried to read it?"

"I've never so much as opened it."

"You know that it's dedicated to you, don't you?"

"Dr. Dominick told me. What was the miracle you worked for?"

The decapitated Davis O'Donnell held his head upon one knee and became a ventriloquist. "It was a delusion. I thought my book would save you. I thought you'd read it. And the magic of the words, like a magnet, would draw the madness from your mind. Would restore you. Save you. And bring you back to my cold bed."

Stunned, I held on to silence and then clutched the Bible to my breasts. "I am already saved."

Davis was derisive. "By Jesus Christ?"

"Yes," I said softly. "Let us sit here, you and I, while I tell you a ghost story."

"I'm listening."

"My religion is a ghost story," I began.

"When did you get religion?"

Undeterred I continued. "You have a superb imagination. But it's tethered in the strength of your being. Do you understand? You mastered your imagination. My imagination was rooted in weakness. And uprooted in crisis. It overwhelmed me. Led me to hallucination, hysteria, and madness. By way of the ghostly, the

260

supernatural, the ethereal. And it was born in the dark where I had lived alone as a child.''

Davis, the consulting physician, spoke. ''Nightmares?''

''No, the terrors of waking moments. Remember, I was an only child and I slept alone. And sleep came hard.'' I conjured up the past. ''The whisper of leaves. The rattle of windows. Moonbeams and shadows. Frosted panes. Creeping fog. Shouts of thunder. The pictures on the walls made by flashes of lightning. The pebbles of rain against the house. The ghosts of snow, rare, white snow in Georgia. The ringing of bells. The creeping ticking of clocks.'' I shuddered like a child. ''And the child's mind never left me. I was always afraid of sleeping in strange beds, in strange hotels, houses, and inns. Always sensing that death had been there before me. Waiting to embrace me. I could never sleep in any room where the shades and curtains were drawn. You know that. And time healed nothing. Not even in those years of whiskey and drugs, or hours torn from sleep and given to experiments in ecstasy. Now I hear voices, I see blood pouring from faucets. What's the formula for madness? Guilt and terror. The sand and oxide that make the glass of hallucination.''

Davis asked, ''What sort of hallucinations do you have now?''

''I'm sorry,'' I apologized. ''I was telling you a ghost story. About my Jesus.'' I turned away from Davis. ''It began last winter. With something Dr. Dominick said to me. He said he wanted me to try to find a beginning of being. A beginning of being! That phrase stayed with me. And I became like a child muttering words by rote, beyond understanding. I remember one night taking the sketch pad and printing in large letters on the very first page, like a first-grader: The Beginning of Being. I filled the page, ripped it out, crumpled it, and threw it away.'' I took a breath and faced Davis again. ''Then I stared at the second page, a fresh page, a blank page. And then I began to make contact with reality, with the past. I found memory. I found you. And I remembered your saying how much you loved the fresh, clean page that invites the imagination to it. And then I remembered your face, and I began to draw like an idiot defacing a — no — I mean I began to draw from memory. A man's

261

face. Not yours. Now, like an idiot, I made wild and angry strokes. Then suddenly I stopped, realizing what I had done was something very, very strange. I had sketched a face I had imagined long before I had met you. It was the face of Jesus, the Jesus of my childhood prayers, that tent of years under which I'd lived in the bosom of my mother, certain of her love, and certain that when my mother wasn't present that Jesus was watching over me." I had to catch my breath again. "Jesus. The Beginning of Being. And so I came to Him. He was my Jesus. Mine alone."

"Shared with no one?"

I ignored his question, for my own reflection had priority. "Dr. Dominick said it. I don't remember who he was quoting. He said: 'Memory is the only paradise from which we cannot be expelled.' Do you understand? By losing my mind, my memory, I lost my paradise." I looked at Davis and saw only the pennies on his eyes. "Then there's another phrase: One always returns to first loves. I returned to my mother. And then to my Jesus."

Davis, the author at work, asked, "And just who is *your* Jesus?"

"Jesus is God. My God, my ghost. And I came to Him singing. 'When I have slept enough in my grave, thou wilt awaken me. Thou wilt save me, resurrect me.'"

Davis, the damned skeptic, said, "You sound as if you actually believe it."

I said, "My faith is a child's faith. I play as a child on the strand, with my pail and shovel, and build my sand-castle heaven. Far from the breaking, smashing waves of reason, intellect, logic, wisdom, and whatnot. Far from the reason of my damned father and the reason of my damned husband. They're both lost to me, and I'm back at the beginning of being. Jesus is my being. He's the rock upon which I stand."

And now Davis, the great compromiser, declared, "Rannah, if you want to go to church again, I'll take you."

I saw myself as a child threatened by an old man's leer, and I remembered not to accept the candy. I said, "I don't want to go anywhere. I don't want to share my Jesus with anyone."

"Not even with me?"

"Does a child wish to share its mother? Why should I wish to share my Jesus?"

Davis relented. "All right, you don't have to share your Jesus with me. Now, shall we talk about your leaving here?"

"No, I don't want to leave."

My reply astounded him. I gave him sufficient time in which to weigh his words. "Why not? Are you afraid of bringing warmth to my cold bed?"

I had refused the candy, and now the stranger was grabbing me and pulling me into his foul embrace. Running from the answer, I said, "When I was truly mad, I believed I had a father who loved me and a husband who loved me. My father came here and left me behind the gates. My husband never came at all."

"I'm here now," he said with contrition.

"You're too late," I told him calmly. "You were too late with your book. You are too late in coming for me."

"Is it that I'm dead, Rannah? Or is it that you're dead?"

I screamed in reply. "*You're* dead! You and my father! I love only Jesus! And He lives!"

Davis looked at me blankly and kept the silence of the dead.

I spoke again, this time with a grace seldom given to the mad. "But thank you for asking me to leave with you. If I can leave, and I choose not to, then I can hardly, even in my most terrible moments, consider Hollow Grove a prison."

I waited for a curtain to descend between us. The actors had declaimed their words, the audience had spent its last response, and it was time to leave the theater to the ruffled dust.

But Davis didn't stir. He was the entranced boy who remained behind to hide under his seat and wait through the night for the curtain to rise on tomorrow's performance. He said, "How'd you like to motor cross country?"

I said nothing to the question that was three years late.

"Rannah, you always loved traveling with me."

Belatedly I confessed, "The strange rooms, the strange beds, they frightened me."

"I was always there."

263

I said, "You and I, we're both on the same course around the sun. You may, if you wish, rush from strange cabin to strange cabin. But you, like me, remain on the same planetary vessel. Yes, you roam where you wish. I prefer it here at Hollow Grove with Dr. Dominick. And Jesus." I rose haughtily and ushered my distant cousin into the far distance. "Thank you so much for dropping by."

Davis got up from his chair more slowly than Lazarus from his tomb. His look and his voice were incredulous. "Do you really want me to go?"

"Please," I said. "I'm tired."

"I love you."

His words winged me to my bedroom on Gedney Street, to the night I had slept with the first novel of Davis O'Donnell in my arms. I said pensively, "You've forgotten something about me. It wasn't your Alexandrian face, your winning personality, your sad smile, your gift for lovemaking, or your class ring that made me truly love you."

"What was it?"

"It was a page, a paragraph, a sentence. A rush of words. It was the magic you brought to a page when you wrote the whispers of God." There were tears in my eyes and a catch in my voice as I faced Davis and cried, "How can I love you now that you're deaf to God's whispers?"

First I heard Davis's mind crack, and then I felt the whip of his words. "God damn it! I wrote a book for you! *In Battalions!* It's sitting right there! Unread! How can you love me and not read it?"

"I can't love the dead."

Again the whip. "Why the hell do you keep it here? Right next to your goddam Bible?"

"Each and every morning," I responded with felicity, "after breakfast, when I sit down to read, I exercise my free will. I choose the living truth of God rather than your dead book."

And now the man who had surrendered his pen to Harry Ingram surrendered the battle to me. "I can't take this any longer."

264

In the boots of General Grant I walked to the window and looked out at the Studebaker. I asked, for no reason but the savoring of my triumph, "Why does your car have New York license plates?"

"I borrowed it. It's Edna's car."

"Edna?"

"Edna Thurlow."

"Oh! If it's not your car, then how were you going to motor across the country?"

Absently, beaten, he said, "I'm taking the train. To quote another Edna: There isn't a train I wouldn't take no matter where it's going." He crossed to the door and opened it. "Excuse me."

"For what?"

"I need a drink."

So saying, he left the cottage. I moved to the open door and stood there. I watched him reach toward the glove compartment and bring out a brown paper sack. From it he withdrew a pint of gin, took the bottle to his mouth, and drained it. Then, in the wash-drawn manner of Frank Merriwell, he held the bottle high over his head, cocked his arm, and threw a touchdown pass that landed unbroken on the shingles of the cottage roof.

Forsaking a last glance at indifferent me, he stuck his head into the oven of the car, accidentally struck the horn with a wild hand, and accelerated frenzy and smoke before departing with the speed of a sophomore racing from the sorority house to the fraternity house to announce how mad the girl was for him.

Within the ensuing hour, without rancor, Dr. Dominick came to the cottage to spank me.

"Turn in your uniform," he said. "You blew the game."

Exhilaration still with me, I told him, "I feel wonderful. I feel free."

"How come?"

"Why shouldn't I, Coach? I just beat Yale."

"You didn't beat him. You merely confused him."

"Did you see him?"

"We talked over coffee. He needed coffee. Rannah, why didn't you leave with him? I was hoping to get rid of you. I'm tired of you, bored with you."

"If you weren't smiling, I'd die."

"I'm jealous of Jesus. I wanted to save you myself."

"Yes, you did talk to Davis."

"Know what he said? He said: 'I was too late. The Calvary man beat me to the rescue.' ''

"That's sacrilegious."

"Spike, they sewed back the wrong head."

"I see you had a long talk. Where's he going now?"

"Back to the mines."

"What does that mean?"

"It was *his* expression. I assume it means he's returning to Hollywood. Which should please you."

I didn't understand. "Why should it please me?"

"If it pleases you to remain here, when you no longer have to, then you should be pleased that someone in Hollywood is working the mines to keep you in luxury." When I failed to react, he added, "Your father doesn't pay your bills. Jesus can't. And I won't."

"Is that where they bury the dead now? In mines? Of course, Doctor, you noticed how dead he was."

Dr. Dominick said, "I hate to contradict you or offend you, but I thought your husband was the resurrection and the life. And I was looking forward to receiving candied fruit from you."

"I hate candied fruit."

"Rannah, what are you afraid of? Being a wife again?"

"He masturbates. He told me."

"Why are you afraid?"

"I didn't say I was afraid."

"Tarragona?"

"What?"

"He knows what happened there."

I ran from the terror of Tarragona. "I want to stay here."

He regarded me sadly. "I'll tell you where they're burying the dead these days. In overpriced prisons like Hollow Grove."

266

My voice was harsh now. "Why do you want me to leave?"

"Because you want to stay."

"Thanks to Jesus."

"You belong with your husband."

"In the same coffin?"

The hook of the question caught Dr. Dominick's neck, ripped into his throat, and left him without a voice. He did an about-face and left.

Shortly after nine that night I went to bed and began to read from my beautiful book.

". . . Jesus answered them, 'Do ye believe now? Behold, the hour cometh, yea, is now come, that ye shall be scattered, every man to his own, and shall leave me alone: and yet I am not alone, because the Father is with me. These things I have spoken unto you, that in me ye shall have peace. In the world ye shall have tribulation: but be of good cheer; I have overcome the world. . . .'"

The Bible closed, my eyes shut, the lamps out, I lay in the warm dark and tempted sleep. Then I heard the blowing of a Klaxon horn. It sounded once, and then again before the return of quiet allowed me to hear the idling of the motor, the singular song of the Apperson.

I cried out, "Mrs. Neff!"

The door to the sitting room burst open, and light spilled past a hulking figure. "Yes, Mrs. O'Donnell?"

"Please. Look out the window."

Mrs. Neff went to the window. "There's nothing there."

I heard the horn again. "Isn't there a car out there?"

"No. No car."

I heard the motor idling. "Do you hear nothing?"

"Nothing at all."

"You don't hear a car?"

"No."

"Thank you, Mrs. Neff."

Mrs. Neff carefully closed the door and returned me to a darkness now tomb cold. Sealed from the sound of the Apperson, I took to the soft of my pillow and listened to the accelerated

267

beat of my heart. Then I turned my head and found the wave length in which the dead whispered.

"Rannah?"

"Yes, Mother."

"The gate is open."

"Where are you, Mother?"

"Rannah, baby, I'm no longer young, have nowhere to run, and no one to run to. Quick, the gate is open! Oh, to be young and running away! Quick, the gate is open! Run!"

"Run where?"

"Quick, Rannah baby, quick, before they close the gates on tomorrow!"

"It's dark, Mother. I can't see."

"Follow me, my voice will lead the way. Oh, dear Jesus, lead us. Run, Rannah, run!"

I ran. I bolted from the bed and ran from the bedroom. In another moment I was beyond the restraining hands of keeper, out of the cottage, and chasing the whisperer to the gate.

As they had taken Jesus down from the cross, so they took me down from the locked gate. They took me to the château, to a room where my body was iced and where the whispers of my mother were crystallized into snowflakes that confounded the roses blooming in the hollow.

4.

To Dr. Dominick the years of my self-imposed incarceration were long and lost. To me it was a time filled with the soft down of asylum.

Within the gates of Hollow Grove, within the salvation of my madness, I entertained the ghost of my dead mother and the visitations of my living Jesus. The gate was a shield against my father's storms of spears, against my husband's death cries rising from a deep and sunless mine shaft in California, and against the confusion and lies authored by the devil in Spain.

Early in the morning of an eventful day Dr. Dominick came to the cottage with a bedside manner that belied the nine years of the War of the Psyche in which we had sometimes been allies but, more often, adversaries. Now he was smiling, and his smile was a mirror in which I saw that, at long last, I was wearing my right head.

"Good morning, Rannah."

"It must be a good morning. You're smiling."

"The sun is shining, and you look good enough to whistle at."

"What's happened?" I asked. "No, let me guess. You've sold the sanitarium."

"No, it's not for sale."

269

"Your wife is leaving you."

His smile was sad now. "No, but one of these days I'll be leaving Marybelle."

"To go with whom?"

"The Army Medical Corps." Noting the blankness of my demeanor, he added, "We'll be in the war before long."

"What war?"

"The Nazis invaded Poland."

"The who?"

"The Germans."

I knew my history. "The Germans invaded Belgium."

"That was 1914. Today is Friday, the fifteenth of September, and the year is 1939."

"The way you're looking at me, I feel fourteen."

He said, "Wear your new summer dress today, and put a ribbon in your hair."

I asked, "What are we going to do today? Collect peach stones for gas masks?"

"Spike, you're being taken for a ride."

"It's been years since you called me Spike. Since I —"

He interrupted me. "Would you like to go for a joyride?"

"Can I be a nurse in the war? Can I go with you when you go to the front?"

"Rannah, I'm talking about today. You're going on a trip."

"Is this some new kind of therapy?"

He shook his head. "I'm playing my last card."

"Is that gangster talk?"

"Your husband's coming this morning."

The news never reached the muscle of my heart. I said nothing.

"No comment?"

"Thank you for underplaying this second coming of the California Christ."

"Please, Rannah, don't be bitter. Not this morning."

"Why is he coming?"

"I'll let him tell you."

"But you know why, don't you?"

270

"He's taking you on a trip."

"Is that what he thinks?"

"I told him you'd go with him."

"Go where?"

"Baltimore, Washington, Richmond, and points south. By car."

"Is the Apperson still running?"

"They don't make Appersons any more. I don't know what he's driving, but he's coming to take his wife on a little vacation."

"Thank you, Thomas Cook."

"I didn't arrange the tour. Davis did."

"Why do you refer to him so familiarly?"

"We're pen pals. Nine years now."

"Nine years?"

"Since you first came here."

I was angry with Dr. Dominick now. "I've done very nicely without clocks, calendars, newspapers or radios. I don't appreciate your coming in here this morning and upsetting me."

"I'll tell you what," he said, "before you leave this morning, you can kick me in the pants."

"I'm not leaving," I said with finality.

Dr. Dominick glanced about the bedroom. "The place needs painting." He turned to me. "We'll do it while you're away. What color would you like?"

"The color of truth. Can your painters mix that? Or would you like to try?"

He said, "I promised Davis I'd persuade you to go with him."

"You haven't succeeded."

"Rannah, what are you afraid of?"

"I'm afraid of the dead."

"Let me tell you a little more about the trip. You'll have lunch in Baltimore. At Miller's. My God, I can smell the fresh French bread, the hot clam chowder and —"

"The food here is excellent," I reminded him.

"From Baltimore you go on to Washington. Davis has a two-bedroom suite reserved at the Carlton. Fine hotel."

271

I had a question. "Two bedrooms? Why?"

"One for you, one for him."

"Can I lock my door?"

"You can lock your door."

"What about tomorrow?"

"You're free to set the course. Davis'll take you where you tell him. North to Hollow Grove or south to wherever."

"Wherever what?"

"Wherever you wish."

I said sharply, "I want to stay here! That's where forever is! Here!"

"Am I your doctor?"

"You're not Thomas Cook."

"If I'm your doctor, then you're obliged to obey my orders."

"Orders? Are we already playing war?"

"We have been for much too long. I want you to get out of bed, bathe, and dress. And be ready to leave the cottage when you hear Davis blow the horn."

"Thank you," I said, "but I'll wait for Gabriel."

He studied me hard. "Repeat that in Miller's. I'm sure Davis'll laugh."

"The dead don't laugh."

"Prepare yourself for his resurrection."

"I don't appreciate that, Doctor," I said.

"Jesus hasn't saved you. I haven't saved you. Give Davis his chance."

"Feeling sorry for yourself?"

"All of us are sick here. Me, I'm sick with disappointment. We made such a lousy fight. All these lousy years we accepted each other's surrender. But not any more. We're fighting this morning. Now get moving."

"Can I come back tomorrow?"

"Yes, you can. But I hope I never see you again."

He turned and hurried away from the sight of me. I ran and caught up with him. "Why did you say that? Why did you say you never wanted to see me again?"

I wept and he embraced me before he said, "Often I blas-

272

pheme, and not so often I pray. Rannah, I don't want to see you here again. That's my prayer.'' He kissed me on the mouth to seal his prayer.

And then he departed.

Less than two hours later, my valise carefully packed and my hair smartly ribboned, I was sitting on the edge of my chair and balancing my mind with the parasol of Biblical wisdom when I heard a strange horn blown by someone who was neither a boy nor blue.

Mrs. Neff, a happy elephant pleased with the prospect of the day, carried my valise as if it were a peanut and led the parade. The circus tent collapsed when, in the center ring, I saw a strange old motorcar beside which stood a strange old man. I was about to turn and flee when, through the mask of time, I saw the bright and smiling eyes that once had shone upon me when Appersons sped down Gedney Street.

Davis greeted and jested with Mrs. Neff, took the valise from her and placed it on the back seat of the two-door coach. Then the coachman held the door open and the princess entered a carriage malodorous with the exhaust of the twentieth century. While Davis jollied Mrs. Neff, I pinched my nostrils and studied the worn, stained upholstery, a speedometer that registered two circumnavigations of the globe, the foot-worn brake, clutch, and gas pedals, and a steering wheel filmed with a mixture of grease and dirt. Finally Davis slid behind the wheel with the look of an aviator settling into the cockpit of his Spad biplane. He wrenched a roar from the motor, a gnashing from the gears, and an unuttered cry of alarm from me as the car took the road, climbing to the gate which opened upon alien roads.

Afraid to speak, I watched the eyes that watched the road. Then, in a voice not as familiar as the brilliant eyes, Davis spoke to me.

"Beautiful morning, isn't it?"

"Yes."

"Comfortable?"

"No."

"Nervous?"

273

"Very. What make car is this?"

"A Plymouth. A 1934 Plymouth."

"Isn't this 1939?"

"Thirty-four was a vintage year for Plymouths."

"Is that when you bought it?"

"No, I bought it yesterday. In New York."

"I thought you were in Hollywood."

"I left Hollywood a week ago."

"Where are we going now?"

"First stop Baltimore. Lunch at Miller's and — I'm sorry. We'll stop sooner, any time you feel like stopping to make a telephone call in a rest room." He laughed, but I refused to share his laughter. Blandly he added, "You just holler."

"Must I holler?"

"No, we'll have a signal. Just tap three times on the dashboard. Like this." He demonstrated.

I noticed his jowls. "How much do you weigh now?"

"You noticed. I weigh enough to make the varsity backfield. One hundred and sixty pounds."

My eyes upon the gray of his temples, I asked, "How old are you?"

"Forty-three."

"When's your birthday?"

"August sixth."

"Do you have a cigarette?"

"Sorry. I gave up smoking. Next time we stop for —"

I continued to cross-examine the impostor. "Do you have a drink?"

"Gave up drinking, too."

"When?"

"About two years now. Hershey bars and Cokes are my vices now."

"Vices?"

"Milk and crackers, that's my dish now."

"What make of car did you have in 1920?"

"An Apperson."

"Where did you spend your honeymoon?"

274

"Atlanta. Clifford Hotel."

"Whom did you telephone that night?"

"My agent. Ellis Mason. In New York. You called him later."

"Where'd we drink champagne?"

"In the bathtub."

"You're very patient with me, aren't you?"

"I feel like singing."

"Sing some Yale songs," I demanded.

What he had failed to do with words he did with music. He sang the college songs and took me to New Haven and to old havens where doubt had not existed. Now, reassured that the man at the wheel was indeed my man, I felt nervous about the kite of my happiness in the high wind of this sudden freedom. Three times I tapped three times on the dashboard before we reached Baltimore.

In Miller's Davis ordered a whiskey sour for me and a glass of orange juice for himself. Then we had tureens of clam chowder, soft-shell crabs, strawberry shortcake, and cups and cups of coffee. And best of all, throughout the meal we took turns remembering all the restaurants and all the unforgettable meals of our shared past.

South from Baltimore we played on flutes of French bread, hid in caves of cheese, and ran in vineyards. It was surprising then when, at the moment I expected to see the environs of Paris, I beheld the marbled vista of Washington. Our entrance into the city was flawed by a supercilious doorman at the Carlton Hotel who, upon regarding the vintage Plymouth, wondered whether we were at the correct hotel and whether we had a reservation. In the Paris of yesteryears Davis would have launched the doorman with a champagne bottle. But now, in Washington, Davis favored him with a benign and forgiving smile.

The suite was perfect for the imperfect arrangement of the evening: two bedrooms flanking a sitting room. I selected my bedroom, accepted Davis's plan for the evening, and then locked him out for two hours during which I bathed with the ghosts of champagne and soap bubbles, lay alone upon the bed naked

275

before the twilight, and dressed for dinner before mirrors that were compassionately tinted.

We dined alone in the sitting room on a table set with flowers and lighted by candles. We had a salad of greens in oil and vinegar, a Chateaubriand with Lyonnaise potatoes and asparagus, a split of burgundy for me, a bottle of Coke for Davis. The dinner conversation was confined to the subject of the Thurlows, with whom Davis had stayed the past two days.

For dessert, as Davis had planned it, we left the hotel, bought ice cream cones and walked streets haunted by American history. As we started back to the hotel we talked of wars, and Davis instructed me in the names of the new chessmen.

In the elevator I had the feeling I was in a balloon rising and drifting away from reality. Davis noted this tensing of fear, and he calmed me and sent me off to bed. Not protesting, I smiled and thanked him politely for a lovely evening. I went then to my bedroom and locked the door against him.

I stood at the door, pressing my face to it, when I heard his voice. My first reaction was that he was talking to someone who had been hiding in his bedroom. And then, in the next moment, I understood that he was talking on the telephone, renting a radio for the night.

Later, as I lay in bed too excited to sleep, I heard a Vincent Youmans song issuing from the sitting room. In another instant I came to believe I was outside a ballroom where Davis was dancing with Liz Cooper. Stealing from the bed, I went to the door and unlocked it.

But the ball was in the box of the radio, and what I beheld was a writer in the throes of creation: Davis, sitting at the antique desk, a pipe in his mouth, a pen in his hand, the lights of hell and heaven in his eyes.

I folded my arms over my nightgown, folded my legs, sat upon the carpeted floor, and silently observed Davis. I found myself questioning the reality of the moment when I saw him suck on his pipe and failed to see blue smoke rise either from the bowl or his pursed mouth.

Davis, discovering me from the corner of an eye, reacted at

276

first with a start and then with a smile as soft as the radio music. "Hello."

My voice was sticky and subdued. "I heard the music."

"I'm sorry. I'll shut it off."

"No, don't. Why isn't there any smoke from your pipe?"

He removed the pipe from his mouth and held it like a periscope. "No tobacco. Just a prop. A pacifier. It gives me the illusion that I'm aflame with inspiration."

"What are you writing?"

"Just making some notes."

"On what?"

"Hollywood."

I watched him return the pipe to his mouth and suck in the air of Hollywood. I asked, "Why did you leave?"

"It's not a fit bedtime story."

"Tell me about the last six years in Hollywood."

"It was nine years."

"I know about the first three." To prove it I said more. "You cheated the studio. You wrote a novel on studio time. The book died. You died. I had a visit. From the dead you. Then you went away, back to Hollywood."

Davis looked at me with a tenderness he would have shown the child he had never had, a child telling its first story to his father. "Very good."

A child, I asked, "What do the dead do in Hollywood?"

He arched his body, stretched out his arms, and laughed, shattering the illusion of Christ upon the cross. He said, "I went out for the team."

"What team?"

"I tried for my varsity M at Metro, my varsity P at Paramount, my varsity W at Warners, and my varsity C at Columbia. I had more chances than at college or prep school."

"Would you please explain?"

Davis said, "Movie-making's a team effort. Rougher than football. What they kick in Hollywood is your ego."

"You felt pain?"

"Agony."

277

"Perhaps you weren't dead after all."

"I wasn't. I cried too much."

"No victories?"

"One. And that was a Pyrrhic victory."

"Tell me about it."

"Are you cold?"

"I'm comfortable. Tell me about the Pyrrhic victory. Please."

I believe he wanted to leave his chair and walk his memory, but, fearful of disturbing the fragile moment, he remained seated and dared not even turn the chair toward me. He said, "About two years ago my telephone rang at three o'clock in the morning. I woke up, and my first thought was: somebody's died. I lifted the phone, said nothing, and then I heard a voice. An apologetic, exuberant voice. It was my producer. He had just finished reading my screenplay. He was —"

I interrupted him. "A screenplay on what?"

"An English novel called *The Day Tomorrow Came*. A first novel by a man named Edmond Morse. A love story told against the background of Armistice Day in London. Anyway, my producer was ecstatic. He promised me a bonus, a boost in salary, and a new contract. All of which I got. He also predicted I would win an Academy Award for my script."

"Which you didn't."

"No," he said. He returned to the memory. "I couldn't sleep any more that night. I didn't want to sleep. I just wanted to lie awake. Laugh. Cry. And taste the secret of my success. Do you know what it was?"

"What?"

"I put Rannah Gedney into the script. I took the heroine and made her you. That was the secret. No, I couldn't sleep that night. And I couldn't sleep in the office the following morning. The telephone kept ringing. The word was out that at last O'Donnell had done it. People were happy for me. I was happy for myself. My happiness lasted three whole days."

"How did it end?"

"The producer called me into his office, did an Irish jig, and announced that Jules Norman, winner of two Academy Awards,

278

was going to direct the picture. Then he asked me what kind of car I was driving. I told him a Studebaker. And he told me I ought to treat myself to a LaSalle. To leave lunch open. We were going to lunch with the great Jules Norman at one o'clock.'' Davis paused. "At one o'clock the producer phoned me. The lunch date was off. The great Jules Norman was tied up with the front office. Big things, big plans. The great Jules Norman was fighting for Gable. Fighting for Shearer."

"I don't understand."

"Every producer and director fights with the front office to get the top stars."

"I see. What happened next?"

"About four o'clock in the afternoon I had a visitor in my office. Tom Jennings. Remember the name?"

I searched. "Jennings? A playwright. We saw a play of his. Nineteen twenty-two. A war play. The title was *Shrapnel and Shrouds*. Morbid. We didn't like it. And, if I remember correctly, I told Jennings how much I disliked it. Was it at Sardi's?"

He nodded. "At Sardi's."

"What happened at four o'clock in your office?"

"Jennings came in to invite me to dinner that night. I accepted."

"Had you been friendly with him?"

"No, he'd been rather cool to me. The way success is cool to failure."

I was back in Sardi's in 1922. "This from Davis O'Donnell?"

"In Hollywood, then and now, Tom Jennings is the success. Davis O'Donnell's the failure."

"Tell me about the dinner."

"I had heard about his big house in Bel Air and his Santa Barbara society wife. I should've suspected something was wrong when he took me to the Beverly Hills Hotel. After the fourth martini, Jennings told me the great things he'd heard about my script. I smiled and I talked too much. Told him too much about my plights and problems. Told him how hard I'd worked on the script. Eight months. How much this new success meant to me. How I hoped it would mean something to my wife.''

I felt a chill. ''Something like what?''

Davis tossed his pipe in the air and caught it. ''Just another O'Donnell folly.''

I persisted. ''Like what?''

''Like making a million dollars. Taking you to Vienna. Giving the money to Freud. And he giving you back to me.''

The daydream had been tossed to me, and I missed it. Hollywood was a long way away from Vienna and I was still pursuing the dénouement of the dinner at the Beverly Hills Hotel. ''What did Jennings say?''

Pronouncing his own death sentence, Davis told me. ''Jennings said Jules Norman had refused to work with me.''

''I don't understand.''

''Directors work with writers on the final script. They direct the writers before they direct the actors.''

''Why didn't the director want to work with you?''

''The great Jules Norman never works with strangers.''

''Davis O'Donnell, a stranger?''

''To Jules Norman, yes. A stranger is by definition someone who's never worked with Jules Norman. A friend is someone who has worked with Jules Norman. On a successful picture. Like, for instance, Tom Jennings.''

''Who took you to dinner to tell you he was going to rewrite your script.''

''Yes.''

''Did you cry in front of him?''

''No.''

''Did you beg him for mercy?''

''No.''

''What did you do?'' I asked in the manner of a mother interrogating a child after the first day at a new school.

''I ordered some Irish whiskey.''

''What did you say to him?''

''I laughed. As if he'd told me a very funny story. As if the joke weren't on me. And insisted on paying the check. Which I did. And then I laughed again."

"Why again?"

"I heard a telephone ring. And I laughed and said to Jennings, 'Why, it must be three o'clock in the morning.'"

"Why didn't you say something to him?"

He said, "Say what? I never said a word to the writer I followed. I was the fifth writer to tackle the script. Get the football vernacular. Tackle a script. Only it's not football, not cricket. It's a daisy chain. A lineup. It's Hollywood."

"Was the picture ever made?"

"Not with Gable and Shearer. With Jimmy Stewart and Carole Lombard. My first picture."

"Your first picture," I reminded him, "was *The Distant Spires* with Richard Barthelmess and —"

"I mean the first one on which I received screenplay credit. The first and only one."

"Didn't Jennings rewrite your script?"

"The credits on the screen read like this: Screenplay by Thomas Jennings and Davis O'Donnell. Adaptation by Lazlo Meyers and Sally Watson. Based on a novel by Edmond Morse." Davis returned the pacifier to his mouth. "When I saw the picture, it was as strange to me as I was to Jules Norman. And I was sick."

"A bad picture?"

"The critics liked it. It made money. The script was nominated for an Academy Award. Which, thankfully, it didn't win."

"Am I in the picture?" I asked.

"Neither of us is in the picture. When another writer touches your work, it becomes his. Not yours."

"What happened next?"

"I —" Davis caught himself and said something else. "I found a friend."

"And who was that?"

"Joel Stone."

In the theater of my mind the screen was filled with the

281

picture of Davis and me driving on a Sunday night to the Long Island mansion. I said softly, "Joel Stone. Wasn't he someone you invented?"

Davis didn't hear me. He was in a theater of his own, where Joel Stone had faded into a screen far from the North Shore. He said, "He found me. In the Brown Derby."

"Brown Derby?"

"A Hollywood restaurant. The Sardi's of the West. Anyway, Joel came over to my table and introduced himself. He was sure I'd forgotten him. Isn't that a remarkable thing? The one man in the world I could never forget. And he was sure I'd forgotten him."

"Did you recognize him?"

"Immediately. By the eyes. He's heavier now than I am. Quite bald."

"What did he have to say?"

"Terrible things."

"Like what?"

"He said I looked wonderful. And he said he'd seen and enjoyed my picture. I thought he meant *North Shore*. What he really meant was *The Day Tomorrow Came*."

"What was Joel doing in Hollywood?"

"I don't know. I never figured out what he was doing in the old days on Long Island. He told me he lives in Las Vegas now."

"What's he doing there?"

"He didn't say. If I had to guess, I'd say he was exposing the underworld to some desert sunshine. Gambling's legal in Nevada. Must be booze and racket money moving in there."

I melted Joel Stone's fat and returned the hair to his handsome head. "Did he ask about me?"

"Yes."

"What did you tell him?"

"He asked me how recently I had seen you — this was only a few weeks ago — and I said I was going to see you shortly. Which was a lie when I said it."

"Did Joel know I was at Hollow Grove?"

282

"He knew."

"Who told him?"

Again I felt he was withholding something from me when he hesitated and said, "I didn't ask him."

"How long did you spend with him?"

"Five to ten minutes. The most important five to ten minutes I've spent in the last fifteen years."

"That's a large statement," I said skeptically.

Davis said, "When Joel went back to his table, I paid my check and left. In a big hurry."

"Were you alone?"

"No. I was with a girl."

"Who was Joel with?"

"A girl."

I summoned the question from home in Stephensville: "Whose girl was the younger and prettier?"

Without a smile, with no pleasure in the memory, Davis said, "Mine. Mine was a girl who smiles only for cameras. The rest of the time she rails against a world that can't see she's another Claudette Colbert."

"Why did you leave in such a hurry?"

"I was too old to cry in the Brown Derby."

"Did you cry on your girl's pillow?"

"I sent her home in a cab."

I asked, "What did Joel say to put you in such a black mood?"

"It was nothing he said. Just his presence. Just the reminder that once, because of him, I climbed my Matterhorn. Just once."

"How drunk did you get that night?"

"I'm on the wagon, Rannah. Been on for two years now."

"Why?"

"Whiskey makes me cry."

"And cigarettes?"

"The smoke gets in my eyes."

"How sick were you?"

Davis paused, wondering, perhaps, how much to tell me. "I was all broken up. And not from laughter."

"Nervous breakdown?"

"I cracked up. First my crankcase went."

"Your crankcase?"

"I leaked blood. From a duodenal ulcer."

"My God!"

"One week in the hospital. Six weeks in my apartment. The studio gave me a layoff. My doctor gave me a diagnosis: acute melancholia of the movies."

"Was it melancholia?"

Davis shook his head. "You should ask the larger question: was it a movie? Yes, the movie was *The Day Tomorrow Came*. As you've undoubtedly guessed."

"How bad were you? Suicidal?"

"Not that bad."

"Manic-depressive," I suggested.

"I only paid the doctor for melancholia. I couldn't afford to be manic-depressive or suicidal. Know what I said to the doctor one day?"

"What?"

"I said we ought to engineer a trade. Between Hollow Grove and Coconut Grove, which is my code name for Hollywood. I told the doctor I ought to take your cottage at Hollow Grove and let you come out here to write for the movies. The way you used to write for the *Post*."

I was incredulous. "You told the doctor our secret?"

"I thought it was a deathbed confession."

"Why did you fail in Hollywood?"

"I didn't fail. Not the way banks fail. I made a lot of money."

"Isn't Hollywood another Waterloo?"

"There are more Waterloos than Middletowns in the —" He broke off to laugh.

"Why are you laughing?"

"About three years ago," said Davis, "a producer I was working for called me in. He had good news for me. He'd just heard from the front office that Robert Young and Madge Evans were set to star in our picture. Well, that gave me a glow for the day, and I took it to the commissary for lunch, to the writers'

284

table. One of the boys — a writer named Paul Marks — noticed my euphoria. He asked me what I was so happy about, and I told him. And this is what he said: 'They always promise you Robert Young and Madge Evans, but you end up with Gable and Garbo.' "

"That's very funny."

Absently Davis continued. "And that's the sad part. One of the reasons I failed. I couldn't consciously write for Gable or Garbo. I couldn't join the assembly line writing vehicles for Gable and Garbo. Gable was Gable, and the writer need never strain for characterization. The character is Gable. So you sit in a projection room and run Gable pictures one after another. And then suddenly you understand. Gable the newspaper reporter, Gable the submarine commander, Gable the test pilot, Gable the cavalry lieutenant. Same expressions, same reactions, same scenes, same results. Pure Gable. Put what you think is a great and original touch in a script and the producer says: 'That's not Gable. Gable wouldn't do this. Not Gable. The movie public wants Gable — 99.44% pure Gable.' "

I said, "You understood it so well, why didn't you adapt to the medium?"

Davis went straight to the truth. "I tried. Real hard. I learned little things. Like putting the star on top of the scene. Giving him the best lines of dialogue, the best pieces of business. The star is the star, and the star belongs on top of the scene. That's just one example. I could go on for days. But the vital thing is this: when I wrote a vehicle for a star, I wasn't writing my best. Far from it. I couldn't pick the fruit of another writer's imagination. Or the bones of another picture's success. Sure, I'd get something down on paper. I'd sweat it out, work it over. I'd listen to the producer and let him put his pencil to the script. I collaborated, cooperated, bent over backwards, controlled my temper, learned to agree, and generated phony enthusiasm. And, in the end, my scripts were either shelved or completely re-written. And, mind you, it wasn't a conspiracy against me. There were some damn fine people out there, rooting for me,

285

wanting to help me, wanting me to succeed. And then there were the bastards.''

He sighed. ''Nine years. Sometimes I feel like a robber. A thief. I took so much money and gave so little value. One producer said to me: 'You can't shoot sweat.' And then there was the director who was given a script I did for an independent producer with a big idea and a small budget. And *he* said: 'How the hell can I shoot character in ten days?' ''

I said, ''I don't understand.''

''It was a Western. And this director had shot scores of them. Always the good guys, the bad guys. He was honest. He couldn't shoot my script in ten days. Not if he had to take time to delineate character. I don't blame him. I blame myself.''

''You make it sound so awful. I mean Hollywood.''

Davis considered this. ''And yet it wasn't. The weather was great. No winters. And the climate for writers was greater. No loneliness. There was always a writer to collaborate on a script with you, play cards with you, play word games, have bull sessions. The writers' table was fun. Like belonging to a fraternity again. Left some good friends there. And some others who might've been good friends if I had given them half a chance.''

''What do you mean?''

''Six years ago, Rannah, you sized me up right. I *was* dead. There was no reality to Hollywood. And I don't mean simply the make-believe of the movies. The thing is that I'd never dreamed of writing for the movies. And if you don't dream something first, you don't appreciate it when you get it. As a boy I dreamed of being a writer, of putting words on paper and then seeing those words in a newspaper, a magazine, or a book. Being a book writer was my special dream. Does that make sense?''

''Yes, it does,'' I said.

''Want to hear something shameful? I stopped reading books. Except those I had to read for an assignment. I avoided book stores. I stopped reading the book review sections in the Sunday *Times* and *Trib*. I avoided literary discussions. Avoided talk of my novels. And, in so doing, offended a lot of people who cared for me. And for my books.''

286

"Did you also avoid talk about me?"

"There wasn't any talk. Not with me. People just knew. And they understood."

I persisted. "Didn't you ever have to explain anything about my madness?"

He pondered the question. "There was one producer at Columbia who was interviewing me for a job. And he asked me: 'What's the inside on Rannah?' I didn't know what to say. I needed a drink. My bowels were boiling. My mind was filled with enthusiasms for the script. I hated myself for being so anxious to get the damned job, and I hated the son of a bitch for his question. And I said this: 'The inside on Rannah? She picked up the depression from Hoover himself.'"

"And what did he say to that?"

"He said no to the assignment."

Now a third voice, rising from the radio, reported on the German armies falling upon Poland. Quickly Davis shut off the radio.

I asked, "Why did you do that?"

"I'm too old," he said. "I can't expend any passion on this war. It's too late for that. A little over a week ago I saw my doctor in Hollywood. I asked him what he thought of my chances of being accepted for enlistment by the RCAF. He told me not to waste my money on a trip to Montreal."

I looked at him with awe. "Did you really want to enlist?"

He nodded. "Not for the medals this time. I wanted to study war. To come home with a war novel."

The name of Harry Ingram remained uninvoked, and I said, "Stendhal, Tolstoi, and Crane. None of them was ever at the battles they committed to literature."

Davis, however, was still at the Battle of Hollywood. "Going to the doctor was just a gesture. It was no surprise when he told me I was a prewar casualty. I know what my war is. And where it is. Not in Hollywood. And not in Europe."

"Where is it?"

"A writer gets his —" His voice fell dead and a shroud fell

287

over his secret. He stood up, his weariness sapping a smile. "A writer gets tired. I've left an early call for us."

I said nothing.

"Rannah, did you have a nice day?"

"Yes, I did. Thank you."

He blew me a kiss. "Sleep well."

I blew him a kiss. "You, too."

Then I shut the door on amenity and locked out the meaning of wedlock. In a few minutes I was in bed, a bed whose feel was strange. I shut my eyes and jumped the wall of night to Hollow Grove. Repressing an urge to call aloud for Mrs. Neff, I opened my eyes, cowered before the strange shapes of the windows, and felt a Presence in the bedroom.

Harry Ingram was there. He had been standing behind Davis in the sitting room when I had opened the door. Thinking back, I now understand that Davis and I weren't talking about Hollywood at all, but about Harry Ingram. And I wondered how Harry Ingram would intercept me in Richmond and take me to Armageddon.

I was working on a scream when I heard again the muted radio, dance music from the ballroom in which Davis waltzed away the night. I relaxed and the phantoms fled.

The morning wore a shawl of clouds, but we enjoyed the sunny side of the eggs and sallied bravely across the Potomac and into Virginia. We drove on to Richmond, stopping occasionally to read historical markers and remembering to stock the woods beyond the highway with clashing armies.

In Richmond we sat down to a luncheon of chicken pot pie and chocolate sundaes, and then walked long enough along Monument Street to wish that one of the fine homes there might be ours. The rain was pattering in the trees and falling on marbled faces before we reached the parked Plymouth and continued the southward advance of the day.

South of Richmond the highway was tawdry with the neons of tourist cabins, greasy spoons, and filling stations. Soon, however, the rain washed the landscape of the sand-clay country where the tobacco farms and the pine forests rolled to the horizon.

We were traveling about fifty miles an hour when the right front tire blew. Davis, reacting with aplomb, remembered not to touch the brake pedal and feathered the car to a halt on the shoulder of the road. The tire was destroyed, the inner tube shredded, and Davis labored long in the rain before the spare was secured to the wheel.

Our faces darkened with the day and the deluge. We lost an hour before we were able to buy a new tire and tube. Another hour was given over to an inept mechanic trying to correct a faulty windshield wiper, and Raleigh, North Carolina, our destination for the night, seemed myriad storms and leagues away.

As night fell, Davis announced to me that we had crossed the border from Virginia to North Carolina. I saw nothing on the map of the moment but the pommeling of rain, the thrashing of the windshield wiper, and the intermittent glare of oncoming vehicles.

Then the bottom fell out. The headlights of the vintage Plymouth began to flicker; they weakened and finally died. Again Davis was equal to the emergency, guiding the car from the highway and onto gravel fronting an abandoned beanery. He found the fuse, then saw to his dismay that the fault lay elsewhere. He braved the rain, raised the hood, and traced wires to no avail before retreating to the interior of the car, where drops of rain now began to seep through a faulty roof.

I said nothing, finding myself more concerned by the agony overtaking Davis than by the unfolding of another nightmare. In precarious command of the situation again, Davis eased the Plymouth close to the edge of the concrete highway. As a hunter watches for skyward explosion of birds, he trained his eyes to the north. When a pair of headlights came over the rise, Davis shifted into low gear and timed his move perfectly, the Plymouth coming up behind a late model Pontiac sedan with North Carolina plates. Davis tailed the Pontiac, which lighted the way for us. About four miles farther south, Davis saw the neon sign that became his star for the night. Deftly he left the stream of light and slowed to a halt before the office of a tourist camp.

The man presiding at a cluttered desk behind a pine counter

was old and sullen, as worn as his cigar. In a far corner of the office sat a young bull of a Negro wearing a rainsoaked painter's cap and a wet mackintosh. Neither of them had a welcome for us.

Davis accosted the old man. "Good evening."

"Howdy." The voice, issuing through a mouth clenching the cigar and teeth the color of tobacco, was as cold as the rain.

"The lights on my car are out. Short in the wires." The old man listened but failed to react or comment. Davis pressed on. "Guess we'll have to spend the night here." Still no comment. Davis tried to be more explicit. "We'll take a cabin."

Now the old man spoke. "Can't give you a cabin."

"You're not filled up, are you?"

"Nope."

"Then what is it?"

"You can't spend the night here."

Davis blew the tire of his temper. "Why the hell not?"

"Watch your talk, mister."

Davis mustered patience. "Why can't we spend the night here?"

"Don't rent my cabins by the night."

"How do you rent them?"

"You folks headed for Raleigh?"

"We were."

"Only forty-three miles to —"

"How do you rent your cabins?"

"Don't like to say. Not in front of the lady."

Davis understood him. "How much do you get by the hour?"

"Mickelson's my name."

"How much by the hour, Mr. Mickelson?"

"This here's Saturday night."

"How much?"

"Dollar an hour."

"How much for the night? For two cabins?"

"What for would you be wantin' *two* cabins?"

Davis turned to me, but my demeanor told him nothing. Grappling with the old man again, Davis said, "One cabin. For the night."

290

"Like I said, I rent 'em —"

Davis interrupted him crisply. "I heard you the first time." He withdrew his wallet, slipped a ten-dollar bill from it, and slapped it down on the counter. "I'm paying you for ten hours."

The old man didn't move for the money. Instead he went for his gold watch. "Just about seven now. You folks be outa here now by five in the mornin'."

"What time is dawn these days?" Davis inquired.

"Better hand over another dollar bill."

Davis hesitated. "You do business that hour of the morning?"

"One hour's like another," the old man said, and Davis, momentarily silenced, came up with additional currency. "Be outa here by six."

"Agreed," Davis said with a smile that was homeless in this haunt of Southern grace and hospitality. "Now what can we get in the way of food?"

"Just what you see," said the old man, indicating a display of cheese crackers and a soft-drink cooler.

Davis asked, "What are *you* having for dinner, Mr. Mickelson?"

"Had my dinner."

"I'll pay you a dollar apiece for some ham sandwiches."

"Let you have some likker. Two dollars a pint. Real likker. Green River."

Davis loftily took six packs of cheese crackers and asked for four Cokes.

The old man said, "Don't carry dopes. Give you four Dr Peppers."

"How about Seven-Up?"

"Just Dr Pepper."

The transaction for provisions concluded, Davis asked for the key to the cabin.

"No keys. There's a latch on the inside." Turning to the Negro, he said, "Boy, take these folks to Number Seven."

"My lucky number," Davis said, deadpan.

The old man didn't react to the irony. The bull Negro got up and opened the door for us. Then he parted the sea of darkness with his flashlight while Davis and I rode the blind Plymouth to the side of Number Seven.

The Negro preceded us into the cabin and pulled the cord that brought the light of a naked bulb to an interior that begged for darkness. The cabin was unfinished, unpainted, and uninviting for anything save a sordid Saturday night assignation. As the rain drummed on the roof, and as Davis brought in the bags, I took in the iron bed salvaged from a departed century, the thin army blanket, the limp pillow, the grainy gray sheets. The cabin also contained a straight chair that was thick with too many coats of paint and too much glue, and an unpainted pine table upon which rested a pitcher of water, two paper cups, and two towels no longer and no softer than table napkins. Needless to report, the place was innocent of any plumbing.

When he had deposited the four bottles and six packs of cheese crackers on the table, Davis turned to me and flashed his best smile. "Welcome to the Plaza."

His gallantry deserved applause, but I only smiled weakly and could think of nothing to say.

"Did I do wrong?" he asked solicitously.

"No."

"No sense cracking up on the road. We're safe for the night."

I looked at the bed again and saw the bull Negro lying there in wait for me. I shivered.

Davis, sensitive as always, said, "I'll sleep in the car."

I said nothing. He brought me two packs of cheese crackers and a bottle of Dr Pepper. While I sat on the bed and remembered the Chateaubriand at the Hotel Carlton in Washington, Davis sat in the chair and blasphemed Detroit in general and the used-car salesman who had sent him into the storm with a Titanic of an automobile in particular.

The four bottles emptied, all but one of the cheese cracker packs consumed, Davis issued the orders of the night: early to bed, early to rise. He then told me the direction and distance of the toilets. Through the yellow pine walls I could see the black mackintosh glistening in the rain. I didn't stir.

"I'll take you," Davis said gently.

292

He held my hand as we walked, and he stood outside the toilet door and waited for me, whistling a Gershwin tune that wilted with my reappearance. Taking me by the hand again, he led me back to our cabin.

Two cabins away from ours, a couple emerged from a Ford and rushed from the rain to the mattress. He was a ponderous man who carried a gallon jug as if it were a demitasse. She was a flaxen-haired, skinny girl whose voice came from the wrong side of the tracks.

Once we were inside our cabin, Davis said, "Will you be all right if I leave you alone for five or ten minutes?"

Warily I asked, "Where are you going?"

"To the toilet. You can latch the door. I'll knock three times when I come back. All right?"

"All right."

He didn't move. "You can get undressed and —"

"I don't want to get undressed."

"Okay, sleep in your clothes. Be warmer that way." He hesitated at the door. "Will you be all right?"

"Yes," I murmured without conviction.

Davis left the cabin and I latched the door but failed to bar terror. In a moment I heard a rapping. My gasp died away before I heard Davis asking me to open the door. The instant I lifted the latch I felt I had been duped by a ventriloquist. I forced the door against Davis's shoulder, lost the struggle, and won back my tenuous sanity when I beheld his singular perplexity.

"Here, take this," he said, handing me a small flashlight taken from the car. "Just in case the lights go in this storm."

I latched the door again, placed the flashlight on the table, sat down on the bed, and allowed the rain on the roof to erode my wits. Above the rain I heard the thunder of laughter and imagined the ponderous man with the skinny girl. I turned from this ugly tableau to the reality of the table. On it I now saw the flashlight, remembered the larger flashlight held by the bull Negro in the black mackintosh, and saw the flashlight on the table as a phallus. Quickly I took the flashlight and rolled it

293

under the bed and out of sight, if not out of mind. Then I recovered it and returned it to the table.

I wanted to lie down, to slide with the rain to sleep, to an awakening from this nightmare that had cornered me in North Carolina.

I heard Davis saying, "We just crossed the border."

And the Renault, with the dust of France upon its hood, sped away from the customs officers and breasted the Mediterranean winds sweeping across the Costa Brava. Alone now, I saw Dandy Flood's face behind the veil of the storm. I saw Dandy Flood wearing a painter's cap and a black mackintosh and holding a flashlight that penetrated the thickest wall of darkness.

"God!" I cried in silence. "Oh my Jesus!"

Leaving the bed, I went and huddled on the floor, close to the latched door. I sat there and tried to tune in the radio music from the Carlton Hotel suite. I wanted to open a door and see Davis sitting at a desk with pen and paper, see the cold pipe from which he sucked inspiration. Instead I heard a broken record. "A writer gets his . . . a writer gets his . . . a writer gets his . . ."

Repeated, urgent rapping upon the cabin door drew me back to imminence. I admitted Davis and watched him prepare for a night on the back seat of the Plymouth. He opened his bag and withdrew a cardigan sweater and two pairs of socks. Sitting down, he removed his wet socks and donned both dry pairs. Then, after shedding his topcoat and jacket, he slipped into the sweater, returned the coats, shook water from his hat, and turned to me.

"Rannah, do you want a sleeping pill?"

"No."

"If you need me, just open the door and holler."

I said nothing.

He said, "Good night."

"Don't go."

"Afraid of being alone?"

I turned away from him, gathered the army blanket, and presented it to him. "Sleep on the floor."

294

Without comment, Davis took the blanket, spread it on the floor, and, after lying down, drew the blanket over him. I took the lone pillow from the bed and placed it under his head.

He smiled and sat up. "Thanks." From the back pockets of his trousers he removed his wallet and key case and handed them to me. "Put these on the table, please. It'll be easier to roll around on the floor without them."

Leaving the wallet and key case on the table, next to the flashlight, I pulled the cord. Darkness. Removing my wet shoes, I chanced the bed.

Davis spoke. "You all right?"

I wasn't. The rain was issuing from monstrous faucets and drowning me in the hell of the château. Fearful of screaming, I kept silent.

"Rannah?"

"I'm all right."

Then, to keep the rain from dominating the night, I asked a question that held only the significance of sound. "Why only Dr Peppers? Why no Coca-Colas, and what was that other drink you asked for?"

"Seven-Up?"

"Yes."

Davis said, "The old man probably gets a cut from the Dr Pepper distributor. Makes more than he can with Cokes. The old bastard, I wonder what crummy brand of condoms he peddles from under the counter to — I'm sorry. Good night, Rannah. Forgive me. Forgive me the storm, the Plymouth, my dirty mouth."

"I forgive you," I said.

Davis yawned, fell silent, and soon I heard the heavy breathing of his sleep. When I turned my head, I saw the blanketed figure on the floor as Dandy Flood, a black panther poised to spring.

Just as Davis had wrestled with the steering wheel when the tire had blown, I now wrestled with a mind blown off course. I had to keep staring at the figure upon the floor and telling myself that it was no one but Davis O'Donnell. I made my case for Davis O'Donnell: I established him at Hollow Grove, in Baltimore, in Washington, in Richmond, and in this very cabin up to the moment I had pulled the string and extinguished the light from the naked bulb.

The rain now began to soothe my nerves and prepare me for sleep, but then my father's voice rose to make the case against Davis O'Donnell.

His voice whispered not to the ears of the walls, but to me alone. "The man on the floor is not Davis O'Donnell. Not the man you took for a husband. You remember Davis O'Donnell. The man drank too much, too often, too hard. The man also led you to drink too much, too often, too hard. He led you to Hollow Grove. Now consider the man on the floor. Have you, since you left Hollow Grove with him, seen him, at any time whatsoever, indulge in spirits? What did he drink at Miller's restaurant? Two Cokes. He also drank Cokes in Washington, and in Richmond. Tonight he drank two Dr Peppers. Out of necessity? No. Out of choice? No. Remember, the old man who calls himself Mickelson offered, in your presence, to sell available whiskey to the man who purports to be Davis O'Donnell. Whiskey for two dollars a pint, brand whiskey, Green River by name. And now consider this carefully, please. Would Davis O'Donnell, on a night of storm and stress, in a time when his confidence was tried by a blown tire, a faulty, leaking chassis, by a short circuit that put him at the mercy of the black night, by a circumstance that put him in the clutches of a greedy old man, and in this most foul nest of illicit love — would Davis O'Donnell, the Davis O'Donnell you knew for a decade as your husband, would he have refused the whiskey?"

I cried, "No!" And my cry, lost in the percussion of rain, never reached the sleep of the sinister, shrouded figure on the floor.

Turning my head to the table, I looked beyond the flashlight to the wallet and the key case. Inspiration stirred my hand to reach out, first for the flashlight, then for the wallet. At the border between doubt and alarm, I was going to subject the blanketed traveler to a scrutiny of his papers. Shielding the light

296

with my coat and the bedsheet, I turned my back on the man in question and carefully examined the contents of his wallet.

In the hot glare of the flashlight I saw a California driving license issued to Davis O'Donnell, an identification card from Paramount Pictures issued to Davis O'Donnell, a Social Security card issued to Davis O'Donnell, a Screen Writers Guild membership card issued to Davis O'Donnell.

Then, at the moment my smile matched the flashlight for light and heat, I saw a photograph of a young and beautiful girl. In the next instant I heard a gruff voice rising from beyond the cabin and above the sound of rain. "Come back! You hear? Come back, you bitch!"

Alarmed that the voice might waken Davis, I snapped the flashlight off. Now, as an automobile horn pierced the storm, I returned the flashlight and the wallet to the table before he awoke and listened to the persisting horn. In the dark Davis rolled toward me. "Rannah?"

"Yes?"

"Were you asleep?"

"Yes."

The horn blared a moment longer before it stopped abruptly and allowed us to hear the high pitch of a girl screaming in pain, followed by the gruff voice intoning obscenities. The next sound was the racing of a motor. The rain, by comparison, seemed to play as softly as the violins at the Plaza.

Davis said, "Good night."

As cool and casual as my father in cross-examination, I asked, "Where are you taking me?"

He was unresponsive. "Where would you like to go?"

"Back."

"To Hollow Grove?"

"Yes," I said.

"This fucking storm. This fucking place for fucking." He sighed, and sadly added, "Maybe the sun'll be shining in the morning. I was hoping to take you south."

"How far south?"

"Stephensville."

On the ceiling I saw the railroad depot and the lieutenant boarding the northbound train. "Why Stephensville?"

"Why Hollow Grove?" Davis countered without rancor.

"Have you talked with my father?"

"I wrote him a letter. Six years ago. He never answered it."

"Why Stephensville?" I insisted.

"For you and me it might be better than Lourdes."

"Where's Harry?"

"What does Harry have to do with Lourdes?"

"You haven't said a word about Harry."

"What's Harry got to do with us?"

"Where is Harry?"

"In Florida."

I saw the map and the border between Georgia and Florida. "Where in Florida?"

"Key West."

"Is that where you're taking me?"

"Harry's working. You know he doesn't have visitors when he's working."

"What's he working on?"

"Another novel. This one's about the Spanish Civil War."

"Harry doesn't write historical novels."

"The Spanish Civil War," Davis advised me, "was fought from 1936 to 1938. Harry fought for the Loyalists, who lost the war."

"I'm glad."

"It was the right side, the right cause."

I was bitter now. "Still defending him?"

"Harry doesn't need me to defend him."

"When did you see him last?"

"A long, long time ago."

"Exactly when and where?"

"Tarragona. April, 1930." He said it as if he were reading my tombstone.

"You correspond with Harry, don't you?"

"Yes."

"When did you write him last?"

"Three years ago."

"Why'd you write to him then?"

"I wrote to tell him how much I enjoyed his latest novel."

"It's nice to know you still enjoy Harry's genius. What did the genius say in reply, if anything?"

"He cabled me from Paris."

"And what did he say?"

"Just one word. Thanks."

"Of course, the book was a smashing success."

"It was."

"Why did you take me away from Hollow Grove?"

He took a moment to answer me. "In Richmond, while we were walking along Monument Avenue, I thought I had done the right thing. For you, and for me. Good-bye Hollow Grove, good-bye Coconut Grove. The O'Donnells are taking Richmond."

Having said it all, Davis said no more. And I had no wish to despoil Monument Avenue. It was raining violins again, and Davis had let his sick heart drift to sleep before I heard another voice.

"Rannah?"

"Yes, Mother."

"Kill him."

"Harry?"

"Davis. I saw the picture. He's in love with this slut of a girl and he wants you dead and out of the way."

"Where is Harry, Mother?"

"In Florida, waiting for Davis to bring him your dead body."

"I'm not dead, Mother."

"If you sleep, you die. Once you're asleep Davis'll unlatch the door for the black bull you didn't recognize as Dandy Flood. And Dandy Flood'll ravish you until you're dead."

"No!"

"Kill Davis before he opens the door."

"How?"

"Take the flashlight and bash his head in."

"Harry's head?"

"*You must kill Davis.*"

299

"Mother, you loved Davis, you wanted me to run away with him."

"Rannah, baby, Davis isn't Davis any more. He's dead."

"Mother, he's been so alive since —"

"Davis only appears to be alive when he thinks he's Harry."

"Mother, I want to go back to Hollow Grove. Davis said he'd take me."

"He won't, Rannah baby."

"He said he would."

"He won't. Davis is tired of wasting money on you. He's had enough. A hundred months or more at a thousand dollars a month. He's tired of mining gold for you in Hollywood and he's tired of you and your madness and your ugliness and he wants you out of the way and dead. He wants the girl in the picture."

"Who is she?"

"You heard Davis in that Washington hotel. *A writer gets his inspiration from a young wife.* Harry told him that, and Davis wants to think he's Harry and go somewhere with the young girl in the picture and write like Harry. Quickly now, Rannah baby, quickly and carefully, take the flashlight —"

"Murder, Mother?"

"Self-defense, as your father would tell you, and I'm telling you now, knowing how Harry and Davis have plotted to have Dandy Flood tear you apart easier than you could tear the picture of the slut of a girl in Davis's wallet."

The last note of my mother's voice fell away. With the drumming of rain in my ears I marched to murder. I peeled off the bedsheet, released the weight of my body from the thin mattress and the creaking springs, and stood shoeless on the floor. After quieting my heart with the awareness that Davis was asleep in a sleep as sound as the death I would shortly deliver unto him, I turned my gaze to the table and the flashlight. Slowly I extended my right hand through the darkness, intending to take up the weapon softly and silently. An instant before my fingers reached the flashlight, my eyes flashed a signal to my brain that the object before me was a black phallus. My mind screamed in Tarragona and my hand collided with the flashlight,

300

scraping it against the table. Committed to frenzy, I clawed the flashlight, wheeled in the dark, fell upon my knees not for mercy but for murder.

I was Ruth Snyder bringing the sash weight down upon her husband's head, but the metal struck a blanketed board instead of flesh and bone. Then I groaned in Tarragona as a black panther clawed the release of the flashlight before savaging my face and silencing my groans.

In another moment, under the sun of the naked bulb, I saw Davis looming above me, flashlight in hand, agony in eye. His breathing was harsh, as audible as the rain. At last he knelt, took up my dead weight, and more gently than I deserved he delivered me to the bed.

Soon he confronted me with a cup of water and a capsule as red as danger. "Take this."

"No."

He held up a small green bottle containing some two dozen capsules. "Dr. Patrone gave this to me. For you."

"No."

"Don't you believe me?"

"I know better," I said, my teeth chattering, my body trembling with cold.

"How do you know?"

"Mother told me."

I had failed to slay Davis with the flashlight, but I did smite him hard with the simplicity of my reply.

"Your mother told you to kill me?"

"Yes."

"Do you think this pill is poison?"

"Yes."

Davis's outstretched hand swung toward his mouth. He swallowed the capsule, washing it down with water. He said, "Anything you care to tell me before I die?"

The orchestra was playing at the country club in Stephensville, and I was standing before the Alexander in the American Army uniform. "Where are you from?"

"I'm the boy who made Milwaukee famous."

301

I heard the secret words and saw the sun shining through the storm of my madness. And I wanted to die. "Will you let me take all the pills at once?"

Solemnly, he shook his head. "I may be remembered as the boy who made Rannah Gedney mad, but I don't want to be remembered as the boy who let her die."

Crossing my trembling arms, I said with resolution, "I'll wait until you fall asleep."

Without a word, Davis opened the green bottle, emptied all the capsules save one into his cupped hand, and went to the door. He unlatched and opened it and flung the handful of capsules to the night. Then he came toward me and handed me the last pill.

I took it and tasted poison. Flinging the cup at Davis, I cried, "You've tricked me! I'll haunt you! I'll haunt you to your grave! Beyond the grave!"

At first Davis said nothing. He merely retrieved the blanket from the floor and spread it over me. Then he said gently, "You comfort me. I was afraid death might mean the end of our relationship."

As Davis reached for the cord, I said, "Leave the light on. So we can watch each other die."

The naked bulb remained burning as Davis sat down, straddling the chair and regarding me with eyes that held no light of life and cried for coins.

And then the bulb fell beyond the horizon and darkness came to Sheol, North Carolina, a darkness through which sleep crept, paid its tribute to death, and passed through the deepest dark to dawn.

I opened my eyes to find Davis shaking me. I looked past him and saw that the night and the rain had fled. Before long, without any exchange of words, we threw our baggage and ourselves into the Plymouth and took to the rain-wet highway. Chauffeured by an old man with dead eyes, I sat in silence, observed the horizon unfolding south to Stephensville, and wondered why the September sun was rising in the west.

5.

The days came again to Hollow Grove as dancers to a masked ball, and I saw only the faces of the four seasons pressed against the one window of time.

Then, on a day captured by guilt and identified by memory as Wednesday, the eighth day of January of the year 1941, I danced with death.

A registered nurse, whose arms I had frequently dismembered in phantasies, left the château, advanced upon my cottage and, without a word, ripped the routine of my morning Bible reading and plunged her puny lance into my flesh. She left without stilling my confusion or alarm. Under sedation now, my mind scrabbled from Jesus to Dr. Dominick to my father.

Carelessly, I divined Dr. Dominick, attired in the uniform of an Army Medical Corps captain, marching into the cottage and off to war. Soon, in a darker presentiment, I saw another entrance for him, this time wearing black solemnity and bearing the yellow envelope containing a telegram telling of the death of my father.

While waiting for Dr. Dominick to catch up with my clairvoyance, I wept and prayed for my father as he paraded before me in a variety of death masks.

303

When, some minutes later, Mrs. Neff opened the cottage door, I thought my mind was at fault again. I saw not Dr. Dominick but Guy Thurlow. Another casting of astonished eyes brought me face to face with Death, who walked in Guy Thurlow's shoes.

Now, as I rushed to embrace Guy and found myself treading deep waters, I knew for certain that Guy Thurlow had come to bid me farewell before dying. I kissed the cold of his lips, and then I stepped back to be chilled by the gray of his face.

It had been three weeks since I had last seen him, but then he bore only a superficial resemblance to the bald-headed Santa Claus who, for eleven straight years, had brought Christmas to Hollow Grove. His ugliness now lost in the shadow of death, I saw Guy in all the beauty of gathering dusk.

Mrs. Neff took herself off to the bedroom and left us alone on the couch. I held one of Guy's cold hands.

"Guy, is this the year of no Christmas?"

"Might be," he said lightly. "We're even having some trouble getting June in January."

"Just a few weeks ago you seemed so well."

"Compared to what?"

"To now. Guy, why are you dying?"

"I'm always dying to see you. You know that."

"I know you're dying."

"Hello, Dr. Kronkite. I'm Dubious."

"Please, no vaudeville."

"No vaudeville. Vaudeville's dead."

"Your heart?"

He shook his head. "Only stands still for you."

"Cancer?"

"You said no vaudeville. And I heard that lousy joke in the Loew's Harkness Pavilion."

"Oh, God!" I wailed. "Oh, my God!"

I embraced him, wept over him, and tried to cure his cancer in the brew of my tears.

Guy, who held the door on death, said, "German propaganda. Cancer of the pancreas? I don't have a pancreas. You have to go to college to get one."

304

"I love you, Guy. I love you." Then, with a sudden pang, I asked, "Are you in pain?"

"As they say in Lindy's, it hurts only when I laugh."

"Seriously, Guy."

His smile unwavering, he said, "Well, I don't drive a car any more. I was chauffeured up here in a limousine. Manufactured by the same outfit that puts out America's most popular hearses."

I summoned yesterday to the deathbed, and I was dancing and laughing and coquetting: "Oh, Guy, you say the most outlandish things."

"It's peculiar, isn't it? I filed some funny stories from Pasadena. Never been funnier. At least that's the opinion from San Simeon."

"Does Edna know?"

"She knows."

"And the girls?"

"They suspect."

"How is Edna taking it?"

"She's a trouper. She'll survive. She'll function as a mother. And, I hope, as a grandmother. By the way, she sends her love to you."

"I like Edna."

"Of course, you were always a little too much for her. I remember she once said to me: 'Rannah's the kind of girl you wish you'd married, isn't she?' And I said: 'Edna, what kind of a girl is Rannah?' And she said: 'A fast girl.' I thought about this, and this is what I said to Edna: 'I'll tell you how fast Rannah is. She's so far out in front of the race of women that it's no longer a race. She's what evolution meant for women to be in the — in what we laughingly call — the twentieth century. The rest of you, with damned few exceptions, show all the ill effects of bondage to foolish men. Foolish men who domesticate their women instead of creating companions in their own image. For their laughter. And their loneliness.'"

I regarded Guy with respect and love. "And you spent your life making jokes about athletes and flagpole sitters."

305

"Look at it this way: I built something. I built circulation for Wee Willie Hearst."

I took the train from San Simeon to Hollywood. "You saw Davis in Hollywood?"

"I did."

"How did he take it? I mean the terrible news about you."

"I didn't tell him."

"Didn't he suspect?"

"Remember that old gag name for a newspaperman? That old gag greeting? I'm Brown from the *Sun*."

"Guy, what are you talking about?"

He said, "I was sitting in the California sun when Davis spotted me. We had lunch at the Ambassador pool. Did you ever hear the story about the two friends passing by the open coffin of a late and mutual friend? And the first one says: 'Looks good, doesn't he?' And the second one answers: 'Why shouldn't he? He just got back from Florida.'"

Unable to laugh, I wept and embraced him again. "Oh, Guy!"

"That's a very funny story," said Guy sadly.

"You'll never be able to make me laugh again."

"I'd settle for a smile."

"Take me to Philadelphia. We'll take a hotel room."

He went back to Broadway and to Lindy's. "That reminds me of another funny story."

"I don't want to hear it. Dr. Dominick'll let me go to Philadelphia. Just for a few hours."

Chained to his booth in Lindy's, Guy began to tell his funny story. "This old man goes to his doctor and complains —"

"I don't want to hear it."

"Do you want to hear about California?"

"Guy, I want to sleep with you. I haven't wanted to sleep with a man since — since Tarragona."

Guy held my hand. "All love begins and ends with hand-holding." He smiled and shook his head. "Get me. That's the damn thing about dying slowly. Makes you sound like Arthur Brisbane."

I said hopelessly, "I'm not attractive any more."

306

"You're beautiful," he said, and I was. "From now on I'll always think kindly of Philadelphia."

"You and your rotten jokes."

"I made Davis laugh."

"Was Davis alone when you saw him?"

"The first time, yes."

"And the second time?"

"No."

My voice rose from a squalid bed in a North Carolina tourist cabin. "Davis has a very young girl, hasn't he?"

"He was with a woman. She's in her thirties. A divorcée. A screenwriter. Canadian."

I wasn't interested in the details. I said, "I know he's terribly interested in a girl. A young girl."

"I know that, too," Guy said calmly.

"Who is she?"

Guy said, "One of my daughters."

"Guy, stop joking."

"Remember Lucy?"

I was on the Long Island beach with three little girls. "There was Ruby. Anita. And Lucy. And I was so young."

"Lucy's nineteen."

A wave swept over the beach and washed away a sand castle. The sun fled and the only light was a flashlight beam on a photograph. "Lucy's very beautiful."

"It's been twelve years since you've seen her."

"She's beautiful," I said, and I heard rain.

"She is."

"What is Lucy doing in California? Is she a starlet?"

"Lucy's never been to California."

I blamed my confusion on the drug coursing through my blood. "Where is she, then?"

"At Smith."

"Which Smith?"

"Smith College. Northampton, Massachusetts. She's a junior."

"Mother wanted me to go to Agnes Scott. That's a college in

307

Atlanta. Father was indifferent. But Wilson wasn't. About the war. Such a brief war."

Idly Guy said, "I think it was called on account of rain."

"So Davis is in love with Lucy?"

"He loves her." I flinched and Guy noted it. "Like a daughter," he amended.

"She's your daughter."

Guy said, "She isn't like her sisters. She's more O'Donnell than Thurlow."

"This — forgive me, I'm drugged. I can't seem to think clearly. What are you trying to say?"

"Lucy's another Rannah Gedney."

"You make it sound like a blessing. Do you mean to?"

"I do," said Guy. "She's bright. Very beautiful. And thinks she knows what she wants out of life."

"And what is that?"

"She wants to write great novels. And, before that, to live them."

"How did Davis take up with her?"

"Lucy wrote to him in the first semester of her freshman year."

My mind contained in a wallet, I said, "And enclosed a snapshot of herself."

"I don't know if she did or not. I do know that Davis answered her promptly. Their correspondence, among other things, took on regularity."

"Among what other things?"

"I've read all the letters. From Davis to Lucy and from Lucy to —"

"How did you get to read them? How did you dare?"

"Lucy showed me Davis's letters. And he showed me his letters from her. And I'm grateful."

"Guy, you're dying very badly. How can you be grateful that your daughter's taken up with an old, dead man married to a madwoman?"

"Davis couldn't save you," Guy said. "But he may save Lucy."

308

"I don't understand you. They're lovers and they write love letters, don't they?"

"Love letters?" Guy weighed the question on the scales of his experience. "Maybe. Maybe about the love of life."

"Guy, what are you trying to say?"

"Those letters are about you."

"Me?"

"Lucy poses a problem. And Davis answers her. Tells her how you'd faced just such a problem. He tells her what you did right, and where you went wrong. Sure, they're love letters. They spell out the love of Davis O'Donnell for Rannah Gedney."

Unmoved, I asked, "What else is in those letters?"

"Evidence."

"Evidence of what?"

"Davis's guilt about your long illness. His shame, his despair."

"Doesn't he love Lucy?"

"Like a daughter," he reiterated with patience.

"Has he helped her?"

"He's been a godsend. Let me say this: Davis owed me for *North Shore*. He dedicated the book to me. But I never considered that full payment of the debt. The debt's paid now with interest. His interest in Lucy."

I turned to the window. "I can't — I simply can't seem to picture Davis as a father. I never really felt badly about being unable to give him children. Or even one child. He was always himself so much the boy, so much the sophomore. He seemed to turn overnight from a sophomore to an Old Blue. No middle age, no maturity, except for writing *North Shore*. And that wasn't truly his own maturity. It was yours, and Freddie's, and Harry's." I paused to catch my breath after the utterance of the devil's name. "In those last years, before Tarragona, I used to be so very thankful that there were no children about to see us — the once dazzling O'Donnells — as drunken, disgusting, revolting derelicts. Dancing on the brimstone of the hell Harry fashioned for us."

309

From the edge of the grave, Guy said, "That was a long time ago."

"Does Lucy remember me?"

"She remembers."

"Fondly?"

"Very."

"She was so young. A child."

"I wasn't," said Guy. "I helped her remember."

"I love you."

"Lucy'd like to write to you."

"To me? Why?"

"She wants you to write to her."

"Why? Has Davis stopped writing to her?"

"He's stopped." I thought I detected a note of profound regret.

"Who stopped him?" I asked. "The Canadian woman?"

"No."

"Is Davis living with this woman?"

"No."

"With another woman?"

"He was living alone. In Santa Monica. In the garage apartment of an old mansion on the palisade."

I was incredulous. "Is that what Davis told you?"

"I was there. I saw the apartment."

"An old mansion?"

"A rooming house."

"When did you see Davis there?"

"A week ago Friday. December 27th."

"And he was alone?"

"Very much alone."

"Don't pity him. He's probably in bed with some starlet right now." Guy said nothing, and neither smiled nor frowned. I asked, "Was he writing?"

"A novel. About Hollywood."

"He'll never finish it. Hollywood! That's no subject matter for a writer who's done *North Shore*. Am I right, Guy?"

"Right. He'll never finish it."

310

"Of course not," I sneered. "His telephone'll ring and he'll run to the nearest studio."

"There's no telephone in the apartment."

"No telephone? Perhaps he's serious about the book. How far along is he?"

"Page 206 was in the typewriter."

"Did Davis ask you to read any of it?"

"No."

"Hollywood," I said with distaste. "The book can't possibly be any good."

"It's good."

"You haven't read it!"

"I read it," Guy said.

"I don't understand. You said —"

"Rannah, let me tell you about my visit. To the garage apartment."

"Which visit was this?"

"The third. I saw him at the Ambassador pool for lunch. I had dinner with him and Felice at Chasen's. And —"

"Felice?"

"Felice Thomson. The Canadian."

"What's she like?"

"I like her. Because she liked Davis."

"Liked? Is the affair over?"

"Over."

"Really," I said as if I couldn't care less. "What happened?"

Guy lowered his head and his voice. "After that dinner at Chasen's, Davis and I arranged to meet at his apartment on Friday afternoon. After my last round of golf with Granny Rice, Braven Dyer, and Ernie Nevers at the Riviera Country Club, which is close to Santa Monica." He paused to catch his breath. "I had to quit after nine holes. It was too much, too late. We all went in, showered, and then sat for an hour or more belting booze at the clubhouse bar. Feeling a little better, thanks to the booze, I took a taxi to Davis's address. My first visit there. And I'll tell you something. When the taxi stopped in front of this old, run-down house, I was so tired again I hoped Davis wasn't

311

at home. I just wanted to get back to my hotel and flop into bed. I paid the driver, but I had him wait. Then, when I saw that Davis's Chevy was in the garage — the garage door was open — I tried to yell to the driver and tell him to go on. I couldn't even yell. I had to wave him away.''

I rushed to the conclusion. "And Davis wasn't in.''

Guy said, "I knocked on the door. For two full minutes.''

"The son of a bitch! Makes an appointment with his best friend and — Guy, why the hell did you bother? Why didn't you just walk away?''

"I could hear radio music through the door.''

"He was in bed! With some tart!''

"No, he wasn't.''

"Where the hell was he?'' I demanded, not certain whether my impatience was with Guy or with Davis.

Guy, the old newspaperman, now seemed to hunt and peck for his words. "I heard a voice. Behind me. I turned and saw this fat old woman standing down below. Asking me who I was and what I wanted. I told her. She told me who she was. The proprietor. I asked her if she'd seen Davis. Maybe he'd gone for a walk. That's why he was living there. He liked to walk on the palisade, look at the ocean. She hadn't seen him. I told her about the radio. Asked her if she could open the door so I could wait for him inside. She complained about climbing the stairs. About letting a stranger in. She found the right key on her key ring. Opened the door. And yelled for Mr. O'Donnell. Then she opened the door wider. Looked in. Screamed. And ran. Right past me and down the stairs. Still screaming.''

I said, "She saw Davis and the tart on the couch.''

Guy gripped my hand, and I wasn't certain which of us was drowning and which of us was the straw. He said prayerfully, "I wish she had.''

"What did she see?''

"Davis. Alone. On the floor. In his pajamas. Not far from the door. And very close to his own vomit.''

"Drunk again!'' Then, as Guy said nothing, I recalled that Davis had disdained liquor on our last journey into catastrophe.

312

Quickly I asked, "Had Davis been drinking the other two times you were with him?"

"No. He was on the wagon."

"What was his excuse for falling off?" When Guy failed to answer, I tried again. "Why the hell did he start drinking again? What was his excuse?"

"He had none," said Guy. "He vomited blood."

I winced and squeezed some pity into my bitterness. "Hemorrhage! What hospital is he in?"

"He never went to a hospital."

"Who's taking care of him? This Canadian bitch?"

I stood in the dark of the Stephensville railroad depot and heard Guy's voice as a train whistle crying over a far horizon. "He's gone. He's dead."

I returned to Hollow Grove to open the Christmas gift brought to me by Guy, to kiss him and send him on his way to California, to his reunion with Davis. My voice, reacting to Guy's voice but detached from awareness, was feeble. "Davis? Dead?"

And Guy, in Santa Monica, said, "I knelt over him. Took his pulse and felt the cold of his wrist. He was dead. I wanted to lie down and die beside him. I wished I'd died the day before. The dying bawl too often. Too much. And I bawled. Then I hit him on the jaw. And I said: 'Get up off the floor, you stupid, potted, Yale bastard. It's *my* day to die. Not yours.'"

Guy had tears now. I had none, nor any words.

Guy continued. "He'd been dead for hours. I got up. Raised the blinds. Opened the windows and shut off the radio. Thinking I was going to be sick myself, I looked for the bathroom. And I found it. The door was open. And there was blood, vomited blood, on the bathroom floor. And a book lying in the vomit. Davis must've gone to the bathroom with the book. Fainted and vomited. Then, some time later, he must've come to. He got up and must've been going to the door. To call for help. Then he probably passed out and vomited again. And then, threw up the ghost."

I felt no emotion, and I told myself I was too old to listen to ghost stories.

313

Guy said, "Then the police came. Get this. Mrs. Overton —"

"Overton?"

"The proprietor."

"Proprietress," I corrected him.

"She told the police — on the phone — that Davis'd been murdered."

"Murdered?"

"The room was dark. A body on the floor. A pool of blood. A young man. Much too young to die. It spelled murder for an old woman, an old widow afraid of being murdered in her bed. After the body was taken to the morgue, she started complaining about her ruined carpet. Which had been ruined before Harding was ruined."

"Did you go to the morgue?"

"No. I hung around. I watched Mrs. Overton and a colored woman clean up the carpet and the bathroom. Then I gave the old bat twenty bucks. For the carpet. And for privacy."

"Privacy?"

"There was an inch of gin in the bottle. The bottle on the table next to the bed. Davis's last bottle. I drank from it. Then I sat down and wiped the blood from the book."

"What book?"

"I told you there was a —"

"I remember. What was the book? *North Shore?*"

Guy spoke slowly. *"November's Leaf Is Red."*

"What?" I couldn't seem to clear away my confusion.

"That's the title of the book. *November's —*"

"Never heard of it. Who wrote it?"

"Harry Ingram," he said. He said it as if he were pronouncing a death sentence, consigning ashes to ashes and dust to dust.

"What's the book about?" I asked, as if I were at a literary tea.

"The Spanish Civil War. Came out last fall."

"Yes, I remember Davis telling me Harry was writing it. Is it good?"

Now Guy appeared as disconcerted as a hangman who has failed to spring the trapdoor. "Sure. It's good."

314

"A hit?"

"A home run. With the bases loaded."

"What did you do with the bloody book? Did you bury it with Davis?"

"No, it's in the trunk."

"What trunk?"

"The steamer trunk. With all those stickers on the outside."

I remembered the trunk, the stickers, and the contents of the days of our travels together. "What else is inside?"

Guy said, "The best of Davis O'Donnell. Letters. Ledgers. Newspaper clippings. Scripts. Unfinished novels. Beginnings for short stories. Essays. Observations. Notes."

"What did you do with his clothes?"

"Salvation Army."

"And where did you bury Davis?"

"We didn't."

"Where is he?"

"His ashes were scattered. Santa Monica Bay."

"Ashes! You cremated him!"

"I checked with Ellis Mason. Davis'd left instructions. He wanted it that way."

"Was there a funeral?"

"No services."

"Also by Davis's instructions?"

"Right."

"Did you stick to the letter of his instructions?"

Guy shook his head, and for an instant I waited for it to topple. "What he asked for was a funeral pyre. On the beach. Like Shelley."

I left Shelley burning on the Italian strand and saw Davis confront Chartres with the awe of a good Catholic boy. "No priest, no prayers?"

"There were prayers," said Guy. "Of a sort. There were ten of us. At Chasen's. Private dining room."

"And you all got drunk," I accused.

"We drank. We ate. And we talked. Of Davis O'Donnell."

"Was the Canadian bitch there?"

315

"She was."

"Did she lead the tears?"

"She loved him."

"And Davis loved her."

"I hope so."

I ground my teeth. "Why do you say that?"

"She's no bitch. She's a fine woman. You should've heard her. At Chasen's. She spoke the last thousand words."

"Garrulous, isn't she?"

Guy said, "She read to us. From *North Shore*. The last thousand words."

"And you all wept."

"When we left Chasen's, we were smiling."

"Smiling?"

"Secret smiles. The ten of us sharing the secret. That Davis wasn't dead. And that the rest of us were more alive. Because of him."

I asked, "Was Freddie there? Harry? Ellis?"

"No. They were too far away."

"Did you hear from any of them?"

"Only what I read in the papers. What they said."

"What did Freddie say?"

"Freddie was quoted in the New York *Times*. Saying he thought Davis had been as careless with his own promise as America has been of its own dream."

"And what did Harry say?"

"Harry talked to a United Press correspondent. Down in Key West. He said Davis's death was only a physical fact. But his life — the life he led — was the crime of the century."

"And of course Harry named me as the culprit."

"No. But the correspondent understood him."

"Were there big headlines?"

"No. It wasn't a page one story."

I asked, "What did you write in your own column?"

Absently Guy said, "I didn't mean to write a word about Davis. My feelings about him wouldn't be understood. Not by my readers."

316

"But you did write something."

"Only in anger."

"Anger? At whom? Harry?"

"No," said Guy. "With my former friend. Morgan Cantwell. Of Colonel McCormick's artillery. Do you remember him? He used to be at my house and in my bottle. Lots of times. Used to be a sportswriter. He's changed now. His major sport is harassing the Roosevelts."

"What did he say about Davis?"

"Called him a snot-nosed sophomore. The kind of drunk who brought on Prohibition. The kind of writer who brought on the Wall Street crash and the depression. And other such nonsense."

"Guy, how did you answer him?"

"I went along with Morgan. And I added to the list of Davis's crimes. I said Davis murdered Harding. Was the cad who sired Nan Britton's daughter. And the cat that got Coolidge's tongue."

I laughed. "That's very funny. What else?"

"Then I told a true story. About the time Morgan and I covered a Yale-Harvard football game at Cambridge. I'd already filed my story. Morgan was sitting next to me in the press box. He hadn't written his lead yet. I just sat there, waiting for his genius to strike the right keys. To come up with a lead better than Granny Rice's about the Four Horsemen. Finally Morgan hit the typewriter. And this is what he wrote: 'Yale beat Harvard today. The score was 6 to 0.'" Guy paused. "The outcome was right. The score was right. The brevity of the lead was worthy of Ecclesiastes. Now — I wrote — I fully expected Morgan to display the same genius in reporting the death of Davis O'Donnell. I, with my lesser talent, might've come up with something like this: 'Death, the only drunk who can lick every man in the house, took on Davis O'Donnell in a fight to the finish.'"

"That's good," I said.

"Then I said I expected Morgan to come up with a lead like this: 'Death beat Davis O'Donnell today. The score was evened.'"

"Beautiful."

Guy said nothing, but he was looking at me as if I were wearing the wrong head.

I ended the silence. "Did Davis talk about me? When you saw him last?"

"He did."

"What did he say?"

"Kept talking about that trip south. In '39. The mystery of the trip."

"What mystery?"

"Do you remember the trip?"

"Of course."

"Remember the night in the tourist cabin?"

"Yes."

"Do you remember trying to kill him?"

"I remember."

"Well, Davis didn't blame you. He blamed himself. He figured his error was mentioning Harry Ingram to you. He thinks — he thought maybe that set you off. He thought maybe you were trying to kill Harry."

I said nothing for a moment, believing it prudent not to tell a dying man that it was the face of his young and beautiful daughter that had brought me to hear my dead mother's voice command me to murder my husband. Finally I lied. "Yes, that's how it was. I thought it was Harry. Paranoia."

"What a shame," Guy said.

I could feel the shame now. "Why can't I cry? It must be the drug. When you leave, I'll take a nap and I'll wake up weeping. I want to. I must cry. I know I must."

Guy rose, went to his overcoat and removed a thick envelope from a pocket. Sitting down again, he took a most familiar ring from the envelope. Davis's class ring.

"I thought you might want this."

In my hand the ring felt as heavy as Davis's dead hand. Too quickly I returned it to Guy. "You keep it."

"It belongs to you."

318

"Give it to Lucy."

"It's yours."

"Please, Guy. I want Lucy to have it. Please!"

Reluctantly Guy pocketed the ring. Then, from the envelope, he withdrew a key case. "Rannah, don't lose this."

The key case was a pound of Davis's flesh. "Why is it so important now? What doors can these keys open now?"

"One key is for the trunk."

"What trunk?"

"The steamer trunk. I shipped it from Santa Monica."

"Shipped it where?"

"To your home. Stephensville."

"My father won't —"

"I spoke with your father. I phoned him. He agreed to take the trunk."

I asked, "What did my father have to say about Davis's death?"

"Not a word. He only thanked me in advance for doing what I'm doing now. He was worried about how you'd take the news."

I laughed, and my laughter was sick. "Needless of Father to worry, wasn't it? Didn't he have anything else to say? Didn't he have any spit for Davis's grave?"

Guy reported, "He asked about the insurance."

Unashamed, I asked, "*Was* there insurance?"

"Davis had a twenty-thousand-dollar policy. The beneficiary is Ellis Mason. Who'll continue to pay your bills as long as the money lasts." Now Guy took a wallet from the envelope. "Here's his wallet. Thirty-three dollars."

I held it, felt it, smelled it. I said, "This isn't Davis's wallet. I remember —"

"It's his. Just look inside."

I counted the thirty-three dollars before extracting these items: a California driver's license issued to Davis O'Donnell, a Social Security card issued to Davis O'Donnell, a Screen Writers Guild card issued to Davis O'Donnell, an automobile insurance card issued to Davis O'Donnell, a card containing the

319

Yale football schedule for the 1940 season, and the snapshot of Lucy Thurlow.

Again I began to laugh. "Yes, it's his. It's his," I repeated and then veered toward the edge of hysteria.

Guy was frightened. "Rannah, what's the matter?"

I controlled myself. "It must be the drug. I keep looking at Lucy and seeing myself."

"Lucy?"

I held the snapshot before his eyes, and I asked, "Is this a good likeness of Lucy?"

Guy exhaled and seemed to rehearse his death. His voice flat, he said, "That's not Lucy."

I looked at the snapshot again and laughed. "It's so much like the daughter I never had."

Guy said, "Rannah, it's you."

More shrill laughter. "Is that what Davis told you?"

"It was taken in 1917. Your face was blown up from a group picture. Davis showed it to me a few years ago."

I listened to Guy and listened to my laughter leak away. "How did Davis get the picture?"

"One of your old friends sent it to —"

"Who?"

"I can't —"

"Who?"

"Gilland. A Mrs. Gilland."

The name failed to register. I got up and stood on leaden feet. "Gilland? Gilland? Jim Gilland! Jim Gilland married Liz Cooper!" My mind was tearing pages from calendars. "June! Nineteen-seventeen! Savannah! Yes, Savannah! After graduation! We went on a motor trip. Mrs. Cooper had a Kodak and —" I looked once again at the snapshot, and this time I vented the wildest and maddest scream of all the screams in all the years at Hollow Grove.

Mrs. Neff rushed in from the bedroom, pressed a button that sounded the alarm in the château, and then came to quiet me. My arms pinioned to the cross of her strength, I cried out, "Oh, God! Oh, my God! Jesus, dear Jesus! God in heaven! I killed

320

Davis! I killed him! He loved me and I killed him! Oh, God, strike me dead! I want to die! I want to die! Please, please, God! Let me die! Now! Now! Jesus, dear Jesus, I betrayed my beloved! Dear Jesus, gather his ashes and bury me in them! *Oh, Jesus!*"

part four

The Battle of the Old Whore

1.

There was at long, long last a window between Dr. Dominick and me. I pressed my face to that window and followed the wave of time sweeping over the Philadelphia railroad station and drowning him in the past. In the tunnel dark, from the aisle seat, I dug out the potato face of Mrs. Neff and desperately held on to the last root of Hollow Grove.

Five months after war had sailed out of Pearl Harbor, I, a prisoner of a private and older war, was being railroaded for internment for the duration in the tower of a castle on Death Street.

I was afraid to come home. I no longer trembled before the wrath of my father. I no longer cowered before the whispers of my ghostly mother. It was Davis who now commanded the specters in the shadows.

And now I was on a sealed train rushing southward on a trunk line to deliver me to the attic of the house on Gedney Street, where Davis was lying in wait to share his death with me. He was concealed in the trunk, a trunk I had opened in a recurring nightmare upon which I had ridden out my nights at Hollow Grove.

The night being long hours away, Stephensville and the attic

325

of my nightmares hundreds upon hundreds of horizons to the south, I borrowed the warmth of the Maytime sun. With Mrs. Neff a few paces behind me, I walked through a long train crowded with war and reviewed the troops.

Lieutenant Davis O'Donnell was absent without leave until the train reached Baltimore. There he returned to break bread with me at Miller's. The Washington I saw this time had no marbled edifices, only a hotel suite which had a pipe for a chimney and ice cream cones for towers.

Across the Potomac, the train outflanked Richmond and denied me the vista of a dream that had once walked Monument Avenue. Then, as we crossed from Virginia to North Carolina, I inspected the troops once again before retiring to my lower berth. While Mrs. Neff slept in the potato bin above me, I lay in the dark looking out the window. Greensboro begat High Point which begat Salisbury which begat Charlotte, but I was in a North Carolina tourist camp somewhere north of Raleigh. Staring at the starry sky beyond the Pullman window, I wondered where the storm was coming from. Turning the other way, I peered through the curtains to see if Davis was sleeping on the floor.

Sleep eluded me through South Carolina, and Georgia welcomed me with a shy dawn. I pulled the bedsheet and blanket over my head and raised the tent of yesterday. But the present returned with the hand of Mrs. Neff, and shortly thereafter we were dressed and marching again to the dining car.

I had no appetite for breakfast, no appetite for the day. The train trembled with speed, and I quaked before the prospect of Stephensville. As I sat at the table, I observed the tempest in the water carafe. I was on the *Titanic,* and I silently implored Jesus to save me. I turned from Jesus to General Sherman and implored him to rise up and burn the tracks between here and Atlanta, or between Atlanta and Stephensville. Home was a dirty word, very much like château.

"Jesus!" I cried in silence. "Save me from Davis!"

The steward heard me, and with the gesture of a white knight he gifted me with a fresh newspaper. I thanked him politely, momentarily held the newspaper with the mystification of an untutored savage, and then began to glance at it cursorily.

It was a copy of the Atlanta *Constitution*. Saturday, May 20, 1942. The datelines from the battlegrounds around the world read May 19. I turned to page two, and then and there I understood I was riding a train sealed by fate.

What I beheld was a three-column photograph of three men standing behind the speakers' table at a hotel banquet. The man being honored — the retiring editor of the Atlanta *Constitution* — stood in the middle, holding a plaque. On his right stood the mayor of Atlanta, on his left the devil from Tarragona.

It was indeed Harry Ingram, his face filling a more imperious mask, his chest straining the staves of the barrel, and his smile golden with the coins in his coffer, the largess of his fame.

I thanked Jesus. I thanked Him for revealing to me the plan of battle. I knew now why I was on a train hurtling toward Atlanta. The battle would be joined there, and I would march to a sea of Harry Ingram's blood.

Folding the newspaper as carefully as if it were a military map, I sat at the table and feasted upon the plums of strategy. This was the plan I evolved: I would slay Harry on a battle-ground of my own choosing; I would slay him on the spot where his presence first shadowed my life.

Atlanta would burn again, put to the torch of my crusade. When the train reached the terminal I led Mrs. Neff to the plat-form, breathed the cannon smoke pouring from locomotive stacks, and marched not to the platform where the Central of Georgia train waited to take me to Stephensville, but beyond the terminal to the taxi stands.

Mrs. Neff carried the two bags without any awareness of burden, but she sensed insurrection. When she protested the upsetting of the timetable, I brought command to my voice and obedience to the ranks.

The cab driver, upon hearing that we wished to be transported to the Clifford Hotel, gaped with incredulity. I repeated the magic name and left him to the concerns of traffic. The grime of years was smeared on the walls of the hotel and the only fresh paint in the lobby was upon the lips of the abounding girls.

I approached the desk as the Maid of Orleans, but the young clerk in his J. C. Penney suit mistook me for a dowager. Seeing Mrs. Neff beyond me, he seemed to recognize my Lesbian partner and my shabby reason for choosing his hotel.

I inquired whether the Governor's Suite was available.

"The what?"

"The Governor's Suite."

"Ma'am, you sure you're at the right hotel?"

"This is the Clifford, isn't it?"

"That's right."

I measured his ignorance and said, "Eight-oh-one. Is eight-oh-one available?"

He said, "I got six rooms that ain't took. Eight-oh-one happens to be one of 'em."

"Thank you. We'll take it."

He hesitated, fearful of imparting the bad news. "That'll be ten dollars."

The desk clerk was reassured by the familiar face of Alexander Hamilton, but betrayed no sign of recognition when I signed the name of Mrs. Davis O'Donnell on the registration card. And he was chagrined when I requested a bellhop. The old Negro, more used to toting beverages on trays, was staggered by the weight of the luggage.

As the bellhop slipped the key into the lock, I shut my eyes and waited for Davis to carry his bride across the threshold. I opened my eyes, entered the sitting room, and smelled the ashes fresh from the crematory. The chess pieces of the room hadn't been moved, but time had soiled and worn the carpet, the furniture, the walls, the ceiling.

After tipping and dismissing the bellhop, I went to the bedroom and saw Davis lying on the floor of a tourist cabin in North Carolina. I went to the bathroom, saw the tub filling with blood pouring from Harry Ingram, and I smiled and fell to my knees.

And I prayed: "Christ with me, Christ before me, Christ behind me, Christ in me, Christ beneath me, Christ above me,

Christ on my right, Christ on my left, Christ when I lie down, Christ when I arise! Be thou my battle shield, sword for the fight! O Lord Jesus, ruler of battles, steel my heart, for I am to contend with the Devil!''

I checked the newspaper again. The banquet had been held at the Peachtree Plaza Hotel. The telephone operator reacted as if I had asked her for the Adlon Hotel in Berlin. While she consulted her directory, I had to spend a moment or two quieting Mrs. Neff. She was firing upon my right flank with expostulations about her orders from Dr. Dominick and about her concern for my father, who was certain to be distraught by my failure to reach Stephensville on schedule.

Compared to the country accents of the Clifford Hotel operator, the voice of the operator at the Peachtree Plaza flowed from a fountain of culture. ''Good morning. Peachtree Plaza.''

''Harry Ingram, please,'' I said resolutely.

''Whom shall I say is calling, please?''

''Mrs. Davis O'Donnell.''

''Thank you. At what number can you be reached?''

''Isn't Mr. Ingram in?''

''Yes, ma'am.''

''Then ring his room, please.''

''I'm sorry, ma'am. I can only take your name and telephone number and give the message to —''

''When will he get the message?''

''The message will be slipped under Mr. Ingram's door.''

''How soon?''

''As soon as I write it out and it's given to a bellhop.''

''I'm an old friend. Can't you ring him for me?''

''I'm sorry. I have my instructions. Would you care to leave your telephone number?''

''Clifford Hotel.''

''Yes, ma'am,'' she said, as if she were an operator at Buckingham Palace replying to a fishmonger calling from Whitechapel.

Replacing the telephone, I asked Mrs. Neff for the time and ended by commandeering her cheap wristwatch. Minute by min-

329

ute, first like a child with a new toy and then like an officer anxiously awaiting zero hour, I kept turning to the small face and the tiny hands that seemed so paralyzed.

I laid waste to the encountered hour by recounting the Battle of Atlanta to Mrs. Neff. I might just as well have sung opera in Italian, for my keeper heard and responded only to the pitch of my excitement.

Leaving Sherman, I again raised the telephone and entered into another colloquy with the same operator at the Peachtree Plaza Hotel. She informed me of her orders and assured me that my message had been delivered to the suite. I thanked her, returned the telephone to its cradle, and rocked Mrs. Neff with the lie that Harry Ingram was waiting for me and I must depart at once.

Mrs. Neff said, "Dr. Dominick, he —"

"This is Atlanta. Not Hollow Grove." I held my smile and the reins of my temper. "Do you know what it means to have a friend?"

"You're excited."

"Of course I am. Can't you understand? I'm being born again. I'm free. I take a train. I read a newspaper. I stop at a hotel. I talk on the telephone. I wear a wristwatch. I'm free. Free to walk away from you and visit an old, dear friend. Who loves me and whom I love dearly. I first met him here in Atlanta. Eighteen years ago! Isn't it wonderful to be able to see old friends? We're old friends now, you and I. Almost twelve years. Think of that, Mrs. Neff! We *are* friends, aren't we?"

"I worry for you."

I said, "And I love you for it. You've been a mother to me. Wouldn't you like to go to a movie?"

"He didn't call you."

"Can't you understand? He's a famous man. He's very busy. He left a message. Told the operator I was to be sure and drop over to his hotel. I'll take a taxi. I'll telephone from there so you won't fret about me. All right?"

Mrs. Neff pinched her broad nostrils as she surveyed the room.

330

"I don't like it here. It's dirty. It's like — I think — like Jersey City."

I understood the pain emanating from the remembrance of her daughter, a prostitute in that city. But I overrode her anyway. "I spent my honeymoon here. Twenty-two years ago." I gathered my coat, hat, and handbag and moved toward the door. "When you get hungry, call room service."

"How long will you be gone?"

"Perhaps you'd best go downstairs. Take a walk. Find a tearoom. Or a cafeteria. It's a wonderful city. I once thought I was going to live here. I was going to marry a boy who lives here. A banker. I'll call you. He was very rich, very handsome. It's a lovely day. And thank you for the lovely watch."

I ran through the smoke screen of my words, opened and shut the door with the magic of certitude, and found myself a wall away from my keeper. But the hounds of hallucination pursued me, and I kept hearing the door opening and Mrs. Neff shouting, "Halt!"

Not daring to wait for the elevator, I took the staircase down to the seventh floor. There I pressed the elevator button, waited, and fled to the staircase again when I heard the sound of a door being thrust open. I took the stairs to the lobby, through which I scuttled to the street.

Driven by urgency but guided by no sense of direction, I walked several blocks into the maze of the city streets before I took refuge in a drugstore. At the fountain I stopped to behold myself in the mirror, and I saw a pale, unpainted face, a straw hat with a bright band, white gloves, and a blue redingote over a navy and white print dress. Although I had left my Bible at the hotel, I looked too much like a matron en route to church.

I went to the cosmetics counter. There I purchased a lipstick called Paul Revere Red.

The clerk who had made the sale was nice enough to escort me to the door of the drugstore and point out the route to the Peachtree Plaza. Quickly I was on my way, but abruptly I was halted by the commanding, cardboard face of Harry Ingram surmounting a column of his latest best-selling novels.

331

I interrupted my descent upon the Peachtree Plaza Hotel to inspect the arms in the windows of a sporting goods store. Momentarily reflected in the plate-glass window was the clairvoyant image of me bringing a brandy bottle down upon Harry's head and attacking Harry's jugular with the jagged teeth of the broken bottle.

Minutes later, armed only with a Queen-of-the-May smile, I entered the lobby of the Peachtree Plaza Hotel and was awed by the majesty of its marble columns and plush carpeting, the sweet, clean cream of its paint, and the magnificence of its clientele.

I found the powder room. In the mirror, as I applied the Paul Revere Red to my lips, I was Louis Napoleon rouging his pallor before Sedan. I peeled the matronly skin of my gloves from my hands, doffed my straw hat, and tried to comb girlhood into my hair. I presented my gloves and hat to the young attendant and rolled my stockings below my trembling knees before I ventured forth again into the lobby. I was a flapper again.

I bought a package of Marlboro cigarettes and a copy of *Vogue,* and then sat down in a soft chair to survey the terrain and plan my next move. I was certain the lackeys at the desk would not divulge the secret number of Harry Ingram's suite. Also I was certain he had received my message, had spewed his obscenities, and had doubled his guard.

And so I sat and waited, my eyes wandering from the magazine to the desk. When a bell sounded and a bellhop stepped to the desk to accept a message envelope, I rose and followed him into an elevator.

There was a button for each floor, and I chose the top button. "Sixteen, please," I announced to the elevator operator.

"Same," said the bellhop.

As my heart ran ahead of the elevator car, my eyes found the message envelope and the typewritten name. On the sixteenth floor I exited and promptly dropped my magazine. The bellhop retrieved it, received my thanks, and went on his way. I took the opposite direction, stopped to fumble with my handbag, and observed the door under which the envelope was slipped. Then I turned a corner of the corridor to take me from the bellhop's view and vigilance.

I glanced at my wristwatch. It was now twenty-five minutes past eleven. Five minutes later I removed the cheap watch and hid it in my bag. Then, taking a deep breath, I advanced upon Harry Ingram, whose battle flag, carried by the doorknob, read: Do Not Disturb.

At the door of his suite, I listened for sound and received silence. I pressed the buzzer lightly, heard it, and was given more silence. Once more into the buzzer, this time activating a more sustained signal. As I waited, I found myself rolling the magazine into a war club. Before I touched the buzzer again, I left the unrolled magazine on the sill of the window at the end of the corridor.

Then, as despair tugged at the silence, I heard the first sound of battle, the tumbling and disengaging of a lock. The door swung open, and there in the shaded dark of hell stood the embodiment of all evil.

He was a stark naked, blind, black Lear standing before me. A better focus revealed his deeply tanned skin, the blue of the pajama bottoms draping his loins, the black shock of his hair, the dark stubble of beard, the salt-and-pepper shield of hair on his massive chest, and the bewilderment in his clouded black eyes.

"Harry?"

"Rannah?"

"Yes."

He opened the door wider, poked a switch, and light spilled over the luxury of the suite. Then, as if he were alone with an apparition, he bent down and took up the envelope. Facing me again with eyes drugged with sleep, he regarded me more with sorrow than with wonder. "Come in," he said.

I entered the sitting room. Gently Harry shut the door, and in the splendor of the room, of his presence, and of the moment, he shut out war and brought me the peace of Eden.

He shut me out of his mind to open the envelope and read his message. Then, without so much as glancing at me, he departed for the bedroom and left me to pine for his return. I sat down

333

and found I was amusing myself with tricks of memory. In a play on hotel names, a young, handsome character named Davis O'Donnell rode out of the bedroom, whipping the bronze horse upon which a bronze Sherman had sat in the plaza.

I was concentrating on the reality of the two bottles of Courvoisier brandy and the basket of fruit on the coffee table when, a minute later, Harry returned to the sitting room. He wore a cotton robe now, and I saw him climbing into the ring at Tarragona to spar with Dandy Flood. He came to me and handed me a telephone message. It read: "Mrs. Davis O'Donnell called at 9:12. She can be reached at the Clifford Hotel."

Before I could say anything, Harry said, "Didn't hit the sack till five this morning."

"Oh."

"And I'm hung over."

"Sorry I woke you."

"I was up at ten. Had to call Washington at ten."

"Washington," I repeated.

Harry sat in a soft chair facing mine across the coffee table. "Went to the door. Found that note. And I said to myself, 'Jesus, what a helluva sense of humor.' Made the call and went back to bed. Damn sure you were still up there in Pennsylvania. Shadow Grove, wasn't it?"

"Hollow Grove."

"What the hell are you doing at the Clifford?"

"Buying memories. Ten dollars worth."

"It's a dive now. This isn't 1924."

"It is here," I said. "This is lovely."

Harry studied me now. He was neither smiling nor frowning. Instead he had the glazed look of a fighter rising from the canvas after being knocked down to blackness and nothingness.

"What are you doing in Atlanta?" he asked.

"Smiling."

"At what?"

"The sun. You. My good fortune."

"What good fortune?"

"Harry, I stole into Atlanta to dance with ghosts. I never expected to see you. Not in the flesh."

"How did you know I was here?"

"It was in the papers. Isn't that remarkable?"

"Why remarkable?"

"Harry, I went almost twelve years without reading a newspaper. And then when —"

He interrupted me. "When did you see the paper?"

"At the hotel," I lied. "This morning. And it seemed so right — so natural — to pick up the telephone. And the threads of the past."

Still probing, Harry asked, "What did you think when I didn't return your call?"

I laughed. "Oh, I told myself Harry'd had a big night. Old friends, good whiskey, good talk, and a good sleep."

He nodded. "That's just what happened."

"I'm sorry I woke you, Harry."

"How'd you get my room number?"

"I charmed a bellhop."

"Rannah, when did you leave Pennsylvania?"

"Yesterday afternoon."

"Traveling alone?"

I laughed. "Really, Harry, I haven't escaped. Mrs. Neff, my keeper, is with me and will remain with me until she delivers me into my father's hands."

"Does she know you're here?"

"Yes," I said. And then, anticipating his next question, I asked, "May I use your telephone, please?"

"Sure."

Harry watched me perform, heard me speak with the telephone operators, and the moment I uttered the name of Mrs. Neff, he relaxed enough to taste brandy. At the other end of the line, however, Mrs. Neff was far from relaxed, for she mistrusted my exuberance.

The telephone conversation concluded, I returned to Harry, sat down, and said, "Mrs. Neff's been a godsend to me. She was with me all the time."

335

"Good to see you so well again."

"Thank you. I feel wonderful."

"Rannah, when did this begin to happen? Your feeling wonderful and *well* again?"

I uttered another untruth. "Oh, it was in 1941. On a Sunday, the seventh day of December."

Harry reacted as if I had told him the date of the Second Coming. "Pearl Harbor?"

"Yes," I said blithely.

"Coincidence?"

"Hardly. Cause and effect."

Harry slopped more brandy into his inhaler. "A flight of Jap planes bombs an American naval base! Cripples our Pacific fleet! Kills thousands and thousands of American kids! Was this the news that caused you to feel *wonderful* and *well* again?"

"Harry, you must remember I had no radio, read no newspapers, had no interest in the world beyond the madhouse gates. Why, I didn't even know the day, the month, the year, or the time of day. Then Dr. Dominick came to my cottage, and I distinctly remember his words. He said, 'Pearl Harbor's been attacked by the Japanese.'"

"Did you understand him?"

"Only his alarm. I said: 'Where is Pearl Harbor and why is it?' And Dr. Dominick said: 'In Hawaii. This means we're in the war.'"

Harry asked, "Did you know what war he meant?"

"Oh, yes, I had heard about the war in Europe."

"From whom?"

"From Dr. Dominick."

"What was your reaction in September of '39 when you —"

I interrupted Harry. "Reaction?"

"Yeah. About World War II."

"Indifference."

"Didn't you give a damn about Europe?"

"Oh, I remember Europe," I laughed. "Does Europe remember me?"

Harry wasn't amused. "Back to Pearl Harbor. How does the

336

knowledge that your country's at war help you to feel *wonderful* and *well* again?"

"It's very simple. I love war."

He was incredulous. "You love war."

I laughed the laughter of the wonderfully well. "Oh, Harry, we're in Atlanta and you're thinking of Sherman and what he said about war. Well, Sherman never knew what hell truly was. He'd never been to Hollow Grove."

With compassion Harry asked, "Was it that bad?"

"It's a garden spot! Just lovely! What makes it hell is the peace and quiet. Peace and quiet are for the dead, not for the living."

"And what's war for?"

My smile was bright with truth. "Wars are made for girls like me. I grew up with war. With the Civil War that gave luster and legend to the name of Gedney. Why, I almost became the wife of an Atlanta banker because I was the granddaughter of a Confederate general. My heritage was worth all the gold in his bank."

"Why didn't you become the banker's wife?"

"Because of another war. Nineteen-seventeen! Nineteen-eighteen! Vintage years! I was so happy in Stephensville when the streets flowered with khaki. I can't wait to get home and see it in bloom again. I consider myself so fortunate to have two great wars in one lifetime."

His compassion splattered by disdain, Harry said, "Can I quote you that war is a ball?"

"It is, Harry," I said with quiet conviction.

"The hell it is!"

"Shall I try to explain?"

"Can you?"

"I want you to understand. But please be patient with me. It's been so long — so very long — since I've voiced my thoughts. Let me see now. In times of peace, a human being is forever at war with his conscience. In a time of war, the same human being escapes the recriminations of his conscience. He can no longer hear his conscience, not above the noise of battle. Of drums beat-

337

ing. Of bands playing. And the sounds of the weeping and the laughter. Am I reaching you?"

Harry was angered. "Are you trying to tell me that Pearl Harbor really *cured* you?"

"Yes, I am."

Harry glared at me as if he had caught me in a lie. "It's been more than five hundred days since Pearl Harbor. You left the madhouse only yesterday. Why did it take you so long?"

Choosing soft words of wisdom, I said, "Harry, my cure was swift. Very swift when you consider all the days from Tarragona to Pearl Harbor. But it's not a question of time. Time didn't heal me, Harry. It wasn't time, Freud, or Jesus. It was war."

Harry addressed his inhaler. "What happens when the war ends?"

"To me?"

His eyes fierce upon me now, he said, "Yeah, to you."

"At the midnight of peace, I'll turn into a peculiar pumpkin again." After a few tinkling notes of laughter, I said, "Seriously, I don't ever think about the war ending. I've never liked for wars or parties to end. Have you?"

"Me? I'm with Sherman."

"War was good to Sherman. And it's been very good to you. Hasn't it, Harry? Hasn't it brought you fame and fortune? Which you well deserve, of course."

Harry regarded me quizzically. "Do I deserve my fame and fortune?"

"Oh, yes. Sherman had command. You were only an enlisted man, a doughboy with one rifle and all the mud you could swallow. Yes, Sherman had command. And I had my lieutenants and captains and all the bands and orchestras playing for me. But when the wars ended for Sherman and me, they began again for you, with your barrage of words that you so deftly and so ably distilled into literature."

More confused than flattered, Harry mumbled his thanks.

Another thought cut in and danced with me. "Last night on the train it was simply wonderful! Exhilarating!"

"What was?"

338

"Walking through the coaches. Seeing all those beautiful girls and handsome boys."

Harry, the twenty-twenty realist, demanded, "Where the hell were the ugly ones?"

I played with my new toy of laughter. "Harry, you miss the point. The uniform makes handsome boys of those who are no longer boys and who were never handsome. And the war makes beautiful girls of women who are neither beautiful nor girls any longer. That's the heaven of war."

Harry responded with the litany of bewilderment. "The heaven of war?"

"The train was so very alive! So very ripe for ecstasy! Oh, yes, Harry, take away the uniforms, take away the war, and what have you? The ugliness of narrow, potted, petty lives, lived as if life were an eternity. As if tomorrow always came wrapped in rainbow ribbons. Oh, the lives that are merely bided away."

"Tell that to the boys at the fronts," Harry said.

"The only sin in time of war is death. The only sin."

Harry poured more brandy. "Rannah, did you make love on the train?"

My toy of laughter broken, my voice distant and sad, I said, "I lay alone in my lower berth, looking out the window, winking back at the stars." No comment forthcoming, I turned to him and found myself saying, "Harry, I've never seen you look so handsome."

His suspicion withered the compliment. "And we're not even on a train."

Then the answer came to me and I rushed to deliver it to Harry. "I never saw you before in a time of war!"

He looked sullen now. "Yeah."

I tried a diversionary tactic. "Where's Charlotte?"

Harry stared at me, spoke not a word, his eyes telling me how disconcerting my question was.

"Did I say something wrong?"

"You have been out of touch, haven't you?"

"Let's not count the days again," I said.

"Charlotte divorced me. In '36."

339

"I'm so sorry."

"I married again in '39." He sniffed the brandy inhaler.

"Who is she?"

"Francine Bard."

"You said that without affection."

"She's in Nevada."

"Is that where you're making your home now?"

"My home's in Key West, Florida. Francine's in Reno."

"Reno? Divorce?"

"Four weeks to go."

"Again, I'm so sorry."

"Fuck her." This was the epitaph for a dead marriage.

I asked, "What happened?"

"Same old story. Three times up, three times out."

"I can't even recall the name of your first wife."

"She's Mrs. Gerald Dreyfuss now. Lives in Houston. Her husband's in advertising."

I said, "I remember when she left you. And why."

Harry was surprised. "You remember?"

"Yes, I remember. Why did Charlotte leave?"

"Franco was coming."

"I don't understand. Who's Franco? Franco who?"

"What Sherman means to you, Franco means to me."

"Are we talking about war or divorce?"

Harry said, "My God, have you been away!"

"Yes, I have."

"We had a civil war in Spain. I sent Charlotte and the kids to —"

"Kids?"

"Charlotte had twins. Billy and Teddy. Jesus, they'll be ten soon. June the twenty-third. Jesus, ten years. Anyway, I sent Charlotte and the kids to Ireland. Dublin. When I joined up with the Loyalists, Charlotte took herself and the kids to Mexico. And got a divorce."

"On what grounds?"

Harry exploded. "Who the fuck knows? When a bitch walks out on you, you don't expect to hear her tell the truth. She said

340

it was desertion. Said that if I loved her and the kids I wouldn't have done what I did."

Quietly I asked, "*Did* you love her and the children?"

"What the fuck do you think?"

"I think you did. But that you loved war more."

"Shit," he said without rancor.

"You had one war. Why did you go to another?"

He flared up now. "Look, Rannah, you've got good reason to forget Tarragona! But it was my home! The first home I had since I left Montana! And my homeland was invaded! Can you get that through your — ?"

"I understand, Harry."

Harry's words now dug a grave for him. "Lost the war. Lost my home. My wife. My kids. My house was leveled by cannon fire. After the battle for Tarragona was over. Leveled by a four-eyed, fucking general."

From the deep pit of my ignorance, I asked, "What was the civil war in Spain all about?"

"Shit and corruption."

I tried again. "Why'd you lose?"

Harry regarded me as if I were a visitor from a far planet. "Didn't you read my book?"

I said, "I've read only one book in the last twelve years."

"*In Battalions?*"

"No, the Bible."

"You would've been on the other side."

"I beg your pardon?"

"Skip it. *November's Leaf Is Red*. That's the title of my latest book. It's about the shit in Spain."

"Then you won the war, didn't you?"

Harry frowned. "I thought you were *well*."

"You survived the cannons, Harry. And you wrote the great novel of that war."

"How the hell would you know?"

"Guy Thurlow told me."

"Told you what?"

"Guy said you hit a home run. With the bases loaded."

Harry dripped with pleasure. "Did he mean it?"

"Yes, indeed."

Meditatively, Harry said, "I liked Guy. More than he liked me. Just couldn't get close to him. Couldn't break him down. Even with a jug of booze. You know he sent us money?"

"Us?"

"The republicans. The Loyalists. My side of the war. Sent us lots of money. And the son of a bitch worked for Hearst."

"I must read the book."

I meant what I had said, but Harry didn't hear me. He was at the bottle again and the tide was raging once more. Fully a minute must have passed before I punctured the silence.

"Harry?" He looked at me. "Why did Francine leave you?"

"That's the way it goes. Love and leave Harry. Want another answer? I enlisted again. Yeah, that's why she left me. I enlisted again."

"Enlisted?"

He corrected himself. "I was sucked in. By the War Department."

"What rank did you hold in Spain?"

"I asked for a machine gun. They gave me a mimeograph machine."

"What are they giving you now, Harry?"

"A division," he said sourly. "I'm going in with a division. Army division. Picking it up at Fort Lewis. That's in Washington. The State of. Gonna stay with the division right through the whole fucking war."

Failing to understand him, I asked, "What are they giving you this time?"

"A general for my next novel. And fifteen thousand troops for my dispatches. I'm gonna be a war correspondent. North American Newspaper Alliance. Hundreds of papers."

"You don't seem enthused, Harry."

"Enthused? Who the fuck gets enthused about war any more? You pick your side, swallow hard, and you go at the fascist bastards again. What the hell! This is just the next chapter of the fighting that went on in China and Spain."

342

"Fascist? Isn't that what Mussolini was in Italy?"

"He's still there."

"I seem to remember something about the Fascisti and trains. Oh, yes, they made the trains run on time."

"Sure, they ran on time. To Ethiopia. To Spain. And now they're running out of Berlin."

"Harry, why a general for your next novel?"

"Because it interests me. I want to get down on paper just how a West Pointer takes thousands of kids who can't spell fascism and makes a fighting division out of them. Soldiers who do and die without knowing what the hell they're laying their lives down for. Do you understand?"

I said, "I understand you. But I don't believe you have an understanding of war. I remember Joel Stone and what he said —"

"Take my word for it, Rannah. You don't understand."

I shrugged. "Not everyone can win glory as a novelist."

"Talking to you is like talking to Rip van Winkle. Rannah, you've been away. Believe me, wars aren't for understanding, they're for enduring. The hell with the songs, the drums, and the medals. No more arches of triumph."

Properly scolded, I smiled and said, "And, of course, wife number three didn't understand you either."

"Francine? She's a cunt."

"What else was there about her that made you marry her?"

The action of Harry's laughter was delayed, but it was warm and flowed on like the Gulf Stream. "That's funny. Hell yeah, that's funny." My laughter was counterpoint to his melody, and I stilled it to listen to his recitative. "I'll tell you what there was about Francine. Beauty. A cold, blonde beauty. Always a fresh, soapy cleanliness about her. She's twenty-four. Put her in a garden and she looks sixteen."

"Any children?"

"One. Francine," he said. We chuckled over that one, then Harry said, "I used to wonder if you'd forgotten how to laugh."

I sighed and exhaled the stale air of the château. "For a time."

343

Harry said, "April, 1930. Now it's May, 1942. And there's rubble outside of Tarragona."

Fleeing the hazelnut grove, I said, "Harry, we're in Atlanta. Sherman and his circus of fire are gone."

Harry went to a window. He raised a blind and looked down upon the city. "It was nice being young here, working on that first novel."

I fell into step with him. "Yes, it was nice being young."

As he left the window, Harry brought a good smile with him. "And it was nice meeting you. Bathsheba in Atlanta."

I laughed. "Harry, you blushed."

"That was the boy from Montana."

"You were a married man."

"The boy from Montana," he insisted.

"Yes, I remember. It was the boy from Montana. The boy with his Christmas rifle alone in the forest."

He regarded me with awe. "Jesus, you remember things about me none of my three wives ever bothered to remember. You know all the words and all the music."

I bowed slightly. "Thank you."

Abruptly he clapped his hands. "Hey, you hungry?"

"Very."

"Shall I order up some chow?"

"That would be lovely."

"Want to see a menu?"

"No, I prefer looking at you."

Harry preened. "I believe you. Why are we so happy to see each other?"

Then I said a wrong thing. "You weren't happy when I walked in."

"I was hung."

"You had the telephone message."

"The guys and me, we were talking about you last night. I figured one of 'em was going on with the gag."

"What gag?"

He scolded me. "The gag of '24. Of being full of piss and ginger. Of being lucky enough to get to interview the dazzling

344

O'Donnells. Sure, they were ribbing me and saying I'd still be making fifty bucks a week on a copy desk if it hadn't been for — "

Harry stopped the flow of his words just before the falls. But I smiled and pushed him over. "For Davis."

He surfaced. "Yeah. If it hadn't been for *Davis*."

I splashed him with laughter. "There, we've said it! Look to the window, Harry! The sun hasn't found a cloud to hide behind!"

"Rannah, why are we laughing so much?"

"It's the war."

"The hell it is."

"It is, Harry. Believe me. The telephone message came by way of Pearl Harbor."

"What does that mean?"

"If we weren't in a state of war, I'd never have called you. Would never have tapped on your door for a cup of kindness."

"A cup of kindness?"

"Just words, Harry, the wrong words. I tapped on your door for the elixir of life. Like that better?"

"Yeah."

"Harry, do you understand me now? You and I, we're at peace with one another. For the sun's shining on war."

Without a word Harry returned to the window and lowered the blind. Turning to me, he said, "The hell with the sun. I know why we're at peace with each other. We're in a hotel room. The door's shut and something's happening. We're remembering who we are, how alive and young we once were, how alive and young we feel right now."

I muttered, "Amen."

Harry hesitated and chilled the room with crisis. "Amen? I'm not preaching in church! This is a hotel room!"

"Then bring on the room service."

Harry lifted the phone and the crisis was past. "Room service, please." He turned to me. "Anything special you want?"

Before I could locate a clever reply, I saw another envelope

345

being slipped under the door. I fetched it and handed it to Harry. "Another message from Garcia."

He said, "Thanks. You want breakfast or lunch?"

I said, "I want a bottle of muscatel. From Tarragona."

There was no reaction from Harry as he vanquished the telephone. "This is Harry Ingram. Listen, I'd like a Sunday breakfast for two. Juice, eggs, ham, bacon, link sausage, and coffee. And listen, heat up some of last night's dinner rolls. Don't bring up any of that fucking tasteless toast." He paused to listen. "That's right, heat 'em up. I want 'em crusty. And listen, pick me up the best bottle of muscatel you can. That's what I said, muscatel. Half hour? Okay." Replacing the telephone, Harry tore the message from the envelope. "From Washington."

"How's the weather in Valley Forge?"

"It's the War Department."

"General Nuisance?"

"Three-star Nuisance. Got to call him right away. Hell, I was going to have a shave and shower."

I said, "Harry, I'll tell you what. You make your call. I'll shave first."

Harry bombarded the walls with laughter, poured more brandy, and burned the telephone lines to Washington. Meanwhile, I left the sitting room and shut the door behind me. I wandered into the bedroom, to the drawn-blind dark, to the erotic disarray of the bed, to the smell of a dead cigar in a cluttered ashtray, to the litter of newspapers and magazines on the carpet. Giddy from all this heavy masculinity, I retreated to the bathroom.

I locked the door and found myself confronted by tiles whose whiteness returned me to the dreaded château. To escape, I clutched at the leather shaving kit resting on the washbasin, embraced it, inhaled its odor and forced myself back to Atlanta.

In a few moments I was playing with it. I removed a wooden bowl of Yardley's shaving soap, a flask of Yardley's after-shave lotion, a Dr. West toothbrush, a can of Dr. Lyon's toothpowder, and I cried for Dr. Dominick when I held an ivory-handled

346

straight razor, opened the long Swedish steel blade, and saw Harry Ingram's blood on it.

Too hastily I returned all of the items to the kit, closed it, and tried to shut murder from my mind. I sank to the floor, my face in my hands, and found myself looking through my fingers at the bathtub which seemed large enough to contain the waters of the Nile.

Rising, I looked at myself in the mirror above the washbasin, saw the years at Hollow Grove faithfully recorded, and promptly took soap and water and blinded the mirror. Then I turned on both tub faucets, and the water began to rise. I calmed as I undressed. I left my clothes on the shore of reality. I was singing and hearing saxophones and banjos as I unlocked the door and displaced the weight of my boldness in the tepid waters of the tub.

I dared not shut my eyes for fear I would be carried back to the château. Instead I opened my mind to laughter. I remembered 1924 and saw Davis open the door to the bathroom at the Clifford Hotel, bringing with him the strange boy from Montana whom he so wanted me to meet.

I went from Bathsheba waiting for David, from Cleopatra waiting for Anthony, to Rannah waiting for Harry. I waited and waited, opening doors and passions in fancy. Then, as I lowered my eyes, I saw the water in the tub growing darker and redder. Harry Ingram's blood was pouring from the faucet. I screamed.

There came a pounding on the bathroom door. "What the hell's wrong? Rannah?" Harry's alarm was manifest.

"Yes!" My voice was distant and strained, but audible.

"What's the matter?"

I countered with a question. "Are you off the phone?"

"Yeah."

"Would you bring me some brandy, please?"

"In there?"

My laughter returning, I said, "Don't wait for me to sail out of the tub."

No answering laughter from Harry. It seemed an eternity

347

before I heard from him again, and all the time I soaped myself softly and pretended I was lying young in the fountain of youth. The soap squirted from a taut hand when again I heard his rap on the bathroom door.

"Who's there?" the sentry within me demanded.

"It's me."

"Enter he who is no slave to grammar."

The door gave way to the commanding presence and the grail golden with brandy. My smile teasing one from Harry, I said, "Welcome to 1924."

Harry handed me the inhaler. "I'm Harry Ingram. From the Atlanta *Constitution*."

"Shut the door. You're letting the war out."

Harry, moving like a marionette whose strings I held, obeyed. Then, moving like a man, he opened and dropped his robe and slid into the bathtub with all the grace of a launched warship. Confronting me with his majesty, he took the brandy from my lips, emptied the inhaler, left it upon the floor, and drew me strongly into his arms, his legs, his hungry mouth.

Then, after a time without measure, I found myself being lifted out of the soapy sea and carried to the bed whose pillows and sheets drank the wetness, and to the forest dark where Lamiel lay with the boy from Montana.

Beyond the forest I found myself weeping and counting the angels on the pin of ecstasy. I wet Harry with my tears, and he held me gently and tenderly and did not stir when the buzzer sounded. Only when I had drained the last of my tears did Harry rise, leave me, and open the door for the entrance of the cart bearing the ambrosia and nectar of Atlanta.

I came to the table, to the room lit with sun, wearing only Harry's pajama shirt, the sleeves rolled to free my hands. The muscatel was from California, but the man across the table was from Tarragona.

Harry observed the bowing of my head, the shutting of my eyes, the movement of my lips, and the stringing of pearl words. "Rannah, you're mumbling."

"I'm saying grace."

348

"The hell you are."

I said, "I've also thanked God for you."

Harry poured muscatel for me. "I'm flying to Washington in the morning."

"Harry, why did you say that?"

"Just getting my bearings."

I sipped the wine. "Your bearings on what?"

His reply came only after the crushing of a crusty roll, the breaking and devouring of eggs, and the sweeping of a linen napkin across his yolk-stained mouth. He said, "Reality."

The California wine was bringing me the heat of Tarragona, and I asked, "What's reality?"

"Eggs getting cold."

"Is *that* reality?"

He smiled. "That's a fact."

I chewed on a crisp slice of bacon. "Harry, what *is* reality?"

He stabbed at a sausage. "Hate," he said. "Hate is reality."

I agreed with him. "And what is love?"

"Love?" He chewed the word with the sausage. "Love's a phantasy."

I took more wine, holding the bottle over the glass until it overflowed. "Poor Harry, his eggs are cold. And his phantasy is colder."

Harry buttered a roll and me. "Today you're my girl."

"Today I love you, Harry," I agreed.

"It's the hotel room."

"It's the war."

Harry shook his head slowly. "The bathtub."

I deliberately spilled more wine. "The fountain of yesterday."

Harry's teeth ground to a halt. "I like that."

"Today is yesterday."

"What's the date?"

"The yesterday before the day Davis danced with me. The yesterday in which he didn't exist for me."

I was in the past, but Harry was in the strawberry jam. "You're not eating."

349

Tapping a fork against the wineglass, I produced a dull note. To Harry I complained, "The orchestras are all gone."

"Gone where?" Harry seemed more concerned that the sausages were gone.

"With the boy who made Milwaukee famous." I drank and spilled and laughed some more. "The boy who made me. Then made me famous, too." After another burst of laughter as bright as the strawberry jam, I added, "The boy who made you hate me."

Harry heard me. He wiped pretense from his face and chose his words with the care he always brought to the blank page. "I love you."

"I love you," I said to Harry and to whoever else might be listening.

Harry heard the tinkle of truth, and he was quick to open another door to another truth. "Getting back to reality. When I got out of bed and opened the door for you, I saw hate. I smelled it."

I didn't refute him. "Why didn't you slam the door in my face?"

The question prompted him back to the brandy, and the dregs were in his mouth when he said, "I've slammed too many doors in too many faces."

"Are all your doors coffin lids?"

"Maybe."

"Doors are doors, Harry, when you touch them with life."

He scowled. "What does that mean?"

"When you let me in, you closed the door tenderly, and you shut the door on the dead. All the dead."

Imagination lit his eyes. "How did Davis get in?"

I sipped muscatel. "You opened the door for the waiter. Harry, did you look closely at the waiter?"

"Did *you* see the waiter?"

I said, "I see the table. I taste the food and the wine, and I assume the waiter came through that door."

"He was colored."

"Undoubtedly a mask. It was Davis. And he's still here with

us. Swirling about in the dust. Dancing with the dust to the tune of our laughter."

Harry brandied his thought. "What do we do now?"

I told him. "Sweep Davis from the field of battle."

"How do we do that?" the boy asked the magician.

"You'll have to do it, Harry," I whispered. "The bedroom door. You can shut that on Davis."

"Can't you do it?"

My voice rose. "I can't shut doors on the dead!"

Harry had the answer. "Better go easy on that muscatel."

"Why, Harry?"

"It's been a long time between drinks."

"You don't think I'm making sense?"

"No, Rannah."

"Did I make love with you?"

He nodded complacently. "Yeah."

"Then I make sense," I concluded.

"Why can't *you* shut the door on the dead?"

Now his question called for more wine for me. "When I don't sleep with Harry Ingram, I sleep with the dead."

"A guy could get drunk just listening to you."

I pointed an accusing finger at Harry. "See? You did it again! You just let in Guy Thurlow!"

"I get it. I said *guy* and *drunk* and you thought of Guy. Now how do we get Guy out of here?"

As I pondered the problem, I drank more wine and found myself distracted by the label on the bottle. "Harry, how far is Livermore, California, from Tarragona?"

"That fucking, four-eyed general. Name was Yague . . . ," muttered Harry.

High up on top of the Peachtree Plaza Hotel, I didn't hear Harry, but he heard me. "I'll tell you how far it is," I said. "It's more than four thousand days and nights away. And all that time I was dead and sleeping only with the dead."

Harry said, "I'm not dead. I'm not even dead drunk."

I answered him with the sign language of fingers playing with buttons. I opened the pajama top and allowed it to fall away from the heat of my body.

Smiling at my breasts, Harry said, "Tarragona."

"Wrong," I said without a smile. "I've just freed us from Guy. Guy runs from my nakedness."

"Tarragona," Harry insisted.

"I didn't like the bedroom in Tarragona."

Harry stood up and dropped his robe. "How about the bedroom in Atlanta?"

I didn't answer him. He watched me rise and weave toward the windows, where I drew the blinds and the draperies.

"What are you doing?" Harry called from the dark.

"Don't stir, Harry. Don't move." I lay down on the carpet and smelled freshly tilled earth. "I'm comely. You're black."

"The bedroom," beckoned Harry.

"The grove. Right here in the hazelnut grove."

Harry cried from hell. "Rannah, don't!"

"Don't stir, Harry. Let me lie here in the grove."

My words flew away on panicked wings, and I lay there, in the soft and silent dark, pressing my thighs into the earth. And then I screamed, "Shut the door, Harry! Shut the door on Davis! He's the dirt under my nails! The stink under my arms! Save me, Harry! Save me again!"

And Harry came and lay beside me, bringing me a tenderness that had no soil in which to grow. I turned fury loose upon him, sank my teeth into the flesh of an arm, and tasted blood.

I was comely, and he was black.

The hills of Atlanta stood in the way of the waning sun when I awoke. I was afloat on a mattress, running the rapids past dismembered nightmares and clutching a still warm, moist hand. I opened my eyes and saw the brandy bottle and the muscatel bottle, both dead soldiers. When I turned and looked the other way, I saw that Dandy Flood had been changed, by the magic of my love, into Harry Ingram.

I woke him with kisses, kisses for the earth turning away from the sun, for the draining of the day, for the momentary stillness

352

of my heart. Harry opened his eyes and seemed to wonder for a moment which of his wives I was.

"Rannah?"

"Yes, I'm Rannah."

"What time is it?"

"It's not tomorrow," I said, and my voice cracked.

My emotion lost upon him, he turned away from me. "Good night."

I dared not lose him to sleep, and I dared not rouse him again, for Davis was in the bedroom with us. He had entered when Harry had opened his eyes and his doors for his three wives.

"Harry?"

"What?"

"Did I ever tell you about Maxim Gorki?"

"Davis told me. Let's get a little more sleep, huh? I'm beat."

"What year is this?"

Harry groaned. "I'm eighty-eight years old."

"When did you have your first girl?"

"Good night."

"When, Harry?"

"I was fourteen."

"Davis was seventeen."

That truly woke Harry. "Who left the door open?"

I asked, "Harry, did you enjoy your wives?"

"I loved them and I hated them. One at a time."

"Who was best in bed?"

"You."

"Thank you, sir. But I'm inquiring about your wives."

"The hell with all three of them."

"Who, Harry?"

"Charlotte."

"Really? She was so frail."

"She wasn't skinny when she carried my sons."

Envy jarred the stillness of my heart. "Know what I wish?"

"What?"

"That you hadn't said that."

"I wish you hadn't asked."

Quickly I took him from his sons and returned him to his devildom in Spain. "Do you remember that last day in Tarragona?"

"Rannah, shut up." His voice was swollen with pain.

"Tell me about it, please."

"Forget it."

I teased him with furtive laughter. "I may remember it differently. From now on."

After a long moment Harry asked, "What the hell does that mean?"

"You raped me in Tarragona," I said.

He turned away again. "Good night."

I traced the curve of his spine with a forefinger. "You knocked out Dandy Flood," I said.

"Hurray for me."

"You made me well again."

"What about Pearl Harbor?"

"You made me a woman again."

"A girl," he corrected me.

The bitch in me now went to work. "Your three wives were girls."

"That's profound."

"More than you think, Harry. They weren't women. Once they were turned by time into women, you ran away from home. From women. You hate women."

"I love you."

"I hear you, Harry. I hear your hate and feel the reality of it. If I keep talking my way into your sleep, your dreams, and your work, I'll turn into a woman. And you'll hate me. Harry, did you hate your mother?"

Harry said harshly, "The door's shut on my mother."

"And on three wives. Shall I tell you why?"

"No."

"I was married to a writer."

Harry sighed. "So?"

"I know all about voids."

"What voids?"

354

I said, "None of your wives — the girls you took for brides — could endure the days, nights, weeks, months, and terrible years of living with a man whose mind and heart were only alive in his imagination. With a man to whom the imagined was more real than reality itself."

Harry looked crossly at me. "What the hell did they expect? They knew who I was and what I was."

"How could they, Harry? They were children! They couldn't understand — couldn't know the clay that writers are made of. They weren't warned about the terrible chasms and voids between the simple, declarative sentences. They couldn't survive the storm clouds of tobacco smoke. The crashing waves of whiskey. They couldn't take the black-on-black moods, the doubts, the dirt of ashtrays and the litter of wastebaskets, or the smell of fear and sweat. They despaired of being alone, being ignored, being left behind while you opened secret doors to secret rooms in secret houses in search of the right words and all those perfect little sentences that make up your books. And your life."

"Yeah," said Harry, "you were married to a writer."

I said, "Your wives weren't tall enough."

"Charlotte was taller than you."

"She and your other wives grew only as tall as your loins. They were children with small breasts and smaller minds. Dream girls. Storybook princesses frightened in the forest of your chest. Harry, did any of them ever express an original idea? Did they ever explore the mystery of Harry Ingram?"

Harry said nothing. He sat up in bed, scratched his chest, and then, without a word, left the bedroom. I lay there and wondered why I felt compelled to return to the reality of hate. I reasoned that tomorrow was closing in on me and drawing me by the force of its gravity.

Holding a fistful of envelopes, Harry returned to the bedroom. He raised a blind, lowered it, turned on a lamp, and dourly read each of the messages. Only when he turned and saw my eyes on him did he realize that he was naked.

He said, without a smile, "Rannah, I've got to make some calls. Why don't you clean up and dress?"

355

Smaller than any of his wives, I asked, "Is this how a day ends?"

He hesitated. "Like some dinner?"

"Yes. And I'd like champagne."

He was uneasy. "You sure?"

I smiled. "I think one bottle every fifteen years isn't too much to ask."

Harry said nothing. He seemed not to see my smile or my nakedness. Gathering his robe, he went to the sitting room to place the first of a series of telephone calls. I went to the bathroom, showered quickly, and spent too much time studying the straight razor and remembering why I had sought out Harry Ingram.

Within an hour, after the razor had been used by Harry himself, we sat down to dine in the sitting room. The candles on the table provided the light of romance, and the champagne delivered the sparkle of a France that had seen us so very young and so very alive. As for the food, Harry had ordered cold shrimps, a thick porterhouse steak rare enough for a lion, a basket of fried chicken, asparagus with hollandaise, Long Branch potatoes, biscuits and honey.

In the iron cage of his silence, Harry tore at the slab of blood-red meat. I sat and nibbled fried chicken, happy to be alive and to be the mate of this king of beasts.

"What a delightful war!" I exclaimed.

The candles heard me and the flames danced. But Harry seemed to be in a deep, dark pit now, where neither the light of my smile nor the sound of my pleasure could reach him.

I tried again. "Harry, remember that song from the First World War? 'Would You Rather Be a Colonel with an Eagle on Your Shoulder, or a Private with a Chicken on Your Knee?'"

"No."

"Something wrong with your steak?"

"No, I was just thinking."

"Excuse me."

"About what you said before. About the mystery of Harry Ingram."

356

"What was that name again?"

"You're drunk."

"Harry, that was a funny song title."

"I want to hear about the mystery."

I wanted to cry. "Harry, please, please laugh."

"Make me. Tell me about myself."

"I'm drunk. I won't make sense."

Harry looked hard at me. "Come on. Unfold the fucking mystery."

I tried again. "Harry, I'm mad. I don't make sense."

"The hell you don't. You make sense. You're wild, all right. But when you get it over the plate it's a sure strike. High and hard, the way the truth's supposed to be. Wind up and let me have it."

"On the bed or on the carpet, Harry?"

"No more screwing, Rannah. I've just opened the door on you. And I see your hate."

"I don't hate you."

"It's tomorrow, Rannah. And hate's the only reality. Remember?"

"Harry, do you hate me?"

"I hated you yesterday in Atlanta. I loved you today. And I'll hate you tomorrow in Washington."

I was sick. "Is it the champagne?"

"Rannah, why'd you come here today?"

I tried to laugh, but the attempt was feeble. "I can't lie, can I?"

"No."

Not daring to smile, I said, "The mystery of Harry Ingram? He's really Judd Gray."

The name eluded the snare of his memory. "Judd Gray?"

"I'm Ruth Snyder."

He understood now. "And Davis *was* Albert Snyder," he said, opening the door to Davis and causing the candles to tremble.

"Yes, Harry."

"Keep pitching."

Choosing a question with care, with care for Harry, I asked,

357

"Do you swear to tell the truth, the seed of truth, and the fruit of truth?"

"Whose truth?" Harry demanded.

"God's truth."

"Fuck that. I fought against that fucking truth in Spain."

Harry's words dirtied me and defiled the food on the table. Flickering candlelight in his eyes, he was again the devil in Spain. I said, "Harry, you fought against me in Tarragona."

"That's right," he said without regret. "I fought for Davis. And made a good case against you."

"I seem to forget your verdict."

"Not guilty by reason of insanity."

I said, "I didn't go mad until the following afternoon."

"I thought you were crazy the first time I ever met you."

"In how many speakeasies have you bellowed that verdict?"

Harry said, "No more speaks. Prohibition's long gone. We drink in bars now. In taverns."

"In how many bars, in how many taverns —?"

"Plenty."

"In how many bars, in how many taverns, have you charged me with the murder of Davis O'Donnell?"

"I get around."

"In all those bottles you've consumed, did you ever find a message? An indictment for Harry Ingram, alias Judd Gray, charging him with being the accomplice of Rannah O'Donnell, alias Ruth Snyder, in the murder of —?"

"No! Now make your goddam case."

I watched Harry rise and return with a full bottle of brandy. Opening it, he poured a dollop into his coffee cup.

"When did you first hear the name of Davis O'Donnell?"

Harry was responsive. "Nineteen-twenty. In Paris."

"What were you doing in Paris?"

"Talking about writing in sidewalk cafés. With other phony writers who drank and talked their books and never wrote."

"Do you recall how you first became aware of Davis?"

"I was sleeping with an American girl who was in love with a book. *The Distant Spires* by Davis O'Donnell."

358

"And she gave you the book to read."

"First she read it to me. I fell in love with the book and married the girl. The bitch."

"What took you from Paris to Atlanta?"

"A train, a boat, and another train."

"Wasn't it the book that drove you to Atlanta? To work on a newspaper? To start your first novel?"

"Yeah, I got a lot of mileage out of that book."

"And how did you come to meet Davis?"

"My city editor, who retired last night, assigned me —"

"Assigned you, Harry? Isn't it the truth that you begged for the assignment? That the assignment had been given to another reporter? And that you bribed this other reporter to relinquish the assignment to you?"

"How the hell did you know that?"

"This other reporter wrote a letter to Davis some years later."

"What else did he say?"

"That you gave him your week's salary."

"That's the truth."

"The best investment you ever made, wasn't it?"

"Yeah."

"You came to use Davis, didn't you?"

"I was there to interview both of you."

I laughed with scorn. "The Inquiring Reporter? No! A book salesman? Yes, indeed! You came to sell Davis the book you'd written."

Harry the lion roared at me. "You were there! I didn't mention the goddam manuscript! Davis took me for just another newspaperman with a whiskey dream of writing the Great American Novel! You heard him! Sounding off about all the reporters who kept telling him —"

I interrupted. "Yes, I was there! And you were very clever! Most clever with your cloak of humility."

"I was nothing," Harry growled. "He was God."

"Who was God?"

"Davis."

"You don't believe in God."

359

"In 1924 Davis O'Donnell was God."

"How did you know he was?"

"Delano Fredericks spread the gospel."

"And how did you serve your God?"

"I made myself over. In his image."

"What image?"

"The image of his books. Not the image of the man. The drunk who laughed too much, sang those fucking Yale songs, marched me to a bathtub to introduce me to his crazy wife."

"Is it mad to bathe? How did you divine that I was mad?"

"I'd heard about you."

"Heard what?"

"About all the hell-raising in New York. America's First Flapper. The Darling of the Tabloids. Always good copy, always good for a picture."

"Then why did the introduction in the bathtub shock you?"

"New York was far away. But when you open a door and shake hands with God — well, you don't expect cathouse hospitality."

"Harry, you liked what you saw in the tub, didn't you?"

"Sure I did. But you were in the wrong tub. In the wrong bathroom. And God was drunk."

"Weren't you also drinking that day?"

"I wasn't drunk. I drank just enough to harden my knuckles. To make a noise on the door to God's suite."

"Were you that afraid of God?"

"I was a boy from Montana. Leading with my chin."

"God was a boy from Milwaukee."

"By way of New Haven."

"You envied him Yale?"

"He was God. You don't envy God."

I said, "No, you don't. Not in 1924. In that crazy year God envied you!"

"In what way?"

"Don't you remember Davis asking you how tall you were and how much you weighed?"

"I remember," he said, "Davis asking me if I'd played foot-

360

ball in college. I was four feet tall when I told him I'd never gone to college."

"But then you said the magic word."

"What word was that?"

"War."

"Yeah, I said something about the war. About going to war instead of college."

"Harry, you hero, you took him overseas. To your trenches, your mud, your battles, and your medals. And your God, standing on his envy, was only two feet tall."

The recollection awed Harry. "Yeah, I sensed that."

"Did you, at that moment, begin to doubt your God?"

"No, I felt Davis was interested in me and the war. So I opened my mouth and told him my manuscript was about the war."

"I was there," I said. "I heard you. And I saw your God die one of his thousand deaths. And then I saw you die."

"Me?"

"Yes, when Davis asked you to let him read the manuscript. You were frightened. You know you were. When Davis told you to get the manuscript, which he wanted to read that very night, you began to stammer. You said something about having to rewrite it. About sending it to him in New York. In a few months."

Harry writhed in remembered torment. "It was just a draft."

"You'd been working on it for three years."

"I brought the manuscript that night, didn't I?"

"Why, Harry? Tell the truth."

"What the hell do you mean?"

"You didn't trust your God. Not out of sight. Out of sight, out of mind. Weren't you afraid that your drunken God and his crazy wife would run back to New York and forget you?"

Harry said, "When I left the hotel, I was wet. Soaked with sweat. With a fear I never felt in the trenches. I had this damn picture in my mind. Davis reading my manuscript and laughing. Davis reading out loud to you, and you laughing with him. I was

361

never so fucking sick and scared in all my life. Never before, never since.''

"Did you expect to hear from God again?"

Harry shook his head. "Hell no. I was goddam sure I'd get a call from the desk clerk telling me to pick up the garbage left for me.''

"How did you feel when Davis telephoned you at the newspaper?"

"Before I talked to him?"

"Yes.''

"I was bleeding. Waiting for the *coup de grace.*"

"And after you talked to him?"

"I didn't believe him.''

"You didn't believe God?"

"No, damn it! No!"

"Why not, Harry?"

"It didn't sound right.''

"Not sincere enough?"

"It was too much. Too much praise. Just sounded wrong.''

I said, "I heard him, Harry. Yes, it was wrong. It was God creating Adam and telling Adam he was superior to his Creator.''

"Yeah. So how the hell could I believe that?"

"You believed him," I reminded Harry. "You trusted Davis with your manuscript.''

"I had a carbon.''

Derision hardening my voice, I said, "A carbon? What kind of an excuse is that? You trusted Davis! He said he'd take the manuscript to Corbell, and you knew he would!''

"I *hoped* he would," Harry corrected me. "After all, he was drunk.''

"God a drunk?" I laughed.

"Drunks are careless.''

"God a careless drunk? But the drunk wasn't careless, was he?"

"No. I sweated for a month. Then I got the letter from old man Corbell. Telling me how pleased he was that he was going to publish the book.''

"The book!" I exclaimed. "Now it's suddenly a book! The manuscript's a book!"

Harry was confused. "What's the point?"

"Oh, I was merely tracing the evolution of an author. The metamorphosis from crawling failure to winged success."

"I never crawled."

"Not even through no-man's-land?"

"Get on with it."

"Did you believe Corbell?"

"There was a check enclosed. Five hundred dollars."

"You have that letter framed, don't you?"

"It's down in Key West. Hanging in my study."

"I know what I can give you for Christmas."

"What?"

"A matching letter. Same letterhead, same typewriter, same signature."

Harry glowered at me. "A letter to whom?"

"Written to Davis. Prior to the one you framed."

Harry feigned disinterest. "Keep it."

"Davis kept it to himself. Had he forwarded that letter to you, you'd have hanged yourself."

"You have that letter?"

"I have all of God's manuscripts, letters, and notebooks."

Harry resorted to the brandy again. "What was in the damn letter?"

"Corbell found your manuscript wanting. Shall I go on?"

"Yeah, I want to hear how wrong he was."

I delivered the words to Harry's jaw. "Corbell said he admired the freshness and crispness of your style, but he chose not to publish your manuscript. He decried your nihilism. He said you made the Great War a confrontation of armies wearing the same uniforms of the same mud."

Reflectively, Harry said, "True. Goddam true. It was different in Spain. It's different now." He stayed with this thought for a long moment, waited in vain for the interruption of my ensuing question, and then was struck by another, darker thought. "Who changed Corbell's mind?"

363

"Divine intervention," I said. "God told Corbell that if he didn't publish Harry Ingram he could go to hell. And God would go elsewhere, to another publishing house."

"Is that in writing, too?"

"God didn't bother to write. The careless drunk drove through traffic signals, got a speeding ticket. But he made it to Corbell's sanctum and unleashed his godlike wrath."

Harry, the little boy lost, said, "He never told me."

"That's why he was God."

The next domino to fall was Harry's literary agent. "Rannah, was there any problem with Mason? Was there a letter to Davis before Mason wrote me?"

"What did Mason write to you?"

"Mason said he was delighted to be handling me. Predicted my book would shake the world. Said the writing was masterful, the finest example of the lean, frontier beauty of the American language." Suddenly Harry's head jerked, as if it had been struck by the strong right hand of Dandy Flood. "Shit! Davis could've written that!" He glowered at me again. "He did, didn't he?"

"Yes," I said with a champagne smile. "And on the seventh day he rested."

Harry whipped his next question. "What did Mason write Davis?"

"They spoke on the telephone."

"And what was said?"

"I only remember what's worth remembering. And at the time nothing they said seemed worth —"

"What did Mason say?"

"Why so anxious, Harry? You know he was wrong."

"Goddam it! How wrong was he?"

I said, "This might give you a laugh. Mason thought Davis was playing a practical joke on him."

"I don't get it."

"You have no humor about yourself, do you?"

"What was the practical joke?"

"Your manuscript."

364

"What the hell was so funny?"

I laughed at the pratfall of his ego. "I'll tell you. Mason couldn't believe there *was* a Harry Ingram. He thought it was a pen name for one of the Jukes. He found the simple declarative simpleminded. He couldn't believe the words of one syllable, the monotones of your dialogue."

A death rattle underlay his next question. "How far did he read?"

"Before Davis read him the riot act? Less than one chapter."

Harry sprang at me with hope. "Did Mason change his mind after finishing the book?"

"Only about handling you. He'd spoken to Corbell. He'd heard Davis's ultimatum. Not wishing to rock his own boat and have his prize passenger jump ship, he allowed God to dictate a letter to you."

"The son of a bitch!"

"Shall I go on?"

He cringed. "There's more?"

I laughed cruelly. "Mason also said — in conversation with God — that Corbell was the wrong publisher for you, all Corbell books have the best bindings, the best quality of paper and printing. Mason said you'd never be as popular as a Sears-Roebuck catalogue in the nation's outhouses."

The beast across the table, who hungered not and thirsted not, was cornered. "That funny, mother-fucking bastard! I'll get him!"

I lashed out at him. "Of course you will! You get everybody! Sooner or later! Even your God!"

Primordial guilt fell over Harry. "How did I do that?"

I began to unravel the past. "You came North to Long Island."

"To take you to bed."

"The charge is murder. Not morals. You took a book to bed. You read *North Shore.*"

"And I praised God in the highest," said Harry.

"But you went South again. To do what?"

"To work."

"No, Harry. You sneaked away to plot against your God. First you offered a sacrifice, a human sacrifice. You sacrificed a child named Nancy, your first wife. And then you sacrificed a precious year of your life."

"I had to. I'd read *North Shore*."

"A masterpiece, wasn't it?"

"Listen, do you know —?" Harry snapped his jaws shut for a moment. Quietly he said, "Yeah, a masterpiece."

"Harry, what were you going to say?"

"Nothing. Nothing important."

"You're lying."

"Make your damn case."

"Wouldn't you consider *North Shore* to be God's highest mountain?"

"His best book," he said.

"Why did you build a higher mountain?"

"Who the hell says I did?"

"Your first novel was Everest."

The Himalayas were a long way from Harry's hell. In the dark of the confessional booth, he said, "*North Shore*'s a better book than *A Pattern Called War*."

"Better than any of your books? *All* of your books?"

Harry tasted his brandy, got the aftertaste of truth, and simply said, "Yeah."

Seeking an end to the case against Harry Ingram, I asked, "Do you now confess to the murder of your God?"

The timbre returning to his voice, the glitter to his eyes; he said, "Hell, no!"

"You had the motive," I accused. "You wanted to be God yourself."

"A God with God, that's all I ever wanted! To be his peer!"

"When Davis drank and puked his way out of your pantheon, what did you do?" I demanded.

"I don't get you."

"Are you drunk, Harry?"

"I can hear you."

366

"But can you understand me? Am I shouting from the tower of Babel?"

"Try me again."

"What did you do when Davis lay there wallowing in his own vomit? Did you try to help him up? Clean him up?"

"You know goddam well I did!"

To quiet the quaking walls I whispered to Harry, "What did you do?"

"You were there! In Tarragona! I said it all in the bedroom!"

Taunting him, I said, "I remember my breasts were exposed. But I don't recall your naked truth."

"You crazy bitch," he said with disgust.

"Harry, you drove me mad. But no matter. You're not charged with that. The charge is murder. The murder of God."

"Like I said, you were crazy the first time I met you."

I said, "Let's pursue that. The first time you met me, was it in a padded cell in a Barcelona hospital?"

"Next question."

"You arranged that hospitality for me in Barcelona, didn't you?"

"The best hospital and the best doctors. I paid the bills."

"Bless you, Harry."

"Fuck you, Rannah."

"Again, Harry?"

Again Harry went for the brandy bottle. He poured, drank, and rode his chair to a far country whose borders were closed to madwomen.

I said, "Harry, you bought the kingdom of God. And you paid for it by paying my bills. Right?"

Harry forced himself to focus on me. "Remember how sick I got when Dandy hit me in the gut, and when you screamed: 'Kill him, kill him?'"

"Oh, yes, my fondest memory."

"I was sick in the ring. But not half as sick as I was in the grove. When we found you."

I shivered as I sensed I was about to learn, for the first time,

367

the details of my fall in the hazelnut grove. "You and who else?"

"Dandy."

"He led you there?"

"Yeah."

"What did he tell you?"

"The sickest story I've ever heard. The early morning walk. Your dirty talk. The punch he hit me. And the punch he hit you."

I said, "You've recovered nicely."

"Yeah."

"How did I leave the grove?"

"Dandy carried you to the house. I drove you to Barcelona. You were folded in the back of my Mercedes. Cradled in Davis's arms. You were catatonic."

"Did Davis know what had happened in the grove?"

"I told him."

"With glee?"

"I told him. He didn't say one word from Tarragona to Barcelona."

"When did you discuss it?"

"We never did."

"Did Davis discuss it with Dandy?"

Harry said icily, "I didn't tell Davis a damn thing until I got Dandy and his white bitch the hell out of there."

"Why? Were you afraid of what Davis might do to Dandy?"

"Damn right. I had guns in the house."

"Weren't you afraid Davis might shoot *you?*"

"Why the hell would he want to shoot me?"

"He was there. In the bedroom. He heard you. He saw you fire the first shot."

Harry seemed in pain now. "I meant well for both of you. I wish to hell I'd gone straight to bed."

I picked at his wound. "When the door of my padded cell was bolted, Davis was free of me. Wasn't that what you wanted? What Davis wanted? Did you both sing and whistle all the way back to Tarragona?"

368

"We stayed at the Hotel Falcón," said Harry absently. "Close to the hospital."

"Just the two of you?"

My question, idly posed, had no meaning beyond arithmetic, but Harry jerked his head with the sudden fear of an antelope sensing the assault of a lion. In an instant, however, he recovered. "Charlotte came down that night. In the Renault. Davis stayed across the hall from us."

"Did you visit me at the hospital?"

"It was two weeks before they let Davis see you."

"And where were you then?"

"Back in Tarragona. We stayed four more days."

"What did the doctors report about me while you were in Barcelona?"

"Why go over it all again?"

"Did you recommend Switzerland?"

Harry sighed. "No."

"What *did* you recommend?" Harry held his brandy and his tongue. "Tell me, Harry."

And he said, "Mattewan."

The name of one of New York State's hospitals for the insane assaulted me. "Mattewan?"

"Do you know what it cost Davis to keep you at Shadow Grove?"

"*Hollow* Grove. And I know what it cost me. Twelve years."

Harry loosed his arrow. "It cost Davis his life!"

I nodded in bland agreement. "Harry, do you now admit that you and I collaborated in his death? His murder?"

"I was three thousand miles away," said the accused.

"You were the new God, and you were in your Heaven."

"While Davis pissed his time away in Hollywood."

I asked, "Why didn't Davis go to San Francisco? You did offer to lend him the money, didn't you?"

"He had to go to Hollywood. To pay your fucking bills."

I laughed. "I did no fucking at Hollow Grove, Harry. There was no one — absolutely no one — between you and Dandy Flood."

369

"You fucked Davis with those Shadow Grove — Hollow Grove — bills."

My laughter soared with courtroom theatricality. "You're coming around, Harry. Soon you'll be able to put Shadow Grove out of your mind. Shortly you'll be able to distinguish the truth from the lie."

"What lie?"

"That Davis was driven to Hollywood by the necessity of paying my madhouse bills."

Harry did his own addition. "Fact one: he did go to Hollywood. Fact two: he did pay the bills. Fact three: he took out a twenty-thousand-dollar life insurance policy, to make sure the bills'd be paid after he was dead."

"Oh, Harry, Harry! A fact is a fact is a fact. But the truth is also the truth, and there's nothing like the truth for shining in the eye of the beholder."

"Thank you, Gertrude Stein."

"The name is Rannah Gedney O'Donnell, you bastard. And the game is called Truth and Nothing But. But first, might I have more champagne?" I asked, holding aloft the empty bottle.

"Hell no!"

Ever so sweetly I tried again, "No more champagne?"

"You're sick already. And I've got a feeling you're about to puke all over me."

I lowered the bottle to the floor and subjected him to a harsh stare. "Shall we return to the truth?"

"You have to get there first."

Accepting that challenge, I began, "Consider this facet of truth: God tells Davis it's right and proper to put his mad-woman in —"

Harry cut me short. "You calling me God now?"

"Yes, of course. The year is 1930. Then, as now, you were the God of what passes for American letters."

"Thanks," he mumbled.

I resumed the assault. "God tells Davis it's right to put his madwoman in a madhouse. It's right to accept a loan from God. Right to take the first train for San Francisco. Right to take the next page to the novel stalled somewhere on the tracks flooded by booze. And what does Davis do? As God commands him? No. He does as his defeated soul implores him. He condemns his sick wife to a plush, expensive prison. And then he takes himself to Hollywood to hack away at the gold. But best of all, he wins his excuse. Are you listening, Harry? The boy who never won his varsity letter at Yale now wins his varsity excuse in Hollywood.''

''What are you raving about?''

I told him. ''The excuse Davis needed to keep from bringing his bankrupt genius to the playing fields where Harry Ingram had already won the match, the cup, the day, the medal, the varsity letter, and all the prerogatives of godhead. Yes, damn you, he won the varsity excuse he needed to keep from facing the blank page.''

Another voice, from another country named Success. ''Davis faced the blank page in Hollywood. He wrote *In Battalions.*''

''A smashing success,'' I said, borrowing the acid from Davis.

I heard Harry's death rattle again. ''A great novel.''

I reached for rhetoric. ''The last will and testament of a pauper who had nothing to leave but his self-pity!''

His face darkening, Harry said, ''Is that what you got out of the book?''

''I never bothered to read it.''

''The hell!''

''I read only the Holy Bible.''

Harry stuck to his jammed guns. ''It's a great novel.''

I sprang at him. ''Is that your message? Well, tell me, God, who got your message about its greatness? Was it printed on the jacket of the book? Were you so quoted in the newspapers and magazines of the nation?''

''No.''

''What did you do, Harry? How far out of your way did you go to serve the God whom —?''

''Shut up about God! No more about gods!''

''One last observation. He who kills God becomes God.''

''Or goes mad.''

"Yes, Harry."

"Let's get back to Hollywood."

"Ah, the culprit wishes to return to the scene of the crime."

Harry said, "I've never been to Hollywood."

"You were there. On the night in question, Harry, you were there."

"What night?"

"The night of December 27, 1940."

"I was in Mexico. Fishing."

"You were in Santa Monica. Hunting. And your prey was Davis."

"He died of a hemorrhage."

"Caused by what?"

"A duodenal ulcer."

"The landlady screamed for the police. She smelled foul play."

Harry tried to hide behind absurdity. "Did the police find my fingerprints?"

"You've read the great detective stories, Harry. You surely must know the police never, never solve murders. It takes the genius of the amateur detective. Sherlock Holmes. Philo Vance. Charlie Chan. Guy Thurlow."

Harry snapped to attention. "Guy?"

"Guy Thurlow," I said. "First upon the scene of the crime."

"Before the police?"

"Yes. He had an appointment with Davis."

"And what did Guy find?"

"The murder weapon. The motive. The incontrovertible evidence that Harry Ingram killed Davis O'Donnell."

"Did Guy take this evidence to his grave?"

"No, but I'll gladly deliver it to *your* grave."

At this the last pretenses of the parlor game were spent. The room smelled of blood, of guilt, of murder. And Harry, the cornered murderer, the lion at bay, clawed at me with his next question: "What damn evidence do you have?"

"Believe me, Harry. I have it."

"What the hell is it?"

372

"I'll get to it," I said coldly. "But let us return to Santa Monica, and to Detective Thurlow. In the apartment he finds an almost empty bottle of gin."

"Gin? Is that what Davis was drinking at the end?"

"Davis had been on the wagon!" I said. "For almost four years! The night he was murdered, the bottle of gin was thrust upon him! Like a dagger!"

"Who the hell by?"

"You!"

"What's this evidence you say you have?"

"Let me put this to you: if a man is murdered and his blood is found on the man to whom all suspicions lead, wouldn't you say the bloodstains were incriminating?"

"What the hell are you trying to say now? That Davis's blood is on me?"

"I have the evidence."

Harry had another thought. "You must've escaped from the madhouse after all."

"The evidence is marked Exhibit A."

"What the hell is it?"

"A book," I whispered.

"Jesus, you're sick!"

I cried aloud, my voice echoing in the corridors of the distant château. "A book by Harry Ingram! *November's Leaf Is Red!* But not so red as the blood of Davis O'Donnell! I have the book! The book Davis was reading the night he was murdered! The book that murdered him. *Your* book! *His* blood! The blood he'd vomited all over your book! The blood he brought up with the gin he was drinking! And why was he drinking this night? Because Harry Ingram was the God before whom there were no other Gods. Because he himself was weary of living with only the ghost of a chance. Yes, he vomited his self-pity and gave up the ghost of a chance. A chance for what? The resurrection of yesterday's glories? He couldn't! You were so high, so mighty. And the boy from Milwaukee who couldn't hold his booze now couldn't hold his blood!"

A long moment of silence intervened before Harry asked, "Where's the book?"

"I have it," I said.

"Where?"

"It's hidden."

"Exhibit A?"

"Yes, Exhibit A."

"Is there an Exhibit B?"

Mixing grains of truth with the venom of malice, I created Exhibit B. I said, "Yes, there most certainly is."

"What is it, you crazy bitch?"

"A letter. A letter from Hollywood. A letter from Davis to me. Written in 1933 after the abysmal failure of *In Battalions*. And this is what Davis wrote. Quote: *I don't write any more. I've surrendered my pen to Harry. He's made my writing unnecessary.* Unquote. Shall I repeat it for you?"

From the canvas floor of the ring at Tarragona, Harry turned upon me his pale and sickly face. "That's a suicide note."

I said, "In 1940 Davis was on the wagon. He was writing a novel. It was seven years later. He was trying to fight back. To come back."

"How far did he get with the book?"

"Not far enough!" I screamed. "He was on page 206 when you murdered him! Murdered him with your six hundred and forty-seven boldly printed pages bound for glory! With your hundreds of thousands of carefully selected words; With your hundreds of thousands of copies! With your hundreds of thousands of Hollywood dollars! With your Pulitzer prizes! With all the thunder you'd stolen from the boy from Milwaukee who'd made you God!"

In vain I waited for the potency of my words to turn Harry to dust. Weak though his flesh was, soft though his bones were, he rose and wove a path leading to my coat. His voice muted by a closed coffin lid, he said, "Come on, I'll put you in a taxi."

I became hysterical. "You want to put me in a hearse! Like you did Davis!"

374

Harry's hands crushed my shoulders, his eyes burned me. "Do you know how dead Davis is?"

Replying not to his question but to my own conscience, I said, "I had Harry in the tub, and I forgot about Charlotte Corday."

Not concerned with the murder of Marat, Harry shook me violently. "Listen to me! I got a telegram from Corbell a few weeks ago! I bawled all over it! And I'm a guy who doesn't bawl! I didn't even bawl when Davis died!"

I let the words pile up like messages slipped under my door, and my answer was directed to Jesus. "O Lord of Battles! I had Harry asleep in bed, and I forgot about Ruth Snyder."

Harry's hand, flying like a hawk, swept down and struck my face. And then he stung me with words. "Listen, you crazy bitch! You know what the fucking telegram said? It said, 'SORRY. ALL OF O'DONNELL'S BOOKS OUT OF PRINT.' Do you hear me? Do you understand?"

I said nothing, understood nothing. I slipped into my coat and moved away from Harry toward one of the steak knives lying on the table. It became a dagger in my hand. And fell to the floor a steak knife again as Harry, reacting all too swiftly, twisted it from me and took my rage for his very own.

With one hand he pushed me, with the other he opened the door. "Get the fuck out of here!"

I was in the corridor, listening to the slamming and bolting of the door and feeling the sting of Harry's hand on my flushed face, when the door was wrenched open again and my handbag flew out and fell to the floor. Slowly, indifferently, I retrieved it. For a long moment I stared at the "Do Not Disturb" sign, and then I turned and walked the narrow course of the corridor.

I opened another door to a staircase, and I took a thousand steps down to the lobby in which I didn't linger. After passing through a door held open for me, I came to the street and the night, and I came as a stranger.

2.

I did not know the name of the city whose lights and sounds assaulted me. I did not know the name of the hotel from which I had been ejected. I did not know the name of the other hotel where my return was awaited. I did not know the day, the week, the month, or the year. And I did not know my own name.

I did know I was cold, lost, and alone. I did remember the waters of the Nile, the naked God, the wines of warmth, the walls of paradise, and the gates of ecstasy which would never again open for me.

I began to walk at random. Hearing music, I followed the strains to a street corner where a Salvation Army band and chorus poured Jesus into the emptiness of the city. Not remaining for the sermon that ensued I walked on until I found myself before a Western Union office. I stopped there, looked through the window, and tried to recall whether I was supposed to send or receive a telegram. Unable to remember anything beyond the lone reality of a telegram, I walked on. With each step I seemed to be moving farther and farther from some vaguely remembered paradise.

I began to tremble from a cold that was within me. I began to cry with tears that tried but failed to tell me who I was, where I

376

was, where I should go. In desperation I grabbed at the sleeve of another human being.

The young soldier withdrew from the filth of my touch, arched his disgust, and spat upon me these words: "Get away from me, you old whore!"

I fled. I stopped at a street corner to watch a man alight from a taxi. Urgently I entered the taxi and shut out all of the evil eyes save those belonging to the hatchet-faced driver.

"Where to?"

"The hotel."

With a patience reserved for drunks, he asked, "Which hotel?"

"Cherokee?"

"Never heard of it."

"It's across the street from the depot."

The driver studied a small, worn booklet. "No Cherokee Hotel in Atlanta."

"Atlanta!" The name was a buoy on a dark and boundless sea. "Yes. It's the — . It begins with a C."

"The Cadillac? The Chambers? The Clifford?"

I felt another and new kind of ecstasy. "Yes! The Clifford!"

Within five minutes the taxi bore me to the protection of the Clifford Hotel, the sight of which caused a gradual return of awareness and memory. It was only when I opened my handbag for the taxi fare that I realized the folly of my amnesia. Within it, among trifles, were the wallet and key case of Davis O'Donnell.

When I entered the lobby I knew who I was, where I was, where I had been, and where I was now going. By the time I had left the elevator on the eighth floor, I was lost again, this time in reverie. Moving in the direction of the music of Paul Whiteman and his orchestra, I rapped upon the door of the Governor's Suite and readied a smile for my handsome husband.

The door opened and my heart fell. Confronting me, in a silence without saxophones, was an ungainly, hulking, perturbed old woman. I felt like a child reading a book and turning ahead a hundred or so pages to steal a glimpse of things to come. I told

377

myself that somewhere, some time, this forbidding creature would come into my life.

Aloud I asked, "What are you doing here?"

"You all right?" Her words seemed more familiar than Whiteman's lost music.

"What in God's name are you doing here?" I cried.

"I sit. I wait." She sighed and her sigh was a bridge I crossed to the reality of the moment.

I sat down, compared this to Harry's suite, and suffered the comparison and the presence of Mrs. Neff. "Did you have your dinner?"

"No," she said.

"What did you have for lunch?"

"No lunch."

"There's a coffee shop downstairs."

"I stay here."

"I'll be all right. You can go down."

"I stay here."

The room seemed to pitch slightly as I got up and went to the telephone meaning to order pheasant under glass for the good woman who had mothered me in my madness. It being 1942 rather than 1920, I was forced to settle for two ham sandwiches, a slice of pecan pie, and a container of coffee. For myself, I ordered music.

The rental radio, with static pervading all wavelengths, issued communiqués from the war fronts, vended bargains and sales, described the pleasures of tobacco, beer, and soda pop, and, when the dial caught music, it did not remind me of Paul Whiteman or of the violins at the Plaza.

Surrendering the dial but not the dissonance, I undressed, changed into my nightgown, gathered my sketch pad and my charcoal, and sat upon the frayed carpet. Mrs. Neff took up her post in a far corner of the room and sat with the stiffness of Ruth Snyder in the electric chair. I touched the charcoal to the paper, and, before long, transmutation brought to me the flesh and blood and flashing eyes of the Alexander who ruled me.

378

In another instant, with my ears suddenly and strangely deaf to the radio, I heard Davis whisper to me. "Rannah?"

Furtively, before answering him, I stole a glance at Mrs. Neff, a chaperon deaf to the whispers of the courtiers.

To Davis I whispered, "Yes, my darling."

"I'm waiting for you."

"Where are you?"

"You know where I am."

"In the attic. In the trunk," I said.

"I expected you tonight."

"Harry's in Atlanta."

"I saw him."

"When?"

"You're mad to think you can shut the door on the dead."

"You saw us?"

"I saw."

"I came to kill Harry. You saw me take up the knife."

"Is Harry dead?"

"No."

"Do you know how dead I am?"

"How dead are you?"

"The telegram told you."

"What telegram?"

"Rannah, what's reality?"

"Harry says it's hate."

"It is for Harry. You shouldn't have made love to him."

"I came to kill him."

"You loved him. He loved you."

"He hates me again. I tried to kill him. I tried to convict him of murdering you."

"Rannah, you only buried me deeper."

"You're in the trunk in the attic."

"I'm out of print. All of my books. Do you understand?"

"Yes, I understand."

"What did I say?"

"The bookstores have only enough shelf space for Harry's books. There's no room on the shelves for —"

"There's room. Harry wanted to make room for me."

"How?"

"The more Harry hated you the more he loved me. He wept when the last of my books died. He made a vow to resurrect my books after the war. Now he won't."

"He will! He hates me all the more! He threw me out!"

"The truth remained."

"What? I don't understand."

"You left the truth with Harry."

"I lied!"

"You told the truth. I heard you. Even old whores tell the truth."

"You heard the soldier?"

"Yes. And he saw you for what you are."

"Forgive me, please. I didn't mean to —"

"Be quiet. Listen to me. The truth you left with Harry. It will destroy Harry's hate for you. Destroy my only chance for resurrection."

"Tell me, tell me, what can I do?"

"The window."

"The window?"

"Remember our honeymoon?"

"Yes, darling."

"Remember the nine moons of Jupiter?"

"Yes, you said there were nine to confuse the lovers."

"You remember well."

"I love you."

"You love Harry. You loved him today."

"I love you."

"Do as I tell you."

"Anything."

"Mrs. Neff is watching you. Be careful."

"I will."

"Rise slowly."

I obeyed. "Now what?"

"Yawn."

I yawned.

380

"Turn off the radio."

I obeyed.

"Tell Mrs. Neff you're going to bed."

I told Mrs. Neff. She trailed me into the bedroom.

"Get into bed," the voice commanded.

"Now what?"

"Pretend sleep. But don't fall asleep. You must fall from the window."

"The window!"

"I'm being kind to you, Rannah. I could command you to open the trunk."

"I don't want to die."

"You must. You're guilty of the murder of Harry's hate."

"Please, I don't want to die."

"Harry and his hate for you could have moved the stone for my resurrection. He can't do it now. Not with all his pity, his shame, and his guilt. If you're sane and wise, you'll choose the window. If you're insane and unwise, you'll open the trunk."

"No!" I screamed, and the scream was loud enough to return me to the ward and the distress of Mrs. Neff.

Seeing her advancing toward me in the dark, I screamed again when I seemed to hear not her voice but the ringing of a telephone. Then, as lamplight burst over the darkness, I saw Mrs. Neff raise the telephone.

"Hello," said Mrs. Neff.

"Is it my father?"

Saying nothing, Mrs. Neff handed the phone to me.

"Rannah?"

Hearing my father's voice, I spoke excitedly. "Father, I'm perfectly all right! Really I am! I'll be home tomorrow! I'm taking the morning train!"

And my father said, "This is Harry."

In the snare of another hallucination I said, all too timidly, "Harry?"

"Yeah," said Harry. "I'm on my way up."

I called his name again, but the connection was severed.

"Who was it?" Mrs. Neff inquired.

381

"The devil," I said.

"Who was it?"

"Harry Ingram. He's on his way up here."

"I don't open the door."

"No, don't open it."

"I send him away."

"No!"

"What is it, Mrs. O'Donnell?"

"Did you hear me praying?"

"No."

"God's been so gracious to me. He's delivered Harry to me, and now I can take the string of his hate for me and tie it again around his little finger. To remind him how dead Davis is, how deeply he's buried, and how he awaits his resurrection." Mrs. Neff, who understood the mad me, said nothing. "Please, Mrs. Neff, open the door."

She brought my robe. Together we went into the sitting room, lit it softly with the warmth of a lamp, and unbolted the door. Gathering my sketch pad and charcoal, I sat, an innocent child, crosslegged upon the floor and continued to work on the portrait of Davis, and on the design of my own demeanor.

Sensing that silence was wrong for the moment, I turned on the radio again, played with the dial, and settled for the recorded but unfamiliar music of Glenn Miller's orchestra.

The shell of tension in the room cracked under the weight of Harry Ingram's knuckles. Mrs. Neff opened the door and admitted the devil to our cottage at Hollow Grove. Graciously Harry introduced himself to Mrs. Neff. She nodded without smiling and, in keeping with her role as a keeper for the mad, retired to her straight chair in a dark corner of the room.

An instant before Harry turned the light and heat of his eyes toward me, I took refuge in the rectangle of the sketch pad. Hearing and feeling the footfalls, I knew he was towering above and behind me. I could feel him, I could smell him, and I had to struggle with a compulsion to run from Hollow Grove and fall upon the lush carpet in the suite at the Peachtree Plaza. I wanted to tear away masks and garments, to blind the charcoal eyes, to turn to Harry for a return to paradise. When I did look away from the pad, it wasn't toward Harry but toward the window through which Davis had wanted me to jump.

Real though he was, Harry spoke in the mode of my auditory hallucinations. "That's good."

"Thank you," I murmured.

"Did you do it from a photograph?"

"There are no photographs of Jesus."

"That's Davis," he insisted.

My eyes remaining on the pad, I said, "It's not very good. Not Jesus. Not Davis."

Then I heard Harry say, "Mrs. Neff, would you mind leaving us alone?"

My head came up and my eyes flew to Harry. He stood eight feet tall, a red-eyed ogre drunk on brandy and thirsting for my blood. I said, "Mrs. Neff's my keeper. She'll stay and keep me from the devil's harm."

Harry shrugged, sat down, glanced about the room, and transformed himself into a melancholy dwarf. "What the hell are you doing here?"

I studied the portrait. "Davis lives here."

"Would you shut that goddam radio off?"

I obeyed. "Is Paul Whiteman still alive?"

"Yeah."

"I don't like Glenn Miller," I said to the portrait.

"Rannah?"

I dared not look at Harry. "Yes?"

"Are you well?"

The truth served me here, and I spoke it. "No. I'll never be well again. There's no cure for schizophrenia."

"What about Pearl Harbor?"

"A delusion I invented. To assuage the sane."

"Why are you going home?"

"My doctor went off to war. His name is Dominick Patrone."

"Why would he send you home if you weren't well?"

"I'm only on furlough. As soon as the war ends, I'll be going back to Hollow Grove."

383

"You say that with relish."

"I want to go back. I wish I'd never left."

Slowed by the brandy and by my singular brand of truth, Harry finally said, "Your doctor, wasn't he afraid for you? For what you might do to yourself?"

"Or to others?" I was thinking of the steak knife.

"Yeah."

I smiled at the charcoal Davis. "Dr. Dominick put it very well. He said: 'Rannah, what could you do? Bomb Pearl Harbor? Sack Warsaw? Burn Rotterdam?' You see, in a world mad with war, I'm not a danger to the world. Rather, the world's a danger to me."

"And you really don't want to go home?"

"No, I don't." I pointed my charcoal at the sketch. "I'm afraid of him."

I heard the springs in the chair squeak as Harry, whose eyes I continued to avoid, apparently twisted around to view the sketch of Davis. "When did you first become afraid of Davis?"

"After he was dead. When he began to haunt me."

In a voice freighted with anguish, Harry said, "He haunts me, too."

I allowed the charcoal eyes to mesmerize me, to keep me from reaching for the sight and the touch of Harry. I asked, "Since when?"

"Since I got that telegram."

"What telegram?"

"The one from Corbell. Telling me that all of Davis's books were out of print."

"Why the telegram?"

"I'd fired off a wire to Corbell. Asking him to forward me two copies of each of Davis's titles. The four novels and the two short-story collections."

"What did you want with them?"

"For my sons. I was getting up a library for them."

"For your sons," I said from a hospital bed in Brooklyn, hard by a speakeasy and so very far, far away from the Japanese lanterns at the country club.

384

"They're too young to read any of the books in the library. I guess what I was doing was building a fire."

"A fire?"

"My father taught me that. We'd build the fire at night. And all it took in the morning was a match to heat the cabin."

"When you were hunting."

"Yeah."

"Are you dying, Harry?"

"Could be my last war."

"And your first death?"

"Yeah. Anyway, I got the books. From a second-hand book dealer in Chicago."

"A copy of each book for each son?"

"We think it's time to separate the twins and make them individuals. We're sending them to different prep schools."

"And separate colleges? Like Princeton and Harvard?"

"Yeah."

"Not Yale."

"No."

"I envy you your boys," I said as I watched the boy from Milwaukee changing trains at Grand Central Terminal for what he had always referred to as the New York, New Haven, and Hard-Fought Railroad.

"Rannah?" Harry's voice was tender.

"Yes, Harry? What do you want of me?"

"Two things."

"What are they?"

Harry said, "My book with Davis's blood on it. And the letter of surrender."

Without rancor I asked, "Also for your sons?"

"For myself."

"And how will the book and the letter serve you?"

"I'll make Corbell put Davis's books back in print."

I feigned ignorance and indifference. "Back in print?"

"I told you. All his books are out of print. Don't you remember?"

"No. But when are you going to do this?"

385

"After the war. Paper's rationed now."

Casually I asked, "Is there paper enough for your books?"

"There is," he said, more with guilt than pride.

"Is Davis out of print because of the paper shortage?"

"He went out of print in '39."

"Did you know that in 1939?"

"No."

"Did Davis know that in 1939?"

"Mason wrote him."

"I saw Davis in September of 1939. He said nothing about it to me."

Harry's curiosity was up and about. "How long did he spend with you?"

I scattered seeds of information. "A weekend. We took a trip."

"How was he?"

I worked on the charcoal eyes. "Very much alive. Very much in love with me. And with life."

"What happened that weekend?"

"I killed him," I said without passion, without guilt, without regret.

"Where?"

"In North Carolina," I said, putting the morning match to the night-built fire of Harry's agony.

"Where in North Carolina?"

"In a tourist cabin. The kind they rent by the hour."

"What the hell were you doing in a hot-bed camp?"

I exchanged secret smiles with the charcoal Davis, and I told Harry a lie. "I asked Davis to take me there."

"Why?"

"Why Harry Ingram? Why Dandy Flood? I'm a whore," I said softly so that the wave of contagion might not reach Mrs. Neff.

"How did you kill Davis?"

"I listened to my mother."

"Your mother?"

386

"I killed her in 1930. I listened to her in 1939. I took a flashlight to use as a sash weight on the sleeping Davis."

"How badly did you hurt him?"

I heard the rain falling in North Carolina. "He woke up in time. But when he woke up again, he was dead."

"Dead?"

I saw the old Plymouth and the young smile. I said, "He came to me from Hollywood. He came to take me to the secret house, to the secret room with the secret window where he would sit and take his direction from the North Star and *North Shore*." I took a deep and needed breath and concluded: "And I struck his dream, and he died. In 1939."

Harry struck a more mundane note. "How was he fixed for money?"

"Oh, he had some money saved. And he was thinking about all the money that would no longer be wasted on Hollow Grove."

Harry asked, "Did Davis have a book to write?"

"Yes, he did."

"What was it about?"

"I don't know. All I remember is the very special light in his eyes. The same light that discovered *North Shore*." No comment or question forthcoming from Harry, I went on. "Davis returned the old whore to Hollow Grove, delivered himself again to Hollywood, and demeaned himself once more to pay for the luxury of my madness."

Harry remained behind in the tourist cabin. "Why'd your mother tell you to kill Davis?"

"She told me Davis was going to kill me."

"Did she say why?"

"She said Davis was in love with a young girl."

"Who?"

I dared not look up, dared not turn to Mrs. Neff, for I was bringing method to my madness. "Mrs. Neff, would you fetch my handbag, please?"

I heard the door to the bedroom being opened before I heard Harry again. "Who was the girl? A Hollywood actress?"

"I don't know. She looks like a schoolgirl to me."

387

"Schoolgirl?"

"Yes, a schoolgirl with bloomers dirtied by boys' hands."

"Rannah, look at me," Harry commanded.

I turned to him, and he, more than Davis, was Christ upon the cross. "Yes, Harry?"

"Do you know what you're saying?"

My words were spears. "You and Davis, you're dirty old men. You like schoolgirls in dirty bloomers. You both hate women."

Harry contained his rage as Mrs. Neff returned with my handbag. Opening it, I found the wallet and from it withdrew the snapshot from Savannah, spat upon it, and handed it to Harry.

He took a handkerchief, wiped away my spit, and once more I seemed to hear his death rattle. "You're beautiful," he said to the snapshot. I pretended not to understand him, and I said nothing. Slowly, Harry turned to me. "This is you," he said.

In anger I reached out, tore the snapshot from his fingers and returned it to the wallet, which I swiftly buried in the handbag, which I deftly flung at Mrs. Neff's feet. My eyes darkening upon Harry, I declared, "Don't humor me, Harry. I'm not that mad."

"That picture," said Harry, "was you."

"You're blind." I looked at the sketch of Davis. "You look at Jesus and see Davis. I love Jesus. I hate Davis. He won't leave me alone. No, he won't let me be until he kills me."

"Rannah, he's dead."

"The dead live. They live in dreams and nightmares. Dreams seldom come true, but nightmares invariably do."

"What sort of nightmares?"

"You're a fool to ask."

"Tell me."

I was in Stephensville. "I dream I'm home again. I'm asleep in my bed, in my own room. I awake when I hear Davis calling me. He whispers for me to leave my bed, to climb the stairs to the attic, to open the trunk."

"What trunk?"

"The trunk from Hollywood."

"What's inside the trunk?"

I said, "In reality, I don't know. In my nightmares, I do know. The first time I opened the trunk I broke the dam on a river of blood! The blood spilled out of the trunk! All over me! And drowned me in the attic!"

Harry prompted me. "And the second time?"

Allowing silence for a moment to create the desired suspense, I finally said, "Again the voice, the climb, and the opening of the trunk. And out fly ashes. Ashes like locusts. Swarming over me. Suffocating me. Burying me alive in Davis's dead ashes." I rocked back and forth, trying to contain the terror. "He won't let me be. Not in dreams, not in nightmares. And now, tonight, for the first time, he spoke to me when I was awake."

"Do you see him?"

"No, I only hear him. The phrase for it at Hollow Grove is auditory hallucination."

"What did Davis say?"

It was now time to change masks. Feigning bemusement, I asked Harry, "You don't really believe the dead communicate with the living, do you?"

"No. But what do you hear?"

I laughed the perfect laughter of the sane. "You have a conscience, Harry. I have a conscience. The difference is that mine goes in for mimicry."

"Rannah, what did Davis say?"

"You *do* believe!"

"What did you hear?"

Trying to induce Harry to see the maggots crawling into my mouth, I said, "A spewing of filth. He damned me for despoiling you. Corrupting you. Infecting you."

"*Infecting* me?"

"Yes. With the virus of my madness."

Harry was obviously relieved. He said, "You're going home tomorrow."

I laughed again. "Home! Do you know what Dr. Dominick said over and over again? Face your fear and your fear dies."

"It's true, Rannah."

389

"Yes! It's true that the attic sits on top of my house!"

Calmly he asked, "What do you expect to find in the trunk?"

"Death! My death!"

"Try again," he urged. "Try to make sense. You can. Sometimes I think you make too much sense."

I said, "That's the magic of the mad. We can, on occasion, make reason stand at attention."

He was implacable. "What do you expect to find in the trunk?"

I allowed Harry to conduct me while I played my solo ever so softly, ever so harrowingly. "Nothingness. Release. An end to nightmares and dreams and hallucinations, to devils and gods, madness and sanity. The moment I raise the lid, I know my heart will fail me. For the last time."

Harry said, "You told me you expected to return to Hollow Grove after the war."

"That's a dream," I said pathetically. "A dream that won't come true."

Undaunted, Harry attacked my western flank. "Who shipped the trunk from Hollywood?"

"Santa Monica. Guy Thurlow."

"Didn't Guy tell you what was in the trunk?"

I lied. "Davis was dead. Guy was dying. Why should he talk of trunks?"

"Didn't Guy tell you he'd found my book with Davis's blood on it?"

I shut my eyes and chose the truth. "Yes, he did."

"Then the book's in the trunk, isn't it?"

"No," I said flatly.

"Did Guy keep it?"

"No, he didn't."

Harry pursued the truth. "Didn't Guy bring the book to you on his last visit?"

"He gave me the wallet and the key case with the key to the trunk."

"But no book?"

"No book."

390

"Because the book was in the trunk."

"He didn't say. What *difference* does it make? You surely don't believe the dead communicate with the living."

"What's that — ?"

I severed the question with the broadsword of my lie. "Guy was dead when he told me about the blood on the book! The bloodstained book exists only in my mad imagination!"

Harry and I listened to Mrs. Neff's nervous cough.

"And the letter from Davis?" he asked.

"What letter?"

"The letter of surrender!"

I looked him full in the eyes. "Forgive me. There's no book. No letter."

His forgiveness tabled, Harry did believe me. "What the hell were you trying to do to me?"

"Kill you," I said. "Mrs. Neff, tell Mr. Ingram when I first read about him in the Atlanta newspaper."

"On the train," she responded in her monotone.

"Where were we supposed to be tonight?"

"In your home."

"Why are we in Atlanta?"

"To see him."

Harry turned from Mrs. Neff to me. "Are you sorry you didn't kill me?"

I hesitated. "No, I'm not. I'm glad I didn't. I think I prefer to see you alive and suffering."

"About the out-of-print books, I still want to do something about them."

"Forget them, Harry. They're dead. Everybody and everything dies. People. Books. Everybody and everything. You and your books, too."

"Books come back from the dead."

"Who's mad, Harry? Is it you or I? What's dead is dead. Davis's books — for a time — were popular. Well, popularity's a kiss of death. Out of style, out of date, out of mind, and, lastly, out of print."

391

"That doesn't have to be. The writers die, but the books live on and —"

"Wishful thinking, Harry. Does Shakespeare know he's immortal? Immortality, I read somewhere, is a concern of the living, not of the dead. And why are we wasting concern on Davis? He wasn't Shakespeare, he wasn't Harry Ingram."

Snatching up the fallen banner of Davis O'Donnell, Harry declared, "He wrote like one of God's spies."

"In what issue of the *Saturday Evening Post?* In what can of Hollywood film? Oh, I know what you're thinking. You're thinking how my extravagances drove him to the *Post.* How my madness forced him to Hollywood. The guilt is mine, Harry, not yours. You, *you* gave him *North Shore.* You showed him the right direction. You didn't point to Philadelphia or to Hollywood. No, Harry, you have no guilt to expiate. Forget Davis. Forget his dead books. You're alive and should concern yourself only with your own immortality. And I don't mean your books. I mean your sons."

"My sons?"

"To whom you've passed your seed. Davis's seed died in me. That's how dead he truly is."

Harry kept on biting the bullet. "Open one of Davis's books and he lives again."

"Harry, you perplex me. Davis, when he died, was the complete atheist. He didn't even believe in himself. I remember the atheism in your first novel. Now you talk of God and his spies, of books and immortality. And one other thing: your belief in yourself. You do believe in yourself, don't you, Harry?"

"I believe in Davis O'Donnell."

I smiled. "Your faith is quite evident. But tell me, Harry, what happened to your bravery?"

"What do you mean?"

"Why aren't you doing as Davis did? Why don't you sow your own destruction?"

"How would I do that?"

I told him. "Find a young and unknown writer. Champion him as Davis championed you. Let him see you as God. As you

392

saw Davis as God. And then take terror to your sleep, and await the sound of voices proclaiming the old God dead, and a new God risen. The dead can't challenge you. Take courage, Harry. Go among the living and name your challenger."

Harry said nothing, and his silence told me that I had said all I had to say to him. As he rose, my heart sank with a sense of defeat. In his eyes I saw no hate for me, but only awe for the truth that the mad sometimes retrieve for the sane.

He turned to study the charcoal sketch of Davis, and he took it from my hands. "Can I have this?"

I hesitated, reforming my lines. "No courage, Harry?"

"What's courage got to do with my wanting this portrait?"

"Do you want it for your sons?"

"For myself. I'll frame it and hang it over my desk."

I brewed the potion with care. "Shall I inscribe it?"

"Please."

"Do you have a pen?"

"No. Here, use this," he said, removing a copy pencil from an inside coat pocket and handing it to me.

Holding the pencil and the sketch pad again, I idly said to Harry, "Where do you keep the pen Davis surrendered to you?"

Harry clenched his teeth. "Where do you keep the letter that told you that?"

I touched the tip of the pencil to my forehead. "Here. In the convoluted gray nest of my fancy." Then, with deliberation, I put the pencil to the pad and wrote my prescription for hate: "For Harry, who loved Davis much, much more than I did. Rannah."

Carefully pulling away the completed and inscribed sketch from the pad, I handed it to Harry. Then I picked up my charcoal again and began to sketch another face, a black face.

There was alarm in Harry's voice. "Rannah?"

"Yes?"

"This isn't true."

"Oh, but it is. I couldn't say this yesterday. I won't repeat it tomorrow. But tonight — in this calm between storms — I can utter the truth."

393

"What truth?" I heard the barrel chair taking the dead weight of Harry Ingram.

"I never loved Davis. I only married his success. He knew it, and he hated me for it."

"Davis loved you."

"He loved you more. Much, much more."

My eyes upon the pad, I could hear Harry's labored breathing. "Explain that."

"It's a very simple, very truthful statement."

I felt the cutting edge of his voice. "You're not making sense!"

"You know I am," I said indifferently. "Deep down, you know I am."

"What the hell do you mean?"

"In the biblical sense, I've known Davis. And I've known you. Harry, remember that night in Tarragona? In the bedroom?"

"What about it?"

"You forced Davis to choose between us."

"I remember warning both of you to stop destroying each other."

"Davis chose you."

"Chose me for what?"

"For his love."

"Christ, you *are* mad!"

"Yesterday and tomorrow. But not today, Harry." His face looked green. "Look at Davis." Harry glanced at the sketch. "Isn't he beautiful, Harry? More beautiful than I ever was. And so sensitive, so very sensitive about his manhood. I used to compare him to you. And I found him wanting."

At last I saw the reality of Harry's hate. "Jesus Christ!"

"I speak as an old whore, Harry. But you were wonderful today." Harry, anointed by my reassurance of his manhood, prepared to take his leave of me. "*Too* wonderful."

The balm fell before the salt of his sweat. "What the hell does *that* mean?"

"Just wondering about you. The running to wars. To the *corrida*. The hunting, the fishing, the boxing ring, the raw

394

whiskey and raw language, the bare chest and the big muscles. The big courage, the strong lovemaking. It all just makes me wonder about—"

"Don't say it!"

"Alex Martin said it first," I retorted, alluding to the suspect poet I had met at Harry's villa in Tarragona.

"Alex Martin!"

"Yes, Alex told me that you and Davis were fairies," I lied, issuing the slime coldly.

Harry jerked his wild head toward Mrs. Neff, sensed her stolidity, and, turning to me again, he crushed the sketch in the press of his hands and threw it at my feet. Restraining rage and wrath, Harry Ingram, god and devil, filled the room with the stench of his hate.

His retreat was orderly. At the door he directed to Mrs. Neff a murmured farewell kited to an apology. And then, with a studied opening and shutting of the door, he was gone from the arena of my madness, the bloody battlefield of my attack.

With the departure of frenzy and fury, of wrath and rage, I took the crumpled sketch, set it into the glass ashtray on the coffee table, and touched it with fire. Mrs. Neff emerged from her dark corner to oversee the flame and the smoke and to keep the high priestess within the radius of her concern.

Taking with me the smoulder of Harry's hate, I allowed Mrs. Neff to convoy me to my bower and the sweet kiss of sleep.

All light extinguished, Mrs. Neff withdrew, fully clothed and unblanketed, to a settee in a distant corner of the bedroom. I lay in the bed, eyes open to the parade of my triumph, ears attuned to the music of the march of my words against Harry and the truth. Soon I took my calm dry hands, joined them in supplication, and thanked Jesus for delivering Harry unto me, and for endowing me with a chance to atone for my sin against Davis's chance for resurrection.

And then, as the earth wheeled from guardian stars, I lost my beatific smile, found terror in the dark, and smelled the too sweet smoke of Davis burning in his crematory oven. My hands, wet and trembling, flew to my mouth and nose to mask the pungent odor. Closing my eyes, I saw the purples and the crimsons and the yellows and the greens against the backdrop of darkness.

The quiet, specked with faraway city sounds, gave way to a static that assaulted me, overcame me. Left me prey to a whisper.

"Rannah?"

"Davis?"

"Yes."

"Davis, I did it! I did it!"

"Did what?"

"Made Harry hate me! Weren't you here? Didn't you see us? Didn't you hear us?"

"Yes."

"I did it!"

"Yes, you did it."

In the muddle of my sense, I heard agony rather than exultation. I said, "Davis, what did I do wrong?"

"You made Harry hate me. Hate the very thought of me, the memory of me. You've covered us both with Alex Martin's slime."

My tears ran with the slime. "I had to! I had to make Harry hate me! That's what you wanted me to do!"

"Harry hates me now."

"Davis, what can I do? What must I do?"

"Come home, Rannah."

"Home?"

"We're waiting for you."

"We?"

"Come home to the moles and the bats, the slime of the snakes."

"No! I won't come to the attic! I won't open the trunk!"

"Come home, Rannah. I'll send armies of maggots to crawl under your door, into your bed, beneath your blankets, under your skin. I'll send succubi to your bed. . . ."

I climbed the knotted rope of my entrails, escaped over the wall of Davis's hell, and ran the last furlong to the window and to the stars of my childhood which waited in the night sky to catch my fall.

Strong arms caught me very close to the window. Instead of huzzas I heard static from Hollow Grove, and, not long after an uneven struggle, I found myself sitting on the floor, cradled in Mrs. Neff's arms, and listening to the hammering of her heart.

As the patron saint of madness rocked me, I began to sing in a voice as thin as the line between life and death. The Salvation Army band and chorus joining me, I sang a spiritual:

> *Mary had a baby, Yes, Lord.*
> *Mary had a baby, Yes, my Lord.*
> *Mary had a baby, Yes, Lord.*
> *De people keep a-comin' and de train done gone. . . .*

My voice shattered the window, and I fell down and down, down and down. Before long I was returned to my bed, given a wafer of sleep and a sip of water, and the vigilance of lamplight and two doleful eyes. This time clasping my hands in prayer, I raised my voice to the deity from Milwaukee.

"Davis above me, Davis below me, Davis in front of me, Davis behind me, Davis inside of me, Davis outside of me, Davis to the left of me, Davis to the right of me, Davis in my mind, Davis in my heart, Davis in my mouth, Davis in my vagina, Davis at my right breast, Davis at my left breast, Davis my God, my Lord, I am thy liege, thy love. I shall come to you. And take your lingering kiss of death."

397

3.

From Atlanta to Stephensville the tracks of the Central of Georgia Railroad ran south by southeast, from the streets paved with Yankee gold to the ruts washed by Confederate defeat. All along the route, at the wayside depots, yesterday and the day before yesterday stood together in their rust and rags and watched the running of trains from one distant war to another.

This was the view from the coach window the morning after the Second Battle of Atlanta. For Harry Ingram the skies were free and clear to Washington. For me there was a frequent drooping of my eyelids, and a tormenting sensation that the roadbed was the bed of a dried, dead river over whose stones I was being dragged.

I opened my eyes again to the pages of the Bible, and the sea was calm as I sailed from Georgia to Bethany, the town fifteen furlongs from Jerusalem. I left behind the huffing and puffing of the steam engine as it consumed the miles, and heard again my Jesus saying: *"Are there not twelve hours in the day? If any man walk in the day, he stumbleth not, because he seeth the light of this world. But if a man walk in the night, he stumbleth, because there is no light in him."*

In time the conductor marched through the coach and an-

398

nounced our approach to Stephensville. And Jesus cried in a loud voice : *"Lazarus, come forth!"*

And I, who was dead, loosened my graveclothes and left the bed of the dead river to move among the living in the hive of the Stephensville depot. The setting called for a first-act curtain, with Lieutenant Davis O'Donnell turning away from Rannah Gedney and blazing a trail for the morrows to follow. From the wings, however, there poured another generation of actors and actresses, boys in khaki and girls in smiles, dancing together on the big bass drum of war.

I was smiling myself, and once more I caught the contagion of laughter. I laughed at the Cherokee Hotel across the street, laughed with the cab driver, giving him the magic incantation : the address on Gedney Street.

To Mrs. Neff, as we rode through streets that had awaited my homecoming all these long years, I said, "I used to own this town!"

In command of the taxi, I ordered the driver to turn corners to the past. When Stephensville High School, its lawns sweeping toward the castle of classrooms, came into view, I wept and called the roll: "Liz! Audrey! Susanna! Helen! Hazel! Harriet! Beverly! Bonnie! Jim! Dinky! Hal! Marty! Flinn! Floyd! Jess! Jack!"

Gedney Street found me trembling. The trunks of the trees seemed swollen and distended. The houses, however, seemed to be cowering and sinking into their foundations. My house in particular seemed desolate and overripe for haunting.

The taxi gone, Mrs. Neff beside me, I avoided raising my eyes to the attic window. Instead, as I had often done as a child, I was careful not to step on the cracks of the walk leading to the porch, to the lovely porch where, as a girl, I had led lieutenants a merry chase.

I kissed the tip of my right forefinger, which gently touched the tarnished bell. Then I turned to Mrs. Neff. "You'll like Hilda. She's — let me see — eighty years old. Makes the best biscuits and pies. I love her. She was always scolding me. She loved me so much. Oh, how she loved to brush my hair and make me say ouch.''

The doorknob turned and the door opened. I rushed to Hilda and a strange, slatternly Negro woman withdrew from me.

''Miss Rannah?''

''Where's Hilda?''

''Ain't no more Hilda. She dead.''

I was still standing just inside the open door. I wanted to turn and run, but there stood the obelisk of Mrs. Neff and behind her the long shadow of time.

I turned to the woman. ''When did she die?''

''Seems like maybe six years. Maybe seven. I been here a long time. Workin' for the Judge.''

''What's your name?''

''Annie. Hey, you was supposed to come yesterday!''

''Was the Judge worried?''

''He don't say nothin' to me. 'Cept yesterday mornin' he told me to look out for you. This mornin' he don't say nothin', and I don't ask him nothin'. I just comes, cooks, cleans, takes my leavin's and goes.''

When Annie had shut the door behind us, I felt that the stone had been placed again before the entrance to the tomb. My graveclothes felt dirty as the darker than remembered walls, and the lower than remembered ceilings closed in upon me.

I remained downstairs while Annie directed Mrs. Neff upstairs to deposit my luggage in my bedroom and her own suitcase in the guest bedroom, where she was to spend the night. In the morning she would go back to Hollow Grove, her mission accomplished.

Rushing into the study, I smiled at the audience of books and frowned at my father's absence. I did, however, detect one change. The telephone had been moved from the entry hall to the desk of the study. With Mother and me gone, this was now father's exclusive link to the world.

The tip of my tongue held the number I now dialed. When a strange voice answered, I thought memory had betrayed me, but it was my father's office, and it was my father's current secretary who informed me that he was in court. I, in turn, had to inform her who I was and where I was.

Lifting the receiver and my spirits again, my forefinger danced upon the dial as another number came to me. I asked for Liz Cooper, and another strange voice, after an exchange of confusions, gave me the correct number for Mrs. James Gilland.

I called Liz Gilland, thought I recognized her voice, and found myself talking to her seventeen-year-old daughter, who told me her parents were in Augusta and not expected at home until the following evening. When I told the girl my name, I waited for recognition but received none. In the background, however, I could hear radio music and the voices of boys.

The next sound I heard was a rapping on the study door. It was Mrs. Neff, and as the door swung open I saw her, for an instant, as a stranger. She, however, brought recognition and recall to me. I took these two bitter pills, refused lunch, and went upstairs to a room that had once been mine. Now the drawers and closet were empty and the walls wore a strange skin of wallpaper and the ceiling a strange coat of paint.

I undressed and came naked to the bed in which I had sailed the subterranean rivers of sleep. Lacking the magic to erase the sun from the sky and lacking the energy to draw the blinds, I pulled the sheet over my head and toyed with sleep and death.

Death lurked in the trunk in the attic, and sleep carried me across the afternoon and into the twilight. It was sound that woke me, the familiar knuckles from Hollow Grove testing an unfamiliar door. Mrs. Neff entered to announce that my father was home.

I tarried. The judge was home, court was now in session, and the prisoner was being dragged by the hands of time to the dock.

I tarried. The haze was gone from the bathroom mirror, and I felt a reluctance to bring the face reflected in it to the mirrors of my father's eyes.

I left my bedroom, I shut the door behind me, I listened to the drumming of my heart and wished I could go directly to the

401

scaffold. But that way led to the attic. I took the other way, the descending stairs to the door of the study.

I didn't knock. Through the closed door I could imagine the audience of books waiting for the entrance of the doomed ingenue. On the cue of chance, I boldly opened the door and found myself confronting a strange actor. The role of my father was being played by an actor of far too many seasons in the sun, and of a talent unseasoned for so demanding a role.

I cried to Jesus and begged him to bring down the curtain. The actor adjusted his mask to a smile that was as wafer thin as his voice. He welcomed me home and sanctified the homecoming by pouring bourbon into glasses that had been long dry. He made no attempt to kiss me, and, as I noted his drawn face, I sensed it to be a face to be kissed again only in death.

We did touch glasses before we put the bourbon to our lips. And then, for the fifteen or so minutes we lingered in the study, and for the hour in which we sat at the dinner table with Mrs. Neff, nothing was said by my father or me that was worthy of remembrance.

There was no cross-examination about Atlanta, no inquisition about Harry Ingram, no questions about the death of Davis O'Donnell. The actor, the inadequate actor portraying my father, revealed his stage fright by reading some wrong lines and garbling others. He talked not as my father, but as my mother had talked, of the immaterial, the irrelevant, and the inconsequential.

At times, when I lowered my eyes to my plate, I heard a stronger voice rising, heard Davis besting my father, pleasing my mother, and thrilling me with his demand for my heart and hand. My own voice began to sound borrowed, borrowed from Liz Cooper, who had never brooked or borrowed a meaningful thought in all the years of her girlhood.

Mrs. Neff, the audience of one, was too overcome with her seat at the table of the king to concern herself with the poverty of the play or with the tastelessness of the food served by the woman named Annie, who was badly miscast as my Hilda.

In the darkness after dinner Mrs. Neff and I walked up and

402

down Gedney Street. In the moments when quiet listened to our footfalls, I had the eerie feeling that the street existed only in the reality of Hollow Grove, that around a corner an institutional gate and fence encircled that reality.

As we approached my house again, I saw it this time as a facade behind which loomed the horrors of the château. I loved my cottage with its low sweep, its sense of belonging to the terrain. I hated the château with its hair standing on end to achieve towers.

Annie was gone for the night. The door to the study was shut, but all the rooms on the ground floor held clouds of pipe smoke, the evidence of a distraught man who was given to pacing his house.

Speaking softly, so as not to distract the man in the study, I took Mrs. Neff on a tour of the ancestral portraits and the storybook past, and she listened like a child hungering for tales of a world beyond her ken. And I spoke as a child kneeling before her mother's bed, offering up a prayer to defer her leavetaking.

The clock struck ten and struck me dumb. Mrs. Neff spoke my name, and I answered the roll of those who dared that night to brave sleep. I bade good night to the shut door of the study.

At the door of the guest bedroom I did something I had never done before: I kissed Mrs. Neff on her potato face. It was not a mere good-night kiss or the kind of kiss a daughter bestows on her mother. It was rather a kiss before parting, a kiss before dying.

As I closed myself into my bedroom, I felt I was not alone. All the lights and lamps were burning, but the shadows were lengthening in my mind. I heard sounds not for what they were but for what they evoked: whiskey splashing into a glass, muffled laughter, and a smacking of lips.

Davis was in the room.

I took my nightgown to the dark of my closet, and there I shed my clothes, sat for too long on the floor, and caressed the softness of the nightgown and the hardness of the planked floorboards.

Reality and reason put their weight against the closet door, opened it, and led me against the night and its legions of furies.

I wound my tarnished old clock and set the alarm. Then, with a brave and steady hand, I extinguished all light and boarded the bed for the voyage to the shore of dawn.

En route to sleep I left Gedney Street and Hollow Grove and went to the Via Dolorosa to help bear the heavy cross of Calvary. I drifted into sleep and into nightmare.

It began with the blaring of a horn, a Klaxon horn, blowing sunlight and springtime through the open windows. I rushed from my bed and saw Lieutenant Davis O'Donnell seated behind the wheel of a white Packard twin-six touring car.

Before I left the bedroom I saw myself in the mirror as I had looked in 1920. Wearing a white motoring costume that was the high fashion of the day, I ran from the house and kissed Davis before getting into the car. Once my door was shut, I noticed the trunk resting on the running board, lashed to the chassis on my side.

The trunk was large and black and strange. I asked Davis about it. The handsome boy behind the wheel answered me in his own voice, but his lips never moved and the sound of his voice issued instead from inside the trunk, telling me the trunk was stuffed with varsity sweaters, trophies, battle flags, and medals.

I was asking Davis what had become of his Apperson when the Packard took a corner too sharply. The trunk fell from the running board and bounced away.

Then I was running along the deserted platform of the Stephensville depot, running after a northbound train. Davis was leaning out a train window and shouting for me to catch the train, to catch up with him. I ran and ran, caught the train, and stepped into darkness. A door slammed shut behind me. Believing I had entered the wrong car, I tried to leave, but my hands pulled the handle from the door and my screams were lost in the shrill cry of the steam whistle. I slumped to the floor, blinded by darkness, crippled by separation from the light of Lieutenant O'Donnell's eyes. I inched forward into the dark and my ten fingers brought enlightenment to my brain. I was touching a trunk, and the instant I touched it I heard a voice from inside. It

404

was Davis, and he was imploring me to open the trunk and let him out.

I opened my handbag, felt for the key case, touched the correct key and guided it to the hole in the lock. The key wouldn't fit.

The voice came again, this time telling me I had the right key but the wrong trunk. I felt my way deeper into the dark, found another trunk, another lock, and another and deeper frustration. I went from trunk to trunk, deeper and deeper into the black chasm of the baggage car, whipped by the voice, frenzied by my failure to release and reclaim my love.

Then, as I reached for yet another trunk, I felt flesh and smelled the sweat of passion. Thrown back between two trunks, I was attacked and ravaged as I clawed at the face of Dandy Flood and tore off the mask that Harry Ingram wore. And then, slashing at Harry's face, I tore off another mask and my father was revealed. Above it rose not the screaming of the steam whistle, but a tormented chorus of voices from all of the trunks, the myriad voices of Davis O'Donnell.

Next I heard the solo ticking of the tarnished clock, and I was thrust into wakefulness. I lay there and took inventory: no wind, no thunder, no lightning, no rain, no moon, no heartbeat, and no sense of motion, save the patient ticking of the clock.

"Mother," I cried to the darkness, "who'll wind my heart when I'm asleep?"

I took myself and my blanket to the window, took a fix upon a star, and reassured myself that the earth was still racing around the invisible sun. The bed was cool to my return, and sleep shunned me.

After a while I left the warmth of the blanket and set forth to confront, once and for all, the reality of the trunk in the attic.

I opened and shut the bedroom door with hardly a sound. My bare feet took the staircase down to the kitchen. Turning on the lights, I sought and found a candle and a dish. The candle lit and set upon the dish, I took to the staircase again. Reason and reality climbed with me, but once I was inside the attic I found they had deserted me.

As the dust danced in the candlelight, my heart fluttered and

405

my eyes caught the green bulk of a trunk hiding behind six parcels shaped at Hollow Grove. Putting the dish on the floor, I methodically moved the parcels and exposed the trunk. I sat down and ran shaky fingers over the faded labels of European hotels and transatlantic steamship lines.

"Davis," I whispered.

But the trunk said nothing.

I kissed the trunk, fondled its lock, and withdrew with a shudder as I realized I had forgotten to bring the key case with me. I stole back into my bedroom and gathered the key case and the courage necessary for the return to the attic.

I found the candle dripping wax as freely as I was beading fear. As I opened the key case, I smelled Davis in the leather and trusted memory to select the correct key. It slipped easily into the lock, which seemed to spring open merely upon the bidding of my thought. After loosening and opening the clasps, I waited for the lid of the trunk to be raised from within.

I saw the lid rising. Quickly I slammed the trunk shut, deftly secured the clasps, and drove the lock home. I sat there watching the distorted shadow of myself on the wall beyond the trunk, dancing with the candle.

I turned away. I turned to chairs only strong enough to hold ghosts, to lamps that burned nothing but memory, to boxes, valises, and cartons that contained only ashes of loss. Once more I noticed the six parcels from Hollow Grove.

"Oh, my God!" I cried, and in that moment I began to build a temple.

I bloodied my fingers tearing the strings from the parcels and ripping away the heavy wrapping paper that protected the forty-seven portraits of Davis O'Donnell. By the light of the candle, with the oils transmuted to blood, I recognized my vengeful God, even in several of those portraits where my schizophrenia had stylized and fragmented the golden face and the blue diamond eyes.

Dancing like a moth about the candle, I built a gallery of the forty-seven portraits, four bright walls to dazzle the shadows.

On the seventh moment I rested. I humbled myself before the

406

trunk, made the three-hundred-and-sixty-degree turn from pleasure to panic, and addressed myself again to the lock.

The lock open, the clasps freed, the candle flickering, I put my perspiring hands to the lid and pressed. Ever so slowly, ever so warily, I raised the lid, lowered my head, shut my eyes, and waited for the consequences beyond metaphors.

The lock that had secured the trunk now blinded my eyes; the wax that had dripped from the candle now sealed my ears; the nails that had held Christ to the cross now paralyzed my hands. But, no longer able to hold my breath, I exhaled the fetid air and felt a spear stab my side before I gasped for life again and drowned my lungs in blood.

4.

Early in August of 1942 I achieved my planned escape from the Elba of the attic in the house on Gedney Street. I boarded a northbound train and forced the gate at Hollow Grove. From there I pushed on to the North Shore before advancing on Manhattan, on a house in Washington Square. With fresh intelligence made available to me there, I commandeered a taxi to Pennsylvania Station, where I boarded a crack train bound west for Cincinnati.

My coach was garish with the uniforms of men at war, but I was the one bearing the standard and rushing into battle, an offensive that began with the rolling of the wheels, with a descent that allowed a river to flow above the train, with a climb to meadows raw and red-faced in the August twilight.

Beyond Newark I rose from my window seat, left the company of a young sailor seated beside me, and carried my oversize handbag as if it were a map case. The dining car was crowded, but the face I sought remained invisible. With some difficulty, caused by an officious steward, I managed to gain safe passage through the car and its traffic of waiters.

In the third Pullman car I came upon my quarry. Although he was wearing the disguise of time and using spectacles to read a leather-bound book, although his shoes boasted a shine, his suit a press, and his tie a certain style, I recognized the Buddha eyes of Delano Fredericks.

He did not see me. Engrossed in his book, he failed to notice my passage up the aisle. I continued to the far end of the car, did an about-face, and rehearsed my strategy before confronting him.

"I beg your pardon."

My voice, soft with uncertainty, never reached his awareness. But I repeated the line exactly as before, and this time he tore his eyes from his book, glanced irritably at me, and pondered the intrusion of this stranger. Saying nothing, he rested the book on his lap. I saw Hebrew letters swarming over the pages before I saw him giving me the attention of his eyes and ears.

"Is your name, perhaps, Delano Fredericks?"

Recognition by a stranger held no charm for him. "Yes, it is."

I trimmed my smile. "I'm Rannah O'Donnell."

Slowly his hands closed the book, and the smile that came to his eyes was genuine. He rose and kissed me with a kiss lost in the rush of years and delivered long years later. Then he sat me down beside him and held my hands to assist him to credulity. When last he had seen me, I was twenty-six years old, wearing a one-piece, cherry colored bathing suit, sipping gin in the Long Island sun, and listening to Vincent Lopez and his orchestra playing Gershwin on a badly scratched record. Now I was forty-two, wearing my years carelessly, savoring his kiss, and listening to the voice I most desperately wanted to hear.

"I can't believe it," said Freddie. "Where are you going?"

"Louisville," I said, naming a city in the path of the lie. "To visit an old friend I grew up with. Liz Cooper." I laughed Liz Cooper's laughter. "And don't say it's a small world. I find it much too large, and much too long between drinks and happenstance. Nineteen-twenty-six and sixteen make 1942."

"What car are you in?"

"Up front. In one of the coaches. The dining car being full up,

409

I decided to inspect the sleeping cars. And, lo and behold, I see you!''

Freddie ran a hand over his graying, balding head. ''Remarkable that you should have recognized me.''

''It was your eyes. Your Buddha eyes. I remember the very first day you came to the Plaza.'' Freddie's smile struck an iceberg, and I sensed I had erred. Abruptly changing course, I asked, ''And where in the West is your station?''

''Cincinnati.''

''Oh, that's where all those German comics go for their vaudeville jokes! I used to love vaudeville! Did you ever see Davis and me do Gallagher and Shean?''

''Yes, I did,'' he said, and I decided against further excursions into nostalgia.

''Why Cincinnati? Or am I being too inquisitive?''

His smile better than ever, Freddie said, ''I'm visiting an old friend. He's eighty-nine years old.''

I said, ''You speak of him as if he were young.''

''He's old, but still very much alive for a man who's lived more than nine hundred years.''

''Methuselah in Cincinnati?''

''His name is Samuel Melnick.''

''You say that as if I should know him.''

''He's the man who discovered a lost page of the Bible.''

''In Cincinnati?'' I asked, tapping the vein of the vaudeville comics and laughing too soon. Again sighting the iceberg, I went into reverse. I said, ''I never knew there *was* a lost page of the Bible. Which page was it?''

''A page from the Song of Songs.''

''Really! And where was it discovered?''

''In Egypt, in the genizah of a synagogue in Alexandria.''

''In the *what* of a synagogue?''

''Genizah.'' He spelled it. ''A Hebrew word. Refers to a place of hiding, of burial. A secret room with secret access to it, in which sacred writings were either deposited or disposed.''

I began to tremble, not from the chill of the iceberg, but from the secret of the genizah. ''Tell me more.''

410

Concerned by my now uncontrollable trembling, Freddie asked, "Is there anything I can do?"

"Yes," I implored him. "Tell me more."

Freddie spoke slowly, as if he were submitting the words to my psyche. He said, "The written word, to the Jews, has always been most sacred. They considered it sacrilege to cast books and scrolls aside, and to expose them to defilement, especially since the writings contained the pseudonyms of the deity."

Still quivering, I said, "The genizah. Tell me about the genizah."

And still cautious, Freddie continued. "The genizahs were repositories not only of holy works, but also of those considered heretical, or, at least, in error. The word *apocrypha* means hidden books."

"Hidden books," I said and my quaking intensified.

"The genizah — Rannah, can I —?"

"The genizah," I begged.

"The genizah preserved good works from harm, and bad works from harming."

"Harming? Harming whom?"

Freddie, clasping his hands as if to keep himself free of my trembling, said, "Each despot rewrites history, censors the truth that doesn't serve him, and burns the books containing the seeds of insurrection."

"Resurrection?"

"Insurrection," Freddie repeated. "For the example of our own times, and our current crisis in history, Adolf Hitler."

"I don't want to hear about Hitler. Tell me more about the genizah."

Freddie said, "To the Jews a book is like a man. When the spirit is gone, the corpse is buried and protected from abuse." His voice dwindled before the sound of my weeping. "Rannah, what *is* it?"

"I'm all right. Really I am. Please, tell me more."

"I seem to be upsetting you."

"No! No, Freddie. I'm sorry I'm so emotional, but please, you

411

must tell me more. Please. You were saying that the corpse is buried and protected from abuse."

"Yes," said Freddie nervously. "When a book is worn with use and age, it is hidden in a genizah to preserve it from profanation. According to the most orthodox scholars, the contents of the book go up to heaven like the soul."

"The soul." With some difficulty I asked, "You don't believe that, do you, Freddie?"

He hesitated. "I'm afraid not."

"I do," I said. "But tell me, Freddie, what does Samuel Melnick believe?"

"He believes the book itself is the soul." Misreading my reaction, he asked, "Does that offend you?"

"Offend me? God, no! That's the truth! The book *is* the soul! The book itself! Freddie, tell me more about this man."

Before he spoke again, Freddie observed the diminution of my distress. "Samuel Melnick was born in 1853, in a Russian Polish town where his father was an architect. At the age of six it became apparent that Melnick was a *Wunderkind*, a child prodigy, particularly in talmudic learning. At the age of twelve there wasn't an elder among the Jews in the village who could match him in depth of perception or in brilliance of debate. One of the elders came to believe the boy was another Moses, meant to deliver the Jews from czarist oppression. And so it was arranged for young Samuel to be sent to Saint Petersburg. There he was adopted by Gregor Golitzen, a lawyer of affluence and a scholar of renown. Melnick was baptized into the Russian Orthodox Church, given the name of Anton Golitzen, and enrolled in a succession of the best schools."

I asked, "Didn't the boy mind all of this?"

"No, he didn't. He understood the nature of his mission with books."

"How did he come to Alexandria? Was he Moses returning to Egypt?"

"No," said Freddie. "In the year 1897 Melnick was the most brilliant lawyer in all of Russia. When a Russian prince became

412

involved in a financial scandal in Alexandria, the czar himself dispatched Melnick to that city.''

I asked, ''How did Melnick get to the genizah?''

''Sir Henry Rosemont, keeper of the collection of Hebraic manuscripts at Cambridge University, was staying at the same hotel in Alexandria. He and Melnick met, and it was a meeting of minds. Once the legal matter was settled — successfully, I might add — Melnick chose not to return to Saint Petersburg immediately. Instead he joined Sir Henry in his search for the genizah.''

''And where did they find it?''

''In an ancient synagogue. Melnick and Sir Henry, who was then sixty-four years old, climbed crude ladders to an opening high up on a wall. Sir Henry took a lantern and looked into the secret recess. Shortly he withdrew and handed the lantern to Melnick. He took it, peered in, and saw what he describes as a battlefield of books.''

''Oh, God!'' I screamed as the train seemed to gather more speed, and I spent more tears.

Apologetically Freddie said, ''I seem to be upsetting you again.''

''No. Believe me, these are tears of joy.''

''I don't understand.''

''I'll explain later. But, please, I must hear about the battlefield of books.''

''Rannah, I don't want to cause —''

''Freddie, I'm all *right*. And, believe me, you're the right medicine for me.''

After watching me dry my eyes and regain my composure, Freddie took up his tale. ''The next step was to obtain permission from the Chief Rabbi to descend into the genizah. Permission was granted, but the beadles warned Sir Henry and Melnick that, lurking in the lightless genizah, were serpents and dragons.''

I screamed again. ''Oh, my God! My God!'' I turned my head and buried it against the back of the seat. But I felt exultancy

413

before I felt the tense hands of Delano Fredericks taking hold of me, trying to keep me from the evil eye of madness.

Fully five minutes later, after much dismay on the part of Freddie and a profusion of apologies from me, Freddie consented to go on with the story. Proceeding as carefully as a printer selecting type from a font, he said, "Sir Henry and Melnick entered the genizah, inhaled the dust of centuries, and spent days and weeks picking among the strewn manuscripts. Sir Henry, who had come to Alexandria a robust man for his age, was literally choked to death by the dust. With the death of Sir Henry, Melnick continued the work alone. And when he left Alexandria, it was not for Saint Petersburg, but for Cambridge, where he took up Sir Henry's post. And, once again, he called himself Samuel Melnick."

"Did he leave a family in Russia?"

"A wife, two sons, and three daughters, all of whom, with his career and his fortune, he renounced."

"Did he become a Jew again?"

Freddie weighed the question. "He'd never stopped being a Jew, in the sense that he was always a man of learning. All that matters to him — call him a bibliomaniac if you will — are books. It matters not what the language, what the culture, what the metaphysics. His interest is man and his civilization, as recorded in his writings, in any language. Language is no barrier to him."

"When did he leave England?"

"In 1936."

"Why?"

"To study recently discovered Babylonian scrolls entrusted to the United Theological Seminary in Cincinnati."

"Freddie, you said — and I love the phrase — that Melnick found *a battlefield of books* in the genizah."

"Yes, the shambles, buried for more than nine hundred years, contained treasures of poetry, philosophy, mathematics, astrology, fiction, legends, medicine, and correspondence of the era. All in all, a testament of a time previously lost to us."

"How did you come to meet Melnick?"

414

"I wrote an article about him for the New York *Times Magazine*. Alfred Knopf read it and prevailed upon me to write a book on the subject, which is the reason for this trip. Or shall I say excuse?" In a moment Freddie told me his secret. "I find I'm more alive, truly alive, in the presence of ancient manuscripts and scrolls, and of scholars like Samuel Melnick."

"Freddie," I asked absently, "do you think you'll ever go searching for a genizah?"

"Someday, perhaps," he said wistfully. "After the war is ended. Yes, I believe I'd find some meaning to my own life in a genizah."

Much too softly, much too casually, I said, "I did."

My declaration of discovery was lost upon Freddie. "Rannah, how've you been?"

I smiled sadly. "I've been mad. Now, suddenly, I'm well again. But you think me mad."

"How long were you in New York?"

"A week. I stayed with Guy Thurlow's widow."

"When did you leave the sanitarium?"

"In May. But I was back there ten days ago. I was also at your house. Today at five o'clock."

My information taken as a shot across his bow, Freddie alerted his senses. "And Irene informed you I'd be on this train."

"Yes. She told me you'd be going to Penn Station directly from Knopf's."

"You had a week in which to phone me."

"I preferred it this way. On a train, on railroad time. In a car sealed from petty concerns and handy excuses."

He tensed. "What do you want of me?"

I was in utter command of myself now. "I want nothing. I wish only to give you something."

Anything but a boy with an unopened Christmas package, Freddie asked, "What is it?"

"You, bless you, told me a story of a beautiful man, and of a strange genizah in far-off Egypt. Now I ask you to listen to me — and weep joyous tears with me — as I tell you of another beautiful man. And another genizah."

415

There was no wonder in his eyes. "Shall we have dinner? I'm famished."

"No, not yet. This is hardly dinner conversation."

He said, "Where is this other genizah?"

"Let me begin at the beginning. In 1914, in the city of Milwaukee —"

"I know the beginning."

"Indeed," I said. "You met the boy from Milwaukee who had come to New Haven to learn the shortest and surest route to the House of Morgan. And you pointed out another road to —"

Unmoved, Freddie said, "I know the middle, too."

"And also the end?" I asked with bitterness.

"The *Times* telephoned me when Davis died."

"Were your tears fit to print?"

A light-year away from a smile, Freddie said, "That's very clever. But my last tear for Davis evaporated in 1926."

"A vintage year for tears."

"Isn't this dinner conversation?"

I restrained my rage. "I'm sorry. Forgive me. You irritate me with your — I don't know — is it impatience or indifference?"

"Impatience."

"You're skeptical, too, aren't you, Freddie?"

"Where is *your* genizah?"

"In the attic of my house in Georgia."

"The attic, then, is your genizah," he said with minimal interest.

"No, the attic is an attic! The genizah is a trunk. A trunk guarded by nightmares and hallucinations. By demons more terrible than serpents and dragons!"

He returned my salvo with a question that limped. "Davis's trunk?"

"Yes."

"Shipped from Hollywood?"

"Santa Monica."

When Freddie spoke again, I heard the bored tone of a Scotland Yard detective questioning a feebleminded upstairs maid in

416

order to satisfy the routine of his investigation. "And what did the trunk contain?"

"I didn't find death! I wasn't drowned in Davis's blood! I wasn't buried in Davis's ashes!"

Freddie took my hands and tried to give me an infusion of his own calm. "Tell me, quietly now, what was in the trunk."

Slowly I freed my hands, opened my handbag, and withdrew a book, which I offered to Freddie. He took it and was bludgeoned by the bloodstained pages.

"Davis's blood?"

"Yes, his vomited blood, which I smelled when I opened the trunk."

Freddie returned the book to me and I returned it to the heavy handbag. He asked, "What else did you find?"

"Davis's soul."

"His soul?"

I wept behind the carriages of my burning and failing cannons. "Don't you believe — as Samuel Melnick and I do — that the book — the book itself — is the soul of the man?"

Evading the question, Freddie asked, "What exactly does the trunk contain?"

I said, "I've raised no dust to make you choke with excitement, have I?"

"Not yet, Rannah."

"The trunk contains thousands upon thousands of pages of typescript. Thousands of pages of handwritten notes."

"Another novel?" Freddie inquired, still without excitement.

"An unfinished novel. Two hundred and six pages of a first draft. And almost five hundred pages of notes on the novel."

"A novel about Hollywood?"

Detecting the sneer in his voice, I said, "No, Freddie. It's a novel about three Jews — a father and two sons — in another Babylon called Hollywood."

"Who were the prototypes?"

"The Selznicks. Lewis, Myron, and David."

The names fell at his feet and raised no dust. "What else was in the trunk?"

417

"Not interested in this novel?"

"It has two faults. It concerns Hollywood, and it's unfinished."

"Oh, you cold piece of cod," I said softly. "The notes themselves are brilliant. And the two-hundred-odd pages contain the best, the very best of Davis. A Davis you and I never knew, the mature Davis, the —"

Freddie trampled on the petals of my bouquet. "What else, Rannah?"

"There's another draft of *In Battalions*. Done several years after publication."

"Anything else?"

"Not interested in the revised *In Battalions?*"

"Not at all."

"It took me eight years before I got around to reading it. How long did it take you?"

"I've read it."

"You said that as if I'd asked you if you'd read yesterday's *Times*. Are you perhaps *not* Delano Fredericks?"

"Anything else?" he asked with indifference.

I took a deep breath. "Yes. A collection of essays. Untitled and relatively simple to title. *The Breakdown. The Downfall.* Or *Madness East and West*."

His interest was captured at last. "East and West? Did Davis have a nervous breakdown?"

"Yes. But he put the pieces together, waited for a second wind to come to his sails, and he voyaged back to the North Shore and beyond."

Freddie's impatience returned. "Rannah, what — "

"In this collection of essays there are long and chilling chapters on me, Harry, Guy, and *you*. The very best chapter is the one on you. It's the first chapter. 'In the beginning there was Freddie. . . .' "

"Rannah, what do you want of me?"

"Harry told me Davis was out of print."

He was incredulous. "Harry Ingram?"

"Yes."

418

"Does Harry write to you?"

"Harry shouts at me. Freddie, did you know that Davis was out of print?"

Unmoved, Freddie said, "No, but it doesn't surprise me. When did you see Harry last?"

My trembling began again. "I don't want to talk about Harry. He's very much in print. Let's talk about Davis. About a resurrection."

"Resurrection?"

"They burned his dead body. They mustn't burn his books with him."

"Rannah, why don't you discuss this with Albert Corbell?"

"Why? Because he's not the one who nominated Davis for God in a smoke-filled room!"

"You're being clever."

"There's a war on. Paper's rationed. Corbell has only enough paper for Harry."

"Who told you that?"

"Harry."

Freddie idly said, "There *is* a war on."

"In Cincinnati?"

"I can't help you, Rannah."

"Freddie, I don't understand what you're saying. Is it that you don't wish to help me? Or is it that you couldn't help me if you wanted to?"

He said, "I couldn't help you if I wanted to."

"Do you want to help?"

"No, I'm afraid I don't consider it any concern of mine."

"You don't care how dead Davis is, do you?"

"The point is there's no current interest in Davis. No one writes or talks about him."

"Harry cares!" I screamed, but the scream availed me nothing. "What happened between Davis and you? Was Davis just another Yale man you outgrew?"

"No, not Davis," he said sadly.

"What was it, Freddie? What happened?"

"Harry Ingram happened."

419

"I don't understand."

Freddie said, "Davis blamed me for the failure of *North Shore*. After the success of *A Pattern Called War*."

"Davis never told me that. When was this?"

"In 1926. Davis came to my flat and took me to task for giving him what he described as a 'bum steer.' "

"And what did that mean?"

"That I had perverted his talent, and that I had led to the writing of a novel that was an attack upon the American Dream."

"He must've been drunk," I said.

"Davis wasn't drunk that day."

"Davis got the idea for the novel from Guy. Not from you."

"Guy gave him his bootlegger hero, Harry the discipline he lacked, and I the heresy that doomed him to failure."

"Freddie, what happened in 1930? Why did you turn your back on Davis?"

"I had no advice to give him. I was, of course, distressed by your illness, for which I blamed Davis."

"Is that why — ?"

"No, Rannah. I had no advice to give him. I thought the idea for *In Battalions* ill advised, ill timed. As for Hollywood, I looked upon it as a Siberia for his crimes against himself and you."

"Freddie, wasn't there someone else?"

"Someone else?"

"Karl Marx."

He looked unhappy. "True."

"Sad but true?"

"Another of my many follies."

"Changing God's name from Davis O'Donnell to Karl Marx?"

In the silence of his meditation, I listened to the train wheels clicking off the miles. Then he said, "When you stray into myth, the names always change. Marx becomes Lenin, who becomes Stalin, who clasps hands with Hitler, who puts the torch to Marx. Am I confusing you?"

420

"No, Freddie."

"I tried to join up again, but my bid for an army commission was denied. My allegiance was suspect."

Taking the opening, I said, "Join my army. God for Davis. Davis for God. Remember what you said to me at the Plaza in 1920? You said: 'Join my church. And believe Davis is God.' "

Reflectively, Freddie said, "I said there are only pseudonyms for the true name of God, and that Davis O'Donnell was the pseudonym of the time."

"No, of the moment. The word you used was *moment*. And you also said this: 'In bed you embrace a man who's obliged to leave more than dust and ashes.' "

Freddie was nonplussed. "How do you remember all of this? It was so long ago."

"The lucidity of the mad." He bit his lip. "Freddie, I escaped from my father, not from the sanitarium. But let me tell you how mad I am. About the time you were embracing Marx I was embracing Jesus for the second time in my life. Now, for the second time, I've given up Jesus. And please don't accuse me of being clever. I'm for Davis now. I opened the trunk — Davis's trunk — and I found life everlasting."

"Rannah, I respect your zeal, but —"

"Freddie, are you still the disappointed novelist? Is envy keeping you from — ?"

"No, not envy."

"Then what is it?"

"A disenchantment with my own times, my own life."

"Where are you running, Freddie? To antiquity? To the fallen columns and the crumbled cities?"

"I know my way now, and it leads to the battlefield of books."

My voice breaking, I cried, "Come to mine! Come to the O'Donnell genizah!"

Intrigued, Freddie studied me for a long moment. "If I were to join your army, what would you expect of me?"

"To aim the cannons and pull the lanyards."

"And when the metaphors are spent?"

"Sorry. I'll be specific. The Davis O'Donnell who wrote for

421

the *Saturday Evening Post,* and who was a hack in Hollywood, must remain dead. The resurrection is meant only for the Davis O'Donnell I found in the trunk. The mature, the serious, the meditative, the nostalgic, the melancholy, the fulfilled Davis O'Donnell. Does that make sense?''

"I'll defer my comments," said Freddie.

"I'd like you to find a proper publisher."

"I'm not Ellis Mason. This is the province of a literary agent."

"Damn Ellis Mason! I don't want Davis peddled! He must be sponsored! By the best literary mind in the country! You!"

Impervious to flattery, Freddie asked, "Is there anything else you require of me?"

"You must contact Harry. Ask him to write a foreword."

"For the unfinished novel?"

"No, for the essays."

"Rannah, why can't you write to Harry?"

I shook my head. "Harry mustn't know. No one must ever know that I had anything to do with Davis's resurrection."

"Why not?"

"I've a more important role to play: the madwoman who bitched up the greatest creative talent of his time."

"The gospel according to Saint Harry," Freddie commented dryly.

"I want that gospel in Harry's foreword."

"Is it the truth?"

"Freddie, I killed Davis."

"That's metaphor."

"I'm the daughter of a trial lawyer. I can convince you I murdered Davis. Even as I convinced Harry *he* murdered Davis."

Startled, Freddie asked, "When was this?"

I ignored the question. "Hate is the only reality for Harry. He told me so himself. If you can, Freddie, urge Harry to pour his hate into the mold of the foreword."

"When did you see Harry?"

422

"In May. And please don't ask me any more about it. We're discussing Davis."

Absently Freddie opened and shut his leather-bound book. "Rannah?"

"Yes."

"Assuming I obtain the desired foreword from Harry, assuming I place the essays with a publisher, what then?"

"Then you must lead your fellow critics in huzzas. And in spreading the message that Davis has arisen."

"To his erstwhile popularity?"

"No, to his rightful place. On bookshelves, within reach."

"Well said."

"Will you do it, Freddie?"

"Question."

"Yes?"

"Wouldn't Harry's foreword be a lie?"

"It'll be Harry's truth."

"Truth or hate?"

"Only for me. Life everlasting for Davis. Eternal damnation for me."

"Rannah, why did you return to Hollow Grove recently?"

"To claim some letters. The file of letters written by Davis, from Hollywood, to my doctor."

"And what have you done with this file?"

"Destroyed what needed to be destroyed and —"

He interrupted me sharply. "What *needed* to be destroyed?"

I said, "In some of the letters, Davis detailed his guilt for my madness. He wrote much the same sort of thing to one of Guy's daughters. I have those letters, too."

Freddie studied me with pain. "And you destroyed what needed to be destroyed."

"Yes. But what remains is a beautiful collection of letters. Letters that will serve Davis well."

Freddie touched a hand to his forehead, and I seemed to sense the ritual gesture of a judge donning his black cloth before delivering a sentence of death.

423

"Rannah?"

"Yes?" My nerves jumped and my eyes strained to read the pale lips.

"In your war," he spoke much too slowly, "your war for Davis, truth has been sacrificed to expediency, hasn't it?"

"It must! For the greater truth! Davis's truth!"

"This, for you, is the ultimate cause, isn't it?"

"Yes!"

"And the cause demands and exacts discipline, doesn't it?"

"Strict discipline!"

Then, as a New York bound train filled the courtroom with a rush of blurred faces, Delano Fredericks delivered his verdict. "Forgive me, Rannah, but you're asking of me what I gave to Marxism. What I'll never again give to any cause. Yours included."

The warning bells were clanging at the crossroads, and the train was passing over the body of Anna Karenina. "Not mine! Davis's cause! Resurrection for Davis!"

Freddie shook his head. "Slogans for dupes, and lies for Davis."

I stood my ground. "That's what war is! Always is and always will be. Banners and slogans. And drums. Who'll march to war without the beat of drums? Freddie, listen to me, it's all a big circus. A county fair. You're the boss at the ticket window. Harry's the barker. And I'm the belly dancer. The last flapper, doing the Charleston while Harry makes the pitch and lures the crowd inside the tent. They come in to see the bitch strip herself naked. And what do they see instead? They see Davis O'Donnell arisen from the dead."

I tore my eyes from Freddie and stared out the window. The tents were down on the New Jersey flatlands, no circuses, no county fairs in sight.

Freddie said, "Let's have dinner."

He was Methuselah shepherding his centuries halfway around the world, laboring up a ladder to an opening high on a synagogue wall, descending into the dust of the days of his youth.

Not to awaken anyone in the bedrooms of the houses beyond the tracks, I spoke softly now. "Tell me about the book you're reading."

"It's seventh-century poetry, written by a Hebrew named Yannai, and recovered from the Alexandrian genizah," he said, caressing the binding.

I sighed. "I must be mad to trust the sound of my voice. And the unsoundness of my mind. Yes, I beat the drums, cry havoc, burn the truth, and parry with my betters. Such as you and Harry. Forgive me, Freddie, for wasting your time. But Freddie . . . one last favor?"

"What is it?"

"Don't be alarmed. It's not for me. It's for Davis."

He said nothing.

I opened my handbag, smelled blood, and carefully withdrew a bulky folder, from which I removed a sheaf of paper and handed it to Freddie. Without emotion I said, "Bring Davis back from the dead. For only fifteen minutes. Take yourself from the seventh century to the twentieth. And read what a writer named O'Donnell had to say about a writer named Fredericks."

Standing, I noted the hour by Mrs. Neff's wristwatch, and I held my tongue and my breath when I saw that Freddie was now reading English rather than Hebrew. Slipping away from him, I followed the aisle to the platform at the rear of the Pullman car.

There, alone, I stood at the window of the train door. I saw not the tracks, not the smoke of war pouring from high stacks, not the lighted windows, not the pattern of the August stars, not the tents of light under which the New Jersey townships played at being cities. Rather, in the reflection of the well of my tears, I saw Delano Fredericks turn one page and then another before, lantern in hand, he went down a sacred road to the battlefield of Davis O'Donnell's books.

Past the platform window, on trembling tracks, a crowded, New York bound passenger train hurtled toward yesterday, all my long, long yesterdays of madness and defeat and death. In

the passing train, in the blur of faces at other windows, I saw the
Buddha eyes fixed upon a newspaper.

Louder than train whistles I screamed, ''Freddie! Come back!
Come back! Oh, Freddie! Save Davis! Save God!''

Stephensville, Georgia
September 1942 – August 1945

Afterword

To this day legend charges Rannah O'Donnell with an escape from an insane asylum, a debauch with a soldier in a hotel room, and an act of arson that destroyed the hotel and one hundred and three lives, including her own.

The truth is more compelling.

In Cincinnati, in August of 1942, after Rannah had met my conditions, which included the writing of her testimony, I agreed to enlist myself in her cause.

The Downfall, by Davis O'Donnell, was published in New York in 1944 by the then obscure Caxton Press. This volume of essays was edited by me and the introduction was mine rather than Harry Ingram's.

Albert Corbell and Son, in the autumn after Hiroshima, returned the name of Davis O'Donnell to its list. The unfinished Hollywood novel and the bulk of his notes, which I had edited, appeared as *A Lantern from Babylon.* In successive publishing seasons *North Shore, In Battalions, The Distant Spires,* and *Violins at the Plaza* reappeared, each bearing an introduction by a different literary critic. I later edited *The Short Stories of Davis O'Donnell* and *The Letters of Davis O'Donnell.*

On November 10, 1947, Rannah telephoned me from Hollow Grove to inform me that her father was dead, and that she was going home to "kiss him in his coffin and bury him." A week

427

later I received a letter from Rannah telling me that matters relating to Judge Gedney's estate would delay, for some weeks, her return to the sanitarium.

Mrs. James Gilland, née Liz Cooper, told me that it was Friday, November 28, before she saw Rannah for the first time since the funeral. Concerned by Rannah's seclusion, Mrs. Gilland prevailed upon her to accompany her husband and her the following morning to Atlanta, to attend the football game between the University of Georgia and Georgia Tech, and to spend the weekend as house guests of the Howard Franklins.

Her onetime fiancé, his wife, and his circle of friends received Rannah graciously. To them she remained Rannah Gedney the Stephensville belle, the granddaughter of a Confederate Army general.

At Grant Field, on the Georgia Tech campus, the Franklin party sat together. During the first half, Rannah, bundled into a borrowed beaver coat, seemed as radiant as a schoolgirl and caught the excitement of the game.

At half time, as the college bands took to the gridiron, Rannah became exuberant as she reminisced to James Gilland about the games she had attended in New Haven, Cambridge, and Princeton with Davis O'Donnell. However, from the time the teams reappeared, according to James Gilland, Rannah appeared blind to the spectacle before her.

Leaving the stadium, the Franklin party moved on to an off-campus tavern crowded with alumni and undergraduates. At the head of the long table reserved for his party, Howard Franklin arranged for Rannah to sit on his right. To this day he remains confounded and perturbed by those last moments with her. This, according to the account he gave me at the Gilland home following Rannah's burial, was what happened:

Howard Franklin began by discussing the football game, but he quickly sensed that Rannah was not at all interested. Then, quite casually, he asked Rannah if she could remember back to the year 1924. Rannah stared at him, but said nothing. Franklin went on to tell her that in 1924 he had happened to be in New York on banking business, and that he had seen her walking

428

alone on Fifth Avenue. He told her he had stopped his taxi, had searched for her, and had not been able to find her on the crowded street.

Rannah, who had listened to this account without apparent amusement or interest, indifferently declared that she had never been to New York. Then, before Franklin was able to resolve his confusion, Rannah inquired if he had any silver in his pockets. Franklin produced some coins. Rannah selected a quarter, rose, and, without a word, left the table. Walking slowly, she went in the direction of the rest rooms. This was the last time Franklin or the Gillands, who also noted her leavetaking, saw her alive.

Some fifteen or twenty minutes later, Franklin left his chair and whispered his apprehensions to Mrs. Gilland, who went to the ladies' room but failed to find Rannah. A search of the interior and exterior of the tavern availed nothing. With contrition, Gilland admitted he had gone so far as to peep into the back seats of the scores of automobiles on the tavern's parking lot.

While the Gillands, bearing the beaver coat abandoned by Rannah, went through the cold, dark streets searching for her, Howard Franklin telephoned the police, concluding his description of Rannah with the intelligence that she was a mental patient.

While the others in the party went on to the Piedmont Driving Club, the Franklins and the Gillands returned to the Franklin home, there to make periodic but futile telephone calls to police headquarters and to Grady Hospital.

It was seven o'clock Sunday morning, November 30, when Franklin received a telephone call urging him to come to the basement morgue of Grady Hospital. Shortly before eight, Franklin and Gilland identified one of the victims of the worst hotel fire in American history.

The Higginson Hotel was a fourteen-story, gray brick building, a "fireproof" commercial hostelry that had first opened its doors in 1915. On that Saturday night in question, because of the big football weekend, the hotel registered three hundred and fourteen guests. At least one occupant was unregistered. Shortly before four o'clock Sunday morning a bellhop named

429

Lem Blake brought a bottle of muscatel, a bottle of ginger ale, and a bucket of ice cubes to Room 620. There he saw the registered occupant of the single room, Master Sergeant Everett Winsett, thirty-four years old. The sergeant was not alone. With him was a woman whom the bellhop was later to identify as Rannah O'Donnell.

As the bellhop left Room 620, he was instantly overwhelmed by smoke. He returned to the room to report the fire. Winsett immediately picked up the telephone to relay the alarm. Rannah, according to the bellhop, rushed out of the room and began pounding on doors and rousing guests from sleep.

By the time the fire department had arrived with all available equipment, the hotel, which had no outside fire escapes, no sprinkler system, and no vented roof, was an open-hearth furnace.

Outside the hotel, firemen ran up spindly ladders and tried to dissuade the panic-stricken from leaping out of high windows. Body after body hurtled to death.

As for Rannah, she was on the twelfth floor when she was trapped. She rushed through Room 1215, opened a window and stepped out upon the ledge. She stood there until a burst of flame caught her hair. In another instant, as thousands in the street below observed, Rannah released her hold on life.

An Atlanta *Journal* photographer took the picture that was carried in thousands of newspapers and on the cover of *Life* magazine. To blanket the lurid photograph, *Life* borrowed its caption from Byron: "To Death, the sable smoke, where vanishes the flame."

In addition to its full coverage of the disaster, *Life* devoted five pages to "The Dazzling O'Donnells" and perpetuated the legend that Davis O'Donnell had been destroyed by his mad wife.

Within weeks of Rannah's death, the O'Donnell revival, discouraging for three years, took a hold it has yet to relinquish. In 1958 this hold became a source of grave concern to Harry Ingram.

In New York, late one autumn afternoon, I received a tele-

430

phone call from a troubled woman who was the fourth Mrs. Harry Ingram. She told me that her husband had made a reservation to dine with me that night at Sharkey's restaurant. When I attempted an excuse, Paula Ingram hinted that her husband was not well, and that my presence would be a mercy.

When, in 1948, the bitter year of his only unrewarding novel, *The Merit of a General,* I had last seen Harry Ingram, I had been morbidly reminded of Eugene Giraud's drawing of Balzac in demise. Now, as I entered Sharkey's, I saw another Harry Ingram, his once thick hair sparse and white, his face drawn by time and fringed with an equally white beard.

He was not alone. He was surrounded by a court of athletes, sportswriters, and Broadway columnists.

Once we were alone, Harry lost his prankish pose. He spoke about the dermatitis that had afflicted him, had made shaving an agony, and had necessitated the growth of the beard. Listening to him, I found myself remembering Rannah's eczema and its relationship to her schizophrenia.

Although his presence ruled the restaurant, he was civil only in speaking of his beloved wife. Then, as he posed questions which explained my audience, his language converted the restaurant into a barracks. Confronted by his peccant attitude, I found myself musing that I would have much preferred the stench of Balzac's death chamber to the paranoia exuded by Harry Ingram.

I vividly recall the thrust and parry of every word, but I offer only an abstract of the dialogue between us, excising all the Anglo-Saxonisms.

Harry began with a lie. "I last saw Rannah in 1930. When did you see her last?"

"I believe it was 1926," I said, matching his lie. "The last time I saw either of the O'Donnells."

"Got a letter from Davis in 1930. Told me he hated your guts."

"He had cause."

"How'd you come to get his stuff?"

"Davis named me as his literary executor."

431

"Was his trunk sent to you?"

"Yes."

"Did you find a book of mine in it?"

"A copy of each of your books."

"Including *November's Leaf Is Red?*"

"Yes."

"Was there blood all over the book?"

"Blood? Who told you — ?"

"I heard it somewhere."

"Whose blood was it supposed — ?"

"I got your letters. Back in '43."

"Why didn't you answer me?"

"There was a war on and I was pounding out dispatches."

"I understood. That's why I wrote the foreword myself."

"I read it. How much is he pulling in now?"

"I don't understand you, Harry."

"How much money did Davis make last year?"

"Davis is dead."

"How much?"

"All of his books are selling well."

"I pulled in sixty-three thousand five hundred and forty-two bucks last year. How much did Davis make?"

"Davis is dead."

"You and your Boston reserve. Give me the figure."

"In excess of ninety thousand dollars."

"Who said he was dead?"

"Guy Thurlow."

"He's more alive than I am. He and Rannah both. They haunt me. They come at night and bring me pus. I scratch and claw at them. You, too, Freddie. You've been at me pretty good with the shaft."

"What shaft?"

"The same shaft you use to carry the banner for your Yale buddy."

"Did you read my article in the *Times Book Review* about your Nobel Prize?"

"I read your review of *General.*"

"Harry, what are you writing now?"

"Suicide notes. How can a guy write when he can't lick the dead? When the dead beat him down?"

"What are you doing in New York?"

"Hunting. Hunting ghosts. I'm a good shot, Freddie. A great shot. But I can't hit the side of a ghost. Ninety thousand dollars. Is that for real?"

"Very real."

"You can't pick up a paper without seeing something about him. The Davis O'Donnell flapper, the Davis O'Donnell bootlegger, the Davis O'Donnell college kids, the Davis O'Donnell style, the Davis O'Donnell era, the Davis O'Donnell genius. The Great American Davis O'Donnell. Davis O'Donnell, the best of the best. You know what it is, don't you? It's death that does it. The living haven't got a chance against the dead. Put death between a writer and his work, and his work loses all of its flaws and takes the shine of a classic. Do you know what I'm driving at, Freddie?"

"Yes, Harry. Shall we order dinner?"

"I've had it. You gave me my dinner. You shoved it right down my throat. I got ninety grand laying like lead in my gut."

I said nothing and tried to pay for the drinks.

Harry said, "Where's the money coming from? The O'Donnells? Do I have to let the dead buy me my drinks?" He reached for his money clip. "I'm still one of the richest live writers around."

"Thank you, Harry."

"I used to think you were my friend. I'd like to take you out in the alley and beat your brains in."

"I'm sorry if I upset you."

"It's a lie about the ninety grand, ain't it?"

I shrugged.

He smiled. "How many years does that fancy figure take in?"

"Four years," I said at random.

Harry was beaming now. "Freddie, let's have another drink before we bust up a couple of big lobsters. How about it, *amigo?*"

433

We had another round of drinks and Harry, banishing the O'Donnell ghosts from his presence, ordered dinner and commanded my attention with a discourse that attempted to prove to me that *The Merit of a General,* the tragedy of an American general relieved of his command, was his greatest novel, if not the greatest of all novels. He ended with maledictions, wishing death for me, my fellow critics, and himself.

Our exit from the restaurant was anything but swift, with Harry stopping at the bar to spar with Ben Sharkey, to have another brandy, and to express opinions on heavyweight boxers, southpaw pitchers, and the generalship of Chief Crazy Horse.

In the taxi, en route to the Hampshire House, where he was staying, Harry asked, "You ever make out with Rannah?"

"No."

"You don't know how lucky you are. How clean you are." I said nothing, and he went on about Rannah. "That picture of her. Her hair on fire. Her dress flying up. Like she was jumping into the fountain at the Plaza. Like she was dancing at the Ziegfeld Follies. That look on her face. I've seen guys die. But I've never seen a look like that. Like she was diving into the fountain at the Plaza. Like Davis was standing around and laughing his head off and applauding."

When the taxi reached his hotel, Harry seemed reluctant to leave. He said, "I hate hotels. Every time the phone rings. Every time I hear a knock on the door. Every time I get a message. Freddie, *amigo,* they don't bury the dead deep enough any more."

Harry said no more. The moment he left the taxi he was engulfed by a group of youngsters seeking to touch him, to wallow in his laughter, to come away with the scrawl of his signature.

Three years later, in his Montana hunting lodge, Harry Ingram made his separate peace. At six o'clock in the morning, September 1, 1961, he left his bed to keep the daily appointment with his typewriter. At twelve minutes past eight that morning Paula Ingram heard a rifle shot. She swore to the coroner that her husband had left no suicide note. There was, however, a

434

blank page in the typewriter. It was a blankness Harry Ingram could no longer endure.

In death, free of the madness that late in life had dwarfed him, he is an American giant.

Rannah's manuscript and her covering letter have both been added to the Davis O'Donnell papers in the Yale library. Lastly, I offer this letter, dated August 18, 1945, as my closing argument in the case for Rannah. Also, for those who are vexed by the mystery of Rannah's last twelve hours, it contains, if not a clue, then surely, an insight into her vagrancy from life.

The letter:

Here it is, the first-class miracle! The miracle is that I didn't burn it. I had such a great fire going yesterday. Fire in August? In Georgia, no less? Yes, the flames were high with the colors of heaven and hell (in the living room fireplace) when I burned the forty-seven portraits of You Know Who. "Thou shalt not make unto thee any graven image. . . ."

Contemplating the ashes, I wondered whether I should have saved one for you. But then I told myself there was no time for the veneration of idols, graven or painted. I'll tell you what I also burned. The book with Harry's words and Davis's blood. I had to. It was a relic. I tell myself that the blood of my beloved runs through the fresh ink and the live pages of The Downfall.

This will surprise you: I sent my Bible to the good woman who was — and will shortly be again — my keeper at the sanitarium. The Downfall *is my Holy Book now. It's the first thing I read when I wake, the last thing I read before I sleep.*

But back to the fire. I ran from it. I ran upstairs to the attic to fetch the pages now in your possession. But you ran with me, shouting reminders of my oath to you. You'd make me very happy, Freddie, if you'd write and tell me how bright the flames grew when you burned my manuscript.

Ah, but you're Freddie, and you don't burn books. Eureka! Why don't you, in your future expedition to the Holy Lands (I know you'll make it) take my manuscript (should I be calling it

435

a typescript?) and give it to the dust of some genizah? Genizah!
I love that word, and I love you for gifting me with it.

Please, think about it. I want the ream of pages, with its riot of
words, hidden, concealed, secreted, covered, buried, and — I'm
fresh out of synonyms. I've got a song for you. With a clever
title. "Yes, We Have No Rannahs." Isn't that horrible? Reminds
me of how Davis used to call the railroad line the New York, New
Haven, and Hard-Fought.

And, please, Freddie, don't write me and tell me what you
think of my writing, of my four battles. Remember, you asked
for it, and you must suffer the consequences.

Seriously, I owe you an apology. You, Davis, Harry, and Guy
— the four men (boys?) who captured my heart. I love all four
of you, but I done you all wrong. When I compare what Davis
accomplished in The Downfall *with the reaming (is this funny?)*
I gave all of you, I feel so small, so tiny, and so very mad.

Anyway, what I want to say is this: Davis, who does write like
one of God's spies, is so fair, so penetrating, so compassionate,
and so just. Oh, my God! You see, I'm using the present tense!
That's what The Downfall *does to me!*

But I'm straying, forgive me. What I want to say (you won't
like it) is that I painted (the alphabet has twenty-six colors for
me) all of you with your pants down, your danders up, and God
knows what. And God, if He knows anything, if He's talked to
his spy from Milwaukee, He surely must know that the best of
all of you (except for Guy) — the true selves, the real identities,
the naked souls — is contained in the pages of your own works.

And you, Freddie, I've neglected to run my brush from the
top to the bottom of the canvas to depict how tall you stand on
the shelves of the Stephensville library. As for Guy, I believe he
comes off the best of all of you. There was no room for his soul in
all of those newspapers in which his laughter was wrapped. He
loved me so, and I love him the more because, after I had run out
of parties, he came to build me bridges to his warmth.

Harry Ingram? There must be a hell waiting for me for having
inflamed his hatred. I'd like to remember how I reached for his
love that afternoon in the Peachtree Plaza Hotel. Harry the

devil? He was only a painted devil in a hell painted by me. No, he's no saint. He's a man who guards the treasure of his talent with brandied dragons. As for his regard for Davis, Harry cares. Harry always cared. And the caring is in all of his books. That he didn't write the foreword to The Downfall *I blame only myself. Just mark down another error for the mad Rannah.*

And Davis? What shall I say? I wish I could've written an entire ream about that last night in Washington. Oh, how I loved him that night! But was that the true Davis? No, I believe not. That was a crayon Davis. Or was it? And what was real? The Apperson and the glory? Or the old Plymouth and the phoenix rising from the California ashes? Or was it (for Davis) the snapshot of the girl he kept in his wallet? And is Rannah Gedney more real than the four heroines of the four novels (who are all Rannahs), whose return to print I wait for in the depot of my dreams? I have a thought, and it cauterizes my tears. It was folly for me to paint Davis, with brushes and oils, or with ribbons and keys. His self-portrait, done in his own blood, is the only good one, once the shadows pass.

And how does Rannah fare with Rannah? The problem of my emerging self-portrait wasn't that I loved myself too much, but that the mirror set me against myself. And, in the duel that must endure to the death, the innocent and the good must fall with the guilty and the evil, the god with the devil.

I'm trying to think of something funny to say here. Oh, yes, you know what? I sometimes see us (me and my men) as the Katzenjammer Kids in the funny papers. I see you, Davis, Harry, and Guy making mud pies with the fresh mud of the twentieth century. Then along comes this little pigtailed brat named Rannah, dancing around the boys, lifting her dress and laughing and throwing all the mud pies in all of your godlike faces.

I should end here, but I must tell you something for you to remember when you try to gray your head with the thought that I've needlessly gone back to the madhouse.

The Gillands threw a party the night President Truman told, on the mountains of radios, of the Japanese surrender. I came to sip forbidden champagne. Found myself confronted by a man of

437

the cloth who urged me to come to his church (which is Liz's church) and heard myself (thinking of Davis, The Downfall, and the resurrection) saying: "To have meaning is to have God."

Leaving this man with egg on his cloth, I listened to a late arrival, a dour Jeremiah, declare that the downtown streets were running with bawdry and strewn with the primroses of dalliance. As I listened, I looked around and saw rot on all the faces in the frame of the room. And I smelled the flowers sweetening the earth of their awaiting graves. Without a word to any of the embalmed faces, I pilfered a bottle of champagne, stole out of the house of the dead, and ran as Lamiel to the forest of the night streets, to the bacchanal in the light of the town square.

Long, long after midnight, with one slipper lost to folly and the other to fetish, with my dress tattered and defiled, with my mouth crushed in the last pressing of the grapes of life, I retraced my steps to Gedney Street.

My father opened the door, and I took his silence to the still waters of my bath. Clean again and nightgowned in chaste white, I climbed to the attic, to the secret room, to the secret window, where I knelt before the altar of the sky.

Conjuring the poisonous mushroom that grew out of Hiroshima, recalling the primordial merriment on the streets of Stephensville, and hearing my regiment of pages marching away from four battles, I cried out to the Christ gone to where the child in me had gone: "Dear Jesus, is this the death of war?"

Mad? Mother always said that blood will tell. And Dr. Dominick thinks me mad to want to be where the mad are supposed to be. But Hollow Grove is the county fair for the likes of me, and when the calliopes break down, I can always escape to the exalted moment when I first looked into the trunk, into the battlefield that is the Yorktown of the American boy from Milwaukee.

I can run to memory's Eden and see the boy lost in Hollywood, estranged from success, happiness, his hearth, his love — a boy weary of listening to alien orchestras playing strange songs for strange dancers — a boy thirsting not for his forbidden gin, but searching for the tweny-six keys to his kingdom to open blank pages and fill them with words so perfect, so enduring.

438

And here are thirty-one words, the first four of which I heard in Washington and heard again from my dead mother the rainswept night before the Carolina sun rose in the west. A quote from a letter received by Dr. Dominick from a man in Santa Monica: "A writer gets his material from his guts, and he can get at his guts only when he is alone. Being alone is a church, the one church, the true Chartres."

Ah, Freddie, to have Davis is to have meaning, to have meaning is to have Davis.

By day, under the one, true sun under which nothing is new, nothing true, I believe that the meaning of madness is the very absence of meaning itself.

By night, under suns seen, unseen, uncounted, unborn, and unimagined, I divine the starlight secret that meaning is nothing but a sweet mirage that lures us on.

But, oh, the earth's sun is shining now, and there is no darkness in the sweet genizahs. Please, remember to write and tell me on what red, red day you will be sending off the sweet trunk. I wish, in fancy, to breach the Pennsylvania walls, to ride with it on the New York, New Haven, and Hard-Fought Railroad, to be there when Davis returns to Yale to take and hold a library shelf, where he may always be reached.

D.F.

Lake Placid, New York
August 10, 1968